'As always the action's the thing – and once Sharpe is surrounded by enemies, both on his own side and the opposition, events move at their usual satisfyingly breathless pace'

Independent on Sunday

SHARPE'S BATTLE

Richard Sharpe and the Battle
of Fuentes de Oñoro, May 1811

BERNARD CORNWELL

HarperCollins*Publishers*

HarperCollins*Publishers* Ltd
1 London Bridge Street
London SE1 9GF

www.harpercollins.co.uk

This paperback edition 2012

4

First published in Great Britain by HarperCollins*Publishers* 1995

A catalogue record for this book is available from the British Library

ISBN 978 0 00 745295 8

This novel is a work of fiction.
The incidents and some of the characters portrayed in it,
while based on real historical events and figures, are
the work of the author's imagination.

Typeset in Minion by Palimpsest Book Production Limited,
Falkirk, Stirlingshire

Printed and bound by
CPI Group (UK) Ltd, Croydon, CR0 4YY

Sharpe's Battle is for Sean Bean

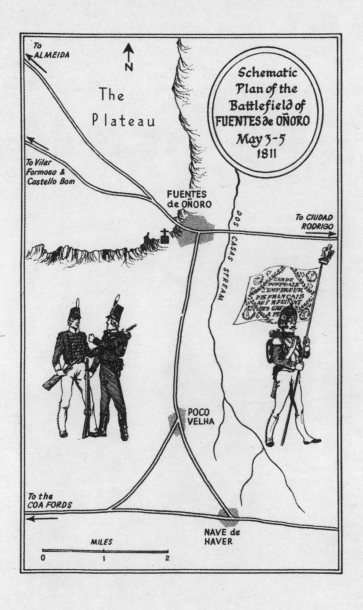

To ALMEIDA

The Plateau

N

To Vilar Formosa & Castello Bom

FUENTES de OÑORO

Schematic Plan of the Battlefield of FUENTES de OÑORO May 3-5 1811

To CIUDAD RODRIGO

DOS CASAS STREAM

GARDE IMPERIALE EMPEREUR DES FRANÇAIS XXVII REGIMENT

POCO VELHA

To the COA FORDS

NAVE de HAVER

MILES

0   1   2

SHARPE'S BATTLE

PART ONE

CHAPTER ONE

Sharpe swore. Then, in desperation, he turned the map upside down. 'Might as well not have a bloody map,' he said, 'for all the bloody use it is.'

'We could light a fire with it,' Sergeant Harper suggested. 'Good kindling's hard to come by in these hills.'

'It's no bloody use for anything else,' Sharpe said. The hand-drawn map showed a scatter of villages, a few spidery lines for roads, streams or rivers, and some vague hatchings denoting hills, whereas all Sharpe could see was mountains. No roads or villages, just grey, bleak, rock-littered mountains with peaks shrouded by mists, and valleys cut by streams turned white and full by the spring rains. Sharpe had led his company into the high ground on the border between Spain and Portugal and there become lost. His company, forty soldiers carrying packs, haversacks, cartridge cases and weapons, seemed not to care. They were just grateful for the rest and so sat or lay beside the grassy track. Some lit pipes, others slept, while Captain Richard Sharpe turned the map right side up and then, in anger, crumpled it into a ball. 'We're bloody lost,' he said and then, in fairness, corrected himself. 'I'm bloody lost.'

'My grand-da got lost once,' Harper said helpfully. 'He'd bought a bullock from a fellow in Cloghanelly Parish and decided to take a short cut home across the Derryveagh Mountains. Then the fog rolled in and grand-da couldn't tell his left from his right. Lost like a wee lamb he was, and then the bullock deserted the ranks and bolted into the fog and jumped clear over a cliff into the Barra Valley. Grand-da said you could hear the poor wee beast bellowing all the way down, then there was a thump just like you'd dropped a bagpipe off a church tower, only louder, he said, because he reckoned they must have heard that thump all the way to Ballybofey. We used to laugh about it later, but not at the time. God, no, it was a tragedy at the time. We couldn't afford to lose a good bullock.'

'Jesus bloody wept!' Sharpe interrupted. 'I can afford to lose a bloody sergeant who's got nothing better to do than blather on about a bloody bullock!'

'It was a valuable beast!' Harper protested. 'Besides, we're lost. We've got nothing better to do than pass the time, sir.'

Lieutenant Price had been at the rear of the column, but now joined his commanding officer at the front. 'Are we lost, sir?'

'No, Harry, I came here for the hell of it. Wherever the hell this is.' Sharpe stared glumly about the damp, bleak valley. He was proud of his sense of direction and his skills at crossing strange country, but now he was comprehensively, utterly lost and the clouds were thick enough to disguise the sun so that he could not even tell which direction was north. 'We need a compass,' he said.

'Or a map?' Lieutenant Price suggested happily.

'We've got a bloody map. Here.' Sharpe thrust the balled-up map into the Lieutenant's hands. 'Major Hogan drew it for me and I can't make head nor tail out of it.'

'I was never any good with maps,' Price confessed. 'I once got lost marching some recruits from Chelmsford to the barracks, and that's a straight road. I had a map that time, too. I think I must have a talent for getting lost.'

'My grand-da was like that,' Harper said proudly. 'He could get lost between one side of a gate and the other. I was telling the Captain here about the time he took a bullock up Slieve Snaght. It was dirty weather, see, and he was taking the short cut –'

'Shut up,' Sharpe said nastily.

'We went wrong at that ruined village,' Price said, frowning over the creased map. 'I think we should have stayed on the other side of the stream, sir.' Price showed Sharpe the map. 'If that is the village. Hard to tell really. But I'm sure we shouldn't have crossed the stream, sir.'

Sharpe half suspected the Lieutenant was right, but he did not want to admit it. They had crossed the stream two hours before, so God only knew where they were now. Sharpe did not even know if they were in Portugal or Spain, though both the scenery and the weather looked more like Scotland. Sharpe was supposedly on his way to Vilar Formoso where his company, the Light Company of the South Essex Regiment, would be attached to the Town Major as a guard unit, a prospect that depressed Sharpe. Town garrison duty was little better than being a provost and provosts were the lowest form of army life, but the South Essex was short of men and so the regiment had been taken out of the battle line and set to administrative duties. Most of the regiment were escorting bullock carts loaded with supplies that had been barged up the Tagus from Lisbon, or else were guarding French prisoners on their way to the ships that would carry them to Britain, but the Light Company was lost, and all because Sharpe had heard a distant cannonade resembling far-away thunder and he had marched towards the sound, only to discover that his ears had played tricks. The noise of the skirmish, if indeed it was a skirmish and not genuine thunder, had faded away and now Sharpe was lost. 'Are you sure that's the ruined village?' he asked Price, pointing to the crosshatched spot on the map that Price had indicated.

'I wouldn't like to swear to it, sir, not being able to read maps. It could be any of those scratchings, sir, or maybe none.'

'Then why the hell are you showing it to me?'

'In a hope for inspiration, sir,' Price said in a wounded voice. 'I was trying to help, sir. Trying to raise our hopes.' He looked down at the map again. 'Maybe it isn't a very good map?' he suggested.

'It would make good kindling,' Harper repeated.

'One thing's certain,' Sharpe said as he took the map back from Price, 'we haven't crossed the watershed which means these streams must be flowing west.' He paused. 'Or they're probably flowing west. Unless the world's bloody upside down which it probably bloody is, but on the chance that it bloody isn't we'll follow the bloody streams. Here' – he tossed the map to Harper – 'kindling.'

'That's what my grand-da did,' Harper said, tucking the crumpled map inside his faded and torn green jacket. 'He followed the water –'

'Shut up,' Sharpe said, but not angrily this time. Rather he spoke quietly, and at the same time gestured with his left hand to make his companions crouch. 'Bloody Crapaud,' he said softly, 'or something. Never seen a uniform like it.'

'Bloody hell,' Price said, and dropped down to the path.

Because a horseman had appeared just two hundred yards away. The man had not seen the British infantrymen, nor did he appear to be on the lookout for enemies. Instead his horse just ambled out of a side valley until the reins checked it, then the rider swung himself wearily out of the saddle and looped the reins over an arm while he unbuttoned his baggy trousers and urinated beside the path. Smoke from his pipe drifted in the damp air.

Harper's rifle clicked as he pulled the cock fully back. Sharpe's men, even those who had been asleep, were all alert now and lying motionless in the grass, keeping so low that even if the horseman had turned he would probably not have noticed the infantry. Sharpe's company was a veteran unit of skirmishers, hardened by two years of fighting in Portugal and Spain and as well trained as any soldiers in Europe. 'Recognize the uniform?' Sharpe asked Price softly.

'Never seen it before, sir.'

'Pat?' Sharpe asked Harper.

'Looks like a bloody Russian,' Harper said. Harper had never seen a Russian soldier, but had a perverse idea that such creatures wore grey and this mysterious horseman was all in grey. He had a short grey dragoon jacket, grey trousers and a grey horsehair plume on his steel-grey helmet. Or maybe, Sharpe thought, it was merely a cloth cover designed to stop the helmet's metal from reflecting the light.

'Spaniard?' Sharpe wondered aloud.

'The dons are always gaudy, sir,' Harper said. 'The dons never did like dying in drab clothes.'

'Maybe he's a partisan,' Sharpe suggested.

'He's got Crapaud weapons,' Price said, 'and trousers.' The pissing horseman was indeed armed just like a French dragoon. He wore a straight sword, had a short-barrelled carbine sheathed in his saddle holster and had a brace of pistols stuck in his belt. He also wore the distinctively baggy *saroual* trousers that the French dragoons liked, but Sharpe had never seen a French dragoon wearing grey ones, and certainly never a grey jacket. Enemy dragoons always wore green coats. Not dark hunting green like the coats of Britain's riflemen, but a lighter and brighter green.

'Maybe the buggers are running out of green dye?' Harper suggested, then fell silent as the horseman buttoned his floppy trousers and hauled himself up onto his saddle. The man looked carefully about the valley, saw nothing to alarm him and so spurred his horse back into the hidden side valley. 'He was scouting,' Harper said softly. 'He was sent to see if anyone was here.'

'He made a bloody bad job of it,' Sharpe commented.

'Even so,' Price said fervently, 'it's a good thing we're going in the other direction.'

'We're not, Harry,' Sharpe said. 'We're going to see who those bastards are and what they're doing.' He pointed uphill. 'You first, Harry. Take your fellows and go halfway up, then wait.'

Lieutenant Price led the redcoats of Sharpe's company up the steep slope. Half of the company wore the red jackets of Britain's line infantry while the other half, like Sharpe himself, had the green jackets of the elite rifle regiments. It had been an accident of war that had stranded Sharpe and his riflemen in a redcoat battalion, but sheer bureaucratic inertia had held them there and now it was sometimes hard to tell the riflemen from the redcoats, so shabby and faded were their respective uniforms. From a distance they all looked like brown uniforms because of the cheap Portuguese cloth that the men were forced to use for repairs.

'You think we've crossed the lines?' Harper asked Sharpe.

'Like as not,' Sharpe said sourly, still angry at himself. 'Not that anyone knows where the damn lines are,' he said defensively, and in part he was right. The French were retreating out of Portugal. Throughout the winter of 1810 the enemy had stayed in front of the Lines of Torres Vedras just a half-day's march from Lisbon, and there they had frozen and half starved to death rather than retreat to their supply depots in Spain. Marshal Masséna had known that retreat would yield all Portugal to the British while to attack the Lines of Torres Vedras would be pure suicide, and so he had just stayed, neither advancing nor retreating, just starving slowly through the winter and staring at the lines' enormous earthworks which had been hacked and scraped from a range of hills across the narrow peninsula just north of Lisbon. The valleys between the hills had been blocked by massive dams or with tangled barricades of thorn, while the hill tops and long slopes had been trenched, embrasured and armed with battery after battery of cannon. The lines, a winter's hunger and the relentless attacks of partisans had finally defeated the French attempt to capture Lisbon and in March they had begun to retreat. Now it was April and the retreat was slowing in the hills of the Spanish frontier, for it was here that Marshal Masséna had decided to make his stand. He would fight and defeat the British in the river-cut hills, and always, at Masséna's back, stood the twin fastnesses of Badajoz and Ciudad Rodrigo. Those two Spanish citadels made the frontier into a mighty barrier, though for now Sharpe's concern was not the grim border campaign that loomed ahead but rather the mysterious grey horseman.

Lieutenant Price had reached a patch of dead ground halfway up the hill where his redcoats concealed themselves as Sharpe waved his riflemen forward. The slope was steep, but the greenjackets climbed fast for, like all experienced infantrymen, they had a healthy fear of enemy cavalry and they knew that steep hillsides were an effective barrier to horsemen and thus the higher the riflemen climbed, the safer and happier they became.

Sharpe passed the resting redcoats and went on up towards the crest of a spur that divided the two valleys. When he was close to the ridge he waved his greenjackets down into the short grass, then crawled up to the skyline to peer down into the smaller valley where the grey horseman had disappeared.

And, two hundred feet beneath him, saw Frenchmen.

The men were all wearing the strange grey uniform, but Sharpe now knew they were French because one of the cavalrymen carried a guidon. This was a small, swallowtailed banner carried on a lance as a rally mark in the chaos of battle, and this particular shabby, frayed flag showed the red, white and blue of the enemy. The standard-bearer was sitting on his horse in the centre of a small abandoned settlement while his dismounted companions searched the half-dozen stone and thatch houses that looked as if they had been built to shelter families during the summer months when the lowland farmers would bring their flocks to graze the high pastures.

There were only a half-dozen horsemen in the settlement, but with them was a handful of French infantrymen, also wearing the drab and plain grey coats, rather than their usual blue. Sharpe counted eighteen infantrymen.

Harper wriggled uphill to join Sharpe. 'Jesus, Mary and Joseph,' he said when he saw the infantry. 'Grey uniforms?'

'Maybe you're right,' Sharpe said, 'maybe the buggers have run out of dye.'

'I wish they'd run out of musket balls,' Harper said. 'So what do we do?'

'Bugger off,' Sharpe said. 'No point in having a fight for the hell of it.'

'Amen to that, sir.' Harper began to slither down from the skyline. 'Are we going now?'

'Give me a minute,' Sharpe said and felt behind his back for his telescope which was stored in a pouch of his French oxhide pack. Then, with the telescope's hood extended to shade the outer lens and so stop even this day's damp light from being reflected downhill, he trained the glass on the tiny cottages. Sharpe was anything but a wealthy man, yet the telescope was a very fine and expensive glass made by Matthew Berge of London, with a brass eyepiece, shutters and a small engraved plate set into its walnut tube. 'In Gratitude,' the plate read, 'AW. September 23rd, 1803.' AW was Arthur Wellesley, now the

Viscount Wellington, a lieutenant general and commander of the British and Portuguese armies which had pursued Marshal Masséna to Spain's frontier, but on September 23rd, 1803, Major General the Honourable Arthur Wellesley had been astride a horse that was piked in the chest and so pitched its rider down into the enemy's front rank. Sharpe could still remember the shrill Indian cries of triumph as the red-jacketed General had fallen among them, though he could remember precious little else about the seconds that followed. Yet it was those few seconds that had plucked him from the ranks and made him, a man born in the gutter, into an officer in Britain's army.

Now he focused Wellington's gift on the French beneath and watched as a dismounted cavalryman carried a canvas pail of water from the stream. For a second or two Sharpe thought that the man was carrying the water to his picketed horse, but instead the dragoon stopped between two of the houses and began to pour the water onto the ground. 'They're foraging,' Sharpe said, 'using the water trick.'

'Hungry bastards,' Harper said.

The French had been driven from Portugal more by hunger than by force of arms. When Wellington had retreated to Torres Vedras he left behind him a devastated countryside with empty barns, poisoned wells and echoing granaries. The French had endured five months of famine partly by ransacking every deserted hamlet and abandoned village for hidden food, and one way to find buried jars of grain was to pour water on the ground, for where the soil had been dug and refilled the water would always drain away more quickly and so betray where the grain jars were hidden.

'No one would be hiding food in these hills,' Harper said scornfully. 'Who do they think would carry it all the way up here?'

Then a woman screamed.

For a few seconds both Sharpe and Harper assumed the sound came from an animal. The scream had been muffled and distorted by distance and there was no sign of any civilians in the tiny settlement, but as the terrible noise echoed back from the far hillside so the full horror of the sound registered on both men. 'Bastards,' Harper said softly.

Sharpe slid the telescope shut. 'She's in one of the houses,' he said. 'Two men with her? Maybe three? Which means there can't be more than thirty of the bastards down there.'

'Forty of us,' Harper said dubiously. It was not that he was frightened by the odds, but the advantage was not so overwhelming as to guarantee a bloodless victory.

The woman screamed again.

'Fetch Lieutenant Price,' Sharpe ordered Harper. 'Tell everyone to be loaded and they're to stay just back from the crest.' He turned round. 'Dan! Thompson! Cooper! Harris! Up here.' The four were his best marksmen. 'Keep your heads down!' he warned the four men, then waited till they reached the crest. 'In a minute I'm taking the rest of the rifles down there. I want you four to stay here and pick off any bastard who looks troublesome.'

'Bastards are going already,' Daniel Hagman said. Hagman was the oldest man in the company and the finest marksman. He was a Cheshire poacher who had been offered a chance to enlist in the army rather than face transportation for stealing a brace of pheasants from an absentee landlord.

Sharpe turned back. The French were leaving, or rather most of them were, for, judging from the way that the men at the rear of the infantry column kept turning and shouting towards the houses, they had left some of their comrades inside the cottage where the woman had screamed. With the half-dozen cavalrymen in the lead, the main group was trudging down the stream towards the larger valley.

12

'They're getting careless,' Thompson said.

Sharpe nodded. Leaving men in the settlement was a risk and it was not like the French to run risks in wild country. Spain and Portugal were riddled with *guerrilleros*, the partisans who fought the *guerrilla*, the little war, and that war was far more bitter and cruel than the more formal battles between the French and the British. Sharpe knew just how cruel for only the previous year he had gone into the wild north country to find Spanish gold and his companions had been partisans whose savagery had been chilling. One of them, Teresa Moreno, was Sharpe's lover, only now she called herself La Aguja, the Needle, and every Frenchman she knifed with her long slim blade was one small part of the endless revenge she had promised to inflict on the soldiers who had raped her.

Teresa was now a long way off, fighting in the country around Badajoz, while in the settlement beneath Sharpe another woman was suffering from the attentions of the French and again Sharpe wondered why these grey-uniformed soldiers thought it safe to leave men to finish their crime in the isolated village. Were they certain that no partisans lurked in these high hills?

Harper came back, breathing hard after leading Price's redcoats up the hill. 'God save Ireland,' he said as he dropped beside Sharpe, 'but the bastards are going already.'

'I think they've left some men behind. Are you ready?'

'Sure I am.' Harper eased back his rifle's doghead.

'Packs off,' Sharpe told his riflemen as he shrugged his own pack off his shoulders, then he twisted to look at Lieutenant Price. 'Wait here, Harry, and listen for the whistle. Two blasts mean I want you to open fire from up here, and three mean I want you down at the village.' He looked at Hagman. 'Don't open fire, Dan, until they see us. If we can get down there without the bastards knowing it'll be easier.' He raised his voice so the rest of his riflemen could hear. 'We go down fast,'

Sharpe said. 'Are you all ready? Are you all loaded? Then come on! Now!'

The riflemen scrambled over the crest and tumbled headlong down the steep hill behind Sharpe. Sharpe kept glancing to his left where the small French column retreated beside the stream, but no one in the column turned and the noise of the horses' hooves and the infantrymen's nailed boots must have smothered the sound of the greenjackets running downhill. It was not until Sharpe was just yards away from the nearest house that a Frenchman turned and shouted in alarm. Hagman fired at the same instant and the sound of his Baker rifle echoed first from the small valley's far slope, then from the distant flank of the larger valley. The echo crackled on, fainter and fainter, until it was drowned as the other riflemen on the hill top opened fire.

Sharpe jumped down the last few feet. He fell as he landed, picked himself up and ran past a dunghill heaped against a house wall. A single horse was tethered to a steel picket pin driven into the ground beside one of the small houses where a French soldier suddenly appeared in the doorway. The man was wearing a shirt and a grey coat, but nothing below the waist. He raised his musket as Sharpe ran into view, but then saw the riflemen behind Sharpe and so dropped the musket and raised his hands in surrender.

Sharpe had drawn his sword as he ran to the house door. Once there he shouldered the surrendering man aside and burst into the hovel that was a bare stone chamber, beamed with wood and roofed with stone and turf. It was dark inside the cottage, but not so dark that Sharpe could not see a naked girl scrambling over the earth floor into a corner. There was blood on her legs. A second Frenchman, this one with cavalry overalls round his ankles, tried to stand and reach for his scabbarded sword, but Sharpe kicked him in the balls. He kicked him so

14

hard that the man screamed and then could not draw breath to scream again and so toppled onto the bloody floor where he whimpered and lay with his knees drawn tight up to his chest. There were two other men on the beaten earth floor, but when Sharpe turned on them with his drawn sword he saw they were both civilians and both dead. Their throats had been cut.

Musketry sounded ragged in the valley. Sharpe went back to the door where the bare-legged French infantryman was crouching with his hands held behind his head. 'Pat!' Sharpe called.

Harper was organizing the riflemen. 'We've got the buggers tamed, sir,' the Sergeant said reassuringly, anticipating Sharpe's question. The riflemen were crouching beside the cottages where they fired, reloaded and fired again. Their Baker rifle muzzles gouted thick spurts of white smoke that smelt of rotted eggs. The French returned the fire, their musket balls smacking on the stone houses as Sharpe ducked back into the hovel. He picked up the two Frenchmen's weapons and tossed them out of the door. 'Perkins!' he shouted.

Rifleman Perkins ran to the door. He was the youngest of Sharpe's men, or was presumed to be the youngest for though Perkins knew neither the day nor the year of his birth, he did not yet need to shave. 'Sir?'

'If either of these bastards move, shoot them.'

Perkins might be young, but the look on his thin face scared the unhurt Frenchman who reached out a placating hand as though begging the young rifleman not to shoot. 'I'll look after the bastards, sir,' Perkins said, then slotted his brass-handled sword bayonet onto his rifle's muzzle.

Sharpe saw the girl's clothing which had been tossed under a crudely sawn table. He picked up the greasy garments and handed them to her. She was pale, terrified and crying, a young thing, scarcely out of childhood. 'Bastards,' Sharpe said to the two prisoners, then ran out into the damp light. A musket ball hissed over his head as he ducked down into cover beside Harper.

'Bastards are good, sir,' the Irishman said ruefully.

'I thought you had them tamed?'

'They've got different ideas on the matter,' Harper said, then broke cover, aimed, fired and ducked back. 'Bastards are good,' he said again as he started to reload.

And the French were good. Sharpe had expected the small group of Frenchmen to hurry away from the rifle fire, but instead they had deployed into a skirmish line and so turned the easy target of a marching column into a scattered series of difficult targets. Meanwhile the half-dozen dragoons accompanying the infantry had dismounted and begun to fight on foot while one man galloped their horses out of rifle range, and now the assorted dragoon carbines and infantry muskets were threatening to overwhelm Sharpe's riflemen. The Baker rifles were far more accurate than the Frenchmen's muskets and carbines, and they could kill at four times the distance, but they were desperately slow to load. The bullets, each one wrapped in a leather patch that was designed to grip the barrel's rifling, had to be forced down the tight grooves and lands of the barrel, whereas a musket ball could be rammed fast down a smoothbore's unrifled gullet. Sharpe's men were already abandoning the leather patches in order to load faster, but without the leather the rifling could not impart spin to the ball and so the rifle was robbed of its one great advantage: its lethal accuracy. Hagman and his three companions were still firing down from the ridge, but their numbers were too few to make much difference and all that was saving Sharpe's riflemen from decimation was the protection of the village's stone walls.

Sharpe took the small whistle from its pouch on his crossbelt.

He blew it twice, then unslung his own rifle, edged round the corner of the house and aimed at a puff of smoke down the valley. He fired. The rifle kicked back hard just as a French musket ball cracked into the wall beside his head. A fleck of stone slashed across his scarred cheek, drawing blood and missing his eyeball by half an inch. 'Bastards are bloody good.' Sharpe echoed Harper's tribute grudgingly, then a crashing musket volley announced that Harry Price had lined his redcoats on the hill top and was firing down at the French.

Price's first volley was enough to decide the fight. Sharpe heard a French voice shouting orders and a second later the enemy skirmish line began to shred and disappear. Harry Price only had time for one more volley before the grey-coated enemy had retreated out of range. 'Green! Horrell! McDonald! Cresacre! Smith! Sergeant Latimer!' Sharpe called to his riflemen. 'Fifty paces down the valley, make a picquet line there, but get the hell back here if the bastards come back for more. Move! Rest of you stay where you are.'

'Jesus, sir, you should see in here.' Harper had pushed open the nearest house door with the muzzle of his seven-barrel gun. The weapon, originally designed to be fired from the fighting tops of Britain's naval ships, was a cluster of seven half-inch barrels fired by a single flint. It was like a miniature cannon and only the biggest, strongest men could fire the gun without permanently damaging their shoulders. Harper was one of the strongest men Sharpe had ever known, but also one of the most sentimental and now the big Irishman looked close to tears. 'Oh, sweet suffering Christ,' Harper said as he crossed himself, 'the living bastards.'

Sharpe had already smelt the blood, now he looked past the Sergeant and felt the disgust make a lump in his throat. 'Oh, my God,' he said softly.

For the small house was drenched in blood, its walls

spattered and its floor soaked with it, while on the floor were sprawled the limp bodies of children. Sharpe tried to count the little bodies, but could not always tell where one blood-boltered corpse began and another ended. The children had evidently been stripped naked and then had their throats cut. A small dog had been killed too, and its blood-matted, curly-haired corpse had been tossed onto the children whose skins appeared unnaturally white against the vivid streaks of black-looking blood.

'Oh, sweet Jesus,' Sharpe said as he backed out of the reeking shadows to draw a breath of fresh air. He had seen more than his share of horror. He had been born to a poorhouse whore in a London gutter and he had followed Britain's drum from Flanders to Madras and through the Indian wars and now from the beaches of Portugal to the frontiers of Spain, but never, not even in the Sultan Tippoo's torture chambers in Seringapatam, had he seen children tossed into a dead pile like so many slaughtered animals.

'There's more here, sir,' Corporal Jackson called. Jackson had just vomited in the doorway of a hovel in which the bodies of two old people lay in a bloody mess. They had been tortured in ways that were only too evident.

Sharpe thought of Teresa who was fighting these same scum who gutted and tormented their victims, then, unable to bear the unbidden images that seared his thoughts, he cupped his hands and shouted up the hill, 'Harris! Down here!'

Rifleman Harris was the company's educated man. He had once been a schoolmaster, even a respectable schoolmaster, but boredom had driven him to drink and drink had been his ruin, or at least the cause of his joining the army where he still loved to demonstrate his erudition. 'Sir?' Harris said as he arrived in the settlement.

'You speak French?'

'Yes, sir.'

'There's two Frogs in that house. Find out what unit they're from, and what the bastards did here. And Harris!'

'Sir?' The lugubrious, red-haired Harris turned back.

'You don't have to be gentle with the bastards.'

Even Harris, who was accustomed to Sharpe, seemed shocked by his Captain's tone. 'No, sir.'

Sharpe walked back across the settlement's tiny plaza. His men had searched the two cottages on the stream's far side, but found no bodies there. The massacre had evidently been confined to the three houses on the nearer bank where Sergeant Harper was standing with a bleak, hurt look on his face. Patrick Harper was an Ulsterman from Donegal and had been driven into the ranks of Britain's army by hunger and poverty. He was a huge man, four inches taller than Sharpe who was himself six feet tall. In battle Harper was an awesome figure, yet in truth he was a kind, humorous and easy-going man whose benevolence disguised his life's central contradiction which was that he had no love for the king for whom he fought and little for the country whose flag he defended, yet there were few better soldiers in all King George's army, and none who was more loyal to his friends. And it was for those friends that Harper fought, and the closest of his friends, despite their disparity in rank, was Sharpe himself. 'They're just wee kiddies,' Harper now said. 'Who'd do such a thing?'

'Them.' Sharpe jerked his head down the small valley to where the stream joined the wider waterway. The grey Frenchmen had stopped there; too far to be threatened by the rifles, but still close enough to watch what happened in the settlement where they had pillaged and murdered.

'Some of those wee ones had been raped,' Harper said.

'I saw,' Sharpe said bleakly.

'How could they do it?'

19

'There isn't an answer, Pat. God knows.' Sharpe felt sick, just like Harper felt sick, but inquiring into the roots of sin would not gain revenge for the dead children, nor would it save the raped girl's sanity, nor bury the blood-soaked dead. Nor would it find a way back to the British lines for one small light company that Sharpe now realized was dangerously exposed on the edge of the French outpost line. 'Ask a goddamn chaplain for an answer, if you can ever find one closer than the Lisbon brothels,' Sharpe said savagely, then turned to look at the charnel houses. 'How the hell are we going to bury this lot?'

'We can't, sir. We'll just tumble the house walls down on top of them,' Harper said. He gazed down the valley. 'I could murder those bastards. What are we going to do with the two we've got?'

'Kill them,' Sharpe said curtly. 'We'll get an answer or two now,' he said as he saw Harris duck out of the cottage. Harris was carrying one of the steel-grey dragoon helmets which Sharpe now saw were not cloth-covered, but were indeed fashioned out of metal and plumed with a long hank of grey horsehair.

Harris ran his right hand through the plume as he walked towards Sharpe. 'I found out who they are, sir,' he said as he drew nearer. 'They belong to the Brigade Loup, the Wolf Brigade. It's named after their commanding officer, sir. Fellow called Loup, Brigadier General Guy Loup. Loup means wolf in French, sir. They reckon they're an elite unit. Their job was to hold the road open through the mountains this past winter and they did it by beating the hell out of the natives. If any of Loup's men get killed then he kills fifty civilians as revenge. That's what they were doing here, sir. A couple of his men were ambushed and killed, and this is the price.' Harris gestured at the houses of the dead. 'And Loup's not far away, sir,' he added in warning. 'Unless these fellows are lying, which I doubt. He left a detachment here and took a squadron to hunt down some fugitives in the next valley.'

Sharpe looked at the cavalryman's horse which was still tethered in the settlement's centre and thought of the infantryman he had captured. 'This Brigade Loup,' he asked, 'is it cavalry or infantry?'

'The brigade has both, sir,' Harris said. 'It's a special brigade, sir, formed to fight the partisans, and Loup's got two battalions of infantry and one regiment of dragoons.'

'And they all wear grey?'

'Like wolves, sir,' Harris said helpfully.

'We all know what to do with wolves,' Sharpe said, then turned as Sergeant Latimer shouted a warning. Latimer was commanding the tiny picquet line that stood between Sharpe and the French, but it was no new attack that had caused Latimer to shout his warning, but rather the approach of four French horsemen. One of them carried the tricolour guidon, though the swallow-tailed flag was now half obscured by a dirty white shirt that had been impaled on the guidon's lance head. 'Bastards want to talk to us,' Sharpe said.

'I'll talk to them,' Harper said viciously and pulled back the cock of his seven-barrelled gun.

'No!' Sharpe said. 'And go round the company and tell everyone to hold their fire, and that's an order.'

'Aye, sir.' Harper lowered the flint, then, with a baleful glance towards the approaching Frenchmen, went to warn the green-jackets to hold their tempers and keep their fingers off their triggers.

Sharpe, his rifle slung on his shoulder and his sword at his side, strolled towards the four Frenchmen. Two of the horsemen were officers, while the flanking pair were standard-bearers, and the ratio of flags to men seemed impertinently high, almost as if the two approaching officers considered themselves greater than other mortals. The tricolour guidon would have been standard enough, but the second banner was extraordinary. It was a French eagle with gilded wings outspread perched atop a pole that had a crosspiece nailed just beneath the eagle's plinth. Most eagles carried a silk tricolour from the staff, but this eagle carried six wolf tails attached to the cross-piece. The standard was somehow barbaric, suggesting the far-off days when pagan armies of horse soldiers had thundered out of the Steppes to rape and ruin Christendom.

And if the wolf-tail standard made Sharpe's blood run chill, then it was nothing compared to the man who now spurred his horse ahead of his companions. Only the man's boots were not grey. His coat was grey, his horse was a grey, his helmet was lavishly plumed in grey and his grey pelisse was edged with grey wolf fur. Bands of wolf pelt encircled his boot tops, his saddle-cloth was a grey skin, his sword's long straight scabbard and his carbine's saddle holster were both sheathed in wolfskin while his horse's nose band was a strip of grey fur. Even the man's beard was grey. It was a short beard, neatly trimmed, but the rest of the face was wild and merciless and scarred fit for nightmare. One bloodshot eye and one blind milky eye stared from that weather-beaten, battle-hardened face as the man curbed his horse beside Sharpe.

'My name is Loup,' he said, 'Brigadier General Guy Loup of His Imperial Majesty's army.' His tone was strangely mild, his intonation courteous and his English touched with a light Scottish accent.

'Sharpe,' the rifleman said. 'Captain Sharpe. British army.'

The three remaining Frenchmen had reined in a dozen yards away. They watched as their Brigadier swung his leg out of the stirrup and dropped lightly down to the path. He was not as tall as Sharpe, but he was still a big man and he was well muscled and agile. Sharpe guessed the French Brigadier was about forty years old, six years older than Sharpe himself. Loup now took two cigars from his fur-edged sabretache and offered one to Sharpe.

'I don't take gifts from murderers,' Sharpe said.

Loup laughed at Sharpe's indignation. 'More fool you, Captain. Is that what you say? More fool you? I was a prisoner, you see, in Scotland. In Edinburgh. A very cold city, but with beautiful women, very beautiful. Some of them taught me English and I taught them how to lie to their drab Calvinist husbands. We paroled officers lived just off Candlemaker Row. Do you know the place? No? You should visit Edinburgh, Captain. Despite the Calvinists and the cooking it is a fine city, very learned and hospitable. When the peace of Amiens was signed I almost stayed there.' Loup paused to strike flint on steel, then to blow the charred linen tinder in his tinderbox into a flame with which he lit his cigar. 'I almost stayed, but you know how it is. She was married to another man and I am a lover of France, so here I am and there she is and doubtless she dreams about me a lot more than I dream about her.' He sighed. 'But this weather reminded me of her. We would so often lie in bed and watch the rain and mist fly past the windows of Candlemaker Row. It is cold today, eh?'

'You're dressed for it, General,' Sharpe said. 'Got as much fur as a Christmas whore, you have.'

Loup smiled. It was not a pleasant smile. He was missing two teeth, and those that remained were stained yellow. He had spoken pleasantly enough to Sharpe, even charmingly, but it was the smooth charm of a cat about to kill. He drew on his cigar, making the tip glow red, while his single bloodshot eye looked hard at Sharpe from beneath the helmet's grey visor.

Loup saw a tall man with a well-used rifle on one shoulder and a battered ugly-bladed sword at his hip. Sharpe's uniform was torn, stained and patched. The jacket's black cord hung in tatters between a few silver buttons that hung by threads, while beneath the jacket Sharpe wore a set of leather-reinforced French cavalry overalls. The remains of an officer's red sash encircled Sharpe's waist, while around his neck was a loosely knotted black choker. It was the uniform of a man who had long discarded the peacetime trappings of soldiering in exchange for the utilitarian comforts of a fighting man. A hard man, too, Loup guessed, not just from the evidence of the scar on Sharpe's cheek, but from the rifleman's demeanour which was awkward and raw-edged as though Sharpe would have preferred to be fighting than talking. Loup shrugged, abandoned his pleasantries and got down to business. 'I came to fetch my two men,' he said.

'Forget them, General,' Sharpe replied. He was determined not to dignify this Frenchman by calling him 'sir' or 'monsieur'.

Loup raised his eyebrows. 'They're dead?'

'They will be.'

Loup waved a persistent fly away. The steel-plated straps of his helmet hung loose beside his face, resembling the *cadenettes* of braided hair that French hussars liked to wear hanging from their temples. He drew on his cigar again, then smiled. 'Might I remind you, Captain, of the rules of war?'

Sharpe offered Loup a word that he doubted the Frenchman had heard much in Edinburgh's learned society. 'I don't take lessons from murderers,' Sharpe went on, 'not in the rules of war. What your men did in that village wasn't war. It was a massacre.'

'Of course it was war,' Loup said equably, 'and I don't need lectures from you, Captain.'

'You might not need a lecture, General, but you damn well need a lesson.'

Loup laughed. He turned and walked to the stream's edge where he stretched his arms, yawned hugely, then stooped to scoop some water to his mouth. He turned back to Sharpe. 'Let me tell you what my job is, Captain, and you will put yourself in my boots. That way, perhaps, you will lose your tedious English moral certainties. My job, Captain, is to police the roads through these mountains and so make the passes safe for the supply wagons of ammunition and food with which we plan to beat you British back to the sea. My enemy is not a soldier dressed in uniform with a colour and a code of honour, but is instead a rabble of civilians who resent my presence. Good! Let them resent me, that is their privilege, but if they attack me, Captain, then I will defend myself and I do it so ferociously, so ruthlessly, so comprehensively, that they will think a thousand times before they attack my men again. You know what the major weapon of the *guerrilla* is? It is horror, Captain, sheer horror, so I make certain I am more horrible than my enemy, and my enemy in this area is horrible indeed. You have heard of El Castrador?'

'The Castrator?' Sharpe guessed the translation.

'Indeed. Because of what he does to French soldiers, only he does it while they are alive and then he lets them bleed to death. El Castrador, I am sorry to say, still lives, but I do assure you that none of my men has been castrated in three months, and do you know why? Because El Castrador's men fear me more than they fear him. I have defeated him, Captain, I have made the mountains secure. In all of Spain, Captain, these are the only hills where Frenchmen can ride safely, and why? Because I have used the *guerrilleros'* weapon against them. I castrate them, just as they would castrate me, only I use a blunter knife.' Brigadier Loup offered Sharpe a grim smile. 'Now tell me, Captain, if you were in my boots, and if your men were being castrated and blinded and disembowelled and skinned alive and left to die, would you not do as I do?'

'To children?' Sharpe jerked his thumb at the village.

25

Loup's one eye widened in surprise, as though he found Sharpe's objection odd in a soldier. 'Would you spare a rat because it's young? Vermin are vermin, Captain, whatever their age.'

'I thought you said the mountains were safe,' Sharpe said, 'so why kill?'

'Because last week two of my men were ambushed and killed in a village not far from here. The families of the murderers came here to take refuge, thinking I would not find them. I did find them, and now I assure you, Captain, that no more of my men will be ambushed in Fuentes de Oñoro.'

'They will if I find them there.'

Loup shook his head sadly. 'You are so quick with your threats, Captain. But fight me and I think you will learn caution. But for now? Give me my men and we shall ride away.'

Sharpe paused, thinking, then finally shrugged and turned. 'Sergeant Harper!'

'Sir?'

'Bring the two Frogs out!'

Harper hesitated as though he wanted to know what Sharpe intended before he obeyed the order, but then he turned reluctantly towards the houses. A moment later he appeared with the two French captives, both of whom were still naked below the waist and one of whom was still half doubled over in pain. 'Is he wounded?' Loup asked.

'I kicked him in the balls,' Sharpe said. 'He was raping a girl.'

Loup seemed amused by the answer. 'You're squeamish about rape, Captain Sharpe?'

'Funny in a man, isn't it? Yes, I am.'

'We have some officers like that,' Loup said, 'but a few months in Spain soon cures their delicacy. The women here fight like the men, and if a woman imagines that her skirts will protect her then she is wrong. And rape is part of the horror, but it also serves a secondary purpose. Release soldiers to rape and they don't care that they're hungry or that their pay is a year in arrears. Rape is a weapon like any other, Captain.'

'I'll remember that, General, when I march into France,' Sharpe said, then he turned back towards the houses. 'Stop there, Sergeant!' The two prisoners had been escorted as far as the village entrance. 'And Sergeant!'

'Sir?'

'Fetch their trousers. Get them dressed properly.'

Loup, pleased with the way his mission was going, smiled at Sharpe. 'You're being sensible, good. I would hate to have to fight you in the same way that I fight the Spanish.'

Sharpe looked at Loup's pagan uniform. It was a costume, he thought, to scare a child, the costume of a wolfman walking out of nightmare, but the wolfman's sword was no longer than Sharpe's and his carbine a good deal less accurate than Sharpe's rifle. 'I don't suppose you could fight us, General,' Sharpe said, 'we're a real army, you see, not a pack of unarmed women and children.'

Loup stiffened. 'You will find, Captain Sharpe, that the Brigade Loup can fight any man, anywhere, anyhow. I do not lose, Captain, not to anyone.'

'So if you never lose, General, how were you taken prisoner?' Sharpe sneered. 'Fast asleep, were you?'

'I was a passenger on my way to Egypt, Captain, when our ship was captured by the Royal Navy. That hardly counts as my defeat.' Loup watched as his two men pulled on their trousers. 'Where is Trooper Godin's horse?'

'Trooper Godin won't need a horse where he's going,' Sharpe said.

'He can walk? I suppose he can. Very well, I yield you the horse,' Loup said magniloquently.

'He's going to hell, General,' Sharpe said. 'I'm dressing them because they're still soldiers, and even your lousy soldiers deserve to die with their trousers on.' He turned back to the settlement. 'Sergeant! Put them against the wall! I want a firing squad, four men for each prisoner. Load up!'

'Captain!' Loup snapped and his hand went to his sword's hilt.

'You don't frighten me, Loup. Not you nor your fancy dress,' Sharpe said. 'You draw that sword and we'll be mopping up your blood with your flag of truce. I've got marksmen up on that ridge who can whip the good eye out of your face at two hundred yards, and one of those marksmen is looking at you right now.'

Loup looked up the hill. He could see Price's redcoats there, and one greenjacket, but he plainly could not tell just how many men were in Sharpe's party. He looked back to Sharpe. 'You're a captain, just a captain. Which means you have what? One company? Maybe two? The British won't entrust more than two companies to a mere captain, but within half a mile I have the rest of my brigade. If you kill my men you'll be hunted down like dogs, and you will die like dogs. I will exempt you from the rules of war, Captain, just as you propose exempting my men, and I will make sure you die in the manner of my Spanish enemies. With a very blunt knife, Captain.'

Sharpe ignored the threat, turning towards the village instead. 'Firing party ready, Sergeant?'

'They're ready, sir. And eager, sir!'

Sharpe looked back to the Frenchman. 'Your brigade is miles away, General. If it was any closer you wouldn't be here talking to me, but leading the attack. Now, if you'll forgive me, I've got some justice to execute.'

'No!' Loup said sharply enough to turn Sharpe back. 'I have made a bargain with my men. You understand that, Captain? You are a leader, I am a leader, and I have promised my men never to abandon them. Don't make me break my promise.'

'I don't give a bugger about your promise,' Sharpe said.

Loup had expected that kind of answer and so shrugged. 'Then maybe you will give a bugger about this, Captain Sharpe. I know who you are, and if you do not return my men I will place a price on your head. I will give every man in Portugal and Spain a reason to hunt you down. Kill those two and you sign your own death warrant.'

Sharpe smiled. 'You're a bad loser, General.'

'And you're not?'

Sharpe walked away. 'I've never lost,' he called back across his shoulder, 'so I wouldn't know.'

'Your death warrant, Sharpe!' Loup called.

Sharpe lifted two fingers. He had heard that the English bowmen at Agincourt, threatened by the French with the loss of their bowstring fingers at the battle's end, had first won the battle and then invented the taunting gesture to show the overweening bastards just who were the better soldiers. Now Sharpe used it again.

Then went to kill the wolfman's men.

Major Michael Hogan discovered Wellington inspecting a bridge over the River Turones where a force of three French battalions had tried to hold off the advancing British. The resulting battle had been swift and brutal, and now a trail of French and British dead told the skirmish's tale. An initial tide line of bodies marked where the sides had clashed, a dreadful smear of bloodied turf showed where two British cannon had enfiladed the enemy, then a further scatter of corpses betrayed the French retreat across the bridge which their engineers had not had time to destroy. 'Fletcher thinks the bridge is Roman work, Hogan,' Wellington greeted the Irish Major.

'I sometimes wonder, my Lord, whether anyone has built a bridge in Portugal or Spain since the Romans.' Hogan, swathed in a cloak because of the day's damp chill, nodded amicably to his Lordship's three aides, then handed the General a sealed letter. The seal, which showed the royal Spanish coat of arms, had been lifted. 'I took the precaution of reading the letter, my Lord,' Hogan explained.

'Trouble?' Wellington asked.

'I wouldn't have bothered you otherwise, my Lord,' Hogan answered gloomily.

Wellington frowned as he read the letter. The General was a handsome man, forty-two years old, but as fit as any in his army. And, Hogan thought, wiser than most. The British army, Hogan knew, had an uncanny knack of finding the least qualified man and promoting him to high command, but somehow the system had gone wrong and Sir Arthur Wellesley, now the Viscount Wellington, had been given command of His Majesty's army in Portugal, thus providing that army with the best possible leadership. At least Hogan thought so, but Michael Hogan allowed that he could be prejudiced in this matter. Wellington, after all, had promoted Hogan's career, making the shrewd Irishman the head of his intelligence department and the result had been a relationship as close as it was fruitful.

The General read the letter again, this time glancing at a translation Hogan had thoughtfully provided. Hogan meanwhile looked about the battlefield where fatigue parties were clearing up the remnants of the skirmish. To the east of the bridge, where the road came delicately down the mountainside in a series of sweeping curves, a dozen work parties were searching the bushes for bodies and abandoned supplies.

30

The French dead were being stripped naked and stacked like cordwood next to a long, shallow grave that a group of diggers was trying to extend. Other men were piling French muskets or else hurling canteens, cartridge boxes, boots and blankets into a cart. Some of the plunder was even more exotic, for the retreating French had weighed themselves down with the loot of a thousand Portuguese villages and Wellington's men were now recovering church vestments, candlesticks and silver plate. 'Astonishing what a soldier will carry on a retreat,' the General remarked to Hogan. 'We found one dead man with a milking stool. A common milking stool! What was he thinking of? Taking it back to France?' He held the letter out to Hogan. 'Damn,' he said mildly, then, more strongly, 'God damn!' He waved his aides away, leaving him alone with Hogan. 'The more I learn about His Most Catholic Majesty King Ferdinand VII, Hogan, the more I become convinced that he should have been drowned at birth.'

Hogan smiled. 'The recognized method, my Lord, is smothering.'

'Is it indeed?'

'It is indeed, my Lord, and no one's ever the wiser. The mother simply explains how she rolled over in her sleep and trapped the blessed little creature beneath her body and thus, the holy church explains, another precious angel is born.'

'In my family,' the General said, 'unwanted children get posted into the army.'

'It has much the same effect, my Lord, except in the matter of angels.'

Wellington gave a brief laugh, then gestured with the letter. 'So how did this reach us?'

'The usual way, my Lord. Smuggled out of Valençay by Ferdinand's servants and brought south to the Pyrenees where it was given to partisans for forwarding to us.'

31

'With a copy to London, eh? Any chance of intercepting the London copy?'

'Alas, sir, gone these two weeks. Probably there already.'

'Hell, damn and hell again. Damn!' Wellington stared gloomily at the bridge where a sling cart was salvaging the fallen barrel of a dismounted French cannon. 'So what to do, eh, Hogan? What to do?'

The problem was simple enough. The letter, copied to the Prince Regent in London, had come from the exiled King Ferdinand of Spain who was now a prisoner of Napoleon in the French château at Valençay. The letter was pleased to announce that His Most Catholic Majesty, in a spirit of cooperation with his cousin of England and in his great desire to drive the French invader from the sacred soil of his kingdom, had directed the Real Compañía Irlandesa of His Most Catholic Majesty's household guard to attach itself to His Britannic Majesty's forces under the command of the Viscount Wellington. Which gesture, though it sounded generous, was not to the Viscount Wellington's taste. He did not need a stray company of royal palace guards. A battalion of trained infantry with full fighting equipment might have been of some service, but a company of ceremonial troops was about as much use to the Viscount Wellington as a choir of psalm-singing eunuchs.

'And they've already arrived,' Hogan said mildly.

'They've what?' Wellington's question could be heard a hundred yards away where a dog, thinking it was being reproved, slunk away from some fly-blackened guts that trailed from the eviscerated body of a French artillery officer. 'Where are they?' Wellington asked fiercely.

'Somewhere on the Tagus, my Lord, being barged towards us.'

'How the hell did they get here?'

'According to my correspondent, my Lord, by ship. Our

ships.' Hogan put a pinch of snuff on his left hand, then sniffed the powder up each nostril. He paused for a second, his eyes suddenly streaming, then sneezed. His horse's ears flicked back at the noise. 'The commander of the Real Compañía Irlandesa claims he marched his men to Spain's east coast, my Lord,' Hogan went on, 'then took ship to Menorca where our Royal Navy collected them.'

Wellington snorted his derision. 'And the French just let that happen? King Joseph just watched half the royal guard march away?' Joseph was Bonaparte's brother and had been elevated to the throne of Spain, though it was taking three hundred thousand French bayonets to keep him there.

'A fifth of the royal guard, my Lord,' Hogan gently corrected the General. 'And yes, that's exactly what Lord Kiely says. Kiely, of course, being their *comandante*.'

'Kiely?'

'Irish peer, my Lord.'

'Damn it, Hogan, I know the Irish peerage. Kiely. Earl of Kiely. An exile, right? And his mother, I remember, gave money to Tone back in the nineties.' Wolfe Tone had been an Irish patriot who had tried to raise money and men in Europe and America to lead a rebellion against the British in his native Ireland. The rebellion had flared into open war in 1798 when Tone had invaded Donegal with a small French army that had been roundly defeated and Tone himself had committed suicide in his Dublin prison rather than hang from a British rope. 'I don't suppose Kiely's any better than his mother,' Wellington said grimly, 'and she's a witch who should have been smothered at birth. Is his Lordship to be trusted, Hogan?'

'So far as I hear, my Lord, he's a drunk and a wastrel,' Hogan said. 'He was given command of the Real Compañía Irlandesa because he's the only Irish aristocrat in Madrid and because his mother had influence over the King. She's dead now, God rest her soul.' He watched a soldier try to fork up the spilt French officer's intestines with his bayonet. The guts kept slipping off the blade and finally a sergeant yelled at the man to either pick the offal up with his bare hands or else leave it for the crows.

'What has this Irish guard been doing since Ferdinand left Madrid?' Wellington asked.

'Living on sufferance, my Lord. Guarding the Escorial, polishing their boots, staying out of trouble, breeding, whoring, drinking and saluting the French.'

'But not fighting the French.'

'Indeed not.' Hogan paused. 'It's all too convenient, my Lord,' he went on. 'The Real Compañía Irlandesa is permitted to leave Madrid, permitted to take ship, and permitted to come to us, and meanwhile a letter is smuggled out of France saying the company is a gift to you from His imprisoned Majesty. I smell Frog paws all over it, my Lord.'

'So we tell these damn guards to go away?'

'I doubt we can. In London the Prince Regent will doubtless be flattered by the gesture and the Foreign Office, you may depend, will consider any slight offered to the Real Compañía Irlandesa to be an insult to our Spanish allies, which means, my Lord, that we are stuck with the bastards.'

'Are they good for anything?'

'I'm sure they'll be decorative,' Hogan allowed dubiously.

'And decoration costs money,' Wellington said. 'I suppose the King of Spain did not think to send his guard's pay chest?'

'No, my Lord.'

'Which means I'm paying them?' Wellington inquired dangerously, and, when Hogan's only answer was a seraphic smile, the General swore. 'God damn their eyes! I'm supposed to pay the bastards? While they stab me in the back? Is that what they're here for, Hogan?'

'I wouldn't know, my Lord. But I suspect as much.'

A gust of laughter sounded from a fatigue party that had just discovered some intimate drawings concealed in a dead Frenchman's coat tails. Wellington winced at the noise and edged his horse further away from the raucous group. Some crows fought over a pile of offal that had once been a French skirmisher. The General stared at the unpleasant sight, then grimaced. 'So what do you know about this Irish guard, Hogan?'

'They're mostly Spanish these days, my Lord, though even the Spanish-born guards have to be descended from Irish exiles. Most of the guardsmen are recruited from the three Irish regiments in Spanish service, but a handful, I imagine, will be deserters from our own army. I'd suspect that most of them are patriotic to Spain and are probably willing to fight against the French, but undoubtedly a handful of them will be *afrancesados*, though in that regard I'd suspect the officers before the men.' An *afrancesado* was a Spaniard who supported the French and almost all such traitors came from the educated classes. Hogan slapped a horsefly that had settled on his horse's neck. 'It's all right, Jeremiah, just a hungry fly,' he explained to his startled horse, then turned back to Wellington. 'I don't know why they've been sent here, my Lord, but I am sure of two things. First, it will be a diplomatic impossibility to get rid of them, and second we have to assume that it's the French who want them here. King Ferdinand, I've no doubt, was gulled into writing the letter. I hear he's not very clever, my Lord.'

'But you are, Hogan. It's why I put up with you. So what do we do? Put them to latrine digging?'

Hogan shook his head. 'If you employ the King of Spain's household guard on menial tasks, my Lord, it will be construed as an insult to our Spanish allies as well as to His Catholic Majesty.'

'Damn His Catholic Majesty,' Wellington growled, then stared balefully towards the trench-like grave where the French dead were now being unceremoniously laid in a long, white, naked row. 'And the *junta*?' he asked. 'What of the *junta*?'

The *junta* in Cadiz was the regency council that ruled unoccupied Spain in their King's absence. Of its patriotism there could be no doubt, but the same could not be said of its efficiency. The *junta* was notorious for its internal squabbles and touchy pride, and few matters had touched that pride more directly than the discreet request that Arthur Wellesley, Viscount Wellington, be made *Generalisimo* of all Spain's armies. Wellington was already the General Marshal of Portugal's army and commander of the British forces in Portugal, and no man of sense denied he was the best general on the allied side, not least because he was the only one who consistently won battles, and no one denied that it made sense for all the armies opposing the French in Spain and Portugal to be under a unified command, but nevertheless, despite the acknowledged sense of the proposal, the *junta* was reluctant to grant Wellington any such powers. Spain's armies, they protested, must be led by a Spaniard, and if no Spaniard had yet proved capable of winning a campaign against the French, then that was no matter; better a defeated Spaniard than a victorious foreigner.

'The *junta*, my Lord,' Hogan answered carefully, 'will think this is the thin end of a very broad wedge. They'll think this is a British plot to take over the Spanish armies piecemeal, and they'll watch like hawks, my Lord, to see how you treat the Real Compañía Irlandesa.'

'The hawk,' Wellington said with a sour twist, 'being Don Luis.'

'Precisely, my Lord,' Hogan said. General Don Luis Valverde was the *junta*'s official observer with the British and Portuguese armies and the man whose recommendation was needed if the Spanish were ever to appoint Wellington as their *Generalisimo*.

It was an approval that was highly unlikely, for General Valverde was a man in whom all the *junta*'s great pride and none of its small sense was concentrated.

'God damn it,' Wellington said, thinking of Valverde. 'Well, Hogan? You're paid to advise me, so earn your damned pay.'

Hogan paused to collect his thoughts. 'I fear we have to welcome Lord Kiely and his men,' he said after a few seconds, 'even while we distrust them, and so it seems to me, my Lord, that we must do our best to make them uncomfortable. So uncomfortable that they either go back to Madrid or else march down to Cadiz.'

'We drive them out?' Wellington said. 'How?'

'Partly, my Lord, by bivouacking them so close to the French that those guardsmen who wish to desert will find it easy. At the same time, my Lord, we say that we have put them in a place of danger as a compliment to their fighting reputation, despite which, my Lord, I think we must assume that the Real Compañía Irlandesa, while undoubtedly skilled at guarding palace gates, will prove less skilled at the more mundane task of fighting the French. We should therefore insist that they submit to a period of strict training under the supervision of someone who can be trusted to make their life a living misery.'

Wellington gave a grim smile. 'Make these ceremonial soldiers stoop, eh? Make them chew on humble pie till it chokes them?'

'Exactly, my Lord. I have no doubt that they expect to be treated with respect and even privilege, so we must disappoint them. We'll have to give them a liaison officer, someone senior enough to smooth Lord Kiely's feathers and allay General Valverde's suspicions, but why not give them a drillmaster too? A tyrant, but someone shrewd enough to smoke out their secrets.'

Wellington smiled, then turned his horse back towards his

aides. He knew exactly who Hogan had in mind. 'I doubt our Lord Kiely will much like Mister Sharpe,' the General said.

'I cannot think they'll take to each other, my Lord, no.'

'Where is Sharpe?'

'He should be on his way to Vilar Formoso today, my Lord. He's an unhappy recruit to the Town Major's staff.'

'So he'll be glad to be cumbered with Kiely instead then, won't he? And who do we appoint as liaison officer?'

'Any emollient fool will do for that post, my Lord.'

'Very well, Hogan, I'll find the fool and you arrange the rest.' The General touched his heels to his horse's flank. His aides, seeing the General ready to move, gathered their reins, then Wellington paused. 'What does a man want with a common milking stool, Hogan?'

'It keeps his arse dry during wet nights of sentry duty, my Lord.'

'Clever thought, Hogan. Can't think why I didn't come up with the idea myself. Well done.' Wellington wheeled his horse and spurred west away from the battle's litter.

Hogan watched the General go, then grimaced. The French, he was sure, had wished trouble on him and now, with God's good help, he would wish some evil back on them. He would welcome the Real Compañía Irlandesa with honeyed words and extravagant promises, then give the bastards Richard Sharpe.

The girl clung to Rifleman Perkins. She was hurt inside, she was bleeding and limping, but she had insisted on coming out of the hovel to watch the two Frenchmen die. Indeed she taunted the two men, spitting and screaming at them, then laughed as one of the two captives dropped to his knees and lifted his bound hands towards Sharpe. 'He says he wasn't raping the girl, sir,' Harris translated.

'So why were the bastard's trousers round his ankles?' Sharpe asked, then looked at his eight-man firing squad. Usually it was hard to find men willing to serve on firing squads, but there had been no difficulty this time. 'Present!' Sharpe called.

'*Non, Monsieur, je vous prie! Monsieur!*' the kneeling Frenchman called. Tears ran down his face.

Eight riflemen lined their sights on the two Frenchmen. The other captive spat his derision and kept his head high. He was a handsome man, though his face was bruised from Harris's ministrations. The first man, realizing that his begging was to go unanswered, dropped his head and sobbed uncontrollably. '*Maman,*' he called pathetically, '*Maman!*' Brigadier General Loup, back in his fur-edged saddle, watched the executions from fifty yards away.

Sharpe knew he had no legal right to shoot prisoners. He knew he might even be endangering his career by this act, but then he thought of the small, blood-blackened bodies of the raped and murdered children. 'Fire!' he called.

The eight rifles snapped. Smoke gusted to form an acrid, filthy-smelling cloud that obscured the skeins of blood splashing high on the hovel's stone wall as the two bodies were thrown hard back, then recoiled forward to flop onto the ground. One of the men twitched for a few seconds, then went still.

'You're a dead man, Sharpe!' Loup shouted.

Sharpe raised his two fingers to the Brigadier, but did not bother to turn round. 'The bloody Frogs can bury those two,' he said of the executed prisoners, 'but we'll collapse the houses on the Spanish dead. They are Spanish, aren't they?' he asked Harris.

Harris nodded. 'We're just inside Spain, sir. Maybe a mile or two. That's what the girl says.'

Sharpe looked at the girl. She was no older than Perkins, maybe sixteen, and had dank, dirty, long black hair, but clean her up, he thought, and she would be a pretty enough thing, and immediately Sharpe felt guilty for the thought. The girl was in pain. She had watched her family slaughtered, then had been used by God knows how many men. Now, with her rag-like clothes held tight about her thin body, she was staring intently at the two dead soldiers. She spat at them, then buried her head in Perkins's shoulder. 'She'll have to come with us, Perkins,' Sharpe said. 'If she stays here she'll be slaughtered by those bastards.'

'Yes, sir.'

'So look after her, lad. Do you know her name?'

'Miranda, sir.'

'Look after Miranda then,' Sharpe said, then he crossed to where Harper was organizing the men who would demolish the houses on top of the dead bodies. The smell of blood was as thick as the mass of flies buzzing inside the charnel houses. 'The bastards will chase us,' Sharpe said, nodding towards the lurking French.

'They will too, sir,' the Sergeant agreed.

'So we'll keep to the hill tops,' Sharpe said. Cavalry could not get to the tops of steep hills, at least not in good order, and certainly not before their leaders had been picked off by Sharpe's best marksmen.

Harper glanced at the two dead Frenchmen. 'Were you supposed to do that, sir?'

'You mean, am I allowed to execute prisoners of war under the King's Regulations? No, of course I'm not. So don't tell anyone.'

'Not a word, sir. Never saw a thing, sir, and I'll make sure the lads say the same.'

'And one day,' Sharpe said as he stared at the distant figure of Brigadier General Loup, 'I'll put him against a wall and shoot him.'

'Amen,' Harper said, 'amen.' He turned and looked at the French horse that was still picketed in the settlement. 'What do we do with the beast?'

'We can't take it with us,' Sharpe said. The hills were too steep, and he planned to keep to the rocky heights where dragoon horses could not follow. 'But I'll be damned before I give a serviceable cavalry horse back to the enemy.' He cocked his rifle. 'I hate to do it.'

'You want me to do it, sir?'

'No,' Sharpe said, though he meant yes for he really did not want to shoot the horse. He did it anyway. The shot echoed back from the hills, fading and crackling while the horse thrashed in its bloody death throes.

The riflemen covered the Spanish dead with stones and thatch, but left the two French soldiers for their own comrades to bury. Then they climbed high into the misty heights to work their way westwards. By nightfall, when they came down into the valley of the River Turones, there was no sign of any pursuit. There was no stink of saddle-sore horses, no glint of grey light from grey steel, indeed there had been no sign nor smell of any pursuit all afternoon except just once, just as the light faded and as the first small candle flames flickered yellow in the cottages beside the river, when suddenly a wolf had howled its melancholy cry in the darkening hills.

Its howl was long and desolate, and the echo lingered.

And Sharpe shivered.

CHAPTER TWO

The view from the castle in Ciudad Rodrigo looked across the River Agueda towards the hills where the British forces gathered, yet this night was so dark and wet that nothing was visible except the flicker of two torches burning deep inside an arched tunnel that burrowed through the city's enormous ramparts. The rain flickered silver-red past the flame light to make the cobbles slick. Every few moments a sentry would appear at the entrance of the tunnel and the fiery light would glint off the shining spike of his fixed bayonet, but otherwise there was no sign of life. The tricolour of France flew above the gate, but there was no light to show it flapping dispiritedly in the rain which was being gusted around the castle walls and sometimes even being driven into the deep embrasured window where a man leaned to watch the arch. The flickering torchlight was reflected in the thick pebbled lenses of his wire-bound spectacles.

'Maybe he's not coming,' the woman said from the fireplace.

'If Loup says he will be here,' the man answered without turning round, 'then he will be here.' The man had a remarkably deep voice that belied his appearance for he was slim, almost fragile-looking, with a thin scholarly face, myopic eyes and cheeks pocked with the scars of childhood smallpox.

He wore a plain dark-blue uniform with no badges of rank, but Pierre Ducos needed no gaudy chains or stars, no tassels or epaulettes or aiguillettes to signify his authority. Major Ducos was Napoleon's man in Spain and everyone who mattered, from King Joseph downwards, knew it.

'Loup,' the woman said. 'It means "wolf", yes?'

This time Ducos did turn round. 'Your countrymen call him El Lobo,' he said, 'and he frightens them.'

'Superstitious people frighten easily,' the woman said scornfully. She was tall and thin, and had a face that was memorable rather than beautiful. A hard, clever and singular face, once seen never forgotten, with a full mouth, deep-set eyes and a scornful expression. She was maybe thirty years old, but it was hard to tell for her skin had been so darkened by the sun that it looked like a peasant woman's. Other well-born women took care to keep their skins as pale as chalk and soft as curds, but this woman did not care for fashionable looks nor for fashionable clothes. Her passion was hunting and when she followed her hounds she rode astride like a man and so she dressed like a man: in breeches, boots and spurs. This night she was uniformed as a French hussar with skin-tight sky-blue breeches that had an intricate pattern of Hungarian lace down the front of the thighs, a plum-coloured dolman with blue cuffs and plaited white-silk cordings and a scarlet pelisse edged with black fur. It was rumoured that Doña Juanita de Elia possessed a uniform from the regiment of every man she had ever slept with and that her wardrobe needed to be as large as most people's parlours. To Major Ducos's eyes the Doña Juanita de Elia was nothing but a flamboyant whore and a soldier's plaything, and in Ducos's murky world flamboyance was a lethal liability, but in Juanita's own eyes she was an adventuress and an *afrancesada*, and any Spaniard willing to side with France in this war was useful to Pierre Ducos. And, he grudgingly

43

allowed, this war-loving adventuress was willing to run great risks for France and so Ducos was willing to treat her with a respect he would not usually accord to women. 'Tell me about El Lobo,' the Doña Juanita demanded.

'He's a brigadier of dragoons,' Ducos said, 'who began his army career as a groom in the royal army. He's brave, he's demanding, he's successful and, above all, he is ruthless.' On the whole Ducos had little time for soldiers whom he considered to be romantic fools much given to posturing and gestures, but he approved of Loup. Loup was single-minded, fierce and utterly without illusions, qualities that Ducos himself possessed, and Ducos liked to think that, had he ever been a proper soldier, he would have been like Loup. It was true that Loup, like Juanita de Elia, affected a certain flamboyance, but Ducos forgave the Brigadier his wolf-fur pretensions because, quite simply, he was the best soldier Ducos had discovered in Spain and the Major was determined that Loup should be properly rewarded. 'Loup will one day be a marshal of France,' Ducos said, 'and the sooner the better.'

'But not if Marshal Masséna can help it?' Juanita asked.

Ducos grunted. He collected gossip more assiduously than any man, but he disliked confirming it, yet Marshal Masséna's dislike of Loup was so well known in the army that Ducos had no need to dissemble about it. 'Soldiers are like stags, madame,' Ducos said. 'They fight to prove they are the best in their tribe and they dislike their fiercest rivals far more than the beasts that offer them no competition. So I would suggest to you, madame, that the Marshal's dislike of Brigadier Loup is confirm-ation of Loup's genuine abilities.' It was also, Ducos thought, a typical piece of wasteful posturing. No wonder the war in Spain was taking so long and proving so troublesome when a marshal of France wasted petulance on the best brigadier in the army.

He turned back to the window as the sound of hooves echoed in the fortress's entrance tunnel. Ducos listened as the challenge was given, then he heard the squeal of the gate hinges opening and a second later he saw a group of grey horsemen appear in the flamelit archway.

The Doña Juanita de Elia had come to stand beside Ducos. She was so close that he could smell the perfume on her gaudy uniform. 'Which one is he?' she asked.

'The one in front,' Ducos replied.

'He rides well,' Juanita de Elia said with grudging respect.

'A natural horseman,' Ducos said. 'Not fancy. He doesn't make his horse dance, he makes it fight.' He moved away from the woman. He disliked perfume as much as he disliked opinionated whores.

The two waited in silent awkwardness. Juanita de Elia had long sensed that her weapons did not work on Ducos. She believed he disliked women, but the truth was that Pierre Ducos was oblivious of them. Once in a while he would use a soldier's brothel, but only after a surgeon had provided him with the name of a clean girl. Most of the time he went without such distractions, preferring a monkish dedication to the Emperor's cause. Now he sat at his table and leafed through papers as he tried to ignore the woman's presence. Somewhere in the town a church clock struck nine, then a sergeant's voice echoed from an inner courtyard as a squad of men was marched towards the ramparts. The rain fell relentlessly. Then, at last, boots and spurs sounded loud on the stairway leading to Ducos's big chamber and the Doña Juanita looked up expectantly.

Brigadier Loup did not bother to knock on Ducos's door. He burst in, already fuming with anger. 'I lost two men! God damn it! Two good men! Lost to riflemen, Ducos, to British riflemen. Executed! They were put against a wall and shot like vermin!' He had crossed to Ducos's table and helped himself from the decanter of brandy. 'I want a price put on the head of their captain, Ducos. I want the man's balls in my men's stewpot.' He stopped suddenly, checked by the exotic sight of the uniformed woman standing beside the fire. For a second Loup had thought the figure in cavalry uniform was an especially effeminate young man, one of the dandified Parisians who spent more money on their tailor than on their horse and weapons, but then he realized that the dandy was a woman and that the cascading black plume was her hair and not a helmet's embellishment. 'Is she yours, Ducos?' Loup asked nastily.

'Monsieur,' Ducos said very formally, 'allow me to name the Doña Juanita de Elia. Madame? This is Brigadier General Guy Loup.'

Brigadier Loup stared at the woman by the fire and what he saw, he liked, and the Doña Juanita de Elia returned the Dragoon General's stare and what she saw, she also liked. She saw a compact, one-eyed man with a brutal, weather-beaten face who wore his grey hair and beard short, and his grey, fur-trimmed uniform like an executioner's costume. The fur glinted with rainwater that had brought out the smell of the pelts, a smell that mingled with the heady aromas of saddles, tobacco, sweat, gun oil, powder and horses. 'Brigadier,' she said politely.

'Madame,' Loup acknowledged her, then shamelessly looked up and down her skin-tight uniform, 'or should it be Colonel?'

'Brigadier at least,' Juanita answered, 'if not *Maréchal*.'

'Two men?' Ducos interrupted the flirtation. 'How did you lose two men?'

Loup told the story of his day. He paced up and down the room as he spoke, biting into an apple he took from Ducos's desk. He told how he had taken a small group of men into the hills to find the fugitives from the village of Fuentes de Oñoro, and how, having taken his revenge on the Spaniards, he had been surprised by the arrival of the greenjackets. 'They were led by a captain called Sharpe,' he said.

'Sharpe,' Ducos repeated, then leafed through an immense ledger in which he recorded every scrap of information about the Emperor's enemies. It was Ducos's job to know about those enemies and to recommend how they could be destroyed, and his intelligence was as copious as his power. 'Sharpe,' he said again as he found the entry he sought. 'A rifleman, you say? I suspect he may be the same man who captured an eagle at Talavera. Was he with greenjackets only? Or did he have redcoats with him?'

'He had redcoats.'

'Then it is the same man. For a reason we have never discovered he serves in a red-jacketed battalion.' Ducos was adding to his notes in the book that contained similar entries on over five hundred enemy officers. Some of the entries were scored through with a single black line denoting that the men were dead and Ducos sometimes imagined a glorious day when all these enemy heroes, British, Portuguese and Spanish alike, would be black-lined by a rampaging French army. 'Captain Sharpe,' Ducos now said, 'is reckoned a famous man in Wellington's forces. He came up from the ranks, Brigadier, a rare feat in Britain.'

'I don't care if he came up from the jakes, Ducos, I want his scalp and I want his balls.'

Ducos disapproved of such private rivalries, fearing that they interfered with more important duties. He closed the ledger. 'Would it not be better,' he suggested coldly, 'if you allowed me to issue a formal complaint about the execution? Wellington will hardly approve.'

'No,' Loup said. 'I don't need lawyers taking revenge for me.' Loup's anger was not caused by the death of his two men, for death was a risk all soldiers learned to abide, but rather by the manner of their death. Soldiers should die in battle or in bed, not against a wall like common criminals. Loup was also piqued that another soldier had got the better of him. 'But if I can't kill him in the next few weeks, Ducos, you can write your damned letter.' The permission was grudging. 'Soldiers are harder to kill than civilians,' Loup went on, 'and we've been fighting civilians too long. Now my brigade will have to learn how to destroy uniformed enemies as well.'

'I thought most French soldiers would rather fight other regulars than fight *guerrilleros*,' the Doña Juanita said.

Loup nodded. 'Most do, but not me, madame. I have specialized in fighting the *guerrilla*.'

'Tell me how,' she asked.

Loup glanced at Ducos as if seeking permission, and Ducos nodded. Ducos was annoyed by the attraction he sensed between these two. It was an attraction as elemental as the lust of a tomcat, a lust so palpable that Ducos almost wrinkled his nose at the stench of it. Leave these two alone for half a minute, he thought, and their uniforms would make a single heap on the floor. It was not their lust that offended him, but rather the fact that it distracted them from their proper business. 'Go on,' he told Loup.

Loup shrugged as though there was no real secret involved. 'I've got the best-trained troops in the army. Better than the Imperial Guard. They fight well, they kill well and they're rewarded well. I keep them separate. They're not billeted with other troops, they don't mix with other troops, and that way no one knows where they are or what they're doing. If you send six hundred men marching from here to Madrid then I guarantee you that every *guerrillero* between here and Seville will know about it before they leave. But not with my men. We don't tell anyone what we're doing or where we're going, we just go there and do it. And we have our own places to live. I emptied a village of its inhabitants and made it my depot, but we don't just stay there. We travel where we will, sleep where we will, and if *guerrilleros* attack us they die, and not just them, but their mothers, their children, their priests and their grandchildren die with them. We horrify them, madame, just as they try to horrify us, and by now my wolf pack is more horrifying than the partisans.'

'Good,' Juanita said simply.

'Brigadier Loup's patrol area is remarkably free of partisans,' Ducos said in generous tribute.

'But not entirely free,' Loup added grimly. 'El Castrador survives, but I'll use his own knife on him yet. Maybe the arrival of the British will encourage him to show his face again.'

'Which is why we are here,' Ducos said, taking command of the room. 'Our job is to make certain that the British do not stay here, but are sent packing.' And then, in his deep and almost hypnotic voice, he described the military situation as he comprehended it. Brigadier General Loup, who had spent the last year fighting to keep the passes through the frontier hills free of partisans and who had thus been spared the disasters that had afflicted Marshal Masséna's army in Portugal, listened raptly as Ducos told the real story and not the patriotic lies that were peddled in the columns of the *Moniteur*. 'Wellington is clever,' Ducos admitted. 'He's not brilliant, but he is clever and we under-estimated him.' The existence of the Lines of Torres Vedras had been unknown to the French until they marched within cannon shot of the defences and there they had waited, ever hungrier, ever colder, through a long winter. Now the army was back on the Spanish frontier and waiting for Wellington's assault.

It was an assault that would be hard and bloody because of the two massive fortresses that barred the only passable roads through the frontier mountains. Ciudad Rodrigo was the northern fastness and Badajoz the southern. Badajoz had been in Spanish hands till a month before and Masséna's engineers had despaired of ever reducing its massive walls, but Ducos had arranged a huge bribe and the Spanish commander had yielded the keys to the fortress. Now both keys of Spain, Badajoz and Ciudad Rodrigo, were firmly in the Emperor's grip.

But there was a third border fortress which also lay in French hands. Almeida was inside Portugal and, though it was not so important as Ciudad Rodrigo or Badajoz, and though its massive castle had been destroyed with the neighbouring cathedral in an earth-shattering explosion of gunpowder just the previous year, the town's thick star-shaped walls and its strong French garrison still presented a formidable obstacle. Any British force laying siege to Ciudad Rodrigo would have to use thousands of men to guard against the threat of Almeida's garrison sallying out to raid the supply roads and Ducos reckoned that Wellington would never abide that menace in his army's rear. 'Wellington's first priority will be to capture Almeida,' Ducos said, 'and Marshal Masséna will do his best to relieve the fortress from the British siege. In other words, Brigadier' – Ducos was speaking more to Loup than to the Doña Juanita – 'there will be a battle fought close to Almeida. Not much is certain in war, but I think we can be certain of that.'

Loup stared at the map, then nodded agreement. 'Unless Marshal Masséna withdraws the garrison?' he said in a tone of contempt suggesting that Masséna, his enemy, was capable of any foolishness.

'He won't,' Ducos said with the certainty of a man who had the power to dictate strategy to marshals of France. 'And the reason he will not is here,' Ducos said, and he tapped the map as he spoke. 'Look,' he said, and Loup bent obediently over the map. The fortress of Almeida was depicted like a star to imitate its jagged, star-shaped fortifications. Around it were the hatch marks of hills, but behind it, between Almeida and the rest of Portugal, ran a deep river. The Coa. 'It runs in a gorge, Brigadier,' Ducos said, 'and is crossed by a single bridge at Castello Bom.'

'I know it well.'

'So if we defeat General Wellington on this side of the river,' Ducos said, 'then the fugitives of his army will be forced to retreat across a single bridge scarce three metres wide. That is why we shall leave the garrison in Almeida, because its presence will force Lord Wellington to fight on this bank of the Coa and when he does fight we shall destroy him. And once the British are gone, Brigadier, we shall employ your tactics of horror to end all resistance in Portugal and Spain.'

Loup straightened up. He was impressed by Ducos's analysis, but also dubious of it. He needed a few seconds to phrase his objection and made the time by lighting a long, dark cigar. He blew smoke out, then decided there was no politic way to voice his doubt, so he just stated it baldly. 'I've not fought the British in battle, Major, but I hear they're stubborn bastards in defence.' Loup tapped the map. 'I know that country well. It's full of hill ranges and river valleys. Give Wellington a hill and you could die of old age before you could shift the bugger loose. That's what I hear, anyway.' Loup finished with a shrug, as if to deprecate his own opinion.

Ducos smiled. 'Supposing, Brigadier, that Wellington's army is rotted from the inside?'

Loup considered the question, then nodded. 'He'll break,' he confirmed simply.

'Good! Because that is precisely why I wanted you to meet the Doña Juanita,' Ducos said, and the lady smiled at the dragoon. 'The Doña Juanita will be crossing the lines,' Ducos continued, 'and living among our enemies. From time to time, Brigadier, she will come to you for certain supplies that I shall provide. I want you to make the provision of those supplies to Doña Juanita your most important duty.'

'Supplies?' Loup asked. 'You mean guns? Ammunition?'

Doña Juanita answered for Ducos. 'Nothing, Brigadier, that cannot be carried in the panniers of a packhorse.'

Loup looked at Ducos. 'You think it's easy to ride from one army to another? Hell, Ducos, the British have a cavalry screen and there are partisans and our own picquets and God knows how many other British sentries. It isn't like riding in the Bois de Boulogne.'

Ducos looked unconcerned. 'The Doña Juanita will make her own arrangements and I have faith in those. What you must do, Brigadier, is acquaint the lady with your lair. She must know where to find you, and how. You can arrange that?'

Loup nodded, then looked at the woman. 'You can ride with me tomorrow?'

'All day, Brigadier.'

'Then we ride tomorrow,' Loup said, 'and maybe the next day too?'

'Maybe, General, maybe,' the woman answered.

Ducos again interrupted their flirtation. It was late, his supper was waiting and he still had several hours of paperwork to be completed. 'Your men,' he said to Loup, 'are now the army's picquet line. So I want you to be alert for the arrival of a new unit in the British army.'

Loup, suspecting he was being taught how to suck eggs, frowned. 'We're always alert to such things, Major. We're soldiers, remember?'

'Especially alert, Brigadier.' Ducos was unruffled by Loup's scorn. 'A Spanish unit, the Real Compañía Irlandesa, is expected to join the British soon and I want to know when they arrive and where they are positioned. It is important, Brigadier.'

Loup glanced at Juanita, suspecting that the Real Compañía

Irlandesa was somehow connected with her mission, but her face gave nothing away. Never mind, Loup thought, the woman would tell him everything before the next two nights were done. He looked back to Ducos. 'If a dog farts in the British lines, Major, you'll know about it.'

'Good!' Ducos said, ending the conversation. 'I won't keep you, Brigadier. I'm sure you have plans for the evening.'

Loup, thus dismissed, picked up his helmet with its plume of wet grey hair. 'Doña,' he said as he reached the staircase door, 'isn't that the title of a married woman?'

'My husband, General, is buried in South America.' Juanita shrugged. 'The yellow fever, alas.'

'And my wife, madame,' Loup said, 'is buried in her kitchen in Besançon. Alas.' He held a hand towards the door, offering to escort her down the winding stairs, but Ducos held the Spanish woman back.

'You're ready to go?' Ducos asked Juanita when Loup was gone out of earshot.

'So soon?' Juanita answered.

Ducos shrugged. 'I suspect the Real Compañía Irlandesa will have reached the British lines by now. Certainly by the month's end.'

Juanita nodded. 'I'm ready.' She paused. 'And the British, Ducos, will surely suspect the Real Compañía Irlandesa's motives?'

'Of course they will. They would be fools not to. And I want them to be suspicious. Our task, madame, is to unsettle our enemy, so let them be wary of the Real Compañía Irlandesa and perhaps they will overlook the real threat?' Ducos took off his spectacles and polished their lenses on the skirts of his plain jacket. 'And Lord Kiely? You're sure of his affections?'

'He is a drunken fool, Major,' Juanita answered. 'He will do whatever I tell him.'

53

'Don't make him jealous,' Ducos warned.

Juanita smiled. 'You may lecture me on many things, Ducos, but when it comes to men and their moods, believe me, I know all there is to know. Do not worry about my Lord Kiely. He will be kept very sweet and very obedient. Is that all?'

Ducos looped his spectacles back into place. 'That is all. May I wish you a good night's rest, madame?'

'I'm sure it will be a splendid night, Ducos.' The Doña Juanita smiled and walked from the room. Ducos listened as her spurs jangled down the steps, then heard her laugh as she encountered Loup who had been waiting at the foot of the steps. Ducos closed the door on the sound of their laughter and walked slowly back to the window. In the night the rain beat on, but in Ducos's busy mind there was nothing but the vision of glory. This did not just depend on Juanita and Loup doing their duty, but rather on the clever scheme of a man whom even Ducos acknowledged as his equal, a man whose passion to defeat the British equalled Ducos's passion to see France triumphant, and a man who was already behind the British lines where he would sow the mischief that would first rot the British army, then lead it into a trap beside a narrow ravine. Ducos's thin body seemed to quiver as the vision unfolded in his imagination. He saw an insolent British army eroded from within, then trapped and beaten. He saw France triumphant. He saw a river gorge crammed to its rocky brim with bloody carcasses. He saw his Emperor ruling over all Europe and then, who could tell, over the whole known world. Alexander had done it, why not Bonaparte?

And it would begin, with a little cunning from Ducos and his most secret agent, on the banks of the Coa near the fortress of Almeida.

*   *   *

'This is a chance, Sharpe, upon my soul it is a chance. A veritable chance. Not many chances come in a man's life and a man must seize them. My father taught me that. He was a bishop, you see, and a fellow doesn't rise from being curate to bishop without seizing his chances. You comprehend me?'

'Yes, sir.'

Colonel Claud Runciman's massive buttocks were well set on the inn bench while before him, on a plain wooden table, were the remnants of a huge meal. There were chicken bones, the straggling stalks of a bunch of grapes, orange peel, rabbit vertebrae, a piece of unidentifiable gristle and a collapsed wineskin. The copious food had forced Colonel Runciman to unbutton his coat, waistcoat and shirt in order to loosen the strings of his corset and the subsequent distending of his belly had stretched a watch chain hung thick with seals tight across a strip of pale, drum-taut flesh. The Colonel belched prodigiously. 'There's a hunchbacked girl somewhere about who serves the food, Sharpe,' Runciman said. 'If you see the lass, tell her I'll take some pie. With some cheese, perhaps. But not if it's goat's cheese. Can't abide goat's cheese; it gives me spleen, d'you see?' Runciman's red coat had the yellow facings and silver lace of the 37th, a good line regiment from Hampshire that had not seen the Colonel's ample shadow in many a year. Recently Runciman had been the Wagon Master General in charge of the drivers and teams of the Royal Wagon Train and their auxiliary Portuguese muleteers, but now he had been appointed liaison officer to the Real Compañía Irlandesa.

'It's an honour, of course,' he told Sharpe, 'but neither unexpected nor undeserved. I told Wellington when he made me Wagon Master General that I'd do the job as a favour to him, but that I expected a reward for it. A fellow doesn't want to spend his life thumping sense into thick-witted wagon drivers, good God, no. There's the hunchback, Sharpe! There she is!

55

Stop her, Sharpe, there's a kind fellow! Tell her I want pie and a proper cheese!'

The pie and cheese were arranged and another wine-skin was fetched, along with a bowl of cherries, to satisfy the last possible vestiges of Runciman's appetite. A group of cavalry officers sitting at a table on the far side of the yard were making wagers on how much food Runciman could consume, but Runciman was oblivious of their mockery. 'It's a chance,' he said again when he was well tucked into his pie. 'I can't tell what's in it for you, of course, because a chap like you probably doesn't expect too much out of life anyway, but I reckon I've got a chance at a Golden Fleece.' He peered up at Sharpe. 'You do know what *real* means, don't you?'

'Royal, sir.'

'So you're not completely uneducated then, eh? Royal indeed, Sharpe. The royal guard! These Irish fellows are royal! Not a pack of common carriers and mule-drivers. They've got royal connections, Sharpe, and that means royal rewards! I've half an idea that the Spanish court might even give a pension with the Order of the Golden Fleece. The thing comes with a nice star and a golden collar, but a pension would be very acceptable. A reward for a job well done, don't you see? And that's just from the Spanish! The good Lord alone knows what London might cough up. A knighthood? The Prince Regent will want to know we've done a good job, Sharpe, he'll take an interest, don't you see? He'll be expecting us to treat these fellows proper, as befits a royal guard. Order of the Bath at the very least, I should think. Maybe even a viscountcy? And why not? There's only one problem.' Colonel Runciman belched again, then raised a buttock for a few seconds. 'My God, but that's better,' he said. 'Let the effusions out, that's what my doctor says. There's no future in keeping noxious effusions in the body, he tells me, in case the body rots from within. Now, Sharpe, the fly in our unguent is the fact these royal guards are all Irish. Have you ever commanded the Irish?'

'A few, sir.'

'Well, I've commanded dozens of the rogues. Ever since they amalgamated the Train with the Irish Corps of Wagoners, and there ain't much about the Irish that I don't know. Ever served in Ireland, Sharpe?'

'No, sir.'

'I was there once. Garrison duty at Dublin Castle. Six months of misery, Sharpe, without a single properly cooked meal. God knows, Sharpe, I strive to be a good Christian and to love my fellow man, but the Irish do sometimes make it difficult. Not that some of them ain't the nicest fellows you could ever meet, but they can be obtuse! Dear me, Sharpe, I sometimes wondered if they were gulling me. Pretending not to understand the simplest orders. Do you find that? And there's something else, Sharpe. We'll have to be politic, you and I. The Irish' – and here Runciman leaned awkwardly forward as though confiding something important to Sharpe – 'are very largely Romish, Sharpe. Papists! We shall have to watch our theological discourse if we're not to unsettle their tempers! You and I might know that the Pope is the reincarnation of the Scarlet Whore of Babylon, but it won't help our cause if we say it out loud. Know what I mean?'

'You mean there'll be no Golden Fleece, sir?'

'Good fellow, knew you'd comprehend. Exactly. We have to be diplomatic, Sharpe. We have to be understanding. We have to treat these fellows as if they were Englishmen.' Runciman thought about that statement, then frowned. 'Or almost English, anyway. You came up from the ranks, ain't that right? So these things might not be obvious to you, but if you just remember to keep silent about the Pope you can't go far wrong. And tell your chaps the same,' he added hastily.

'A fair number of my fellows are Catholics themselves, sir,' Sharpe said. 'And Irish.'

'They would be, they would be. A third of this army is Irish! If there was ever a mutiny, Sharpe . . .' Colonel Runciman shuddered at the prospect of the papist redcoats running wild. 'Well, it doesn't bear thinking about, does it?' he went on. 'So ignore their infamous heresies, Sharpe, just ignore them. Ignorance is the only possible cause for papism, my dear father always said, and a burning at the stake the only known cure. He was a bishop, so he understood these matters. Oh, and one other thing, Sharpe, I'd be obliged if you didn't call me Colonel Runciman. They haven't replaced me yet, so I'm still the Wagon Master General, so it ought to be General Runciman.'

'Of course, General,' Sharpe said, hiding a smile. After nineteen years in the army he knew Colonel Runciman's type. The man had purchased his promotions all the way to lieutenant colonel and there got stuck because promotion above that rank depended entirely on seniority and merit, but if Runciman wanted to be called General then Sharpe would play along for a while. He also sensed that Runciman was hardly likely to prove a difficult man so there was small point in antagonizing him.

'Good fellow! Ah! You see that scrawny chap who's just going?' Runciman pointed to a man leaving the inn through its arched entrance. 'I swear he's left half a skin of wine on his table. See it? Go and snaffle it, Sharpe, there's a stout fellow, before that hunchbacked girl gets her paws on it. I'd go myself, but the damn gout is pinching me something hard today. Off you go, man, I'm thirsty!'

Sharpe was saved the indignity of scavenging the tables like a beggar by the arrival of Major Michael Hogan who waved Sharpe back towards the wreckage of Runciman's luncheon. 'Good afternoon to you, Colonel,' Hogan said, 'and it's a grand day too, is it not?' Hogan, Sharpe noticed, was deliberately exaggerating his Irish accent.

'Hot,' Runciman said, dabbing with his napkin at the perspiration that dripped down his plump cheeks and then, suddenly conscious of his naked belly, he vainly tried to tug the edges of his corset together. 'Damnably hot,' he said.

'It's the sun, Colonel,' Hogan said very earnestly. 'I've noticed that the sun seems to heat up the day. Have you noticed that?'

'Well, of course it's the sun!' Runciman said, confused.

'So I'm right! Isn't that amazing? But what about winter, Colonel?'

Runciman threw an anguished glance towards the abandoned wineskin. He was about to order Sharpe to fetch it when the serving girl whisked it away. 'Damn,' Runciman said sadly.

'You spoke, Colonel?' Hogan asked, helping himself to a handful of Runciman's cherries.

'Nothing, Hogan, nothing but a twinge of gout. I need some more Husson's Water, but the stuff is damned hard to find. Maybe you could put a request to the Horse Guards in London? They must realize we need medication here? And one other thing, Hogan?'

'Speak, Colonel. I am ever yours to command.'

Runciman coloured. He knew he was being mocked but, though he outranked the Irishman, he was nervous of Hogan's intimacy with Wellington. 'I am still, as you know, Wagon Master General,' Runciman said heavily.

'So you are, Colonel, so you are. And a damned fine one too, I might say. The Peer was only saying to me the other day. Hogan, says he, have you ever seen wagons so finely mastered in all your born days?'

'Wellington said that?' Runciman asked in astonishment.

'He did, Colonel, he did.'

'Well, I'm not really surprised,' Runciman said. 'My dear

mother always said I had a talent for organization, Hogan. But the thing is, Major,' Runciman went on, 'that until a replacement is found then I am still the Wagon Master General' – he stressed the word 'General' – 'and I would be vastly obliged if you addressed me as –'

'My dear Wagon Master,' Hogan interrupted Runciman's laborious request, 'why didn't you say so earlier? Of course I shall address you as Wagon Master, and I apologize for not thinking of that simple courtesy myself. But now, Wagon Master, if you'll excuse me, the Real Compañía Irlandesa have reached the edge of town and we need to review them. If you're ready?' Hogan gestured to the inn's gateway.

Runciman quailed at the prospect of exerting himself. 'Right now, Hogan? This minute? But I can't. Doctor's orders. A man of my constitution needs to take a rest after . . .' He paused, seeking the right word. 'After . . .' he went on and failed again.

'Rest after labour?' Hogan suggested sweetly. 'Very well, Wagon Master, I'll tell Lord Kiely you'll meet him and his officers at General Valverde's reception this evening while Sharpe takes the men up to San Isidro.'

'This evening at Valverde's, Hogan,' Runciman agreed. 'Very good. And Hogan. About my being Wagon Master General –'

'No need to thank me, Wagon Master. You'd just embarrass me with gratitude, so not another word! I shall respect your wishes and tell everyone else to do the same. Now come, Richard! Where are your green fellows?'

'In a taproom at the front of the inn, sir,' Sharpe said. His riflemen were to join Sharpe in the San Isidro Fort, an abandoned stronghold on the Portuguese border, where they would help train the Real Compañía Irlandesa in musketry and skirmishing.

'My God, Richard, but Runciman's a fool!' Hogan said happily as the two men walked through the inn's gateway. 'He's a genial fool, but he must have been the worst Wagon Master General in history. McGilligan's dog would have done a better job, and McGilligan's dog was famously blind, epileptic and frequently drunk. You never knew McGilligan, did you? A good engineer, but he fell off the Old Mole at Gibraltar and drowned himself after drinking two quarts of sherry, God rest his soul. The poor dog was inconsolable and had to be shot. The 73rd Highlanders did the deed with a full firing party and military honours to follow. But Runciman's just the fellow to flatter the Irish and make them think we're taking them seriously, but that's not your job. You understand me?'

'No, sir,' Sharpe said, 'don't understand you in the least, sir.'

'You're being awkward, Richard,' Hogan said, then stopped and took hold of one of Sharpe's silver coat buttons to emphasize his next words. 'The object of all we now do is to upset Lord Kiely. Your job is to insert yourself into Lord Kiely's fundament and be an irritant. We don't want him here and we don't want his bloody Royal Company here, but we can't tell them to bugger off because it wouldn't be diplomatic, so your job is to make them go away voluntarily. Oh! Sorry now,' he apologized because the button had come away in his fingers. 'The buggers are up to no good, Richard, and we have to find a diplomatic way of getting rid of them, so whatever you can do to upset them, do it, and rely on Runciman the Rotund to smooth things over so they don't think we're being deliberately rude.' Hogan smiled. 'They'll just blame you for not being a gentleman.'

'But I'm not, am I?'

'As it happens, you are, it's one of your faults, but let's not worry about that now. Just get rid of Kiely for me, Richard, with all his merry men. Make them cringe! Make them suffer! But above all, Richard, please, please make the bastards go away.'

* * *

61

The Real Compañía Irlandesa might be called a company, but in fact it was a small battalion, one of the five that made up the household guard of Spain's royalty. Three hundred and four guardsmen had been on the company's books when it had last served in the Escorial Palace outside Madrid, but the imprisonment of Spain's king and benign neglect by the occupying French had reduced its ranks, and the journey by sea around Spain to join the British army had thinned the files even more, so that by the time the Real Compañía Irlandesa paraded on the outskirts of Vilar Formoso there were a mere one hundred and sixty-three men left. The one hundred and sixty-three men were accompanied by thirteen officers, a chaplain, eighty-nine wives, seventy-four children, sixteen servants, twenty-two horses, a dozen mules, 'and one mistress,' Hogan told Sharpe.

'One mistress?' Sharpe asked in disbelief.

'There's probably a score of mistresses,' Hogan said, 'two score! A walking brothel, in all likelihood, but his Lordship tells me we have to arrange accommodation suitable for himself and a lady friend. Not that she's here yet, you understand, but his Lordship tells me she's coming. The Doña Juanita de Elia is supposed to charm her way across the enemy lines in order to warm his Lordship's bed and if she's the same Juanita de Elia that I've heard about then she's well practised in bed warming. You know what they say of her? That she collects a uniform from the regiment of every man she sleeps with!' Hogan chuckled.

'If she crosses the lines here,' Sharpe said, 'she'll be damned lucky to escape the Loup Brigade.'

'How the hell do you know about Loup?' Hogan asked instantly. For most of the time the Irishman was a genial and witty soul, but Sharpe knew the bonhomie disguised a very keen mind and the tone of the question was a sudden baring of that steel.

Yet Hogan was also a friend and for a split second Sharpe was tempted to confess how he had met the Brigadier and illegally executed two of his grey-uniformed soldiers, but then decided that was a deed best forgotten. 'Everyone knows about Loup here,' he answered instead. 'You can't spend a day on this frontier without hearing about Loup.'

'That's true enough,' Hogan admitted, his suspicions allayed. 'But don't be tempted to inquire further, Richard. He's a bad boy. Let me worry about Loup while you worry about that shambles.' Hogan and Sharpe, followed by the riflemen, had turned a corner to see the Real Compañía Irlandesa slouching in parade order on a patch of waste land opposite a half-finished church. 'Our new allies,' Hogan said sourly, 'believe it or not, in fatigue dress.'

Fatigue dress was meant to be a soldier's duty uniform for everyday wear, but the fatigue uniform of the Real Compañía Irlandesa was much gaudier and smarter than the full dress finery of most British line battalions. The guardsmen wore short red jackets with black-edged, gilt-fringed swallowtails behind. The same gold-trimmed black cord edged their button-holes and collars, while the facings, cuffs and turnbacks of their coats were of emerald green. Their breeches and waistcoats had once been white, their calf-length boots, belts and crossbelts were of black leather, while their sashes were green, the same green as the high plume that each man wore on the side of his black bicorne hat. The gilded hat badges showed a tower and a rearing lion, the same symbols that were displayed on the gorgeous green and gold shoulder sashes worn by the sergeants and drummer boys. As Sharpe walked closer he saw that the splendid uniforms were frayed, patched and discoloured, yet they still made a brave display in the bright spring sunshine. The men themselves looked anything but brave, instead appearing dispirited, weary and aggravated.

'Where are their officers?' Sharpe asked Hogan.

'Gone to a tavern for luncheon.'

'They don't eat with their men?'

'Evidently not.' Hogan's disapproval was acid, but not as bitter as Sharpe's. 'Now don't be getting sympathetic, Richard,' Hogan warned. 'You're not supposed to like these boys, remember?'

'Do they speak English?' Sharpe asked.

'As well as you or I. About half of them are Irish born, the other half are descended from Irish emigrants, and a good few, I have to say, once wore red coats,' Hogan said, meaning that they were deserters from the British army.

Sharpe turned and beckoned Harper towards him. 'Let's have a look at this palace guard, Sergeant,' he said. 'Put 'em in open order.'

'What do I call them?' Harper asked.

'Battalion?' Sharpe guessed.

Harper took a deep breath. ''Talion! 'Shun!' His voice was loud enough to make the closest men wince and the further ones jump in surprise, but only a few men snapped to attention. 'For inspection! Open order march!' Harper bellowed, and again very few guardsmen moved. Some just gaped at Harper while the majority looked towards their own sergeants for guidance. One of those gorgeously sashed sergeants came towards Sharpe, evidently to inquire what authority the riflemen possessed, but Harper did not wait for explanations. 'Move, you bastards!' he bellowed in his Donegal accent. 'You're in a war now, not guarding the royal pisspot. Behave like the good whores we all are and open up, now!'

'And I can remember when you didn't want to be a sergeant,' Sharpe said to Harper under his breath as the startled guards at last obeyed the greenjacket Sergeant's command. 'Are you coming, Major?' Sharpe asked Hogan.

'I'll wait here, Richard.'

'Come on then, Pat,' Sharpe said, and the two men began inspecting the company's front rank. An inevitable band of small mocking boys from the town fell into step behind the two greenjackets and pretended to be officers, but a thump on the ear from the Irishman's fist sent the boldest boy snivelling away and the others dispersed rather than face more punishment.

Sharpe inspected the muskets rather than the men, though he made sure that he looked into each soldier's eyes in an attempt to gauge what kind of confidence and willingness these men had. The soldiers returned his inspection resentfully, and no wonder, Sharpe thought, for many of these guards were Irishmen who must have been feeling all kinds of confusion at being attached to the British army. They had volunteered for the Real Compañía Irlandesa to protect a Most Catholic King, yet here they were being harried by the army of a Protestant monarch. Worse still, many of them would be avid Irish patriots, fierce for their country as only exiles can be, yet now they were being asked to fight alongside the ranks of that country's foreign oppressors. Yet, as Sharpe walked down the rank, he sensed more nervousness than anger and he wondered if these men were simply fearful of being asked to become proper soldiers for, if their muskets were any indication, the Real Compañía Irlandesa had long abandoned any pretensions to soldiering. Their muskets were a disgrace. The men carried the serviceable and sturdy Spanish-issue musket with its straight-backed hammer; however these guns were anything but serviceable, for there was rust on the locks and fouling caked inside the barrels. Some of them had no flints, others had no leather flint-seatings, while one gun did not even have the doghead screw to hold the flint in place. 'Did you ever fire this musket, son?' Sharpe asked the soldier.

'No, sir.'

'Have you ever fired a musket, son?'

The boy looked nervously towards his own sergeant. 'Answer the officer, lad!' Harper growled.

'Once, sir. One day,' the soldier said. 'Just the once.'

'If you wanted to kill someone with this gun, son, you'd have to beat them over the head with it. Mind you' – Sharpe pushed the musket back into the soldier's hands – 'you look big enough for that.'

'What's your name, soldier?' Harper asked him.

'Rourke, sir.'

'Don't call me "sir". I'm a sergeant. Where are you from?'

'My da's from Galway, Sergeant.'

'And I'm from Tangaveane in County Donegal and I'm ashamed, boy, ashamed, that a fellow Irishman can't keep a gun in half decent order. Jesus, boy, you couldn't shoot a Frenchman with that thing, let alone an Englishman.' Harper unslung his own rifle and held it under Rourke's nose. 'Look at that, boy! Clean enough to pick the dirt out of King George's nose. That's how a gun should look! 'Ware right, sir.' Harper added the last three words under his breath.

Sharpe turned to see two horsemen galloping across the waste ground towards him. The horses' hooves spurted dust. The leading horse was a fine black stallion being ridden by an officer who was wearing the gorgeous uniform of the Real Compañía Irlandesa and whose coat, saddlecloth, hat and trappings fairly dripped with gold tassels, fringes and loops. The second horseman was equally splendidly uniformed and mounted, while behind them a small group of other riders curbed their horses when Hogan intercepted them. The Irish Major, still on foot, hurried after the two leading horsemen, but was too late to stop them from reaching Sharpe. 'What the hell are you doing?' the first man asked as he reined in above

Sharpe. He had a thin, tanned face with a moustache trained and greased into fine points. Sharpe guessed the man was still in his twenties, but despite his youth he possessed a sour and ravaged face that had all the effortless superiority of a creature born to high office.

'I'm making an inspection,' Sharpe answered coldly.

The second man reined in on Sharpe's other side. He was older than his companion and was wearing the bright-yellow coat and breeches of a Spanish dragoon, though the uniform was so crusted with looped chains and gold frogging that Sharpe assumed the man had to be at least a general. His thin, moustached face had the same imperious air as his companion's. 'Haven't you learned to ask a commanding officer's permission before inspecting his men?' he asked with a distinct Spanish accent, then snapped an order in Spanish to his younger companion.

'Sergeant Major Noonan,' the younger man shouted, evidently relaying the older man's command, 'close order, now!'

The Real Compañía Irlandesa's Sergeant Major obediently marched the men back into close order just as Hogan reached Sharpe's side. 'There you are, my Lords' – Hogan was addressing both horsemen – 'and how was your Lordships' luncheon?'

'It was shit, Hogan. I wouldn't feed it to a hound,' the younger man, whom Sharpe assumed was Lord Kiely, said in a brittle voice that dripped with aloofness but was also touched by the faint slur of alcohol. His Lordship, Sharpe decided, had drunk well at lunch, well enough to loosen whatever inhibitions he might have possessed. 'You know this creature, Hogan?' His Lordship now waved towards Sharpe.

'Indeed I do, my Lord. Allow me to name Captain Richard Sharpe of the South Essex, the man Wellington himself chose to be your tactical adviser. And Richard? I have the honour to present the Earl of Kiely, Colonel of the Real Compañía Irlandesa.'

Kiely looked grimly at the tattered rifleman. 'So you're supposed to be our drillmaster?' He sounded dubious.

'I give lessons in killing too, my Lord,' Sharpe said.

The older Spaniard in the yellow uniform scoffed at Sharpe's claim. 'These men don't need lessons in killing,' he said in his accented English. 'They're soldiers of Spain and they know how to kill. They need lessons in dying.'

Hogan interrupted. 'Allow me to name His Excellency Don Luis Valverde,' he said to Sharpe. 'The General is Spain's most valued representative to our army.' Hogan gave Sharpe a wink that neither horseman could see.

'Lessons in dying, my Lord?' Sharpe asked the General, puzzled by the man's statement and wondering whether it sprang from an incomplete mastery of English.

For answer the yellow-uniformed General touched his horse's flanks with the tips of his spurs to make the animal walk obediently along the line of the Real Compañía Irlandesa's front rank and, superbly oblivious of whether Sharpe was following him or not, lectured the rifleman from his saddle. 'These men are going to war, Captain Sharpe,' General Valverde said in a voice loud enough for a good portion of the guard to hear him. 'They are going to fight for Spain, for King Ferdinand and Saint James, and fighting means standing tall and straight in front of your enemy. Fighting means staring your enemy in the eye while he shoots at you, and the side that wins, Captain Sharpe, is the side that stands tallest, straightest and longest. So you don't teach men how to kill or how to fight, but rather how to stand still while all hell comes at them. That's what you teach them, Captain Sharpe. Teach them drill. Teach them obedience. Teach them to stand longer than the French. Teach them' – the General at last twisted in his saddle to look down on the rifleman – 'to die.'

'I'd rather teach them to shoot,' Sharpe said.

The General scoffed at the remark. 'Of course they can shoot,' he said. 'They're soldiers!'

'They can shoot with those muskets?' Sharpe asked derisively.

Valverde stared down at Sharpe with a look of pity on his face. 'For the last two years, Captain Sharpe, these men have stayed at their post of duty on the sufferance of the French.' Valverde spoke in the tone he might have used to a small and unintelligent child. 'Do you really think they would have been allowed to stay there if they had posed a threat to Bonaparte? The more their weapons decayed, the more the French trusted them, but now they are here and you can provide them with new weapons.'

'To do what with?' Sharpe asked. 'To stand and die like bullocks?'

'So how would you like them to fight?' Lord Kiely had followed the two men and asked the question from behind Sharpe.

'Like my men, my Lord,' Sharpe said, 'smartly. And you begin fighting smartly by killing the enemy officers.' Sharpe raised his voice so that the whole of the Real Compañía Irlandesa could hear him. 'You don't go into battle to stand and die like bullocks in a slaughteryard, you go to win, and you begin to win when you drop the enemy officers dead.' Sharpe had walked away from Kiely and Valverde now and was using the voice he had developed as a sergeant, a voice pitched to cut across windy parade grounds and through the deadly clamour of battlefields. 'You start by looking for the enemy officers. They're easy to recognize because they're the overpaid, overdressed bastards with swords and you aim for them first. Kill them any way you can. Shoot them, club them, bayonet them, strangle them if you must, but kill the bastards and after that you kill the sergeants and then you can begin murdering the

69

rest of the poor leaderless bastards. Isn't that right, Sergeant Harper?'

'That's the way of it, sure enough,' Harper called back.

'And how many officers have you killed in battle, Sergeant?' Sharpe asked, without looking at the rifle Sergeant.

'More than I can number, sir.'

'And were they all Frog officers, Sergeant Harper?' Sharpe asked, and Harper, surprised by the question, did not answer, so Sharpe provided the answer himself. 'Of course they were not. We've killed officers in blue coats, officers in white coats and even officers in red coats, because I don't care what army an officer fights for, or what colour coat he wears or what king he serves, a bad officer is better off dead and a good soldier had better learn how to kill him. Ain't that right, Sergeant Harper?'

'Right as rain, sir.'

'My name is Captain Sharpe.' Sharpe stood in the centre front of the Real Compañía Irlandesa. The faces watching him showed a mixture of astonishment and surprise, but he had their attention now and neither Kiely nor Valverde had dared to interfere. 'My name is Captain Sharpe,' he said again, 'and I began where you are. In the ranks, and I'm going to end up where he is, in the saddle.' He pointed at Lord Kiely. 'But in the meantime my job is to teach you to be soldiers. I dare say there are some good killers among you and some fine fighters too, but soon you're going to be good soldiers as well. But for tonight we've all got a fair step to go before dark and once we're there you'll get food, shelter and we'll find out when you were last paid. Sergeant Harper! We'll finish the inspection later. Get them moving!'

'Sir!' Harper shouted. ''Talion will turn to the right. Right turn! By the left! March!'

Sharpe did not even look at Lord Kiely, let alone seek his

Lordship's permission to march the Real Compañía Irlandesa away. Instead he just watched as Harper led the guard off the waste ground towards the main road. He heard footsteps behind, but still he did not turn. 'By God, Sharpe, but you push your luck.' It was Major Hogan who spoke.

'It's all I've got to push, sir,' Sharpe said bitterly. 'I wasn't born to rank, sir, I don't have a purse to buy it and I don't have the privileges to attract it, so I need to push what bit of luck I've got.'

'By giving lectures on assassinating officers?' Hogan's voice was frigid with disapproval. 'The Peer won't like that, Richard. It smacks of republicanism.'

'Bugger republicanism,' Sharpe said savagely. 'But you were the one who told me the Real Compañía Irlandesa can't be trusted. But I tell you, sir, that if there's any mischief there, it isn't coming from the ranks. Those soldiers weren't trusted with French mischief. They don't have enough power. Those men are what soldiers always are: victims of their officers, and if you want to find where the French have sown their mischief, sir, then you look among those damned, overpaid, overdressed, overfed bloody officers,' and Sharpe threw a scornful glance towards the Real Compañía Irlandesa's officers who seemed unsure whether or not they were supposed to follow their men northwards. 'That's where your rotten apples are, sir,' Sharpe went on, 'not in the ranks. I'd as happily fight alongside those guardsmen as alongside any other soldier in the world, but I wouldn't trust my life to that rabble of perfumed fools.'

Hogan made a calming gesture with his hand, as if he feared Sharpe's voice might reach the worried officers. 'You make your point, Richard.'

'My point, sir, is that you told me to make them miserable. So that's what I'm doing.'

'I just wasn't sure I wanted you to start a revolution in the

71

process, Richard,' Hogan said, 'and certainly not in front of Valverde. You have to be nice to Valverde. One day, with any luck, you can kill him for me, but until that happy day arrives you have to butter the bastard up. If we're ever going to get proper command of the Spanish armies, Richard, then bastards like Don Luis Valverde have to be well buttered, so please don't preach revolution in front of him. He's just a simple-minded aristocrat who isn't capable of thinking much beyond his next meal or his last mistress, but if we're going to beat the French we need his support. And he expects us to treat the Real Compañía Irlandesa well, so when he's nearby, Richard, be diplomatic, will you?' Hogan turned as the group of Real Compañía Irlandesa's officers led by Lord Kiely and General Valverde came close. Riding between the two aristocrats was a tall, plump, white-haired priest mounted on a bony roan mare.

'This is Father Sarsfield' – Kiely introduced the priest to Hogan, conspicuously ignoring Sharpe – 'who is our chaplain. Father Sarsfield and Captain Donaju will travel with the company tonight, the rest of the company's officers will attend General Valverde's reception.'

'Where you'll meet Colonel Runciman,' Hogan promised. 'I think you'll find him much to your Lordship's taste.'

'You mean he knows how to treat royal troops?' General Valverde asked, looking pointedly at Sharpe as he spoke.

'I know how to treat royal guards, sir,' Sharpe intervened. 'This isn't the first royal bodyguard I've met.'

Kiely and Valverde both stared down at Sharpe with looks little short of loathing, but Kiely could not resist the bait of Sharpe's comment. 'You refer, I suppose, to the Hanoverian's lackeys?' he said in his half-drunken voice.

'No, my Lord,' Sharpe said. 'This was in India. They were royal guards protecting a fat little royal bugger called the Sultan Tippoo.'

'And you trained them too, no doubt?' Valverde inquired.

'I killed them,' Sharpe said, 'and the fat little bugger too.' His words wiped the supercilious look off both men's thin faces, while Sharpe himself was suddenly overwhelmed with a memory of the Tippoo's water-tunnel filled with the shouting bodyguard armed with jewelled muskets and broad-bladed sabres. Sharpe had been thigh-deep in scummy water, fighting in the shadows, digging out the bodyguard one by one to reach that fat, glittering-eyed, buttery-skinned bastard who had tortured some of Sharpe's companions to death. He remembered the echoing shouts, the musket flashes reflecting from the broken water and the glint of the gems draped over the Tippoo's silk clothes. He remembered the Tippoo's death too, one of the few killings that had ever lodged in Sharpe's memory as a thing of comfort. 'He was a right royal bastard,' Sharpe said feelingly, 'but he died like a man.'

'Captain Sharpe,' Hogan put in hastily, 'has something of a reputation in our army. Indeed, you may have heard of him yourself, my Lord? It was Captain Sharpe who took the Talavera eagle.'

'With Sergeant Harper,' Sharpe put in, and Kiely's officers stared at Sharpe with a new curiosity. Any soldier who had taken an enemy standard was a man of renown and the faces of most of the guards' officers showed that respect, but it was the chaplain, Father Sarsfield, who reacted most fulsomely.

'My God and don't I remember it!' he said enthusiastically. 'And didn't it just excite all the Spanish patriots in Madrid?' He climbed clumsily down from his horse and held a plump hand out to Sharpe. 'It's an honour, Captain, an honour! Even though you are a heathen Protestant!' This last was said with a broad and friendly grin. 'Are you a heathen, Sharpe?' the priest asked more earnestly.

'I'm nothing, Father.'

'We're all something in God's eyes, my son, and loved for it. You and I shall talk, Sharpe. I shall tell you of God and you shall tell me how to strip the damned French of their eagles.' The chaplain turned a smiling face on Hogan. 'By God, Major, but you do us proud by giving us a man like Sharpe!' The priest's approval of the rifleman had made the other officers of the Real Compañía Irlandesa relax, though Kiely's face was still dark with distaste.

'Have you finished, Father?' Kiely asked sarcastically.

'I shall be on my way with Captain Sharpe, my Lord, and we shall see you in the morning?'

Kiely nodded, then turned his horse away. His other officers followed, leaving Sharpe, the priest and Captain Donaju to follow the straggling column formed by the Real Compañía Irlandesa's baggage, wives and servants.

By nightfall the Real Compañía Irlandesa was safe inside the remote San Isidro Fort that Wellington had chosen to be their new barracks. The fort was old, outdated and had long been abandoned by the Portuguese so that the tired, newly arrived men first had to clean out the filthy stone barracks rooms that were to be their new home. The fort's towering gatehouse was reserved for the officers, and Father Sarsfield and Donaju made themselves comfortable there while Sharpe and his riflemen took possession of one of the magazines for their own lodgings. Sarsfield had brought a royal banner of Spain in his baggage that was proudly hoisted on the old fort's ramparts next to the union flag of Britain. 'I'm sixty years old,' the chaplain told Sharpe as he stood beneath Britain's flag, 'and I never thought the day would come when I'd serve under that banner.'

Sharpe looked up at the British flag. 'Does it worry you, Father?'

'Napoleon worries me more, my son. Defeat Napoleon, then we can start on the lesser enemies like yourself!' The comment

74

was made in a friendly tone. 'What also worries me, my son,' Father Sarsfield went on, 'is that I've eight bottles of decent red wine and a handful of good cigars and only Captain Donaju to share them with. Will you do me the honour of joining us for supper now? And tell me, do you play an instrument, perhaps? No? Sad. I used to have a violin, but it was lost somewhere, but Sergeant Connors is a rare man on the flute and the men in his section sing most beautifully. They sing of home, Captain.'

'Of Madrid?' Sharpe asked mischievously.

Sarsfield smiled. 'Of Ireland, Captain, of our home across the water where few of us have ever set foot and most of us never shall. Come, let's have supper.' Father Sarsfield put a companionable arm across Sharpe's shoulder and steered him towards the gatehouse. A cold wind blew over the bare mountains as night fell and the first cooking fires curled their blue smoke into the sky. Wolves howled in the hills. There were wolves throughout Spain and Portugal and in winter they would sometimes come right up to the picquet line in the hope of snatching a meal from an unwary soldier, but this night the wolves reminded Sharpe of the grey-uniformed Frenchmen in Loup's brigade. Sharpe supped with the chaplain and afterwards, under a star-shining sky, he toured the ramparts with Harper. Beneath them the Real Compañía Irlandesa grumbled about their accommodations and about the fate that had stranded them on this inhospitable border between Spain and Portugal, but Sharpe, who had orders to make them miserable, wondered if instead he could make them into real soldiers who would follow him over the hills and far into Spain to where a wolf needed to be hunted, trapped and slaughtered.

Pierre Ducos waited nervously for news of the Real Compañía Irlandesa's arrival in Wellington's army. The Frenchman's greatest fear was that the unit would be positioned so far behind the fighting front that it would be useless for his purposes, but that was a risk Ducos was forced to run. Ever since French intelligence had intercepted Lord Kiely's letter requesting King Ferdinand's permission to take the Real Compañía Irlandesa to war on the allied side, Ducos had known that the success of his scheme depended as much on the allies' unwitting cooperation as on his own cleverness. Yet Ducos's cleverness would achieve nothing if the Irishmen failed to arrive, and so he waited with mounting impatience.

Little news came from behind the British lines. There had been a time when Loup's men could ride with impunity on either side of the frontier, but now the British and Portuguese armies were firmly clamped along the border and Loup had to depend for his intelligence on the unreliable and minuscule handful of civilians willing to sell information to the hated French, on interrogations of deserters and on educated guesses formed from the observations of his own men as they peered through spyglasses across the mountainous border.

And it was one of those scouts who first brought Loup news of the Real Compañía Irlandesa. A troop of grey dragoons had gone to one of the lonely hill tops which offered a long view into Portugal, and from where, with luck, a patrol might see some evidence of a British concentration of forces that could signal a new advance. The lookout post dominated a wide, barren valley where a stream glittered before the land rose to the rocky ridge on which the long-abandoned fort of San Isidro stood. The fort was of little military value for the road it guarded had long fallen into disuse and a century of neglect had eroded its ramparts and ditches into mockeries of their former strength so that now the San Isidro was home to ravens, foxes, bats, wandering shepherds, lawless men, and the occasional patrol of Loup's grey dragoons who might spend a night in one of the cavernous barracks rooms to stay out of the rain.

Yet now there were men in the fort, and the patrol leader brought Loup news of them. The new garrison was not a full battalion, he said, just a couple of hundred men. The fort itself, as Loup well knew, would need at least a thousand men to man its crumbling walls, so a mere two hundred hardly constituted a garrison, yet strangely the newcomers had brought their wives and children with them. The dragoons' troop leader, a Captain Braudel, thought the men were British. 'They're wearing red coats,' he said, 'but not the usual stovepipe hats.' He meant shakoes. 'They've got bicornes.'

'Infantry, you say?'

'Yes, sir.'

'No cavalry? Any artillery?'

'Didn't see any.'

Loup picked at his teeth with a sliver of wood. 'So what were they doing?'

'Doing drill,' Braudel said. Loup grunted. He was not much interested in a group of strange soldiers taking up residence in San Isidro. The fort did not threaten him and if the newcomers were content to sit tight and make themselves comfortable then Loup would not stir them into wakefulness. Then Captain Braudel stirred Loup himself into wakefulness. 'But some of them were unblocking a well,' the Captain said, 'only they weren't redcoats. They were wearing green.'

Loup stared at him. 'Dark green?'

'Yes, sir.'

Riflemen. Damned riflemen. And Loup remembered the insolent face of the man who had insulted him, the man who had once insulted all France by taking an eagle touched by the Emperor himself. Maybe Sharpe was in the San Isidro Fort? Ducos had denigrated Loup's thirst for vengeance, calling it unworthy of a great soldier, but Loup believed that a soldier made his reputation by picking his fights and winning them famously. Sharpe had defied Loup, the first man to openly defy him in many a long month, and Sharpe was a champion among France's enemies, so Loup's vengeance was not just personal, but would send ripples throughout the armies that waited to fight the battle that would decide whether Britain lunged into Spain or was sent reeling back into Portugal.

So that afternoon Loup himself visited the hill top, taking his finest spyglass which he trained on the old fort with its weed-grown walls and half-filled dry moat. Two flags hung limply in the windless air. One flag was British, but Loup could not tell what the second was. Beyond the flags the red-coated soldiers were doing musket drill, but Loup did not watch them long, instead he inched the telescope southwards until, at last, he saw two men in green coats strolling along the deserted ramparts. He could not see their faces at this distance, but he could tell that one of the men was wearing a long straight sword and Loup knew that British light infantry officers wore curved sabres. 'Sharpe,' he said aloud as he collapsed the telescope.

A scuffle behind made him turn round. Four of his wolf-grey men were guarding a pair of prisoners. One captive was in a gaudily trimmed red coat while the other was presumably the man's wife or lover. 'Found them hiding in the rocks down there,' said the Sergeant who was holding one of the soldier's arms.

'He says he's a deserter, sir,' Captain Braudel added, 'and that's his wife.' Braudel spat a stream of tobacco juice onto a rock.

Loup scrambled down from the ridge. The soldier's uniform, he now saw, was not British. The waistcoat and sash, the half boots and the plumed bicorne were all too fancy for British taste, indeed they were so fancy that for a second Loup wondered if the captive was an officer, then he realized that Braudel would never have treated a captured officer with such disdain. Braudel clearly liked the woman who now raised shy eyes to stare at Loup. She was dark-haired, attractive and probably, Loup guessed, about fifteen or sixteen. Loup had heard that the Spanish and Portuguese peasants sold such daughters as wives to allied soldiers for a hundred francs apiece, the cost of a good meal in Paris. The French army, on the other hand, just took their girls for nothing. 'What's your name?' Loup asked the deserter in Spanish.

'Grogan, sir. Sean Grogan.'

'Your unit, Grogan?'

'Real Compañía Irlandesa, *señor.*' Guardsman Grogan was plainly willing to cooperate with his captors and so Loup signalled the Sergeant to release him.

Loup questioned Grogan for ten minutes, hearing how the Real Compañía Irlandesa had travelled by sea from Valencia, and how the men had been happy enough with the idea of joining the rest of the Spanish army at Cadiz, but how they resented being forced to serve with the British. Many of the men, the fugitive claimed, had fled from British servitude, and they had not enlisted with the King of Spain just to return to King George's tyranny.

Loup cut short the protests. 'When did you run?' he asked.

'Last night, sir. Half a dozen of us did. And a good many ran the night before.'

'There is an Englishman in the fort, a rifle officer. You know him?'

Grogan frowned, as though he found the question odd, but then he nodded. 'Captain Sharpe, sir. He's supposed to be training us.'

'To do what?'

79

'To fight, sir,' Grogan said nervously. He found this one-eyed, calm-spoken Frenchman very disconcerting. 'But we know how to fight already,' he added defiantly.

'I'm sure you do,' Loup said sympathetically. He poked at his teeth for a second, then spat the makeshift toothpick away. 'So you ran away, soldier, because you didn't want to serve King George, is that it?'

'Yes, sir.'

'But you'd certainly fight for His Majesty the Emperor?'

Grogan hesitated. 'I would, sir,' he finally said, but without any conviction.

'Is that why you deserted?' Loup asked. 'To fight for the Emperor? Or were you hoping to get back to your comfortable barracks in the Escorial?'

Grogan shrugged. 'We were going to her family's house in Madrid, sir.' He jerked his head towards his wife. 'Her father's a cobbler, and I'm not such a bad hand with a needle and thread myself. I thought I'd learn the trade.'

'It's always good to have a trade, soldier,' Loup said with a smile. He took a pistol from his belt and toyed with it for a moment before he pulled back the heavy cock. 'My trade is killing,' he added in the same pleasant voice and then, without showing a trace of emotion, he lifted the gun, aimed it at Grogan's forehead and pulled the trigger.

The woman screamed as her husband's blood splashed across her face. Grogan was thrown violently back, blood spraying and misting the air, then his body thumped and slid backwards down the hill. 'He didn't really want to fight for us at all,' Loup said. 'He'd have been just another useless mouth to feed.'

'And the woman, sir?' Braudel asked. She was bending over her dead husband and screaming at the French.

'She's yours, Paul,' Loup said. 'But only after you have delivered a message to Madame Juanita de Elia. Give madame my undying compliments, tell her that her toy Irish soldiers have arrived and are conveniently close to us, and that tomorrow morning we shall mount a little drama for their amusement. Tell her also that she would do well to spend the night with us.'

Braudel smirked. 'She'll be pleased, sir.'

'Which is more than your woman will be,' Loup said, glancing at the howling Spanish girl. 'Tell this widow, Paul, that if she does not shut up I will tear her tongue out and feed it to the Doña Juanita's hounds. Now come on.' He led his men down the hill to where the horses had been picketed. Tonight the Doña Juanita de Elia would come to the wolf's stronghold, and tomorrow she would ride to the enemy like a plague rat sent to destroy them from within.

And somewhere, some time before victory was final, Sharpe would feel France's vengeance for two dead men. For Loup was a soldier, and he did not forget, did not forgive and never lost.

CHAPTER THREE

Eleven men deserted during the Real Compañía Irlandesa's first night in the San Isidro Fort and eight men, including four picquets set to stop such desertions, ran on the second night. The guardsmen were providing their own sentries and Colonel Runciman suggested Sharpe's riflemen took over the duty. Sharpe argued against such a change. His riflemen were supposed to be training the Real Compañía Irlandesa and they could not work all day and stand guard all night. 'I'm sure you're right, General,' Sharpe said tactfully, 'but unless headquarters sends us more men we can't work round the clock.'

Colonel Runciman, Sharpe had discovered, was malleable so long as he was addressed as 'General'. He only wanted to be left alone to sleep, to eat and to grumble about the amount of work expected from him. 'Even a general is only human,' he liked to inform Sharpe, then he would inquire how he was supposed to discharge the onerous duties of liaising with the Real Compañía Irlandesa while he was also expected to be responsible for the Royal Wagon Train. In truth the Colonel's deputy still ran the wagon train with the same efficiency he had always displayed, but until a new Wagon Master General was formally appointed Colonel Runciman's signature and seal were necessary on a handful of administrative documents.

'You could surrender the seals of office to your deputy, General?' Sharpe suggested.

'Never! Never let it be said that a Runciman evaded his duty, Sharpe. Never!' The Colonel glanced anxiously out of his quarters to see how his cook was proceeding with a hare shot by Daniel Hagman. Runciman's lethargy meant that the Colonel was quite content to let Sharpe deal with the Real Compañía Irlandesa, but even for a man of Runciman's idle nonchalance, nineteen deserters in two nights was cause to worry. 'Damn it, man' – he leaned back after inspecting the cook's progress – 'it reflects on our efficiency, don't you see? We must do something, Sharpe! In another fortnight we won't have a soul left!'

Which, Sharpe reflected silently, was exactly what Hogan wanted. The Real Compañía Irlandesa was supposed to self-destruct, yet Richard Sharpe had been put in command of their training and there was a stubborn streak in Sharpe's soul that would not let him permit a unit for which he was responsible to slide into ruin. Damn it, he would make the guards into soldiers whether Hogan wanted him to or not.

Sharpe doubted he would get much help from Lord Kiely. Each morning his Lordship woke in a foul ill-temper that lasted until his steady intake of alcohol gave him a burst of high spirits that would usually stretch into the evening, but then be replaced by a morose sullenness aggravated by his losses at cards. Then he would sleep till late in the morning and so begin the cycle again. 'How in hell,' Sharpe asked Kiely's second-in-command, Captain Donaju, 'did he get command of the guard?'

'Birth,' Donaju said. He was a pale, thin man with a worried face who looked more like an impoverished student than a soldier, but of all the officers in the Real Compañía Irlandesa he seemed the most promising. 'You can't have a royal guard commanded by a commoner, Sharpe,' Donaju said with a touch

of sarcasm, 'but when Kiely's sober he can be quite impressive.'
The last sentence contained no sarcasm at all.

'Impressive?' Sharpe asked dubiously.

'He's a good swordsman,' Donaju replied. 'He detests the
French, and in his heart he would like to be a good man.'

'Kiely detests the French?' Sharpe asked without bothering
to disguise his scepticism.

'The French, Sharpe, are destroying Kiely's privileged world,'
Donaju explained. 'He's from the *ancien régime*, so of course
he hates them. He has no money, but under the *ancien régime*
that didn't matter because birth and title were enough to get
a man a royal appointment and exemption from taxes. But the
French preach equality and advancement on merit, and that
threatens Kiely's world so he escapes the threat by drinking,
whoring and gambling. The flesh is very weak, Sharpe, and it's
especially feeble if you're bored, under-employed and also
suspect that you're a relic of a bygone world.' Donaju shrugged,
as though ashamed of having offered Sharpe such a long and
high-minded sermon. The Captain was a modest man, but
efficient, and it was on Donaju's slender shoulders that the
day-to-day running of the guard had devolved. He now told
Sharpe how he would attempt to stem the desertions by
doubling the sentries and using only men he believed were
reliable as picquets, but at the same time he blamed the British
for his men's predicament. 'Why did they put us in this godforsaken place?' Donaju asked. 'It's almost as if your General wants
our men to run.'

That was a shrewd thrust and Sharpe had no real answer.
Instead he mumbled something about the fort being a strategic
outpost and needing a garrison, but he was unconvincing and
Donaju's only response was to politely ignore the fiction.

For the San Isidro Fort was indeed a godforsaken place. It
might have had strategic value once, but now the main road

between Spain and Portugal ran leagues to the south and so the once huge fastness had been abandoned to decay. Weeds grew thick in the dry moat that had been eroded by rainfall so that the once formidable obstacle had become little more than a shallow ditch. Frost had crumbled the walls, toppling their stones into the ditch to make countless bridges to what was left of the glacis. A white owl roosted in the remains of the chapel's bell tower while the once-tended graves of the garrison's officers had become nothing but shallow declivities in a stony meadow. The only serviceable parts of San Isidro were the old barracks buildings that had been kept in a state of crude repair thanks to the infrequent visits of Portuguese regiments which had been stationed there in times of political crisis. During those crises the men would block the holes in the barracks walls to protect themselves from the cold winds, while the officers took up quarters in the twin-towered gatehouse that had somehow survived the years of neglect. There were even gates that Runciman solemnly ordered closed and barred each night, though employing such a precaution against desertion was like stopping up one earth of a mighty rabbit warren.

Yet, for all its decay, the fort still held a mouldering grandeur. The impressive twin-towered gateway was embellished with royal escutcheons and approached by a four-arched causeway that spanned the only section of the dry moat still capable of checking an assault. The chapel ruins were laced with delicate carved stonework while the gun platforms were still hugely massive. Most impressive of all was the fort's location for its ramparts offered sky-born views deep across shadowy peaks to horizons unimaginable distances away. The eastern walls looked deep into Spain and it was on those eastern battlements, beneath the flags of Spain and Britain, that Lord Kiely discovered Sharpe on the third morning of the guard's stay in the fort. It seemed that even Kiely had become worried about the rate of desertion.

'We didn't come here to be destroyed by desertion,' Kiely snapped at Sharpe. The wind quivered the waxed tips of his moustaches.

Sharpe fought back the comment that Kiely was responsible for his men, not Sharpe, and instead asked his Lordship just why he had come to join the British forces.

And, to Sharpe's surprise, the young Lord Kiely took the question seriously. 'I want to fight, Sharpe. That's why I wrote to His Majesty.'

'So you're in the right place, my Lord,' Sharpe said sourly. 'The Crapauds are just the other side of that valley.' He gestured towards the deep, bare glen that separated the San Isidro from the nearest hills. Sharpe suspected that French scouts must be active on the valley's far side and would already have seen the movement in the old fort.

'We're not in the right place, Sharpe,' Kiely said. 'I asked King Ferdinand to order us to Cadiz, to be in our own army and among our own kind, but he sent us to Wellington instead. We don't want to be here, but we have royal orders and we obey those orders.'

'Then give your men a royal order not to desert,' Sharpe said glibly.

'They're bored! They're worried! They feel betrayed!' Kiely shuddered, not with emotion, but because he had just risen from his bed and was still trying to shake off his morning hangover. 'They didn't come here to be trained, Sharpe,' he snarled, 'but to fight! They're proud men, a bodyguard, not a pack of raw recruits. Their job is to fight for the King, to show Europe that Ferdinand still has teeth.'

Sharpe pointed east. 'See that track, my Lord? The one that climbs to that saddle in the hills? March your men up there, keep them marching for half a day and I'll guarantee you a fight. The French will love it. It'll be easier for them than fighting

86

choirboys. Half your men don't even have working muskets! And the other half can't use them. You tell me they're trained? I've seen militia companies better trained in Britain! And all those plump militia bastards do is parade in the market place once a week and then beat a retreat to the nearest bloody tavern. Your men aren't trained, my Lord, whatever you might think, but you give them to me for a month and I'll have them sharper than a bloody razor.'

'They're merely out of practice,' Kiely said loftily. His immense pride would not let him concede that Sharpe was right and that his vaunted palace guards were a shambles. He turned and gazed at his men who were being drilled on the weed-thick flagstones of the fort's plaza. Beyond the company, hard by the gatehouse towers, grooms were bringing saddled horses ready for the officers' midday exercises in horsemanship, while just inside the gate, on a stretch of smooth flagstones, Father Sarsfield was teaching the catechism to some of the company's children. The learning process evidently involved a deal of laughter; indeed, Sharpe had noticed, wherever the chaplain went, good humour followed. 'If they were just given an opportunity,' Kiely said of his men, 'they'd fight.'

'I'm sure they would,' Sharpe said, 'and they'd lose. What do you want of them? Suicide?'

'If necessary,' Kiely said seriously. He had been staring east into enemy-held country, but now looked Sharpe in the eye. 'If necessary,' he said again, 'yes.'

Sharpe gazed at the dissolute, ravaged young face. 'You're mad, my Lord.'

Kiely did not take offence at the accusation. 'Would you call Roland's defence of Roncesvalles the suicide of a madman? Did Leonidas's Spartans do nothing but throw away their lives in a fit of imbecility? What about your own Sir Richard Grenville? Was he just mad? Sometimes, Sharpe, a great name and undying fame can only come from a grand gesture.' He pointed at the far hills. 'There are three hundred thousand Frenchmen over there, and how many British here? Thirty thousand? The war is lost, Sharpe, it is lost. A great Christian kingdom is going down to mediocrity, and all because of a Corsican upstart. All the glory and the valour and the splendour of a royal world are about to become commonplace and tawdry. All the nasty, mean things – republicanism, democracy, equality – are crawling into the light and claiming that they can replace a lineage of great kings. We are seeing the end of history, Sharpe, and the beginnings of chaos, but maybe, just maybe, King Ferdinand's household guard can bring the curtain down with one last act of shining glory.' For a few seconds the drunken Kiely had betrayed his younger, nobler self. 'That's why we're here, Sharpe, to make a story that will still be told when men have forgotten the very name of Bonaparte.'

'Christ,' Sharpe said, 'no wonder your boys are deserting. Jesus! I would too. If I take a man into battle, my Lord, I like to offer him a better than evens chance that he'll march away with his skin intact. If I wanted to kill the buggers I'd just strangle them in their sleep. It's kinder.' He turned and watched the Real Compañía Irlandesa. The men were taking it in turns to use the forty or so serviceable muskets and, with a handful of exceptions, they were virtually useless. A good soldier could shoot a smoothbore musket every twenty seconds, but these men were lucky to get a shot away every forty seconds. The guards had spent too long wearing powdered wigs and standing outside gilded doors, and not long enough learning the simple habits of priming, ramming, firing and loading. 'But I'll train them,' Sharpe said when the echo of another straggling volley had faded across the fort, 'and I'll stop the buggers deserting.' He knew he was undermining Hogan's stratagem, but Sharpe liked the rank and file of the Real Compañía Irlandesa. They were soldiers like any others, not so well trained maybe, and with more confused loyalties than most, but the majority of the men were willing enough. There was no mischief there, and it cut against Sharpe's grain to betray good men. He wanted to train them. He wanted to make the company into a unit of which any army could be proud.

'So how will you stop them deserting?' Kiely asked.

'By my own method,' Sharpe said, 'and you don't want to know what it is, my Lord, because it isn't a method Roland would have much liked.'

Lord Kiely did not respond to Sharpe's taunt. Instead he was staring eastwards at something that had just claimed his attention. He took a small telescope from his uniform pocket, snapped it open and trained it across the wide bare valley to where Sharpe, staring into the morning sun, could just make out the figure of a lone horseman picking his way down the track which zigzagged from the saddle. Kiely turned. 'Gentlemen!' he shouted at his officers. 'To horse!' His Lordship, energized by a sudden excitement, ran down one of the ammunition ramps and shouted for a groom to bring his big black stallion.

Sharpe turned back east and took out his own telescope. It took him a moment or two to train the cumbersome instrument, then he managed to trap the distant rider in the lens. The horseman was in the uniform of the Real Compañía Irlandesa and he was also in trouble. Till now the man had been following the course of the steep track as it twisted down the valley's side, but now he abandoned the track and put his horse to the precipitous slope and slashed back with his whip to drive the beast down that dangerous descent. Half a dozen dogs raced ahead of the horseman, but Sharpe was more interested in what had prompted the man's sudden, dangerous plunge down the mountainside and so he raised the telescope to the skyline and there, silhouetted against the cloudless sky's hard brilliance, he saw dragoons. French dragoons. The lone horseman was a fugitive and the French were close behind.

'Are you coming, Sharpe?' Colonel Runciman, mounted on his carthorse-like mare, had thoughtfully provided his spare horse for Sharpe. Runciman was relying more and more on Sharpe as a companion to stave off the necessity of dealing with the sardonic Lord Kiely whose tart comments constantly dispirited Runciman. 'D'you know what's happening, Sharpe?' Runciman asked as his nemesis led a ragged procession of mounted officers out of the fort's imposing entrance-way. 'Is it an attack?' The Colonel's uncommon display of energy was doubtless caused by fear rather than curiosity.

'There's a fellow in company uniform coming towards us, General, with a pack of Frogs on his tail.'

'My word!' Runciman looked alarmed. As Wagon Master General he had been given few opportunities to see the enemy and he was not certain he wanted to remedy that lack now, but he could hardly display timidity in front of the guards and so he spurred his horse into a lumbering walk. 'You'll stay close to me, Sharpe! As an aide, you understand?'

'Of course, General.' Sharpe, uncomfortable as ever on horseback, followed Runciman across the entrance bridge. Sergeant Harper, curious about the excitement that had stirred the fort into sudden activity, led the Real Compañía Irlandesa onto the ramparts, ostensibly to stand guard, but in reality so they could watch whatever event had prompted this sudden exodus of officers from San Isidro.

By the time Sharpe had negotiated the causeway over the half-filled dry moat and had persuaded his horse to turn east off the road, the adventure seemed over. The fugitive had already crossed the stream and was now closer to Lord Kiely's rescue party than to his French pursuers, and as Kiely was attended

90

by a dozen officers and there were only half a dozen dragoons, the horseman was clearly safe. Sharpe watched the fugitive's dogs lope excitedly round the rescue party, then he saw that the pursuing Frenchmen were dressed in the mysterious grey coats of Brigadier General Loup's brigade. 'That fellow had a lucky escape, General,' Sharpe said, 'those are Loup's dragoons.'

'Loop?' Runciman asked.

'Brigadier Loup, General. He's a nasty Frog who dresses his men in wolf fur and likes to cut off his enemies' balls before they die.'

'Oh, my word.' Runciman paled. 'Are you sure?'

'I've met him, General. He threatened to geld me.'

Runciman was driven to fortify himself by taking a handful of sugared almonds from a pocket and putting them one by one into his mouth. 'I do sometimes wonder if my dear father was not right,' he said between mouthfuls, 'and that perhaps I should have chosen a churchman's career. I would have made a very serviceable bishop, I think, though perhaps a bishop's life might not have proved full enough for a man of my energies. There's little real work to do as a prelate, Sharpe. One preaches the odd sermon, of course, and makes oneself pleasant to the better sort of people in the county, and from time to time a fellow has to whip the lesser clergy into line, but there's not much else to the job. It's hardly a demanding life, Sharpe, and, quite frankly, most episcopal palaces are inhabited by very mediocre men. My dear father excepted, of course. Oh, my word, what's happening?'

Lord Kiely had ridden ahead to greet the fugitive, but, after stretching out a hand and offering a hasty word, his Lordship had spurred on towards the French pursuers who, recognizing that their quarry had escaped, had already reined in their horses. But now Kiely crossed the stream, drew his sword and shouted a challenge to the Frenchmen.

Every man in the valley knew what Kiely intended. He was challenging an enemy officer to a duel. Men of sense, like infantrymen or anyone given half a set of wits, disapproved of the practice, but cavalrymen could rarely resist the challenge. To take part in such a combat required pride and bravery, but to win such a fight was to forge a name as a warrior and every cavalry regiment in every army had officers whose fame went back to just such a fight: one man against one man, single sword against single sword, a duel between strangers that invited fame or death. 'Kiely's trying to get himself killed, General,' Sharpe told Runciman. Sharpe sounded sour, yet he could not deny a reluctant admiration for Kiely who, for this moment at least, had thrown off his hangover and his morose bitterness to become what he was in his own daydreams: the perfect knight and king's champion. 'Kiely's got a fancy to die famous,' Sharpe said. 'He wants to be Roland or that Spartan fellow who thumped the Persians.'

'Leonidas, Sharpe, King Leonidas,' Runciman said. 'Mind you, Sharpe, Kiely's a fine swordsman. I've watched him at practice, and the drink scarcely slows him a beat! Not that we'll see any evidence of that today,' Runciman said as Kiely turned away from the unmoving Frenchmen. 'None of them will fight!' Runciman sounded surprised, but also a little relieved that he would not have to witness any bloodshed.

'Kiely hardly gave them time to accept,' Sharpe said. And Kiely had indeed stayed only a few seconds, almost as though he had wanted to make the defiant gesture, but was scared lest any of the enemy might accept his challenge.

Then one of the enemy did accept. Kiely had reached the stream's bank when a shout sounded behind him and a dragoon officer spurred out from among his companions. Kiely twisted in his saddle and Sharpe could have sworn that his Lordship blanched as the Frenchman rode towards him. 'Oh, my word,' Runciman said in alarm.

Kiely could not refuse to fight now, not without losing face, and so he returned to the grey dragoon who threw back his wolf-fur pelisse, tugged down on his helmet's brim, then drew his long-bladed straight sword. He twisted its strap about his wrist, then held the blade upright in salute of the man who would be either his killer or his victim. Lord Kiely returned the salute with his own straight blade. His Lordship might have made the challenge as a gesture that he never expected to be taken up, but now that he was committed to the fight he showed neither reluctance nor nervousness.

'They're both bloody fools,' Sharpe said, 'dying for bloody nothing.' He and Runciman had joined the Real Compañía Irlandesa's officers as had Father Sarsfield who had abandoned his catechism class to follow Kiely into the valley. The priest heard Sharpe's scorn and offered the rifleman a surprised glance. The priest, like Runciman, seemed uncomfortable with the imminent duel and was running the beads of his rosary through plump fingers as he watched the two horsemen face each other across a fifty-yard gap. Lord Kiely dropped his blade from the salute and both men put spurs to their horses' flanks.

'Oh, my word,' Runciman said. He fumbled another handful of almonds from his pocket.

The two horses closed slowly at first. Only at the very last moment did their riders release them to the full gallop. Both men were right-handed and looked to Sharpe to be well-matched in size, though Lord Kiely's black horse was the bigger by a clear hand.

The dragoon cut first. He seemed to have put his faith in a savage sweeping slash that would have disembowelled an ox, except that at the last moment he checked the swing to reverse the blade and cut back at his enemy's unprotected neck. It was done as fast as a man could blink and on the back of a horse at full gallop, and against any other rider it might have worked, but Lord Kiely simply turned his horse into his opponent's mount without even bothering to parry. The dragoon's smaller horse staggered as the weight of the stallion hit its hindquarters. The Frenchman's backslash cut thin air, then the horses parted and both men were sawing on their reins. Kiely turned faster and rammed his spurs back to add the horse's weight to the lunge of his straight sword. Masters-at-arms always taught that the point beats the edge, and Kiely now lanced his sword's point at the grey dragoon's belly and for a second Sharpe thought the lunge would surely pierce the Frenchman's defence, but somehow the dragoon parried and a second later the sound of the blades' ringing clash carried to Sharpe. By the time the harsh sound had echoed back from the far hills the two horses were already twenty yards apart and being turned into the attack again. Neither man had dared ride too far from his opponent in case he should be pursued and attacked from behind, so from now on the duel would be fought at close quarters and it would depend as much on the training of the two horses as on the riders' swordsmanship.

'Oh, dear,' Runciman said. He feared to watch the horror of a man dying, yet dared not take his eyes from the spectacle. It was a sight as old as warfare: two champions clashing in full view of their comrades. 'It's a wonder Kiely can fight at all,' Runciman continued, 'considering how much he drank last night. Five bottles of claret by my count.'

'He's young,' Sharpe said sourly, 'and he was born with natural gifts for riding horses and fighting with swords. But as he gets older, General, those gifts will waste away and he knows it. He's living on borrowed time and that's why he wants to die young.'

'I can't believe that,' Runciman said, then winced as the two men hammered at each other with their swords.

'Kiely should go for the bastard's horse, not the man,' Sharpe said. 'You can always beat a horseman by crippling his bloody horse.'

'It isn't the way a gentleman fights, Captain,' Father Sarsfield said. The priest had edged his horse close to the two British officers.

'There's no future in being a gentleman in a fight, Father,' Sharpe said. 'If you think wars should only be fought by gentlemen then you should stop recruiting people like me out of the gutter.'

'No need to mention your origins, Sharpe,' Runciman hissed reprovingly. 'You are an officer now, remember!'

'I pray for the day when no gentleman fights at all, nor other men either,' Father Sarsfield said. 'I do so dislike fighting.'

'Yet you're a chaplain in the army?' Sharpe asked.

'I go where the need is greatest,' the chaplain said, 'and where will a man of God look to find the greatest concentration of sinners outside of a prison? In an army, I would suggest, begging your presence.' Sarsfield smiled, then flinched as the duellists charged and their long swords clashed again. Lord Kiely's stallion instinctively ducked its head to avoid the blades that hissed above its ears. Lord Kiely lunged at his opponent and one of Kiely's officers cheered when he thought that his Lordship had skewered the Frenchman, but the sword had merely pierced the cloak that was rolled onto the cantle of the dragoon's saddle. Kiely dragged his sword free of the cloak just in time to parry a vicious backslash from the dragoon's heavier blade.

'Will Kiely win, do you think?' Runciman asked Sharpe anxiously.

'God knows, General,' Sharpe said. The two horses were virtually motionless now, just standing still as the riders exchanged blows. The sound of the steel was continuous and Sharpe knew the men would be getting tired for swordfighting was damned hard work. Their arms would be weary from the weight and Sharpe could imagine the breath rasping in their throats, the grunts as they cut down with the steel and the pain as the sweat stung their eyes. And every now and then, Sharpe knew, each man would feel the strange sensation of catching the dispassionate gaze of the stranger he was trying to kill. The blades clashed and scraped for another few seconds, then the grey dragoon yielded that phase of the fight by touching spurs to his horse.

The Frenchman's horse started forward, then put a hoof into a rabbit's hole.

The horse stumbled. Kiely spurred forward as he saw his opportunity. He slashed down hard, rising out of the saddle to put all the weight of his body behind the killing blow, but somehow the dragoon parried the cut, even though the strength of it almost knocked him out of the saddle. His tired horse struggled to rise as the dragoon parried again and again, then suddenly the Frenchman abandoned his defence and lunged hard at Kiely. His sword tip caught in the hilt of Kiely's sword and drove it clear out of Kiely's grip. Kiely had looped the silk-tasselled sword strap around his wrist so the sword just hung loose, but it would take his Lordship a few seconds to retrieve the snakeskin-wrapped hilt and to give himself that time he wheeled his horse desperately away. The Frenchman scented victory and spurred his tired horse after his opponent.

Then the carbine cracked. The report was startling and it echoed back from the steep hill slope before anyone reacted.

The dragoon gave a gasp as the bullet struck him. The shot had taken him in the ribs and knocked him back in his saddle. The dying man recovered his balance then shook his head in disbelief that someone had interfered in the duel. His own sword fell to dangle from its strap as his companions shouted in protest that anyone should have dared break the convention that such duellists should be left alone on the battlefield, then the dragoon's mouth fell open and a wash of dark blood soaked the front of his grey jacket as he collapsed backwards off his tired horse.

An astonished Lord Kiely took one look at the vengeful dragoons spurring towards their fallen companion, then fled across the stream. 'I don't understand,' Colonel Runciman said.

'Someone broke the rules, General,' Sharpe said, 'and they saved Kiely's bacon by doing it. He was a dead man till that shot was fired.' The French were still shouting protests, and one of them rode to the stream bank and dared any of the allied officers to face him in a second duel. No one accepted his offer so he began to call taunts and insults, all of which Sharpe reckoned were deserved because whoever had fired the carbine had killed the Frenchman unfairly. 'So who did fire?' Sharpe asked aloud.

It had been the single officer who had been pursued by the dragoons and whose arrival in the valley had prompted the duel who had ended it so unsportingly. Sharpe could see the carbine in the fugitive's hands, but what surprised him was that no one was chiding the officer for his interference in the duel. Instead the other officers of the Real Compañía Irlandesa clustered about the newcomer in evident welcome. Sharpe urged his horse closer to see that the fugitive was a slim young officer with what Sharpe took to be a plume of shining black horsehair reaching down his back, but then Sharpe saw that it was not horsehair at all, but real hair, and that the officer was not an officer either, but a woman.

'He was going for his pistol,' the woman offered in explanation, 'so I shot him.'

'Bravo!' one of the admiring officers called. The taunting Frenchman had turned away in disgust.

'Is that . . . ? Is she . . . ? Is it . . . ?' Runciman asked incoherently.

'It's a woman, General,' Sharpe said drily.

'Oh, my word, Sharpe! So he . . . she is.'

She was a striking-looking woman too, Sharpe thought, whose fierce looks were made even more noticeable by the man's uniform that had been tailored to her trim figure. She swept off her plumed hat to salute Lord Kiely, then leaned over to kiss his Lordship. 'It's the mistress, General,' Sharpe said. 'Major Hogan told me about her. She collects uniforms from all her lovers' regiments.'

'Oh, my word. You mean they're not married and we're to be introduced?' Runciman asked in alarm, but it was too late to escape, for Lord Kiely was already beckoning the two English officers forward. He introduced Runciman first, then gestured towards Sharpe. 'Captain Richard Sharpe, my dear, our tutor in modern fighting.' Kiely did not try to disguise the sneer as he so described Sharpe.

'Ma'am,' Sharpe said awkwardly. Juanita gave Runciman one withering glance, then appraised Sharpe for a long time while her pack of hunting dogs sniffed about his horse's legs. The woman's gaze was unfriendly and she finally turned away without even acknowledging the rifleman's presence. 'So why did you shoot the dragoon, ma'am?' Sharpe asked, trying to provoke her.

She turned back to him. 'Because he was going to shoot my Lord Kiely,' she answered defiantly. 'I saw him reach for his pistol.'

She had not seen anything of the kind, Sharpe thought, but he would achieve nothing by challenging her bare-faced lie. She had shot to preserve her lover's life, nothing else, and Sharpe felt a pang of jealousy that the wastrel Kiely should have found himself such a brazen, defiant and remarkable woman. She was no beauty, but something in her clever, feral face stirred Sharpe, though he would be damned before he let her know she had that power. 'You've come far, ma'am?' he asked.

'From Madrid, Captain,' she said frostily.

'And the French didn't stop you?' Sharpe asked pointedly.

'I don't need French permission to travel in my own country, Captain, nor, in my own country, do I need explain myself to impertinent British officers.' She spurred away, summoning her shaggy-haired, long-legged hounds to follow her.

'She doesn't like you, Sharpe,' Runciman said.

'It's a mutual thing, General,' Sharpe said. 'I wouldn't trust the bitch an inch.' It was mainly jealousy that made him say it and he knew it.

'She's a fine-looking woman, though, ain't she?' Runciman sounded wistful as though he understood he was not the man to donate a uniform of the 37th Line to Juanita's wardrobe. 'I can't say as I've ever seen a woman in breeches before,' Runciman said, 'let alone astride a saddle. Doesn't happen much in Hampshire.'

'And I've never seen a woman ride from Madrid to Portugal without a servant or a lick of luggage,' Sharpe said. 'I wouldn't trust her, General.'

'You wouldn't trust who, Sharpe?' Lord Kiely asked. He was riding back towards the British officers.

'Brigadier Loup, sir,' Sharpe lied smoothly. 'I was explaining to General Runciman the significance of the grey uniforms.' Sharpe pointed towards the dragoons who were now carrying the dead man's body back up the hillside.

'A grey uniform didn't help that dragoon today!' Kiely was still animated by the duel and apparently unashamed of the way it had ended. His face seemed younger and more attractive as though the arrival of his mistress had restored the lustre of youth to Kiely's drink-ravaged looks.

'Chivalry didn't help him either,' Sharpe said sourly. Runciman, suspecting that Sharpe's words might provoke another duel, hissed in remonstrance.

Kiely just sneered at Sharpe. 'He broke the rules of chivalry, Sharpe. Not me! The man was evidently going for his pistol. I reckon he knew he would be dead the moment I recovered my sword.' His expression dared Sharpe to contradict him.

'Funny how chivalry becomes sordid, isn't it, my Lord?' Sharpe said instead. 'But then war is sordid. It might start with chivalrous intentions, but it always ends with men screaming for their mothers and having their guts flensed out by cannon balls. You can dress a man in scarlet and gold, my Lord, and tell him it's a noble cause he graces, but he'll still end up bleeding to death and shitting himself in a panic. Chivalry stinks, my Lord, because it's the most sordid bloody thing on earth.'

Kiely was still holding his sword, but now he slid the long blade home into its scabbard. 'I don't need lectures on chivalry from you, Sharpe. Your job is to be a drillmaster. And to stop my rogues from deserting. If, indeed, you can stop them.'

'I can do that, my Lord,' Sharpe promised. 'I can do that.'

And that afternoon he went to keep his word.

Sharpe walked south from San Isidro following the spine of the hills as they dropped ever lower towards the main border road. Where the hills petered out into rolling meadowland there was a small village of narrow twisting streets, stone-walled gardens and low-roofed cottages that huddled on a slope climbing from a fast-flowing stream up to a rocky ridge where the village church was crowned by the ragged sticks of a stork's nest. The village was called Fuentes de Oñoro, the village that had provoked Loup's fury, and it lay only two miles from Wellington's headquarters in the town of Vilar Formoso. That proximity worried Sharpe who feared his errand might be questioned by an inquisitive staff officer, but the only British troops in Fuentes de Oñoro were a small picquet of the 60th

Rifles who were positioned just north of the village and took no notice of Sharpe. On the stream's eastern bank were a few scattered houses, some walled gardens and orchards and a small chapel that were all reached from the main village by a foot-bridge constructed of stone slabs supported on boulders standing beside a ford where a patrol of King's German Legion cavalry was watering its horses. The Germans warned Sharpe that there were no allied troops on the further bank. 'Nothing but French over there,' the cavalry's Captain said and then, when he discovered Sharpe's identity, he insisted on sharing a flask of brandy with the rifleman. They exchanged news of Von Lossow, a KGL friend of Sharpe's, then the Captain led his men out of the stream and onto the long straight road that led towards Ciudad Rodrigo. 'I'm looking for trouble,' he called over his shoulder as he pulled himself up into the saddle, 'and with God's help I'll find it!'

Sharpe turned the other way and climbed the village street to where a tiny inn served a robust red wine. It was not much of an inn, but then Fuentes de Oñoro was not much of a village. The place lay just inside the Spanish border and had been plundered by the French as they had marched into Portugal then raked over again as they marched back out, and the villagers were justifiably suspicious of all soldiers. Sharpe took his wineskin out of the inn's smoky interior to a small vegetable garden where he sat beneath a grapevine with a half severed trunk. The damage seemed not to have affected the plant which was putting out vigorous new tendrils and bright fresh leaves. He dozed there, almost too weary to lift the wineskin.

'The French tried to cut the vine down.' A voice spoke in sudden Spanish behind Sharpe. 'They tried to destroy every-thing. Bastards.' The man belched. It was a vast belch, loud enough to stir a cat sleeping on the garden's far wall. Sharpe turned to see a mountainous creature dressed in filthy brown leggings, a blood-stained cotton shirt, a green French dragoon coat that had split at all the seams in order to accommodate its new owner's bulk, and a leather apron that was caked black and stiff with dried blood. The man and his clothes stank of old food, bad breath, stale blood and decay. At his belt there hung an old-fashioned, unscabbarded sabre with a blade as dark, thick and filthy as a pole-axe, a horse pistol, a small bone-handled knife with a curiously hooked blade and a wooden whistle. 'You're Captain Sharpe?' the enormous man asked as Sharpe rose to greet him.

'Yes.'

'And my whistle tells you who I am, does it not?'

Sharpe shook his head. 'No.'

'You mean that castrators in England don't signal their coming with a blast on the whistle?'

'I've never heard of them doing it,' Sharpe said.

El Castrador sat heavily on a bench opposite Sharpe. 'No whistles? Where would I be without my little whistle? It tells a village I am coming. I blow it and the villagers bring out their hogs, beeves and foals, and I bring out my little knife.' The man flicked the small, wickedly curved blade and laughed. He had brought his own wineskin which he now squirted into his mouth before shaking his head in rueful nostalgia. 'And in the old days, my friend,' El Castrador went on wistfully, 'the mothers would bring out their little boys to be cut, and two years later the boys would travel to Lisbon or Madrid to sing so sweetly! My father, now, he cut many boys. One of his youngsters even sang for the Pope! Can you imagine? For the Pope in Rome! And all because of this little knife.' He fingered the small bone-handled cutter.

'And sometimes the boys died?' Sharpe guessed.

El Castrador shrugged. 'Boys are easily replaced, my friend. One cannot afford to be sentimental about small children.' He

102

jetted more red wine down his vast gullet. 'I had eight boys, only three survived and that, believe me, is two too many.'

'No girls?'

'Four.' El Castrador fell silent for a second or two, then sighed. 'That French bastard Loup took them. You know of Loup?'

'I know him.'

'He took them and gave them to his men. El Lobo and his men like young girls.' He touched the knife at his belt, then gave Sharpe a long speculative look. 'So you are La Aguja's Englishman.'

Sharpe nodded.

'Ah! Teresa!' The Spaniard sighed. 'We were angry when we heard she had given herself to an Englishman, but now I see you, Captain, I can understand. How is she?'

'Fighting the French near Badajoz, but she sends her greetings.' In fact Teresa had not written to Sharpe in weeks, but her name was a talisman among all the partisans and had been sufficient to arrange this meeting with the man who had been so roundly defeated by Brigadier Loup. Loup had tamed this part of the Spanish frontier and wherever Sharpe went he heard the Frenchman's name mentioned with an awed hatred. Every piece of mischief was the fault of Loup, every death, every house fire, every flood, every sick child, every robbed hive, every stillborn calf, every unseasonable frost; all were the wolf's work.

'She will be proud of you, Englishman,' El Castrador said.

'She will?' Sharpe asked. 'Why?'

'Because El Lobo has placed a price on your head,' El Castrador said. 'Did you not know?'

'I didn't know.'

'One hundred dollars,' El Castrador said slowly, with relish, as though he was tempted by the price himself.

'A pittance,' Sharpe said disparagingly. Twenty-five pounds

might be a small fortune to most people, a good year's pay indeed for most working folk, but still Sharpe reckoned his life was worth more than twenty-five pounds. 'The reward on Teresa's head is two hundred dollars,' he said resentfully.

'But we partisans kill more French than you English,' El Castrador said, 'so it is only right that we should be worth more.' Sharpe tactfully refrained from asking whether there was any reward on El Castrador's own matted and lice-ridden head. Sharpe suspected the man had lost most of his power because of his defeats, but at least, Sharpe thought, El Castrador lived while most of his men were dead, killed by the wolf after being cut in the same way that El Castrador had cut his captives. There were times when Sharpe was very glad he did not fight the *guerrilla*.

El Castrador raised the wineskin again, spurted the wine into his mouth, swallowed, belched again, then breathed an effluent gust towards Sharpe. 'So why do you want to see me, Englishman?'

Sharpe told him. The telling took a good while for though El Castrador was a brutal man, he was not especially clever and Sharpe had to explain his requirements several times before the big man understood. In the end, though, El Castrador nodded. 'Tonight, you say?'

'I would be pleased. And grateful.'

'But how grateful?' El Castrador shot a sly look at the Englishman. 'Shall I tell you what I need? Muskets! Or even rifles like that!' He touched the barrel of Sharpe's Baker rifle which was propped against the vine's trunk.

'I can bring you muskets,' Sharpe said, though he did not yet know how. The Real Compañía Irlandesa needed muskets much more desperately than this great butcher of a man did, and Sharpe did not even know how he was to supply those weapons. Hogan would never agree to give the Real Compañía

Irlandesa new muskets, yet if Sharpe was to turn King Ferdinand's palace guard into a decent infantry unit then he would need to find them guns somehow. 'Rifles I can't get,' he said, 'but muskets, yes. But I'll need a week.'

'Muskets, then,' El Castrador agreed, 'and there is something else.'

'Go on,' Sharpe said warily.

'I want revenge for my daughters,' El Castrador said with tears in his eyes. 'I want Brigadier Loup and this knife to meet each other.' He held up the small, bone-handled cutter. 'I want your help, Englishman. Teresa says you can fight, so fight with me and help me catch El Lobo.'

Sharpe suspected this second request would prove even more difficult than the first, but he nodded anyway. 'You know where Loup can be found?'

El Castrador nodded. 'Usually at a village called San Cristóbal. He drove out the inhabitants, blocked the streets and fortified the houses. A stoat could not get near without being spotted. Sanchez says it would take a thousand men and a battery of artillery to take San Cristóbal.'

Sharpe grunted at the news. Sanchez was one of the best *guerrilla* leaders and if Sanchez reckoned San Cristóbal was virtually impregnable, then Sharpe would believe him. 'You said "usually". So he's not always at San Cristóbal?'

'He goes where he likes, *señor*,' El Castrador said moodily. 'Sometimes he takes over a village for a few nights, sometimes he would put his men in the fort where you now live, sometimes he would use Fort Concepción. Loup, *señor*, is a law to himself.' El Castrador paused. 'But La Aguja says you are also a law unto yourself. If any man can defeat El Lobo, *señor*, it must be you. And there is a place near San Cristóbal, a defile, where he can be ambushed.'

El Castrador offered this last detail as an enticement,

but Sharpe ignored the lure. 'I will do all a man can do,' he promised.

'Then I shall help you tonight,' El Castrador assured Sharpe in return. 'Look for my gift in the morning, *señor*,' he said, then stood and shouted a command to the men he had evidently left outside the inn. Hooves clattered loud in the little street. 'And next week,' the partisan added, 'I shall come for my reward. Don't let me down, Captain.'

Sharpe watched the gross man go, then hefted the wineskin. He was tempted to drain it, but knew that a bellyful of sour wine would make his journey back to San Isidro doubly hard and so, instead, he poured the liquid over the roots of the ravaged vine. Maybe, he thought, it would help the vine repair itself. Wine to grapes, ashes to ashes and dust to dust. He picked up his hat, slung his rifle, and walked home.

That night, despite all Captain Donaju's precautions, three more guardsmen deserted. More men might have tried, but shortly after midnight a series of terrible screams sounded from the valley and any other men tempted to try their luck across the frontier decided to wait for another day. At dawn next morning, when Rifleman Harris was leading a convoy down the mountainside to fetch water from the stream to augment the trickle that the fort's well provided, he found the three men. He came back to Sharpe white-faced. 'It's horrible, sir. Horrible.'

'See that cart?' Sharpe pointed across the fort's courtyard to a handcart. 'Get it down there, put them in and bring them back.'

'Do we have to?' Rifleman Thompson asked, aghast.

'Yes, you bloody do. And Harris?'

'Sir?'

'Put this in with them,' and Sharpe handed Harris a sack

holding a heavy object. Harris began to untie the sack's mouth. 'Not here, Harris,' Sharpe said, 'do it down there. And only you and our lads to see what you're doing.'

By eight o'clock Sharpe had the one hundred and twenty-seven remaining guardsmen on parade, together with all their junior officers. Sharpe was the senior officer left inside the fort, for both Lord Kiely and Colonel Runciman had spent the night at army headquarters where they had gone to plead with the Assistant Commissary General for muskets and ammunition. Father Sarsfield was visiting a fellow priest in Guarda, while both Kiely's majors and three of his captains had gone hunting. Doña Juanita de Elia had also taken her hounds in search of hares, but had spurned the company of the Irish officers. 'I hunt alone,' she said, and then had scorned Sharpe's warning of patrolling Frenchmen. 'In coming here, Captain,' she told Sharpe, 'I escaped every Frenchman in Spain. Worry about yourself, not me.' Then she had spurred away with her hounds loping behind.

So now, bereft of their senior officers, the Real Compañía Irlandesa lined in four ranks beneath one of the empty gun platforms that served Sharpe as a podium. It had rained in the night and the flags on the crumbling battlements lifted reluctantly to the morning wind as Harris and Thompson manoeuvred the handcart up one of the ramps which led from the magazines to the gun platforms. They pushed the vehicle with its sordid cargo to Sharpe's side, then tipped the handles up so that the cart's bed faced the four ranks. There was an intake of breath, then a communal groan sounded from the ranks. At least one guardsman vomited while most just looked away or closed their eyes. 'Look at them!' Sharpe snapped. 'Look!'

He forced the guardsmen to look at the three mutilated naked bodies, and especially at the bloody, gut-churning mess dug out of the centre of each corpse and at the rictus of horror and pain on each dead face. Then Sharpe reached past one of the cold, white, stiff shoulders to drag free a steel-grey helmet plumed with coarse grey hair. He set it on one of the uptilted cart shafts. It was the same helmet that Harris had collected as a keepsake from the high settlement where Sharpe had discovered the massacred villagers and where Perkins had met Miranda who now followed the young rifleman with a touching and pathetic devotion. It was the same helmet that Sharpe had given back to Harris in the sack earlier that morning.

'Look at the bodies!' Sharpe ordered the Real Compañía Irlandesa. 'And listen! The French believe there are two kinds of people in Spain: those who are for them and those who are against them, and there ain't a man among you who can escape that judgement. Either you fight for the French or you fight against them, and that isn't my decision, that's what the French have decided.' He pointed to the three bodies. 'That's what the French do. They know you're here now. They're watching you, they're wondering who and what you are, and until they know the answers they'll treat you like an enemy. And that's how the Frogs treat their enemies.' He pointed to the bloody holes carved into the dead men's crotches.

'Which leaves you lot with three choices,' Sharpe went on. 'You can run east and have your manhood sliced off by the Frogs, or you can run west and risk being arrested by my army and shot as a deserter, or else you can stay here and learn to be soldiers. And don't tell me this isn't your war. You swore an oath to serve the King of Spain, and the King of Spain is a prisoner in France and you were supposed to be his guard. By God, this is your war far more than it's my war. I never swore an oath to protect Spain, I never had a woman raped by a Frenchman or a child murdered by a dragoon or a harvest stolen and a house burned by a Crapaud forage party. Your country has suffered all those things, and your country is Spain, and if you'd rather fight for Ireland than for Spain then why in the name of Almighty God did you take the Spanish oath?' He paused. He knew that not every man in the company was a would-be deserter. Many, like Lord Kiely himself, wanted to fight, but there were enough troublemakers to sap the company's usefulness and Sharpe had decided that this shock treatment was the only way to jar the troublemakers into obedience.

'Or does the oath mean nothing to you?' Sharpe demanded. 'Because I'll tell you what the rest of this army thinks about you, and I mean the rest of this army, including the Connaught Rangers and the Inniskilling Dragoons and the Royal Irish Regiment and the Royal County Down Regiment and the Prince of Wales's Own Irish Regiment and the Tipperary Regiment and the County of Dublin Regiment and the Duke of York's Irish Regiment. They say you lot are soft. They say you're powder-puff soldiers, good for guarding a pisspot in a palace, but not good for a fight. They say you ran away from Ireland once and you'll run away again. They say you're about as much use to an army as a pack of singing nuns. They say you're overdressed and over-coddled. But that's going to change, because one day you and I will go into battle together and on that day you're going to have to be good! Bloody good!'

Sharpe hated making speeches, but he had seized these men's attention or at least the three castrated bodies had gripped their interest and Sharpe's words were making some kind of sense to them. He pointed east. 'Over there,' Sharpe said, and he plucked the helmet off the cart's shaft, 'there's a man called Loup, a Frenchman, and he leads a regiment of dragoons called the wolf pack, and they wear these helmets and they leave that mark on the men they kill. So we're going to kill them. We're going to prove that there isn't a French regiment in the world that can stand up to an Irish regiment, and we're going to do that together. And we're going to do it because this is your war, and your only damned choice is whether you want to die like gelded dogs or fight like men. Now you make up your damned minds what you're going to do. Sergeant Harper?'

'Sir!'

'One half-hour for breakfast. I want a burial party for these three men, then we begin work.'

'Yes, sir!'

Harris caught Sharpe's eye as the officer turned away. 'Not one word, Harris,' Sharpe said, thrusting the helmet into the rifleman's belly, 'not one bloody word.'

Captain Donaju stopped Sharpe as he walked away from the ramparts. 'How do we fight without muskets?'

'I'll get you muskets, Donaju.'

'How?'

'The same way a soldier gets everything that isn't issued to him,' Sharpe said, 'by theft.'

That night not a single man deserted.

And next morning, though Sharpe did not recognize it at first, the trouble began.

'It's a bad business, Sharpe,' Colonel Runciman said. 'My God, man, but it's a bad business.'

'What is, General?'

'You haven't heard?' Runciman asked.

'About the muskets, you mean?' Sharpe asked, assuming that Runciman must be referring to his visit to the army headquarters, a visit that had ended in predictable failure. Runciman and Kiely had returned with no muskets, no ammunition, no blankets, no pipe clay, no boots, no knapsacks and not even a promise of money for the unit's back pay. Wellington's parsimony was doubtless intended to draw the fangs of the Real

Compañía Irlandesa, but it gave Sharpe horrid problems. He was struggling to raise the guardsmen's morale, but without weapons and equipment that morale was doomed. Worse still Sharpe knew he was close to enemy lines and if the French did attack then it would be no consolation to know that the Real Compañía Irlandesa's defeat had been a part of Hogan's plans, not if Sharpe was himself involved in the debacle. Hogan might want the Real Compañía Irlandesa destroyed, but Sharpe needed it armed and dangerous in case Brigadier Loup came calling.

'I wasn't talking about muskets, Sharpe,' Runciman said, 'but about the news from Ireland. You really haven't heard?'

'No, sir.'

Runciman shook his head, making his jowls wobble. 'It seems there are new problems in Ireland, Sharpe. Damned bad business. Bloody rebels making trouble, troops fighting back, women and children dead. River Erne blocked with bodies at Belleek. Talk of rape. Dear me. I really thought that '98 had settled the Irish business once and for all, but it seems not. The damned papists are making trouble again. Dear me, dear me. Why did God allow the papists to flourish? They try us Christians so sorely. Ah, well.' Runciman sighed. 'We'll have to break some skulls over there, just as we did when Tone rebelled in '98.'

Sharpe reflected that if the remedy had failed in 1798 then it was just as likely to be ineffective in 1811, but he thought it tactful not to say as much. 'It might mean trouble here, General,' he said instead, 'when the Irish troops hear about it?'

'That's why we have the lash, Sharpe.'

'We might have the lash, General, but we don't have muskets. And I was just wondering, sir, exactly how a Wagon Master General orders his convoys about.'

Runciman goggled at Sharpe, amazed at the apparently inappropriate question. 'Paper, of course, paper! Orders!'

Sharpe smiled. 'And you're still Wagon Master General, sir, isn't that so? Because they haven't replaced you. I doubt they can find a man to fill your shoes, sir.'

'Kind of you to say so, Sharpe, most kind.' Runciman looked slightly surprised at receiving a compliment, but tried not to show too much unfamiliarity with the experience. 'And it's probably true,' he added.

'And I was wondering, General, how we might divert a wagon or two of weapons up to the fort here?'

Runciman gaped at Sharpe. 'Steal them, you mean?'

'I wouldn't call it theft, General,' Sharpe said reproachfully, 'not when they're being employed against the enemy. We're just re-allocating the guns, sir, if you see what I mean. Eventually, sir, the army will have to equip us, so why don't we anticipate the order now? We can always catch up with the paperwork later.'

Runciman shook his head wildly, dislodging the careful strands of long hair that he obsessively brushed over his balding pate. 'It can't be done, Sharpe, it can't be done! It's against all precedence. Against all arrangements! Damn it, man, it's against regulations! I could be court-martialled! Think of the disgrace!' Runciman shuddered at the thought. 'I'm astonished, Sharpe,' he went on, 'even disappointed, that you should make such a suggestion. I know you were denied a gentleman's breeding or even an education, but I had still expected better from you! A gentleman does not steal, he does not lie, he does not demean a woman, he honours God and the King. These attributes are not beyond you, Sharpe!'

Sharpe went to the door of Runciman's quarters. The Colonel's day parlour was the old guard room in one of the gatehouse towers and, with the fortress's ancient gates propped open, the doorway offered a stunning view south. Sharpe leaned on a doorpost. 'What happened, General,' he asked when

Runciman's sermon had petered out, 'when a wagon went missing? You must have lost some wagons to thieves?'

'A few, very few. Hardly one. Two, maybe. A handful, possibly.'

'So then —' Sharpe began.

Colonel Runciman held up a hand to interrupt him. 'Don't suggest it, Sharpe! I am an honest man, a God-fearing man, and I won't contrive to cheat His Majesty's exchequer of a wagonload of muskets. No, I won't. I have never dealt in untruths and I shall not start now. Indeed, I expressly forbid you to continue talking of the matter, and that is a direct order, Sharpe!'

'Two wagonloads of muskets,' Sharpe offered the correction, 'and three ammunition carts.'

'No! I have already forbidden you to speak of the matter, and that is an end of it. You will say no more!'

Sharpe took out the penknife he used to clean the fouling off his rifle's lock. He unfolded the blade and ran his thumb along the edge. 'Brigadier Loup knows we're here now, General, and he's going to be upset about that young fellow that Kiely's whore killed. It wouldn't surprise me if he tried to take revenge. Let's see now? A night assault? Probably. And he's got two full battalions of infantry and each and every one of those bastards will be trying to earn the reward Loup's put on my head. If I was Loup I'd attack from the north because the walls have virtually disappeared there, and I'd have the dragoons waiting down there to cut off the survivors.' Sharpe nodded down the steep approach road, then chuckled. 'Just imagine it, can't you? Being hunted down in the dawn by a pack of grey dragoons, each of them with a newly sharpened castrating knife in his sabretache. Loup doesn't give quarter, you see. He's not known for taking prisoners, General. He just pulls out the knife, yanks down your breeches and slices off your —'

'Sharpe! Please! Please!' A wan Runciman stared at Sharpe's penknife. 'Do you have to be so graphic?'

'General! I'm raising a serious matter! I can't hold off a brigade of Frenchmen with my handful of riflemen. I might do some damage if the Irish boys had muskets, but without muskets, bayonets and ammunition?' Sharpe shook his head, then snapped the blade shut. 'It's your choice, General, but if I was the senior British officer in this fort then I'd find a way to get some decent weapons up here as fast as possible. Unless, of course, I wanted to be singing the high notes in the church choir when I got back to Hampshire.'

Runciman gaped at Sharpe. The Colonel was sweating now, overwhelmed by a vision of castrating Frenchmen running wild inside the crumbling fort. 'But they won't give us muskets, Sharpe. We tried! Kiely and I tried together! And that awkward man General Valverde pleaded for us as well, but the Quartermaster General says there's a temporary shortage of spare weapons. He hoped General Valverde might persuade Cadiz to send us some Spanish muskets.'

Sharpe shook his head at Runciman's despair. 'So we have to borrow some muskets, General, till the Spanish ones arrive. We just need to divert a wagon or two with the help of those seals you've still got.'

'But I can't issue orders to the wagon train, Sharpe! Not any longer! I have new duties, new responsibilities.'

'You've got too many responsibilities, General,' Sharpe said, 'because you're too valuable a man, but really, sir, you shouldn't be worrying yourself over details. Your job is to look after the big decisions and let me look after the small.' Sharpe tossed the penknife in the air and caught it. 'And let me look after the Crapauds if they come, sir. You've got better things to do.'

Runciman leaned back in his folding chair, making it creak dangerously. 'You have a point, Sharpe, you do indeed have a point.' Runciman shuddered as he contemplated the enormity of the crime. 'But you think I am merely anticipating an order rather than breaking one?'

Sharpe stared at the Colonel with feigned admiration. 'I wish I had your mind, General, I really do. That's a brilliant way of putting it. "Anticipating an order." I wish I'd thought of that.'

Runciman preened at the compliment. 'My dear mother always maintained I could have been a lawyer,' he said proudly, 'maybe even Lord Chancellor! But my father preferred me to take an honest career.' He pulled some empty papers across his makeshift desk and began writing orders. From time to time the horror of his conduct made him pause, but each time Sharpe snapped the small blade open and shut and the noise prompted the Colonel to dip his quill's tip into the inkwell.

And next day four ox-drawn wagons with puzzled drivers and beds loaded with weapons, ammunition and supplies arrived at the San Isidro Fort.

And the Real Compañía Irlandesa was armed at last.

And thinking of mutiny.

CHAPTER FOUR

Next morning, just after dawn, a delegation discovered Sharpe at the deserted northern end of the fort. The sun was slicing across the valley to gild the small mist that sifted above the stream where Sharpe was watching a harrier float effortlessly in the light wind with its gaze trained down on the hillside. The eight men of the delegation halted awkwardly behind Sharpe who, after one sour glance at their serious faces, looked back to the valley. 'There's some rabbits down there,' Sharpe said to no one in particular, 'and that daft bird keeps losing them in the mist.'

'He won't go hungry for long though,' Harper said, 'I've never seen a hawk dafter than a rabbit.' The greenjacket Sergeant was the only delegate from Sharpe's company: the other men were all from the Real Compañía Irlandesa. 'It's a nice morning,' Harper said, sounding uncharacteristically nervous. He plainly believed that either Father Sarsfield, Captain Donaju or Captain Lacy should broach the delicate subject that had caused this delegation to seek Sharpe out, but the chaplain and the two embarrassed officers were silent. 'A grand morning,' Harper said, breaking the silence again.

'Is it?' Sharpe responded. He had been standing on a merlon beside a gun embrasure, but now he jumped down to the firing platform and from there into the bed of the dry ditch. Years of rainfall had eroded the glacis and filled the ditch, just as

116

frost had degraded and crumbled the stonework of the ramparts. 'I've seen hovels built better than this,' Sharpe said. He kicked at the wall's base and one of the larger stones shifted perceptibly. 'There's no bloody mortar there!' he said.

'There wasn't enough water in the mix,' Harper explained. He took a deep breath, then, realizing that his companions would not speak up, took the plunge himself. 'We wanted to see you, sir. It's important, sir.'

Sharpe clambered back up to the ramparts and brushed his hands together. 'Is it about the new muskets?'

'No, sir. The muskets are just grand, sir.'

'The training?'

'No, sir.'

'Then the man you want to see is Colonel Runciman,' Sharpe said curtly. 'Call him "General" and he'll give you anything.' Sharpe was deliberately dissembling. He knew exactly why the delegation was here, but he had small appetite for their worries. 'Talk to Runciman after breakfast and he'll be in a good enough mood,' he said.

'We've spoken to the Colonel,' Captain Donaju spoke at last, 'and the Colonel said we should speak with you.'

Father Sarsfield smiled. 'I think we knew he would say that, Captain, when we approached him. I don't think Colonel Runciman is particularly sympathetic to the problems of Ireland.'

Sharpe looked from Sarsfield to Donaju, from Donaju to Lacy, then from Lacy to the sullen faces of the four rank and file guardsmen. 'So it's about Ireland, is it?' Sharpe said. 'Well, go on. I haven't got any other problems to solve today.'

The chaplain ignored the sarcasm, offering Sharpe a folded newspaper instead. 'It is about that, Captain Sharpe,' Sarsfield said respectfully.

Sharpe took the paper which, to his surprise, came from Philadelphia. The front page was a dense mass of black type:

lists of ships arriving or departing from the city wharves; news from Europe; reports of Congress and tales of Indian atrocities suffered by settlers in the western territories.

'It's at the bottom of the page,' Donaju offered.

'"The Melancholy Effects of Intemperance"?' Sharpe read a headline aloud.

'No, Sharpe. Just before that,' Donaju said, and Sharpe sighed as he read the words 'New Massacres in Ireland'. What followed was a more lurid version of the tale Runciman had already told Sharpe: a catalogue of rape and slaughter, of innocent children cut down by English dragoons and of praying women dragged out of houses by drink-crazed grenadiers. The newspaper claimed that the ghosts of Cromwell's troopers had come back to life to turn Ireland into a blood-drenched misery again. Ireland, the English government had announced, would be pacified once and for all, and the newspaper commented that the English were choosing to make that pacification when so many Irishmen were fighting against France in the King's army in Portugal. Sharpe read the piece through twice. 'What did Lord Kiely say?' he asked Father Sarsfield, not because he cared one fig what Kiely thought, but the question bought him a few seconds while he thought how to respond. He also wanted to encourage Sarsfield to do the delegation's talking, for the Real Compañía Irlandesa's chaplain had struck Sharpe as a friendly, sensible and cool-headed man and if he could get the priest on his side then he reckoned the rest of the company would follow.

'His Lordship hasn't seen the newspaper,' Sarsfield said. 'He has gone hunting with the Doña Juanita.'

Sharpe handed the paper back to the priest. 'Well, I've seen the newspaper,' he said, 'and I can tell you it's bloody rubbish.' One of the guardsmen stirred indignantly, then stiffened when Sharpe gave him a threatening look. 'It's a fairy tale for idiots,' Sharpe said provocatively, 'pure bloody make-believe.'

118

'How do you know?' Donaju asked resentfully.

'Because if there was trouble in Ireland, Captain, we'd have heard about it before the Americans. And since when did the Americans have a good word to say about the British?'

'But we have heard about it,' Captain Lacy intervened. Lacy was a stocky young man with a pugnacious demeanour and scarred knuckles. 'There've been rumours,' Lacy insisted.

'There have too,' Harper added loyally.

Sharpe looked at his friend. 'Oh, Christ,' he said as he realized just how hurt Harper was, though he also realized that Harper must have come to him hoping that the stories were not true. If Harper had wanted a fight he would not have chosen Sharpe, but some other representative of the enemy race. 'Oh, Christ,' Sharpe swore again. He was plagued with more than enough problems already. The Real Compañía Irlandesa had been promised pay and given none; every time it rained the old barracks ran with damp; the food in the fort was dreadful and the only well provided nothing but a trickle of bitter water. Now, on top of those problems and the added threat of Loup's vengeance, there was this sudden menace of an Irish mutiny. 'Give me back the newspaper, Father,' Sharpe said to the chaplain, then stabbed a dirty fingernail at the date printed at the top of the sheet. 'When was this published?' He showed the date to Sarsfield.

'A month ago,' the priest said.

'So?' Lacy asked belligerently.

'So how many bloody drafts have arrived from Ireland in the last month?' Sharpe asked, his voice as scornful as it was forceful. 'Ten? Fifteen? And not one of those men thought to tell us about his sister being raped or his mother being buggered witless by some dragoon? Yet suddenly some bloody American newspaper knows all about it?' Sharpe had addressed his words to Harper more than to the others, for Harper alone could be expected to know how frequently replacement drafts arrived from Ireland. 'Come on, Pat! It doesn't make bloody sense, and if you don't believe me then I'll give you a pass and you can go down to the main camps and find some newly arrived Irishmen and ask them for news of home. Maybe you'll believe them if you don't believe me.'

Harper looked at the date on the paper, thought about Sharpe's words, and nodded reluctantly. 'It doesn't make sense, sir, you're right. But not everything in this world needs to make sense.'

'Of course it bloody does,' Sharpe snapped. 'That's how you and I live. We're practical men, Pat, not bloody dreamers! We believe in the Baker rifle, the Tower musket and twenty-three inches of bayonet. You can leave superstitions to women and children, and these things' – he slapped the newspaper – 'are worse than superstitions. They're downright lies!' He looked at Donaju. 'Your job, Captain, is to go to your men and tell them that they're lies. And if you don't believe me then you ride down to the camps. Go to the Connaught Rangers and ask their new recruits. Go to the Inniskillings. Go wherever you like, but be back here by dusk. And in the meantime, Captain, tell your men they've got a full day of musket training. Loading and firing till their shoulders are raw meat. Is that clear?'

The men from the Real Compañía Irlandesa nodded reluctantly. Sharpe had won the argument, at least until the evening when Donaju returned from his reconnaissance. Father Sarsfield took the paper from Sharpe. 'Are you saying this is a forgery?' the priest asked.

'How would I know, Father? I'm just saying it isn't true. Where did you get it?'

Sarsfield shrugged. 'They're scattered throughout the army, Sharpe.'

'And when did you and I ever see a newspaper from America, Pat?' Sharpe asked Harper. 'And funny, isn't it, that the first one we ever see is all about Britain being bloody to Ireland? It smacks of mischief to me.'

Father Sarsfield folded the paper. 'I think you're probably right, Sharpe, and praise be to God for it. But you won't mind, will you, if I ride with Captain Donaju today?'

'It isn't up to me what you do, Father,' Sharpe said. 'But for the rest of you, let's get to work!'

Sharpe waited while the delegation left. He motioned Harper to stay behind, but Father Sarsfield also lingered for Sharpe's attention. 'I'm sorry, Sharpe,' the priest said.

'Why?'

Sarsfield flinched at Sharpe's harsh tone. 'I imagine you do not need Irish problems intruding on your life.'

'I don't need any damn problems, Father. I've got a job to do, and the job is to turn your boys into soldiers, good soldiers.'

Sarsfield smiled. 'I think you are a rare thing, Captain Sharpe: an honest man.'

'Of course I'm not,' Sharpe said, almost blushing as he remembered the horrors done to the three men caught by El Castrador at Sharpe's request. 'I'm not a bloody saint, Father, but I do like to get things done. If I spent my damn life dreaming dreams I'd still be in the ranks. You can only afford dreams if you're rich and privileged.' He added the last words viciously.

'You speak of Kiely,' Sarsfield said and started walking slowly back along the ramparts beside Sharpe. The skirts of the priest's soutane were wet with the dew from the ragweed and grass that grew inside the fort. 'Lord Kiely is a very weak man, Captain,' Sarsfield went on. 'He had a very strong mother' – the priest grimaced at the memory – 'and you would not know, Captain, what a trial to the church strong women can be, but I think they can be even more of a trial to their sons. Lady Kiely wanted her son to be a great Catholic warrior, an Irish warrior! The Catholic warlord who would succeed where the Protestant lawyer Wolfe Tone failed, but instead she drove him into drink, pettiness and whoring. I buried her last year' – he made a quick sign of the cross – 'and I fear her son did not mourn her as a son should mourn his mother nor, alas, will he ever be the Christian she wanted him to be. He told me last night that he intends to marry the Lady Juanita and his mother, I think, will be weeping in purgatory at the thought of such a match.' The priest sighed. 'Still, I didn't want to talk to you about Kiely. Instead, Captain, I beg you to be a little patient with us.'

'I thought I was being patient with you,' Sharpe said defensively.

'With us Irish,' Father Sarsfield explained. 'You are a man with a country, Captain, and you don't know what it's like to be an exile. You cannot know what it is like to be listening to the harps beside the waters of Babylon.' Sarsfield smiled at the phrase, then shrugged. 'It's like a wound, Captain Sharpe, that never heals, and I pray to God that you never have to feel that wound for yourself.'

Sharpe felt a stab of embarrassed pity as he looked into the priest's kindly face. 'Were you never in Ireland, Father?'

'Once, my son, years ago. Long years ago, but if I live a thousand years that one brief stay will always seem like yesterday.' He smiled ruefully, then hitched up his damp soutane. 'I must join Donaju for our expedition! Think about my words, Captain!' The priest hurried away, his white hair lifting in the breeze.

Harper joined Sharpe. 'A nice man, that,' Harper said, nodding at the priest's receding back. 'He was telling me how he was in Donegal once. Up in Lough Swilly. I had an aunt who lived that way, God rest her poor soul. She was in Rathmullen.'

'I never was in Donegal,' Sharpe said, 'and I'll probably never get there, and frankly, Sergeant, right at this moment I don't care. I've got enough bloody troubles without the bloody Irish going moody on me. We need blankets, food and money which means I'm going to have to get Runciman to write another of his magic orders, but it won't be easy because the fat bugger's scared shitless of being court-martialled. Lord bloody Kiely's no bloody help. All he does is suck brandy, dream about bloody glory and trail around behind that black-haired whore like a mooncalf.' Sharpe, despite Sarsfield's advice about patience, was losing his temper. 'The priest is telling me to feel sorry for you all, Hogan wants me to kick these lads in the teeth and there's a fat Spaniard with a castrating knife who thinks I'm going to hold Loup down while he cuts off his bloody balls. Everyone expects me to solve all their bloody problems, so for God's sake give me some bloody help.'

'I always do,' Harper said resentfully.

'Yes, you do, Pat, and I'm sorry.'

'And if the stories were true –' Harper began.

'They're not!' Sharpe shouted.

'All right! All right! God save Ireland.' Harper blew out a long breath, then there was an awkward silence between the two men. Sharpe just glowered to the north while Harper clambered down into a nearby gun embrasure and kicked at a loosened stone. 'God knows why they built a fort up here,' he said at last.

'There used to be a main road down there.' Sharpe nodded to the pass which lay to the north. 'It was a way to avoid Ciudad Rodrigo and Almeida, but half the road got washed away and what's left of it can't take modern guns so it's no use these days. But the road eastwards is still all there, Pat, and Loup's bloody brigade can use it. Down there' – he pointed to the route as he spoke – 'up this slope, over these walls and straight down on us and there's bugger all here to stop them.'

'Why would Loup do that?' Harper asked.

'Because he's a mad, brave, ruthless bugger, that's why. And because he hates me and because kicking the lights out of us would be a cheap victory for the bastard.' Sharpe had become preoccupied by the threat of a night raid by Loup's brigade. He had first thought of the raid merely as a means of frightening Colonel Runciman into signing his fraudulent wagon orders, but the more Sharpe had thought about it, the more likely such a raid seemed. And the San Isidro Fort was hopelessly ill prepared for such an attack. A thousand men might have been able to hold its degraded ramparts, but the Real Compañía Irlandesa was far too small a unit to offer any real resistance. They would be trapped within the vast, crumbling walls like rats in a terrier's fighting ring. 'Which is just what Hogan and Wellington want,' Sharpe said aloud.

'What's that, sir?'

'They don't bloody trust your Irishmen, see? They want them out of the way and I'm supposed to help get rid of the buggers, but the trouble is I like them. Damn it, Pat. If Loup comes we'll all be dead.'

'You think he's coming?'

'I bloody well know he's coming,' Sharpe said fervently, and suddenly the vague suspicions hardened into an utter certainty. He might have just made a vigorous proclamation of his practicality, but in truth he relied on instinct most of the time. Sometimes, Sharpe knew, the wise soldier listened to his superstitions and fears because they were a better guide than mere practicality. Good flat hard sense dictated that Loup would not waste valuable effort by raiding the San Isidro Fort, but Sharpe rejected that good sense because his every instinct told him there was trouble coming. 'I don't know when or how he'll come,' he told Harper, 'but I'm not trusting a palace guard to serve picquet. I want our boys up here.' He meant he wanted riflemen guarding the fort's northern extremity. 'And I want a night picquet too, so make sure a couple of the lads get some sleep today.'

124

Harper gazed down the long northern slope. 'You think they'll come this way?'

'It's the easiest. West and east are too steep, the southern end is too strong, but a cripple could waltz across this wall. Jesus.' This last imprecation was torn from Sharpe as he realized just how vulnerable the fort was. He stared eastwards. 'I'll bet that bastard is watching us right now.' From the far peaks a Frenchman armed with a good telescope could probably count the buttons on Sharpe's jacket.

'You really think he'll come?' Harper asked.

'I think we're damn lucky he hasn't come already. I think we're damn lucky to be alive.' Sharpe jumped off the ramparts onto the grass inside the fort. There was nothing but grass and weed-strewn waste land for a hundred yards, then the red stone barracks buildings began. There were eight long buildings and the Real Compañía Irlandesa bivouacked in the two that had been kept in best repair while Sharpe's riflemen camped in one of the magazines close to the gate tower. That tower, Sharpe decided, was the key to the defence, for whoever held the tower would dominate the fight. 'All we need is three or four minutes' warning,' Sharpe said, 'and we can make the bugger wish he'd stayed in bed.'

'You can beat him?' Harper asked.

'He thinks he can surprise us. He thinks he can break into the barracks and slaughter us in our beds, Pat, but if we just have some warning we can turn that gate tower into a fortress and without artillery Loup can't do a damn thing about it.' Sharpe was suddenly enthusiastic. 'Don't you always say that a good fight is a tonic to an Irishman?' he asked.

'Only when I'm drunk,' Harper said.

'Let's pray for a fight anyway,' Sharpe said eagerly, 'and a victory. My God, that'll put some confidence into these guards!'

But then, at dusk, just as the last red-gold rays were shrinking behind the western hills, everything changed.

The Portuguese battalion arrived unannounced. They were *caçadores*, skirmishers like the greenjackets, only these troops were outfitted in blood-brown jackets and grey British trousers. They carried Baker rifles and looked as if they knew how to use them. They marched into the fort with the easy, lazy step of veteran troops, while behind them came a convoy of three ox-drawn wagons loaded with rations, firewood and spare ammunition. The battalion was a little over half strength, mustering just four hundred rank and file, but the men still made a brave show as they paraded on the fort's old plaza.

Their Colonel was a thin-faced man called Oliveira. 'For a few days every year,' he explained off-handedly to Lord Kiely, 'we occupy the San Isidro. Just as a way of reminding ourselves that the fort exists and to discourage anyone else from setting up house here. No, don't move your men out of the barracks. My men don't need roofs. And we won't be in your way, Colonel. I'll exercise my rogues across the frontier for the next few days.'

Behind the last supply wagons the fort's great gates creaked shut. They crashed together, then one of Kiely's men lifted the locking bar into position. Colonel Runciman hurried out of the gatehouse to offer his greeting to Colonel Oliveira and to invite the Portuguese officer to supper, but Oliveira declined. 'I share my men's supper, Colonel. No offence.' Oliveira spoke good English and nearly half his officers were British, the result of a policy to integrate the Portuguese army into Wellington's forces. To Sharpe's delight one of the *caçador* officers was Thomas Garrard, a man who had served with Sharpe in the ranks of the 33rd and who had taken advantage of the promotion prospects offered to British sergeants willing to join the

Portuguese army. The two men had last met at Almeida when the great fortress had exploded in a horror that had led to the garrison's surrender. Garrard had been among the men forced to lay down his arms.

'Bloody Crapaud bastards,' he said feelingly. 'Kept us in Burgos with hardly enough food to feed a rat, and what food there was was all rotted. Christ, Dick, you and I have eaten some bad meals in our time, but this was really bad. And all because that damned cathedral exploded. I'd like to meet the French gunner who did that and wring his bloody neck.'

In truth it had been Sharpe who had caused the magazine in the cathedral's crypt to explode, but it did not seem a politic admission to make. 'It was a bad business,' Sharpe agreed mildly.

'You got out next morning, didn't you?' Garrard asked. 'Cox wouldn't let us go. We wanted to fight our way out, but he said we had to do the decent thing and surrender.' He shook his head in disgust. 'Not that it matters now,' he went on. 'The Crapauds exchanged me and Oliveira asked me to join his regiment and now I'm a captain like you.'

'Well done.'

'They're good lads,' Garrard said fondly of his company which was bivouacking in the open space inside the northern ramparts where the Portuguese campfires burned bright in the dusk. Oliveira's picquets were on every rampart save the gate tower. Such efficient sentries meant that Sharpe no longer needed to deploy his own riflemen on picquet duty, but he was still apprehensive and told Garrard his fears as the two men strolled round the darkening ramparts.

'I've heard of Loup,' Garrard said. 'He's a right bastard.'

'Nasty as hell.'

'And you think he's coming here?'

'Just an instinct, Tom.'

'Hell, ignore those and you might as well dig your own grave, eh? Let's go and see the Colonel.'

But Oliveira was not so easily convinced of Sharpe's fears, nor did Juanita de Elia help Sharpe's cause. Juanita and Lord Kiely had returned from a day's hunting and, with Father Sarsfield, Colonel Runciman and a half-dozen of the Real Compañía Irlandesa's officers, were guests at the Portuguese supper. Juanita scorned Sharpe's warning. 'You think a French brigadier would bother himself with an English captain?' she asked mockingly.

Sharpe suppressed a stab of evil temper. He had been speaking to Oliveira, not to Kiely's whore, but this was not the time or the place to pick a quarrel. Besides, he recognized that in some obscure way his and Juanita's dislike of each other was bred into the bone and probably unavoidable. She would talk to any other officer in the fort, even to Runciman, but at Sharpe's very appearance she would turn and walk away rather than offer a polite greeting. 'I think he'll bother with me, ma'am, yes,' Sharpe said mildly.

'Why?' Oliveira demanded.

'Go on, man, answer!' Kiely said when Sharpe hesitated.

'Well, Captain?' Juanita mocked Sharpe. 'Lost your tongue?'

'I think he'll bother with me, ma'am,' Sharpe said, stung into an answer, 'because I killed two of his men.'

'Oh, my God!' Juanita pretended to be shocked. 'Anyone would think there was a war happening!'

Kiely and some of the Portuguese officers smiled, but Colonel Oliveira just stared at Sharpe as though weighing the warning carefully. Finally he shrugged. 'Why would he worry that you killed two of his men?' he asked.

Sharpe hesitated to confess to what he knew was a crime against military justice, but he could hardly withdraw now. The safety of the fort and all the men inside depended on him convincing Oliveira of the genuine danger and so, very reluctantly, he described the raped and massacred village and how he had captured two of Loup's men and stood them up against a wall.

'You had orders to shoot them?' Oliveira asked presciently.

'No, sir,' Sharpe said, aware of the eyes staring at him. He knew it might prove a horrid mistake to have admitted the executions, but he desperately needed to persuade Oliveira of the danger and so he described how Loup had ridden to the small upland village to plead for his men's lives and how, despite that appeal, Sharpe had ordered them shot. Colonel Runciman, hearing the tale for the first time, shook his head in disbelief.

'You shot the men in front of Loup?' Oliveira asked, surprised.

'Yes, sir.'

'So this rivalry between you and Loup is a personal vendetta, Captain Sharpe?' the Portuguese Colonel asked.

'In a way, sir.'

'Either yes or no!' Oliveira snapped. He was a forceful, quick-tempered man who reminded Sharpe of General Crauford, the Light Division's commander. Oliveira had the same impatience with evasive answers.

'I believe Brigadier Loup will attack very soon, sir,' Sharpe insisted.

'Proof?'

'Our vulnerability,' Sharpe said, 'and because he's put a price on my head, sir.' He knew it sounded feeble and he blushed when Juanita laughed aloud. She was wearing her Real Compañía Irlandesa uniform, though she had unbuttoned the coat and shirt so that the flamelight glowed on her long neck. Every officer around the fire seemed fascinated by her, and no wonder, for she was a flamboyantly exotic creature in this place

129

of guns and powder and stone. She sat close to Kiely, an arm resting on his knee, and Sharpe wondered if perhaps they had announced their betrothal. Something seemed to have put the supper guests into a holiday mood. 'How much is the price, Captain?' she asked mockingly.

Sharpe bit back a retort that the reward would prove more than enough to hire her services for a night. 'I don't know,' he lied instead.

'Can't be very much,' Kiely said. 'Over-age captain like you, Sharpe? Couple of dollars maybe? Bag of salt?'

Oliveira glanced at Kiely and the glance expressed disapproval of his Lordship's drunken gibes. The Colonel sucked on a cigar, then blew smoke across the fire. 'I have doubled the sentries, Captain,' he said to Sharpe, 'and if this Loup does come to claim your head then we'll give him a fight.'

'When he comes, sir,' Sharpe insisted, 'can I suggest, with respect, sir, that you get your men into the gatehouse?'

'You don't give up, do you, Sharpe?' Kiely interrupted. Before the Portuguese battalion's arrival Sharpe had asked Kiely to move the whole Real Compañía Irlandesa into the gatehouse, a request that Kiely had peremptorily turned down. 'No one's going to attack us here,' Kiely now said, reiterating his earlier argument, 'and anyway, if they do, we should fight the bastards from the ramparts, not the gatehouse.'

'We can't fight from the ramparts –' Sharpe began.

'Don't tell me where we can fight! God damn you!' Kiely shouted, startling Juanita. 'You're a jumped-up corporal, Sharpe, not a bloody general. If the French come, damn it, I'll fight them how I like and beat them how I like and I won't need your help!'

The outburst embarrassed the assembled officers. Father Sarsfield frowned as though he was looking for some emollient words, but it was Oliveira who finally broke the awkward silence. 'If they come, Captain Sharpe,' he said gravely, 'I shall seek the

130

refuge you advise. And thank you for your advice.' Oliveira nodded his dismissal.

'Good night, sir,' Sharpe said, then walked away.

'Ten guineas to the price on your head says Loup won't come, Sharpe!' Kiely called after the rifleman. 'What is it? Lost your damn nerve? Don't want to take a wager like a gentleman?' Kiely and Juanita laughed. Sharpe tried to ignore them.

Tom Garrard had followed Sharpe. 'I'm sorry, Dick,' Garrard said and then, after a pause, 'Did you really shoot two Crapauds?'

'Aye.'

'Good for you. But I wouldn't tell too many people about it.'

'I know, I know,' Sharpe said, then shook his head. 'Bloody Kiely.'

'His woman's a rare one though,' Garrard said. 'Reminds me of that girl you took up with at Gawilghur. You remember her?'

'This one's a bitch, that's the difference,' Sharpe said. God, he thought, but his temper was being abraded to a raw bloody edge. 'I'm sorry, Tom,' he said, 'it's like fighting with wet powder, trying to shake sense into this bloody place.'

'Join the Portuguese, Dick,' Garrard said. 'Good as gold they are and no bloody over-born buggers like Kiely making life hard.' He offered Sharpe a cigar. The two men bent their heads over Garrard's tinderbox and, when the charred linen caught the spark to flare bright, Sharpe saw a picture chased into the inner side of the lid.

'Hold it there, Tom,' he said, stopping his friend from closing the lid. He stared at the picture for a few seconds. 'I'd forgotten those boxes,' Sharpe said. The tinderboxes were made of a cheap metal that had to be protected from rust by gun oil, but Garrard had somehow kept this box safe for twelve years. There had once been scores like it, all made by a tinsmith in captured Seringapatam and all with explicit pictures etched crudely into the lids. Garrard's box showed a British soldier on top of a long-legged girl whose back was arched in apparent ecstasy. 'Bugger might have taken his hat off first,' Sharpe said.

Garrard laughed and snapped the box shut to preserve the linen. 'Still got yours?'

Sharpe shook his head. 'It was stolen off me years ago, Tom. I reckon it was that bastard Hakeswill that had it. Remember him? He was a thieving sod.'

'Jesus God,' Garrard said, 'I'd half forgotten the bastard.' He drew on the cigar, then shook his head in wonder. 'Who'd ever believe it, Dick? You and me captains? And I can remember when you were broken down from corporal for farting on church parade.'

'They were good days, Tom,' Sharpe said.

'Only because they're a long way back. Nothing like distant memory for putting green leaves on a bare life, Dick.'

Sharpe held the smoke in his mouth, then breathed out. 'Let's hope it's a long life, Tom. Let's hope Loup isn't halfway here already. It would be a damned pity for you all to come up here for an exercise only to be slaughtered by Loup's brigade.'

'We're not really here for an exercise,' Garrard said. There was a long awkward silence. 'Can you keep a secret?' Garrard asked eventually. The two men had reached a dark open space, out of earshot of any of the bivouacked *caçadores*. 'We didn't come here by accident, Richard,' Garrard admitted. 'We were sent.'

Sharpe heard footfalls on the nearest rampart where a Portuguese officer made his rounds. A challenge rang out and was answered. It was comforting to hear such military efficiency. 'By Wellington?' Sharpe asked.

Garrard shrugged. 'I suppose so. His Lordship doesn't talk to me, but not much happens in this army without Nosey's say-so.'

'So why did he send you?'

'Because he doesn't trust your Spanish Irishmen, that's why. There have been some odd stories going round the army these last few days. Stories of English troops burning Irish priests and raping Irish women, and –'

'I've heard the tales,' Sharpe interrupted, 'and they're not true. Hell, I even sent a captain down to the camps today and he found out for himself.' Captain Donaju, returning from the army's cantonments with Father Sarsfield, had possessed enough grace to apologize to Sharpe. Wherever Donaju and Sarsfield had visited and whoever they had asked, even men fresh out of Ireland, they could find no confirmation of the stories printed in the American newspaper. 'No one can believe the stories!' Sharpe now protested to Garrard.

'But true or not,' Garrard said, 'the stories worry someone high up, and they think the stories are coming from your men. So we've been sent to keep an eye on you.'

'Guard us, you mean?' Sharpe asked bitterly.

'Keep an eye on you,' Garrard said again. 'No one's really sure what we're supposed to do except stay here until their Lordships make up their mind what to do. Oliveira thinks your lads will probably be sent to Cadiz. Not you, Dick,' Garrard hastened to add reassuringly, 'you're not one of the Irish, are you? We'll just make sure these Irish lads can't make mischief and then your lads can go back to some proper soldiering.'

'I like these Irish lads,' Sharpe said flatly, 'and they're not making mischief. I can warrant that.'

'I'm not the one you have to convince, Dick.'

It was Hogan or Wellington, Sharpe supposed. And how clever of Hogan or Wellington to send a Portuguese battalion to do the dirty work so that General Valverde could not say that a British regiment had persecuted the Royal Irish Company of the King of Spain's household guard. Sharpe blew out cigar smoke. 'So those sentries on the wall, Tom,' he said, 'they're not looking outwards for Loup, are they, but looking in at us?'

'They're looking both ways, Dick.'

'Well, make sure they're looking outwards. Because if Loup comes, Tom, there'll be hell to pay.'

'They'll do their duty,' Garrard said doggedly.

And they did. The diligent Portuguese picquets watched from the walls as the night chill spread down into the eastern valley where a ghostly mist worked its way upstream. They watched the long slopes, always alert to the smallest motion in the vaporous dark while in the fort some children of the Real Compañía Irlandesa cried in their sleep, a horse whinnied and a dog barked briefly. Two hours after midnight the sentries changed and the new men settled into their posts and gazed down the hillsides.

At three in the morning the owl flew back to its roost in the ruined chapel, its great white wings beating above the smouldering remnants of the Portuguese fires. Sharpe had been walking the sentries' beat and staring into the long shadowed night for the first sign of danger. Kiely and his whore were in bed, as was Runciman, but Sharpe stayed awake. He had taken what precautions he could, moving vast quantities of the Real Compañía Irlandesa's spare ammunition into Colonel Runciman's day parlour and issuing the rest to the men. He had talked a long while with Donaju, rehearsing what they should do if an attack did come and then, when he believed he had done all he could, he had walked with Tom Garrard. Now, following the owl, Sharpe went to his bed. It was less than three hours till dawn and Loup, he decided, would not come now. He lay down and fell fast asleep.

And ten minutes later woke to gunfire.

As the wolf, at last, attacked.

The first Sharpe knew of the attack was when Miranda, the girl rescued from the high border settlement, screamed like a banshee and for a second Sharpe thought he was dreaming, then he became aware of the gunshot that had preceded the scream by a split second and he opened his eyes to see that Rifleman Thompson was dying, shot in the head and bleeding like a stuck pig. Thompson had been hurled clear down the flight of ten steps that led from the magazine's crooked entrance and now lay twitching as a flood of gore spurted from his matted hair. He had been carrying his rifle when he was shot and now the weapon skidded over the floor to stop beside Sharpe.

Shadows loomed at the stairhead. The magazine's main entrance led into a short tunnel which would have been equipped with two doors when the fort had been properly garrisoned and its magazine filled with shot and powder. Where the second door should have hung the tunnel turned in an abrupt right angle, then reversed back to the stairhead. The pair of turns had been designed to baffle any enemy shell that might have breached the magazine's entrance and in the bleak darkness the double angle had succeeded in slowing down Thompson's killers who now erupted into the tiny rushlight that burned in the great underground chamber.

Grey uniforms. This was not a dream but a nightmare, for the grey killers had come.

Sharpe seized Thompson's rifle, pointed the muzzle and pulled the trigger.

An explosion crashed through the cellar as a cluster of flames speared through a smoke cloud towards the French at the top of the stair. Patrick Harper had fired his seven-barrelled gun and the volley of pistol balls slammed into the attackers to throw them back into the angle of the corridor's last turn where they went down in a welter of blood and pain. Two more riflemen fired. The magazine echoed with the shots and the air was stinking and thick with the choking smoke. A man was screaming, so was a girl. 'Back way! Back way!' Sharpe shouted.

'Shut that bloody girl up, Perkins!' He seized his own rifle and fired it up the stairs. He could see nothing now except for the small shining spots where the tiny rushlights glimmered in the smoke. The French seemed to have vanished, though in truth they were merely trying to negotiate the barricade of screaming, bleeding, twitching men who had been hurled back by Harper's volley and the fusillade of rifle bullets.

There was a second stair at the magazine's end, a stair that twisted up to the ramparts and was designed to let ammunition be delivered direct to the firestep rather than be carried through the fort's courtyard. 'Sergeant Latimer!' Sharpe shouted. 'Count them up! Thompson's out of it. Go, go!' If the French already held the ramparts, Sharpe reflected, then he and his riflemen were already trapped and doomed to die like rats in a hole, but he dared not abandon hope. 'Go!' he shouted at his men. 'Out! Out!' He had been sleeping with his boots on, so all he needed to do was snatch up his belt, pouches and sword. He slung the belt over his shoulder and began reloading the rifle. His eyes were smarting from the smoke. A French musket coughed more smoke at the top of the stairs and the bullet ricocheted harmlessly off the back wall.

'Just you and Harps, sir!' Latimer called from the back stair.

'Go, Pat!' Sharpe said.

Boots clattered on the stairs. Sharpe abandoned his attempt to load the rifle, reversed the weapon instead and hammered its butt at the shadow that appeared in the smoke. The man went down silently and hard, felled instantly by the brass-weighted blow. Harper, his rifle reloaded, fired blindly up the stairs, then grabbed Sharpe's elbow. 'For the love of God, sir. Come on!'

Grey attackers were pouring down the stairs into the smoky darkness. A pistol fired, a man shouted in urgent French and another tripped over Thompson's corpse. The damp cave-like space stank of urine, rotted eggs and sweat. Harper pulled Sharpe through the cloying smoke to the foot of the back stairs where Latimer crouched. 'Go on, sir!' Latimer had a loaded rifle that would serve as the parting shot.

Sharpe pounded up the stairs towards the cool and blessedly clean night air. Latimer fired into the chaos, then followed Harper up the crooked stair. Cresacre and Hagman were waiting at the stairhead with pointed rifles. 'Don't shoot!' Sharpe called as he neared the stairhead, then pushed past the two riflemen and ran to the inner edge of the firestep to try and understand the night's full horror.

Harper ran to the door that led into the gate tower, only to find it was barred from the inside. He hammered on the wood with the butt of his volley gun. 'Open up!' he shouted. 'Open up!'

Hagman fired down the winding stair and a scream echoed up the steps.

'Behind us, sir!' Perkins called. He was sheltering a terrified Miranda in one of the machicolations, 'and there's more on the road, sir!'

Sharpe swore. The gatehouse, which he had thought would be the night's salvation, was already captured. He could see that the gate was wide open and being guarded by grey-uniformed soldiers. Sharpe guessed two companies of Loup's *voltigeurs*, distinguished by the red epaulettes they wore, had led the attack and both were now inside the fort. One company had gone straight to the magazine where Sharpe and his men were bivouacking while most of the second company had spread into a skirmish line that was now advancing fast among the barracks blocks. Another squad of the grey-clad infantry was running up a ramp which led to the wall's wide firestep.

Harper kept trying to break the door down, but no one inside the gatehouse responded. Sharpe shouldered his half-loaded rifle and drew his sword. 'Leave it, Pat!' he shouted.

'Rifles! Line on me!' The real danger now was the section of men coming up to the wall. If those men got a lodging in the gun platforms then Sharpe's riflemen would be trapped while the rest of Loup's men swarmed into the San Isidro. That main enemy force was now hurrying up the approach road and, from the one quick southward glance that he could spare, Sharpe could see that Loup had sent his whole brigade into this attack which had been spearheaded by two companies of light infantry. God damn it, Sharpe thought, but he had got everything wrong. The French had not attacked from the north, but from the south, and in so doing they had already captured the fort's strongest point, the place Sharpe had planned to turn into an impregnable stronghold. He guessed that the two elite companies had crept up the approach road and rushed the causeway before any sentry called the alarm. And doubtless, too, the gates had been unbarred from inside by the same person who had betrayed where Sharpe, Loup's sworn enemy, was to be found and where Loup, seeking his revenge, had sent one of the two attacking companies.

Now, though, was not the time to analyse Loup's tactics, but to clear the ramparts of the Frenchmen who threatened to isolate Sharpe's riflemen. 'Fix swords,' he ordered, and waited while his men slotted the long, sword-handled bayonets onto their rifles' muzzles. 'Be calm, lads,' he said. He knew his men were frightened and excited after being woken to nightmare by a clever enemy, but this was no time for panic. It was a time for very cool heads and murderous fighting. 'Let's get the bastards! Come on!' Sharpe called and he led his men in a ragged line down the moonlit battlements. The first Frenchmen to reach the firestep dropped to their knees and took aim, but they were outnumbered, in the dark and nervous and so they fired early and their bullets flew wide or high. Then, fearing to be overwhelmed by the dark mass of riflemen, the *voltigeurs* turned and ran down the ramp to join the skirmish line that was advancing between the barracks blocks towards Oliveira's *caçadores*.

The Portuguese, Sharpe decided, must fend for themselves. His duty lay with the Real Compañía Irlandesa whose twin barracks had already been surrounded by the French skirmishers. The *voltigeurs* were firing at the barracks from the shelter of the other buildings, but they dared not attack, for the Irish guardsmen had opened a brisk return fire. Sharpe assumed the Real Compañía Irlandesa's officers were already either dead or prisoners, though it was possible that a few might have escaped out of the gatehouse's rampart doors as the French streamed into the lower rooms. 'Listen, lads!' Sharpe raised his voice so that all his riflemen could hear. 'We can't stay here. The buggers will be up from the magazine soon so we're going over to join the Irish boys. We'll barricade ourselves inside and keep firing.' He would have liked to split his greenjackets into two groups, one for each of the besieged barracks, but he doubted any man could reach the further barracks alive. The nearer of the two was less infested by *voltigeurs*, but it was also the barracks where the wives and children were quartered and thus the more in need of extra firepower. 'Are you ready?' Sharpe called. 'Let's go!'

They ran down the ramp just as Oliveira's skirmishers attacked from the right. The appearance of the *caçadores* distracted the *voltigeurs* and gave Sharpe's riflemen the chance to cross to the barracks without fighting through a whole *voltigeur* company, but it was a narrow chance, for even as Harper began shouting in Gaelic to order the Real Compañía Irlandesa to open their door a huge cheer from the gatehouse on Sharpe's left announced the arrival of Loup's main force. Sharpe was among the barracks now where the *voltigeurs* were retreating from the attack of the Portuguese skirmishers.

The Frenchmen's retreat drove them at right angles across Sharpe's path. Loup's men realized their danger too late. A sergeant screamed a warning, then was clubbed to the ground by Harper's volley gun. The Frenchman tried to stand, then the butt of the heavy gun slammed sickeningly into his skull. Another Frenchman tried to turn and run in the opposite direction, then realized in his panic that he was running towards the Portuguese and so turned back again only to find Rifleman Harris's sword bayonet at his throat. '*Non, monsieur!*' the Frenchman cried as he dropped his musket and raised his hands.

'Don't speak bloody Crapaud, do I?' Harris lied and pulled his trigger. Sharpe swerved past the falling body, parried a clumsy bayonet thrust and hammered his attacker down with his heavy sword. The man tried to stab his bayonet up at Sharpe who gave him two furious slashes with the big sword and left him screaming and bleeding and curled into a ball. He back-cut another French skirmisher, then ran on to the moon-cast shadow of the next empty barracks block where a huddle of riflemen were protecting Miranda. Harper still shouted in Gaelic, one of the precautions Sharpe had agreed with Donaju in case the French used an English speaker to confuse the defenders. The Sergeant's shouting had at last gained the attention of the guardsmen in the nearest barracks and the end door opened a crack. A rifle flared and crashed close beside Sharpe, a bullet hissed through the dark overhead while behind him a man screamed. Hagman was already at the barracks door where he crouched and counted the riflemen inside. 'Come on, Perks!' he called, and Perkins and Miranda scuttled over the open space, followed by a rush of riflemen. 'They're all safe, sir, all safe,' the Cheshireman called to Sharpe, 'just you and Harps.'

'Go, Pat,' Sharpe said, and just as the Irishman began to run a *voltigeur* came round the corner of the building, saw the big rifle Sergeant running away and dropped to one knee as he levelled his musket. He saw Sharpe a second later, but it was already too late. Sharpe came out of the dark shadow with the sword already swinging. The blade caught the *voltigeur* just above the eyes and such was the anger and strength in the blow that the top of the man's skull came away like a decapitated boiled egg.

'God save England,' Hagman said, watching the blow from the barracks door. 'Come in, Harps! Come on, sir! Hurry!' The panic started among the *voltigeurs* by the counterattacking Portuguese had helped the riflemen escape Loup's first assault, but that panic was subsiding as Loup's main force arrived through the captured gatehouse. That force would soon have Sharpe's men trapped in the barracks.

'Mattresses! Packs!' Sharpe shouted. 'Pile 'em behind the doors! Pat! Look to the windows! Move, woman!' he snarled at a screaming wife who was trying to leave the barracks altogether. He unceremoniously pushed her back. Bullets cracked on the stone walls and splintered the door. There were two small windows on either side of the long room and Harper was stuffing them with blankets. Rifleman Cresacre pushed his rifle through one of the half-blocked windows and fired towards the gatehouse.

Sharpe and Donaju had discussed earlier what might happen if the French attacked and they had gloomily agreed that the Real Compañía Irlandesa might be trapped inside their barracks and so Donaju had ordered his men to make loopholes in the walls. The work had been done half-heartedly, but at least the loopholes existed and gave the defenders a chance to fire back. Even so, in the rushlit gloom of the tunnel-like barracks, this was a nightmarish place to be trapped. The women and children were crying, the guardsmen were nervous and the barricades behind the two end doors flimsy.

'You all know what to do,' Sharpe called to the guardsmen. 'The French can't get in here, and they can't blow the walls down and they can't shoot through stone. You keep up a good fire and you'll drive the bastards away.' He was not sure that anything he had said was true, but he had to do his best to restore the men's spirits.

There were ten loopholes in the barracks, five on each long side, and each loophole was manned by at least eight men. Few of the men were as efficient as Sharpe would have liked at loading a musket, but with so many men using each loophole their fire would still be virtually continuous. He hoped the men in the second barracks were making similar preparations for he expected the French to assault both barracks at any moment. 'Someone opened that damned gate for them,' Sharpe told Harper. Harper had no time to answer, for instead a great howling noise announced the advance of Loup's main body of troops. Sharpe peered through a chink in one of the blocked windows and saw the flood of grey uniforms surge past the barracks. Behind them, pale in the moonlight, Loup's horsemen rode under their wolf-tail banner. 'It's my own fault,' Sharpe said ruefully.

'Yours, why?' Harper was ramming the last barrel of his volley gun.

'What does a good soldier do, Pat? He goes for surprise. It was so obvious that Loup had to attack from the north that I forgot about the south. Damn it.' He pushed his rifle through the gap and looked for the one-eyed Loup. Kill Loup, he thought, and this attack would stall, but he could not see the Brigadier among the mass of grey uniforms into which he fired his rifle indiscriminately. The enemy's fire crackled harmlessly against the stone walls, while inside the barracks muskets crashed loud at loopholes and children wailed. 'Keep those damn kids quiet!' Sharpe snapped. The dark, chill barracks room became foul with the acrid smell of powder smoke that

142

scared the children almost as much as the deafening gunfire. 'Quiet!' Sharpe roared, and there was a sudden gasping silence except for one baby that screamed incessantly. 'Keep the damn thing quiet!' Sharpe shouted at the mother. 'Hit it if you have to!' The mother plunged a breast into the baby's mouth instead, effectively stifling it. Some of the women and older children were usefully loading spare muskets and stacking them beside the windows. 'Can't stand bloody children crying,' Sharpe grumbled as he reloaded his rifle, 'never have and never will.'

'You were a baby once, sir,' Daniel Hagman said reprovingly. The poacher turned rifleman was liable to such sententious moments.

'I was sick once, damn it, but that doesn't mean I have to like disease, does it? Has anyone seen that bastard Loup?'

No one had, and by now the mass of the Loup Brigade had swept past the two barracks in pursuit of the Portuguese who had called back their skirmish line and formed two ranks so that they could trade volleys with their attackers. The fight was lit by a half-moon and the guttering flicker of what remained of the campfires. The Frenchmen had ceased their wolf-like howling as the fight became grim, but it was still a one-sided affair. The newly woken Portuguese were outnumbered and facing men armed with a quick-loading musket, while they were equipped with the slow-loading Baker rifle. Even if they tap-loaded the rifle, abandoning the rammer and the leather patch that gripped the barrel's rifling, they still could not compete with the speed of the well-trained French force. Besides, Oliveira's *caçadores* were trained to fight in open country, to harass and to hide, to run and to shoot, and not to trade heavy volleys in the killing confrontation of the main battle line.

Yet even so the *caçadores* did not break easily. The French infantry found it hard to pinpoint the Portuguese infantry in the half-dark, and when they did establish where the line was formed it took time for the scattered French companies to come together and make their own line of three ranks. But once the two French battalions were in line they overlapped the small Portuguese battalion and so the flanks of the French pressed inwards. The Portuguese fought back hard. Rifle flames stabbed the night. The sergeants shouted at the files to close to the centre as men were hurled back by the heavy French musket balls. One man fell into the smouldering embers of a fire and screamed terribly as his cartridge pouch exploded to tear a haversack-sized hole in his back. His blood hissed and bubbled in the red-hot ashes as he died. Colonel Oliveira paced behind his men, weighing the fight's progress and judging it lost. That damned English rifleman had been right. He should have taken refuge in the barracks blocks, but now the French were between him and that salvation and Oliveira sensed the coming calamity and knew there was little he could do to prevent it. He had even fewer options when he heard the ominous and unmistakable sound of hooves. The French even had cavalry inside the fort.

The Colonel sent his colour party back to the northern ramparts. 'Find somewhere to hide,' he ordered them. There were old magazines in the bastions, and fallen walls that had made dark caves amidst the ruins, and it was possible that the regiment's colours might be preserved from capture if they were hidden in the tangle of damp cellars and tumbled stone. Oliveira waited as his hard-pressed men fired two more volleys then gave the order to retreat. 'Steady now!' he called. 'Steady! Back to the walls!' He was forced to abandon his wounded, though some bleeding and broken men still tried to crawl or limp back with the retreating line. The French uniforms pressed closer, then came the moment Oliveira feared most as a trumpet blared in the dark to the accompaniment of swords scraping out of scabbards. 'Go!' Oliveira shouted to his men. 'Go!'

His men broke ranks and ran to the walls just as the cavalry charged, and thus the *caçadores* became the dream target of all horsemen: a broken unit of scattered men. The grey dragoons slashed into the retreating ranks with their heavy swords. Loup himself led the charge and deliberately led it wide so that he could turn and herd the fugitives back towards his advancing infantry.

Some of Oliveira's left-hand companies reached the ramparts safely. Loup saw the dark uniforms streaming up an ammunition ramp and was content to let them go. If they crossed the wall and fled out into the valleys then the remainder of his dragoons would hunt them down like vermin, while if they stayed on the ramparts his men inside the San Isidro Fort would do the same. Loup's immediate concern was the men who were trying to surrender. Dozens of Portuguese soldiers, their rifles unloaded, stood with hands raised. Loup rode at one such man, smiled, then cut down with a backswing that half severed the man's head. 'No prisoners!' Loup called to his men. 'No prisoners!' His withdrawal from the fort could not be slowed by prisoners and, besides, the slaughter of a whole battalion would serve to warn Wellington's army that in reaching the Spanish frontier they had encountered a new and harder enemy than the troops they had chased away from Lisbon. 'Kill them all!' Loup shouted. A *caçador* aimed at Loup, fired, and the bullet slapped inches past the Brigadier's short grey beard. Loup laughed, spurred his grey horse and threaded his way through the panicking infantry to hunt down the wretch who had dared try to kill him. The man ran desperately, but Loup cantered up behind and slashed his sword in an underhand swing that laid the man's spine open to the night. The man fell, writhing and screaming. 'Leave him!' Loup called to a French infantryman tempted to give the wretch his *coup de grâce*. 'Let him die hard,' Loup said. 'He deserves it.'

Some of the survivors of Oliveira's battalion opened a galling rifle fire from the walls and Loup wheeled away from it. 'Dragoons! Dismount!' He would let his dismounted cavalry hunt down the defiant survivors while his infantry dealt with the Real Compañía Irlandesa and the riflemen who seemed to have taken refuge in the barracks buildings. That was a pity. Loup had hoped that his advance guard would have trapped Sharpe and his damned greenjackets in the magazine, and that by now Loup would have had the pleasure of meting out an exquisitely painful revenge for the two men Sharpe had killed, but instead the rifleman had temporarily escaped and would need to be dug out of the barracks like a fox being unearthed at the end of a day's good run. Loup tilted his watch's face to the moon as he tried to work out just how much time he had left to break the barracks apart.

'*Monsieur!*' a voice shouted as the Brigadier closed his watch and slid out of his saddle. '*Monsieur!*'

Loup turned to see a thin-faced and angry Portuguese officer in the firm grip of a tall French corporal. '*Monsieur?*' Loup responded politely.

'My name is Colonel Oliveira, and I must protest, *monsieur!* My men are surrendering and your men are killing still! We are your prisoners!'

Loup fished a cigar from his sabretache and stooped to a dying fire to find an ember that would serve to light the tobacco. 'Good soldiers don't surrender,' he said to Oliveira, 'they just die.'

'But we are surrendering,' Oliveira insisted bitterly. 'Take my sword.'

Loup straightened, sucked on the cigar and nodded to the Corporal. 'Let him go, Jean.'

Oliveira shook himself free of the Corporal's grip. 'I must protest, *monsieur,*' he said angrily. 'Your soldiers are killing men who have their hands raised.'

146

Loup shrugged. 'Terrible things happen in war, Colonel. Now give me your sword.'

Oliveira drew his sabre, reversed the blade and held the hilt towards the hard-faced dragoon. 'I am your prisoner, *monsieur*,' he said in a voice thickened by shame and anger.

'You hear that!' Loup shouted so that all his men could hear. 'They have surrendered! They are our prisoners! See? I have their Colonel's sabre!' He took the sabre from Oliveira and flourished it in the smoky air. Gallantry insisted he should now give the weapon back to his defeated enemy on a promise of parole, but instead Loup hefted the blade as though judging its effectiveness. 'A passable weapon,' he said grudgingly, then looked into Oliveira's eyes. 'Where are your colours, Colonel?'

'We destroyed them,' Oliveira said defiantly. 'We burned them.'

The sabre slashed silver in the moonlight and blood seeped black from the slash on Oliveira's face where the steel had sliced across his left eye and his nose. 'I don't believe you,' Loup said, then waited until the shocked and bleeding Colonel had recovered his wits. 'Where are your colours, Colonel?' Loup asked again.

'Go to hell,' Oliveira said. 'You and your filthy country.' He had one hand pressed over his wounded eye.

Loup tossed the sabre to the Corporal. 'Find out where the colours are, Jean, then kill the fool. Cut him if he won't tell you. A man usually loosens his tongue to keep his balls screwed on tight. And the rest of you,' he shouted at his men who had paused to watch the confrontation between the two commanding officers, 'this isn't a damned harvest festival, it's a battle. So start doing your job! Kill the bastards!'

The screams began again. Loup drew on his cigar, brushed his hands and walked towards the barracks.

* * *

The Doña Juanita's hounds began to howl. The sound set more children crying, but one glance from Sharpe was enough to make the mothers quell their infants' misery. A horse whinnied. Through one of the loopholes Sharpe could see that the French were leading away the horses captured from the Portuguese officers. He assumed the Irish company's horses had already been taken away. It had gone quiet in the barracks. Most of the French attackers had pursued the Portuguese, leaving just enough infantrymen behind to keep the trapped men blocked inside the barracks. Every few seconds a musket ball cracked against the stone, a reminder to Sharpe and his men that the French were still watching every blocked-up door and window.

'Bastards will have captured poor old Runcibubble,' Hagman said. 'I can't see the General living on prisoners' rations.'

'Runciman's an officer, Dan,' Cooper said. Cooper was aiming his rifle through one of the loopholes, stalking a target. 'He won't live on rations. He'll give his parole and be feeding on proper Frog victuals. He'll get even fatter. Got you, you bastard.' He pulled his trigger, then slid the rifle inside to let another man take his place. Sharpe suspected that the erstwhile Wagon Master General would be lucky to be a prisoner because if Loup was fighting true to his reputation then it was more likely that Runciman was lying slaughtered in his bed with his flannel nightdress and tasselled woollen cap soaked in blood.

'Captain Sharpe, sir!' Harper called from the far end of the block. 'Here, sir!'

Sharpe worked his way between the straw mattresses that lay on the beaten earth floor. The air inside the blocked-up barracks was fetid and the few wicks still alight were guttering. A woman spat as Sharpe went by and Sharpe turned on her. 'You'd rather be out there being raped, you stupid bitch? I'll bloody well throw you out, if that's what you want.'

'No, *señor*,' she shrank away from his anger.

The woman's husband, crouching at a loophole, tried to apologize for his wife. 'It's just that the women are frightened, sir.'

'So are we. Anyone but a fool would be frightened, but that doesn't mean you lose your manners.' Sharpe hurried on to where Harper was kneeling beside the pile of straw-filled sacks that had served as mattresses and which now blocked the door.

'There's a man calling you, sir,' Harper said. 'I think it's Captain Donaju.'

Sharpe crouched near the loophole next to the barricaded door. 'Donaju! Is that you?'

'I'm in the men's barracks, Sharpe. Just to let you know that we're all well.'

'How did you escape the gatehouse?'

'Through the door to the ramparts. There's half a dozen officers here.'

'Is Kiely with you?'

'No. Don't know what's happened to him.'

And Sharpe did not much care. 'Is Sarsfield there?' he asked Donaju.

''Fraid not,' Donaju answered.

'Keep the faith, Donaju!' Sharpe called. 'These buggers will be gone at first light!' He felt oddly relieved that Donaju had taken over the defence of the other barracks, for Donaju, for all his shy and retiring appearance, was proving to be a very good soldier. 'Pity about Father Sarsfield,' Sharpe said to Harper.

'He'll have gone straight to heaven, that one,' Harper said. 'Not many priests you can say that about. Most of them are proper devils for whiskey, women or boys, but Sarsfield, he was a good man, a real good man.' The firing at the northern end of the fort died away and Harper crossed himself. 'Pity about the poor Portuguese bastards too,' he said, realizing what the lull in the sound of fighting meant.

Poor Tom Garrard, Sharpe thought. Unless Garrard lived? Tom Garrard had always had a charmed life. He and Sharpe had crouched in the fiery red dust of Gawilghur's breach as blood from their comrades' corpses trickled past like rivulets flowing down a rock-fall. Sergeant Hakeswill had been there, gibbering like a monkey as he tried to hide under a drummer boy's corpse. Damn Obadiah Hakeswill, who had also claimed to bear a charmed life, though Sharpe could not believe the bastard still lived. Dead of the pox, like as not, or, if there was even a trace of justice in a bad world, gutted by the bullets of a firing squad. 'Watch the roof,' Sharpe said to Harper. The barracks roof was a continuous arch of masonry designed to resist the fall of an enemy mortar shell, but time and neglect had weakened the tough construction. 'They'll find a weak spot,' Sharpe said, 'and try and break through to us.' And it would be soon, he thought to himself, for the heavy silence in the fort betrayed that Loup had finished off Oliveira and would now be coming for his real prize, Sharpe. The next hour promised to be grim. Sharpe raised his voice as he walked back to the other end of the room. 'When the attack comes just keep firing! Don't aim, don't wait, just fire and make room at your loophole for another man. They're going to reach the barracks walls, we can't stop that, and they're going to try to break open the roof, so keep a good ear above you. Soon as you see starlight, fire. And remember, it'll be light soon and they won't stay after sunrise. They'll be feared that our cavalry will cut off their retreat. Now, good luck, boys.'

'And God bless you all,' Harper added from the gloom at the far end of the room.

The attack came with a roar like a rush of water released by lifting a sluice gate. Loup had massed his men in the cover of some nearby barracks, then released them in a desperate charge against the two barracks' north-facing walls. The rush was designed to carry the French infantry fast across the dangerous patch of ground covered by Sharpe's muskets and rifles. Those guns cracked to fill the barracks with yet more filthy smoke, but the third or fourth shot from each loophole sounded perversely loud and suddenly a man reeled back cursing from his musket's wrist-shattering recoil. 'They're blocking the holes!' another man called.

Sharpe ran to the nearest loophole on the north wall and rammed his rifle into the hole. The muzzle cracked on stone. The French were holding masonry blocks against the loophole's outer opening, effectively ending Sharpe's fire. More Frenchmen were climbing onto the roof where their boots made a muffled, scraping sound like rats in an attic. 'Jesus Christ!' A man stared wanly upwards. 'Mary, Mother of God,' he began to pray in a wailing voice.

'Shut up!' Sharpe snapped. He could hear the ringing noise of metal working on stone. How long before the roof collapsed and let in a flood of vengeful Frenchmen? Inside the barracks a hundred pale faces stared at Sharpe, willing an answer he did not possess.

Harper came up with the solution instead. He clambered up on the monstrous pile of straw-filled sacks by the door so that he could reach the topmost point of the end wall where a small hole served as a chimney and ventilator. The hole was too high for the French to block, and high enough to give Harper a clear shot along the roofline of Donaju's barracks. The bullets would be rising and so would be more of a threat to those Frenchmen nearest Harper, but if he could fire enough bullets he could at least slow down the assault on Donaju and pray that Donaju would return the compliment.

Harper opened with his seven-barrelled gun. The crash echoed through the barracks with the sound of a thirty-two-pounder cannon. A scream answered the blast that had whipped like canister shot across the other roof. Now, one by one, muskets and rifles were handed up to the big Sergeant who fired again and again, not bothering to aim, but just cracking the bullets into the grey mass that swarmed on the neighbouring roof. After a half-dozen shots the mass began to shred as men sought shelter on the ground. The answering fire smacked all around Harper's loophole, creating more dust than danger. Perkins had reloaded the volley gun and Harper now fired it again just as a musket flashed from the equivalent venthole in Donaju's barracks. Sharpe heard a scraping sound above him as a Frenchman's boots slid down the outer curve to the wall's base.

A man screamed in the barracks as he was hurled backwards by a musket ball. The French were randomly unmasking the loopholes and firing into the room where the wives and children crouched and whimpered. The besieged huddled away from the loopholes' lines of fire, the only defence they had. Harper kept firing while a group of men and women loaded for him, but most of the barracks' occupants could only wait in the smoky gloom and pray. The noise was hellish: a banging, ringing, scraping cacophony, and always, like an eerie promise of the horrid death that defeat promised, the feral wolf howl of Loup's men all around the barracks.

Dust sifted down from a patch of the ceiling. Sharpe moved everyone away from the threatened area, then ringed it with men armed with loaded muskets. 'If a stone falls,' he told them, 'shoot like hell and keep shooting.' The air was difficult to breathe. It was filled with dust, smoke and the stench of urine. The cheap rushlight candles were guttering. Children were crying throughout the length of the barracks now and Sharpe could not stop them. Women were crying too, while muffled French voices mocked their victims, doubtless promising that they would give the women something better than mere smoke to cry about.

Hagman coughed, then spat onto the floor. 'Like a coal mine, it is,' he said.

'You ever been in a coal mine, Dan?' Sharpe asked.

'I was a year down a mine in Derbyshire,' Hagman said, then flinched as a musket flash speared through a nearby loophole. The ball spread itself harmlessly on the opposite wall. 'I was just a littl'un,' Hagman went on. 'If my dad hadn't gone and died and my mam moved back to her sister's in Handbridge I'd be there still. Or more likely dead. Only the luckiest see their thirtieth birthday down the mines.' He shuddered as a huge, rhythmic crashing began to reverberate through the tunnel-like barracks. Either the French had brought a sledgehammer, or else they were using a boulder like a battering ram. 'Like the little pigs in the house, aren't we,' Hagman said in the echoing dark, 'with the big bad wolf huffing and puffing outside?'

Sharpe gripped his rifle. He was sweating, and his rifle's stock felt greasy. 'When I was a child,' he said, 'I never believed the pigs could really see off the wolf.'

'Pigs don't, as a rule,' Hagman said grimly. 'If the bastards go on banging like that they'll give me a headache.'

'Dawn can't be far off,' Sharpe said, though whether Loup would truly withdraw in the first light, Sharpe did not know. He had told his men that the French would go at dawn to give them hope, but maybe there was no hope. Maybe they were all condemned to die in a wretched fight in the scrabbling ruins of an abandoned barracks where they would be bayoneted and shot by an elite French brigade who had come to destroy this scratch force of unhappy Irishmen.

'Mind out!' a man called. More dust streamed down from the ceiling. So far the old barracks had stood the assault astonishingly well, but the first breach in the masonry was imminent.

'Hold your fire!' Sharpe ordered. 'Wait till they break through!'

A huddle of kneeling women were telling their beads, rocking back and forth on their knees as they said the Hail Mary. Nearby a circle of men waited with expectant faces, muskets aimed up at the threatened patch of ceiling. Behind them an outer ring of men waited with more loaded guns.

'I hated the coal mine,' Hagman said. 'I was always frightened from the moment I went down the shaft. Men used to die there for no reason. None at all! We'd just find them dead, peaceful as you like, sleeping like babes. I used to think the devils came from the earth's centre to take their souls.'

A woman screamed as a masonry block in the ceiling jarred and threatened to fall. 'At least you didn't have screaming women in the mines,' Sharpe said to Hagman.

'But we did, sir. Some worked with us and some were ladies working for themselves, if you follow my meaning. There was one called Dwarf Babs, I remember. A penny a time, she charged. She'd sing to us every Sunday. Maybe a psalm or perhaps one of Mr Wesley's hymns. "Hide me, O my Saviour, hide, till the storm of life be past". Hagman grinned in the sultry dark. 'Maybe Mr Wesley had some trouble with the Frenchies, sir? Sounds like it. Do you know Mr Wesley's hymns, sir?' he asked Sharpe.

'I was never one for church, Dan.'

'Dwarf Babs wasn't exactly church, sir.'

'But she was your first woman?' Sharpe guessed.

In the dark Hagman blushed. 'And she didn't even charge me.'

'Good for Dwarf Babs,' Sharpe said, then raised his rifle as, at last, a section of the roof gave way and crashed to the floor in a welter of dust, screams and noise. The ragged hole was two or three feet across and obscured by dust beyond which the wraith-like shapes of French soldiers loomed like giants. 'Fire!' Sharpe yelled.

The ring of muskets blazed, followed, a second later, by the second ring of guns as more men fired into the void. The French reply was oddly muted, almost as if the attackers had been surprised by the amount of musket fire that now poured up from the newly opened vent. Men and women reloaded frantically and passed the newly charged guns forward, and the French, driven from the hole's edge by the sheer volume of fire, began hurling rocks into the barracks. The stones crashed harmlessly onto the floor. 'Block the loopholes!' Sharpe ordered, and men rammed the French-delivered stones into the loopholes to stop the intermittent bullets. Better still the air began to feel fresh. Even the candle flames took on new life and glowed into the darker recesses of the packed, fearful barracks.

'Sharpe!' a voice called outside the barracks. 'Sharpe!'

The French had momentarily stopped firing and Sharpe ordered his men to hold their own fire. 'Reload, lads!' He sounded cheerful. 'It's always a good sign when the bastards want to talk instead of fight.' He walked closer to the hole in the roof. 'Loup?' he called.

'Come out, Sharpe,' the Brigadier said, 'and we will spare your men.' It was a shrewd enough offer even though Loup must have known that Sharpe would not accept, but he did not expect Sharpe to accept, instead he wanted the rifleman's companions to surrender him as Jonah had been surrendered to the ocean by his shipmates.

'Loup?' Sharpe called. 'Go to hell. Pat? Open fire!'

Harper crashed a volley of half-inch balls at the other barracks. Donaju's men were still alive and still fighting, and now Loup's men came back to life as the fighting renewed itself. A frustrated volley of musketry cracked against the wall around Harper's loophole. One of the bullets ricocheted inside and slapped against the stock of Harper's rifle. He swore because the blow stung, then fired the rifle at the opposite roof.

Another rush of feet on the roof announced a new attack. The men beneath the broken masonry fired upwards, but suddenly a blast of gunfire swamped down through the hole. Loup had sent every man possible onto the roof and the attackers were able to match the fury of the defenders' fusillades. The Real Compañía Irlandesa's guardsmen shrank back from the musketry. 'Bastards are everywhere!' Harper said, then ducked as a crash sounded on the stone roof just above his head. The French were now trying to break through the roof right over Harper's eyrie. Women screamed and covered their eyes. A child was bleeding from a ricochet.

The fight, Sharpe knew, was ending. He could sense the defeat. He supposed it had been inevitable, right from the moment that Loup had outguessed and out-manoeuvred the San Isidro's defenders. Any second now, Sharpe knew, and a wave of Frenchmen would swarm through the hole in the roof and though the first few enemy to enter the barracks would surely die, the second wave would live to fight over their comrades' bodies and so win the battle. And what then? Sharpe flinched from the thought of Loup's revenge, the knife at his groin, the slicing cut and the pain beyond all pain. He watched the hole in the roof with his rifle ready for one last shot and he wondered whether it would not be better to put the muzzle beneath his chin and blow the top of his skull away.

And then the world shook. Dust started from every masonry joint as a flash of light seared across the hole in the barracks' roof. A second later the boom and thunderous bellow of a great explosion rolled over the barracks, drowning even the furious crack of the French muskets outside and the desperate sobbing of the children inside. The vast noise reverberated against the gate tower to roll back again over the fort's interior while scraps of wood dropped from the sky to clatter on the roof.

A kind of ragged silence followed. The French fire had stopped. Somewhere close to the barracks a man was sighing as he breathed in and whimpering as he breathed out. The sky looked lighter, but the light was vivid and red. A piece of stone or wood scraped and rattled its way down the curving side of the barracks. Men were moaning and crying, while further off there was the crackle of flame. Daniel Hagman cleared away some of the straw mattresses that blocked the end door and peered through a ragged bullet hole driven through the timber. 'It's the Portuguese ammunition,' Hagman said. 'Two wagons of the stuff were parked over there, sir, and some silly bastard of a Frog must have been playing with fire.'

Sharpe unblocked a loophole and found it open at the far side. A Frenchman, his grey uniform burning, staggered past Sharpe's view. Now, in the silence after the great explosion, he could hear more men crying and gasping. 'That blast scraped the buggers clean off the roofs, sir!' Harper called.

Sharpe ran to the hole in the roof and ordered a man to crouch on the ground. Then, using the man's back as a step, he leaped up and caught the broken edge of the masonry. 'Heave me up!' he ordered.

Someone pushed his legs and he scrambled awkwardly over the broken lip. The fort's interior seemed to be scorched and smoking. The two carts of ammunition had blown themselves to smithereens and blasted the victorious French into chaos. Blood was smeared on the roof and a tangle of dead lay on the ground near the barracks where the explosion's survivors wandered in a daze. A naked man, blackened and bleeding, reeled among those shocked Frenchmen. One of the confused infantrymen saw Sharpe on the roof but did not have the strength or maybe lacked the sense to raise his musket. There appeared to be some thirty or forty dead, and maybe as many again badly injured; not many casualties out of the thousand men that Loup had brought to the San Isidro Fort, but the disaster had whipped the confidence clean out of the wolf's brigade.

And, Sharpe saw, there was better news still. For through the swirling smoke and dust, through the greydark of night and the sullen glow of fire, a silver line showed in the east. The dawn light was shining and with the rising sun would come an allied cavalry picquet to discover why so much smoke plumed up from the San Isidro Fort.

'We've won, boys,' Sharpe said as he jumped back down to the barracks floor. That was not quite true. They had not won, they had merely survived, but survival felt uncommonly like victory and never more so than when, a half-hour later, Loup's men left the fort. They had made two more attacks on the barracks, but the assaults were feeble, mere gestures, for the explosion had ripped the enthusiasm out of Loup's brigade. So, in the first light, the Frenchmen went and they carried their wounded with them. Sharpe helped dismantle the barrier inside the nearest barracks door, then stepped cautiously into a chill and smoky morning that stank of blood and fire. He carried his loaded rifle in case Loup had left some marksmen behind, but no one shot at him in the pearly light. Behind Sharpe, like men released from nightmare, the guardsmen stepped cautiously into the dawn. Donaju emerged from the second barracks and insisted on shaking Sharpe's hand, almost as though the rifleman had won some kind of victory. He had not. Indeed Sharpe had come within a hand's breadth of ignominious defeat.

But now, instead, he was alive and the enemy was gone.

Which meant, Sharpe knew, that the real trouble was about to begin.

CHAPTER FIVE

Caçadores trailed into the fort all morning. A few had escaped by hiding in ruined parts of the northern ramparts, but most of the survivors had fled across the ramparts and found a refuge among the thorns or in the dead, stony ground at the foot of the ridge dominated by the San Isidro Fort. Those lucky ones had watched aghast from their hiding places as other fugitives were hunted and slaughtered by the grey dragoons.

Oliveira had brought over four hundred riflemen to the fort. Now more than a hundred and fifty were dead, seventy were wounded and as many others missing. Just over a quarter of the Portuguese regiment paraded at midday. They had suffered a terrible defeat after being overwhelmed in a confined space by an enemy four times their number, yet they were not wholly destroyed and their colours still flew. Those flags had stayed hidden all night despite Loup's efforts to find the banners. Colonel Oliveira was dead and his body carried horrific evidence of the manner of his dying. Most of the other officers were also dead.

The Real Compañía Irlandesa had lost no officers, not one. The French, it appeared, had not bothered to assault the gate tower. Loup's men had streamed through the gates and ransacked the fort, but not one man had tried to enter the imposing tower. The enemy had not even taken the officers' horses from their stables next to the gatehouse. 'We had the doors barred,' Lord Kiely lamely explained the survival of the gatehouse's occupants.

'And the Crapauds didn't try to break them down?' Sharpe asked, not bothering to hide his scepticism.

'Be careful of what you suggest, Captain,' Kiely said in a supercilious tone.

Sharpe reacted like a dog smelling blood. 'Listen, you bastard,' he said, astonished to hear himself saying it, 'I fought my way up from the gutter and I don't care if I have to fight you to get another bloody step up. I'll slaughter you, you drunken bugger, and then I'll feed your damned guts to your whore's dogs.' He took a step towards Kiely who, scared of the rifleman's sudden vehemence, stepped back. 'What I'm suggesting,' Sharpe went on, 'is that one of your bloody friends in the bloody gatehouse opened the bloody gates to the bloody French and that they didn't attack you, my Lord' – he spoke the honorific title as rudely as he could – 'because they didn't want to kill their friends as well as their enemies. And don't tell me I'm wrong!' By now Sharpe was walking after Kiely who was trying to escape Sharpe's diatribe that had attracted the attention of a large number of riflemen and guardsmen. 'Last night you said you'd beat the enemy without my help.' Sharpe caught Kiely by the shoulder and turned him round so violently that Kiely was forced to stagger to keep his balance. 'But you didn't even fight, you bastard,' Sharpe went on. 'You skulked inside while your men did the fighting for you.'

Kiely's hand went to his sword hilt. 'Do you want a duel, Sharpe?' he asked, his face flushed with embarrassment. His dignity was being flayed in front of his men and what made it worse was that he knew he had deserved their scorn, yet pride would never permit Lord Kiely to admit as much. For a second it looked as if he would flick his hand to strike

160

Sharpe's cheek, but instead he settled for words. 'I'll send you my second.'

'No!' Sharpe said. 'A pox on your bloody second, my Lord. If you want to fight me, then fight me now. Here. Right here! And I don't care what bloody weapons we use. Swords, pistols, muskets, rifles, bayonets, fists, feet.' He was walking towards Kiely, who backed away. 'I'll fight you into the ground, my Lord, and I'll beat the offal out of your yellow hide, but I'll only do it here and now. Right here. Right now!' Sharpe had not meant to lose his temper, but he was glad that he had. Kiely seemed dumbstruck, helpless in the face of a fury he had never suspected existed.

'I won't fight like an animal,' Kiely said weakly.

'You won't fight at all,' Sharpe said, then laughed at the aristocrat. 'Run away, my Lord. Go on. I'm done with you.'

Kiely, utterly defeated, tried to walk away with some dignity, but reddened as some of the watching men cheered his departure. Sharpe shouted at them to shut the hell up, then turned to Harper. 'The bloody French didn't try to get into the gatehouse,' he told Harper, 'because they knew their bloody friends were inside, just as they didn't steal their friends' horses.'

'Stands to reason, sir,' Harper agreed. He was watching Kiely walk away. 'He's yellow, isn't he?'

'Front to back,' Sharpe agreed.

'But what Captain Lacy says, sir,' Harper went on, 'is that it wasn't his Lordship who gave the order not to fight last night, but his woman. She said the French didn't know there was anyone in the gatehouse and so they should all keep quiet.'

'A woman giving orders?' Sharpe asked in disgust.

Harper shrugged. 'A rare hard woman, that one, sir. Captain Lacy says she was watching the fighting and loving every second of it.'

'I'd have the witch on a bonfire fast enough, I can tell you,' Sharpe said. 'Bloody damn hellbitch.'

'Damn what, Sharpe?' It was Colonel Runciman who asked the question, but who did not wait to hear an answer. Instead Runciman, who at last had a genuine war story to tell, hastened to describe how he had survived the attack. The Colonel, it seemed, had locked his door and hidden behind the great pile of spare ammunition that Sharpe had stacked in his day parlour, though now, in the daylight, the Colonel ascribed his salvation to divine intervention rather than to the fortuitous hiding place. 'Maybe I am intended for higher things, Sharpe? My mother always believed as much. How else do you explain my survival?' Sharpe was more inclined to believe that the Colonel had lived because the French had been under orders to leave the whole gatehouse complex untouched, but he did not think it kind to say as much.

'I'm just glad you're alive, General,' Sharpe said instead.

'I would have died hard, Sharpe! I had both my pistols double-shotted! I would have taken some of them with me, believe you me. No one can say a Runciman goes into eternity alone!' The Colonel shuddered as the night's horrors came back to him. 'Have you seen any evidence of breakfast, Sharpe?' he asked in an attempt to restore his spirits.

'Try Lord Kiely's cook, General. He was frying bacon not ten minutes ago and I don't suppose his Lordship's got much of an appetite. I just challenged the yellow bastard to a fight.'

Runciman looked shocked. 'You did what, Sharpe? A duel? Don't you know duelling is illegal in the army?'

'I never said anything about a duel, General. I just offered to beat the hell out of him right here and now, but he seemed to have other things on his mind.'

Runciman shook his head. 'Dear me, Sharpe, dear me. I can't think you'll come to a good end, but I shall be sad when it happens. What a scamp you are! Bacon? Lord Kiely's cook, you said?'

Runciman waddled away and Sharpe watched him go. 'In ten years' time, Pat,' Sharpe said, 'he'll have turned last night's mess into a rare old story. How General Runciman saved the fort, armed to the jowls and fighting off the whole Loup Brigade.'

'Runcibubble's harmless,' Harper said.

'He's harmless, Pat,' Sharpe agreed, 'so long as you keep the fool out of harm's way. And I almost failed to do that, didn't I?'

'You, sir? You didn't fail last night.'

'Oh, but I did, Pat. I failed. I failed badly. I didn't see that Loup would out-clever me, and I didn't hammer the truth into Oliveira's skull, and I never saw how dangerously trapped we were in those barracks.' He flinched, remembering the fetid, humid, dust-laden darkness of the night and the awful, scrabbling sound as the French tried to break through the thin masonry shell. 'We survived because some poor fool set light to an ammunition wagon,' Sharpe admitted, 'not because we outfought Loup. We didn't. He won and we got beat.'

'But we're alive, sir.'

'So's Loup, Pat, so's Loup, God damn him.'

But Tom Garrard was not alive. Tom Garrard had died, though at first Sharpe did not recognize his friend, for the body was so scorched and mutilated by fire. Garrard was lying face down in the very centre of the blackened spot where one of the ammunition wagons had stood and at first the only clue to his identity was the bent, blackened scrap of metal in an outstretched hand that had been fire-shrunken into a charred claw. Sharpe spotted the glint of metal and stepped through the still hot ashes to prise the box clear of the shrivelled grip. Two fingers snapped off the hand as Sharpe freed the tinder box. He brushed the black fingers aside, then levered open the lid to see that though all the linen kindling had long been consumed the picture of the redcoat was undamaged. Sharpe cleaned the engraving with a hand, then wiped a tear from his eye. 'Tom Garrard saved our lives last night, Pat.'

'He did?'

'He blew up the ammunition on purpose and killed himself doing it.' The presence of the tinderbox could mean nothing else. Tom Garrard, in the wake of his battalion's defeat, had somehow managed to reach the ammunition wagons and light a fire he had known would blow his own soul clear into eternity. 'Oh, dear God,' Sharpe said, then fell silent as he remembered the years of friendship. 'He was at Assaye with me,' he went on after a while, 'and at Gawilghur too. He was from Ripon, a farmer's boy, only his father was a tenant and the landlord threw him out when he was three days late with the rent after a bad harvest so Tom saved his folks the need to feed another mouth by joining the 33rd. He used to send money home, God knows how on a soldier's pay. In another two years, Pat, he'd have made colonel in the Portuguese, and then he planned to go home to Ripon and beat ten kinds of hell out of the landlord who drove him into the army in the first place. That's what he told me last night.'

'Now you'll have to do it for him,' Harper said.

'Aye. That bugger'll get a thumping he never dreamed of,' Sharpe said. He tried to close the tinderbox, but the heat had distorted the metal. He took a last glance at the picture, then tossed the box back into the ashes. Then he and Harper climbed the ramparts where they had charged the small group of *voltigeurs* the night before and from where the full horror of the night could be seen. The San Isidro was a smoking, blackened wreck, littered with bodies and reeking of blood. Rifleman Thompson, the only greenjacket to die in the night, was being carried in a blanket towards a hastily dug grave beside the fort's ruined church.

'Poor Thompson,' Harper said. 'I gave him hell for waking me last night. Poor bugger was only going outside for a piss and tripped over me.'

'Lucky he did,' Sharpe said.

Harper walked to the tower door that still had the dents driven into it by the butt of his volley gun. The big Irishman fingered the marks ruefully. 'Those bastards must have known we were trying to get refuge, sir,' he said.

'At least one of those bastards wanted us dead, Pat. And if I ever find out who, then God help him,' Sharpe said. He noticed that no one had thought to raise any flags on the battlements.

'Rifleman Cooper!' Sharpe called.

'Sir?'

'Flags!'

The first outsiders to arrive at San Isidro were a strong troop of King's German Legion cavalry who scouted the valley before climbing to the fort. Their captain reported a score of dead at the foot of the slope, then saw the far greater number of bodies lying in the fort's open area. '*Mein Gott!* What happened?'

'Ask Colonel the Lord Kiely,' Sharpe said, and jerked a thumb at Kiely who was visible on the gatehouse turret. Other Real Compañía Irlandesa officers were supervising the squads collecting the Portuguese dead, while Father Sarsfield had taken charge of a dozen men and their wives who were caring for the Portuguese wounded, though without a surgeon there was little they could do except bandage, pray and fetch water. One by one the wounded died, some crying out in delirium, but most staying calm as the priest held their hands, asked their names and gave them the viaticum.

The next outsiders to arrive were a group of staff officers, mostly British, some Portuguese and one Spaniard, General Valverde. Hogan led the party, and for a solemn half-hour the Irish Major walked about the horror with an appalled expression, but when he left the other staff officers to join Sharpe he was grinning with an inappropriate cheerfulness. 'A tragedy, Richard!' Hogan said happily.

Sharpe was offended by his friend's cheerfulness. 'It was a bloody hard night, sir.'

'I'm sure, I'm sure,' Hogan said, trying and failing to sound sympathetic. The Major could not contain his happiness. 'Though it's a pity about Oliveira's *caçadores*. He was a good man and it was a fine battalion.'

'I warned him.'

'I'm sure you did, Richard, I'm sure you did. But it's always the same in war, isn't it? The wrong people get the hind teat. If only the Real Compañía Irlandesa could have been decimated, Richard, that would have been a great convenience right now, a real convenience. Still and all, still and all, this will do. This will do very well.'

'Do for what?' Sharpe asked fiercely. 'Do you know what happened here last night, sir? We were betrayed. Some bastard opened the gates to Loup.'

'Of course he did, Richard!' Hogan said soothingly. 'Haven't I been saying all along that they couldn't be trusted? The Real Compañía Irlandesa aren't here to help us, Richard, but to help the French.' He pointed to the dead. 'You need further proof? But of course this is good news. Until this morning it was impossible to send the bastards packing because that would have offended London and the Spanish court. But now, don't you see, we can thank the Spanish King for the valued assistance of his personal guard, we can claim that the Real Compañía Irlandesa was instrumental in seeing off a strong French raid over the frontier, and then, honours even, we can send the

166

treacherous buggers to Cadiz and let them rot.' Hogan was positively exultant. 'We are off the hook, Richard, the French malevolence is defeated, and all because of last night. The French made a mistake. They should have left you alone, but plainly Monsieur Loup couldn't resist the bait. It's all so clever, Richard, that I wish I'd thought of it myself, but I didn't. But no matter; this'll mean goodbye to our gallant allies and an end to all those rumours about Ireland.'

'My men didn't spread those rumours,' Sharpe insisted.

'Your men?' Hogan mocked. 'These aren't your men, Richard. They're Kiely's, or more likely Bonaparte's, but they're not your men.'

'They're good men, sir, and they fought well.'

Hogan shook his head at the anger in Sharpe's voice, then steered his friend along the eastern battlements with a touch on the rifleman's elbow. 'Let me try and explain something to you, Richard,' Hogan said. 'One third of this army is Irish. There's not a battalion that doesn't have its ranks full of my countrymen and most of those Irishmen are not lovers of King George. Why should they be? But they're here because there's no work at home and because there's no food at home and because the army, God bless it, has the sense to treat the Irish well. But just suppose, Richard, just suppose, that we can upset all those good men from County Cork and County Offaly, and all those brave souls from Inniskilling and Ballybofey, and suppose we can upset them so badly that they mutiny. How long will this army hold together? A week? Two days? One hour? The French, Richard, very nearly ripped this army into two parts and don't think they won't try again, because they will. Only the next rumour will be more subtle, and the only way I can stop that next rumour is by ridding the army of the Real Compañía Irlandesa, because even if you're right and they didn't spread the tales of rape and massacre, then someone

167

close to them did. So tomorrow morning, Richard, you're going to march these bastards down to headquarters where they will surrender those nice new muskets you somehow filched for them and draw rations for a long march. In effect, Richard, they are under arrest until we can find the transport to carry them to Cadiz and there's nothing you can do about it. It's all been ordered.' Hogan took a piece of paper from his pouch and gave it to the rifleman. 'And it isn't an order from me, Richard, but from the Peer.'

Sharpe unfolded the paper. He felt aggrieved at what he perceived to be an injustice. Men like Captain Donaju only wanted to fight the French, but instead they were to be shuffled aside. They were to be marched down to headquarters and disarmed like a battalion of turncoats. Sharpe felt a temptation to crumple Wellington's written order into a ball, but sensibly resisted the impulse. 'If you want to get rid of the trouble-makers,' he said instead, 'then start with Kiely and his bloody whore, start with the –'

'Don't teach me my job,' Hogan interrupted tartly. 'I can't act against Kiely and his whore because they're not in the British army. Valverde could get rid of them, but he won't, so the easy thing to do, the politic thing, is to get rid of the whole damned pack of them. And tomorrow morning, Richard, you do just that.'

Sharpe took a deep breath to curb his anger. 'Why tomorrow?' he asked when he trusted himself to speak again. 'Why not now?'

'Because it will take you the rest of today to bury the dead.'

'And why order me to do it?' Sharpe asked sullenly. 'Why not Runciman, or Kiely?'

'Because those two gentlemen,' Hogan answered, 'will be going back with me to make their reports. There's going to be a court of inquiry and I need to make damn sure that the court discovers exactly what I want it to discover.'

'Why the hell do we want a court of inquiry?' Sharpe asked sourly. 'We know what happened. We got beat.'

Hogan sighed. 'We need a court of inquiry, Richard, because a decent Portuguese battalion got torn to scraps, and the Portuguese government is not going to like that. Worse still, our enemies in the Spanish *junta* will love it. They'll say the events of last night prove that foreign troops can't be trusted under British command, and right now, Richard, what we want more than anything else is to have the Peer made the *Generalisimo* of Spain. We won't win otherwise. So what we need to do now, just to make sure that bloody Valverde doesn't have too much sunshine in which to make his hay, is hold a solemn court of inquiry and find a British officer on whom all the blame can be laid. We need, God bless the poor bastard, a scapegoat.'

Sharpe felt the long, slow dawning of disaster. The Portuguese and Spanish wanted a scapegoat, and Richard Sharpe would make a fine victim, a victim who would be trussed and basted by the reports Hogan would concoct this afternoon at head-quarters. 'I tried to tell Oliveira that Loup was going to attack,' Sharpe said, 'but he wouldn't believe me –'

'Richard! Richard!' Hogan interrupted in a long-suffering tone. 'You're not the scapegoat! Good God, man, you're nothing but a captain, and only a captain on sufferance. Aren't you a lieutenant on the list? You think we can go to the Portuguese government and say we allowed a greenjacket lieutenant to destroy a prime regiment of *caçadores*? Good Lord alive, man, if we're going to make a sacrifice then the very least we can do is find a big, plump beast with enough fat on its carcass to make the fire sizzle when we throw it on the flames.'

'Runciman,' Sharpe said.

Hogan smiled wolfishly. 'Exactly. Our Wagon Master will be sacrificed to make the Portuguese happy and to persuade the

Spanish that Wellington can be trusted not to massacre their precious soldiers. I can't sacrifice Kiely, though I'd love to, because that will upset the Spaniards and I can't sacrifice you because you're too junior and, besides, I need you for the next time I've got a fool's errand, but Colonel Claud Runciman was born for this moment, Richard. This is Claud's proud and sole purpose in life: to sacrifice his honour, his rank and his reputation to keep Lisbon and Cadiz happy.' Hogan paused, thinking. 'Maybe we'll even shoot him. Only *pour encourager les autres.*'

Sharpe guessed he was supposed to recognize the French phrase, but it meant nothing to him and he was too depressed to ask for a translation. He also felt desperately sorry for Runciman. 'Whatever you do, sir,' Sharpe said, 'don't shoot him. It wasn't his fault. It was mine.'

'If anyone's,' Hogan said brusquely, 'it was Oliveira's responsibility. He was a good man, but he should have listened to you, but I dare not blame Oliveira. The Portuguese need him as a hero, just as the Spanish need Kiely. So we'll pick on Runciman instead. It ain't justice, Richard, but politics, and like all politics it ain't pretty, but well done it can work wonders. I'll leave you to bury the dead and tomorrow morning you report to headquarters with all your Irishmen disarmed. We're looking for a place to billet them where they can't get into trouble, and you, of course, can then go back to some proper soldiering.'

Sharpe again felt a pang at the injustice of the solution. 'Suppose Runciman wants to call me as a witness?' he asked. 'I won't lie. I like the man.'

'You have perverse tastes. Runciman won't call you, no one will call you. I'll make sure of that. This court of inquiry isn't supposed to establish the truth, Richard, but to ease Wellington and me off a painful hook that is presently inserted deep into our joint fundament.' Hogan grinned, then turned and walked away. 'I'll send you some picks and shovels to bury the dead,' he called in callous farewell.

'You couldn't send us what we needed, could you?' Sharpe shouted after the Major in bitterness. 'But you can find bloody shovels fast enough.'

'I'm a miracle worker, that's why! Come and have lunch with me tomorrow!'

The smell of the dead was already rank in the fort. Carrion birds wheeled overhead or perched on the crumbling ramparts. There were a few entrenching tools in the fort already and Sharpe ordered the Real Compañía Irlandesa to start digging a long trench for a grave. He made his own riflemen join the diggers. The greenjackets grumbled that such labouring was beneath their dignity as elite troops, but Sharpe insisted. 'We do it because they're doing it,' he told his unhappy men, jerking his thumb towards the Irish guardsmen. Sharpe even took a hand himself, stripping to the waist and wielding a pickaxe as though it was an instrument of vengeance. He slammed the point repeatedly into the hard, rocky soil, wrenched it loose and swung again until the sweat poured off him.

'Sharpe?' A sad Colonel Runciman, mounted on his big horse, peered down at the sweating, bare-backed rifleman. 'Is that really you, Sharpe?'

Sharpe straightened and pushed the hair out of his eyes. 'Yes, General. It's me.'

'You were flogged?' Runciman was staring aghast at the thick scars on Sharpe's back.

'In India, General, for something I didn't do.'

'You shouldn't be digging now! It's beneath an officer's dignity to dig, Sharpe. You must learn to behave as an officer.'

Sharpe wiped the sweat off his face. 'I like digging, General. It's honest work. I always fancied that one day I might have a

171

farm. Just a small one, but with nothing but honest work to do from sun-up to lights-out. Are you here to say goodbye?'

Runciman nodded. 'You know there's going to be a court of inquiry?'

'I heard, sir.'

'They need someone to blame, I suppose,' Runciman said. 'General Valverde says someone should hang for this.' Runciman fidgeted with his reins, then turned in his saddle to stare at the Spanish General who was a hundred paces away and deep in conversation with Lord Kiely. Kiely seemed to be doing most of the talking, gesticulating wildly, but also pointing towards Sharpe every few seconds. 'You don't think they'll hang me, do you, Sharpe?' Runciman asked. He seemed very close to tears.

'They won't hang you, General,' Sharpe said.

'But it'll mean disgrace all the same,' Runciman said, sounding broken-hearted.

'So fight back,' Sharpe said.

'How?'

'Tell them you ordered me to warn Oliveira. Which I did.'

Runciman frowned. 'But I didn't order you to do that, Sharpe.'

'So? They won't know that, sir.'

'I can't tell a lie!' Runciman said, shocked at the thought.

'It's your honour that's at stake, sir, and there'll be enough bastards telling lies about you.'

'I won't tell lies,' Runciman insisted.

'Then bend the truth, for God's sake, sir. Tell them how you had to play tricks to get some decent muskets, and if it hadn't been for those muskets then no one would have lived last night! Play the hero, sir, make the bastards wriggle!'

Runciman shook his head slowly. 'I'm not a hero, Sharpe. I'd like to think there's a valued contribution I can make to the army, as my dear father made to the church, but I'm not sure I've

172

found my real calling yet. But I can't pretend to be what I'm not.' He took off his cocked hat to wipe his brow. 'I just came to say goodbye.'

'Good luck, sir.'

Runciman smiled ruefully. 'I never had that, Sharpe, never. Except in my parents. I was lucky in my dear parents and in being blessed with a healthy appetite. But otherwise . . . ?' He shrugged as though the question was unanswerable, put his hat on again and then, with a forlorn wave, turned and rode to join Hogan. Two ox-drawn wagons had come to the fort with spades and picks and as soon as the tools were unloaded Father Sarsfield commandeered the two vehicles so that the wounded could be carried to doctors and hospitals.

Hogan waved goodbye to Sharpe and led the wagons out of the fort. The surviving *caçadores* followed, marching beneath their flags. Lord Kiely said nothing to his men, but just rode southwards. Juanita, who had not shown her face outside the gatehouse all morning, rode beside him with her dogs running behind. General Valverde touched his hat to greet Juanita, then pulled his reins sharply around and spurred his horse across the fire-blackened grass of the fort's yard until he came to where Sharpe was digging. 'Captain Sharpe?' he said.

'General?' Sharpe had to shade his eyes to look up at the tall, thin, yellow-uniformed man in his high saddle.

'What reason did General Loup have for his attack last night?'

'You must ask him, General,' Sharpe said.

Valverde smiled. 'Maybe I shall. Now back to your digging, Captain. Or should it be Lieutenant?' Valverde waited for an answer, but when none came he turned his horse and rammed his spurs hard back.

'What was all that about?' Harper asked.

'God knows,' Sharpe said, watching the elegant Spaniard gallop to catch up with the wagons and the other horsemen.

Except he did know, and he knew it meant trouble. He swore, then plucked the pick out of the soil and rammed it hard down again. A spark flew from a scrap of flint as the pick's spike slashed deep. Sharpe let go of the handle. 'But I'll tell you what I do know, Pat. Everyone loses out of last night's business except goddamned Loup, and Loup's still out there and that gives me the gripe.'

'So what can you do about it, sir?'

'At this moment, Pat, nothing. I don't even know where to find the bastard.'

Then El Castrador arrived.

'El Lobo is in San Cristóbal, *señor*,' El Castrador said. The partisan had come with five of his men to collect the muskets Sharpe had promised him. The Spaniard claimed he needed a hundred weapons, though Sharpe doubted whether the man had even a dozen followers any more, yet doubtless any extra guns would be sold for a healthy profit. Sharpe gave El Castrador thirty of the muskets he had stored overnight in Runciman's quarters.

'I cannot spare more,' he had told El Castrador, who had shrugged acceptance in the manner of a man accustomed to disappointments.

Now El Castrador was poking among the Portuguese dead, searching for plunder. He picked up a rifle horn, turned it over and saw it had been holed by a bullet. He nevertheless wrenched off the horn's metal spout and shoved it into a capacious pocket of his blood-stained apron. 'El Lobo is in San Cristóbal,' he said again.

'How do you know?' Sharpe asked.

'I am El Castrador!' the gross man said boastfully, then squatted beside a blackening corpse. He prised open the dead man's jaws with his big fingers. 'Is it true, *señor*, that you can sell the teeth of the dead?'

'In London, yes.'

'For gold?'

'They pay gold, yes. Or silver,' Sharpe said. The plundered teeth were made into sets of dentures for rich clients who wanted something better than replacement teeth made from bone or ivory.

El Castrador peeled the corpse's lips back to reveal a handsome set of incisors. 'If I take the teeth out, *señor*, will you buy them from me? Then you can send them to London for a profit. You and me, eh? We can do business.'

'I'm too busy to do business,' Sharpe said, hiding his distaste. 'Besides, we only take French teeth.'

'And the French take British teeth to sell in Paris, yes? So the French bite with your teeth and you bite with theirs, and neither of you will bite with your own.' El Castrador laughed as he straightened from the corpse. 'Maybe they will buy teeth in Madrid,' he said speculatively.

'Where's San Cristóbal?' Sharpe changed the subject.

'Over the hills,' El Castrador said vaguely.

'Show me.' Sharpe pulled the big man towards the eastern ramparts. 'Show me,' he said again as they reached the firestep.

El Castrador indicated the track that twisted up into the hills on the valley's far side, the same track down which Juanita de Elia had fled from the pursuing dragoons. 'You follow that path for five miles,' El Castrador said, 'and you will come to San Cristóbal. It is not a big place, but it is the only place you can reach by that road.'

'And how do you know Loup is there?' Sharpe asked.

'Because my cousin saw him arrive there this morning. My cousin said he was carrying wounded men with him.'

Sharpe gazed eastwards. Five miles. Say two hours if the moon was unclouded or six hours if it was jet dark. 'What was your cousin doing there?' he asked.

'He once lived in the village, *señor*. He goes to watch it from time to time.'

A pity, Sharpe thought, that no one had been watching Loup the previous evening. 'Tell me about San Cristóbal,' he said.

It was a village, the Spaniard said, high in the hills. Not a large village, but prosperous with a fine church, a plaza, and a number of substantial stone houses. The place had once been famous for rearing bulls destined for the fighting rings of the small frontier towns. 'But no more,' El Castrador said. 'The French stewed the last bulls.'

'Is it a hill-top village?' Sharpe asked.

El Castrador shook his head. 'It sits in a valley like that one' – he waved at the eastern valley – 'but not so deep. No trees grow there, *señor*, and a man cannot get close to San Cristóbal without being seen. And El Lobo has built walls across all the gaps between the houses and he keeps watchmen in the church's bell tower. You cannot get close.' El Castrador issued the warning in a worried voice. 'You are thinking of going there?'

Sharpe did not answer for a long time. Of course he was thinking of going there, but to what purpose? Loup had a brigade of men while Sharpe had half a company. 'How close can I get without being seen?' he asked.

El Castrador shrugged. 'A half-mile? But there is also a defile there, a valley where the road runs. I've often thought we could trap Loup there. He used to scout the valley before he rode through it, but not now. Now he is too confident.'

So go to the defile, Sharpe thought, and watch. Just watch. Nothing else. No attack, no ambush, no disobedience, no heroics, just a reconnaissance. And after all, he told himself, Wellington's order to take the Real Compañía Irlandesa to the army headquarters at Vilar Formoso did not detail the route he must take. Nothing specifically forbade Sharpe taking a long, circuitous journey via San Cristóbal, but he knew, even as he thought of that evasion, that it was specious. The sensible thing was to forget Loup, but it cut against all his instincts to be beaten and just lie down and accept the beating. 'Does Loup have artillery at San Cristóbal?' he asked the partisan.

'No, *señor*.'

Sharpe wondered if Loup had arranged for this intelligence to reach him. Was Loup enticing Sharpe into a trap? 'Would you come with us, *señor*?' he asked El Castrador, suspecting that the partisan would never come if Loup was the inspiration behind this news of the brigade's whereabouts.

'To watch Loup,' the Spaniard asked guardedly, 'or to fight him?'

'To watch him,' Sharpe said, knowing it was not the honest answer.

The Spaniard nodded. 'You haven't enough men to fight him,' he added to explain his cautious question.

Privately Sharpe agreed. He did not have enough men, not unless he could surprise Loup or maybe ambush him in the defile. One rifle bullet, well aimed, would kill a man as surely as a full battalion attack, and when Sharpe thought of Oliveira's mangled and tortured body he reckoned that Loup deserved that bullet. So maybe tonight, Sharpe thought, he could take his riflemen to San Cristóbal and pray for a private revenge in the defile at dawn. 'I would welcome your help,' Sharpe told El Castrador, flattering the man.

'In a week's time, *señor*,' El Castrador said, 'I can assemble a respectable troop.'

'We go tonight,' Sharpe said.

'Tonight?' The Spaniard was appalled.

'I saw a bullfight once,' Sharpe said, 'and the matador gave the bull the killing stroke, the one over the neck and down through the shoulders, and the bull staggered, then sank to its knees. The man pulled the sword out and turned away with his arms raised in triumph. You can guess what happened.'

El Castrador nodded. 'The bull rose?'

'A horn in the small of the man's back,' Sharpe confirmed. 'Well, I am the bull, *señor*, and I confess to being wounded, but Loup's back is turned. So tonight, when he thinks we're too weak to move, we march.'

'But only to watch him,' the partisan said cautiously. He had been scorched by Loup too often to risk a fight.

'To watch,' Sharpe lied, 'just to watch.'

He was truthful with Harper. He took his friend to the top of the gatehouse tower from where the two riflemen stared across the eastern valley towards the hazed country where the village of San Cristóbal was hidden. 'I don't honestly know why I'm going,' Sharpe confessed, 'and we've got no orders to go and I'm not even sure we can do a damned thing when we get there. But there's a reason for going.' He paused, suddenly feeling awkward. Sharpe found it hard to articulate his more private thoughts, perhaps because to do so exposed a vulnerability and few soldiers were good at doing that, and what he wanted to say was that a soldier was only as good as his last battle and Sharpe's last battle had been this disaster that had left San Isidro smoking and bloody. And there were plenty of carping fools in the army who would be glad that the upstart from the ranks had at last got his comeuppance, all of which meant that Sharpe must strike back at Loup or else lose his reputation as a lucky and victorious soldier.

'You have to beat the blood out of Loup?' Harper broke the silence with his suggestion.

'I don't have enough men to do that,' Sharpe said. 'The riflemen will come with me, but I can't order Donaju's men to

San Cristóbal. The whole idea's probably a waste of time, Pat, but there's a chance, a half-chance, that I can get that one-eyed bastard in my rifle sight.'

'You'd be surprised,' Harper said. 'There's more than a few of the Real Compañía Irlandesa who'd love to come with us. I don't know about the officers, but Sergeant Major Noonan will come, and that fellow Rourke, and there's a wild bugger called Leon O'Reilly who wants nothing more than to kill Crapauds and there's plenty more like him. They've got something to prove, you see. That they're not all as yellow as Kiely.'

Sharpe smiled, then shrugged. 'It probably is all a waste of time, Pat,' he repeated.

'So what else were you planning on doing tonight?'

'Nothing,' Sharpe said, 'nothing at all.' Yet he knew that if he marched to another defeat he would risk everything he had ever earned, but he also knew that not to go, however hopeless the prospect of revenge, was to accept the beating Loup had administered and Sharpe was too proud to accept that licking. He would most likely achieve nothing by marching to San Cristóbal, yet march he must.

They marched after dark. Donaju insisted on coming, and fifty of his men came too. More would have marched, but Sharpe wanted most of the Real Compañía Irlandesa to stay behind and guard the families and baggage. Everyone and everything left in the San Isidro Fort had been moved into the gatehouse just in case Loup did come back to finish off his previous night's work. 'Which would just be my bloody luck,' Sharpe said. 'Me marching to shoot him and him marching to geld me.' He had his riflemen ranging ahead as scouts just in case the French were returning to the San Isidro.

'What do we do if we meet them?' Donaju asked.

'Hide,' Sharpe said. 'Seventy of us can't beat a thousand of them, not in the open.' An ambush might work this night, but not a firefight on open, level moonlit ground against an overwhelming enemy. 'And I hate night fighting,' Sharpe went on. 'I was captured in a bloody night fight in India. We were blundering around in the sodding dark with no one knowing what they were doing or why except for the Indians, and they knew well enough. They were firing rockets at us. The things were no bloody use as weapons, but at night their fire blinded us and the next thing I knew there were twenty big buggers with fixed bayonets all around me.'

'Where was that?' Donaju asked.

'Seringapatam.'

'What business did you have in India?' Donaju asked in evident disapproval.

'Same business I've got here,' Sharpe said curtly. 'Killing the King's enemies.'

El Castrador wanted to know what they were talking about, so Donaju translated. The partisan was suffering because Sharpe had refused to let anyone ride a horse so El Castrador's horse, like the horses of the Spanish-Irish officers, was being led at the column's rear. Sharpe had insisted on the precaution because men on horses were liable to ride away from the line of march and the sight of a mounted man on a crest could easily serve to alert a French patrol. Sharpe had similarly insisted that no man carry a loaded musket in case a stumble snapped a lock and fired a shot that would carry far in the still, almost windless night.

The march was not hard. The first hour was the worst, for they had to climb the steep hill opposite the San Isidro, but once over the crest the road kept to fairly level ground. It was a drover's road, grassy, wide and easy marching in the cool night air. The route wound lazily between rocky outcrops where enemy picquets could have been hidden. Normally Sharpe would have reconnoitred such dangerous places, but this night he pushed his scouts urgently ahead. He was in a dangerous and fatalistic mood. Maybe, he thought, this reckless march was the aftermath of defeat, a kind of shocked reaction in which a man lashed out blindly, and this daft expedition under the half-moon was undoubtedly blind, for Sharpe knew in his inmost soul that the unfinished business between himself and Brigadier Loup would almost certainly stay unfinished. No man could expect to march by night towards a fortified village that he had not reconnoitred and then spring an ambush. The odds were that the small expedition would watch the village from afar, Sharpe would conclude that nothing could be achieved against its walls or in the nearby defile, and in the dawn the guards and riflemen would march back to San Isidro with nothing but sore feet and a wasted night.

It was just after midnight when the column reached the low ridge that overlooked the valley of San Cristóbal. Sharpe rested the men behind the crest while he climbed to the top with El Castrador, Donaju and Harper. The four men lay in the rocks and watched.

The grey stone of the village was blanched near white by the moonlight which cast stark shadows from the intricate web of stone walls that marked the fields around the small settlement. The limewashed bell tower of the church seemed to glow, so clear was the night, and so bright the half-moon that hung above the glimmering hills. Sharpe trained his telescope on the tower and, though he could plainly see the untidy stork's nest on top and the sheen of the moon glancing from a bell suspended in the tower's arched opening, he could see no sentries there. But nor would he necessarily expect to see a picquet, for any man keeping watch through a cold long night in a high vulnerable place would be likely to huddle for shelter in a corner of the tower.

San Cristóbal looked as though it had been a pleasant village before Loup's brigade came to evict the inhabitants and destroy their livelihood. The sturdy field walls had been built to keep fighting bulls safely penned, and those bulls had paid for the church and houses that all showed a touch of affluence in the lens of Sharpe's telescope. At Fuentes de Oñoro, the tiny village where he had first met El Castrador, the cottages had been mostly low and virtually windowless, but some of San Cristóbal's houses had two storeys and nearly all the outward-facing walls possessed windows and even, in one case, a small balcony. Sharpe assumed there would be picquets in half those windows.

He traced the line of the drover's road with his telescope to see that where a track left the road to become the village's main street a stone wall had been built between two houses. There was a gap in the wall, but Sharpe could just make out the shadowy hint of a second wall beyond the first. He made a zigzag motion with his hand as he looked at El Castrador. 'The gate, *señor?*'

'*Sí.* Three walls!' El Castrador exaggerated the zigzag gesture to show how complicated the maze-like entrance was. Such a maze would slow down any attacker while Loup's men poured musket fire down from the upper windows.

'How do they get their horses inside?' Donaju asked in Spanish.

'Around the far side,' El Castrador answered. 'There is a gate. Very strong. And the defile, *señor*, is on the far side of the village. Where the road goes into the hills, see? We should go there?'

'Christ, no,' Sharpe said. His hope in El Castrador's defile had vanished the moment he saw where it was. The gorge might be a perfect place for a surprise attack, but it was too far away and Sharpe knew he would have no chance of reaching it before daylight. So much for his hopes of ambush.

He turned the spyglass back to the village just in time to see a flicker of motion. He tensed, then saw it was merely a puff of smoke coming from a chimney deep in the village. The smoke had been there all the time, but someone must have dumped wood on the fire or else tried to revive a hearth of smouldering embers with a pair of bellows and so provoked the sudden gust of smoke.

'They're all tucked up in bed,' Donaju said. 'Safe and sound.'

Sharpe edged the telescope across the village roofs. 'No flag,' he said at last. 'Does he usually fly a flag?' he asked El Castrador.

The big man shrugged. 'Sometimes yes, sometimes no.' He plainly did not know the answer.

Sharpe collapsed the telescope. 'Put a dozen men on guard, Donaju,' he ordered, 'and tell the rest to sleep a while. Pat? Send Latimer and a couple of the lads to that knoll.' He indicated a rocky height that would offer the best view of the surrounding country. 'And you and the rest of the rifles will come with me.'

Harper paused as though he wanted to ask for details of what they planned to do, then decided mute obedience was the best course and slid back off the crest. Donaju frowned. 'I can't come with you?'

'Someone has to take charge if I die,' Sharpe said. 'So keep watch, stay here till three in the morning, and if you haven't heard from me by then, go home.'

'And what do you plan to do there?' Donaju asked, gesturing towards the village.

'It doesn't smell right,' Sharpe said. 'I can't explain it, but it doesn't smell right. So I'm just going to take a look. Nothing more, Donaju, just a look.'

Captain Donaju was still unhappy at being excluded from Sharpe's patrol, yet he did not like to contradict Sharpe's plans.

Sharpe, after all, was a fighting soldier and Donaju had only one night's experience of battle. 'What do I tell the British if you die?' he asked Sharpe chidingly.

'To take my boots off before they bury me,' Sharpe said. 'I don't want blisters through eternity.' He turned to see Harper leading a file of riflemen up the slope. 'Ready, Pat?'

'Aye, sir.'

'You'll stay here,' Sharpe said to El Castrador, not quite as a question, but not quite a direct order either.

'I shall wait here, *señor*.' The partisan's tone betrayed that he had no wish to get any closer to the wolf's lair.

Sharpe led his men southwards behind the crest until a broken stretch of rocks offered a patch of shadow that took them safe down to the nearest stone wall. They moved fast, despite having to go at a crouch, for the shadows of the stone walls offered black lanes of invisibility that angled towards the village. Halfway across the valley floor Sharpe stopped and made a cautious reconnaissance with his telescope. He could see now that all the lower windows in the village had been blocked with stone, leaving only the inaccessible upper windows free for lookouts. He could also see the foundations of houses that had been demolished outside the village's defensive perimeter so that no attacker would have shelter close to San Cristóbal. Loup had taken the additional precaution of knocking down the drystone walls that lay within close musket range of the village. Sharpe could get as near as sixty or seventy paces, but after that he would be as visible as a blowfly on a limewashed wall.

'Bugger's taking no chances,' Harper said.

'Can you blame him?' Sharpe answered. 'I'd knock down a few walls to stop El Castrador practising his technique on me.'

'So what do we do?' Harper asked.

'Don't know yet.'

Nor did Sharpe know. He had come to within rifle range of his enemy's stronghold and he could feel no prickle of fear. Indeed, he could feel no apprehension at all. Maybe, he thought, Loup was not here. Or maybe, more worryingly, Sharpe's instincts were out of kilter. Maybe Loup was the puppetmaster here and he was enticing Sharpe ever closer, lulling his victim into a fatal sense of security.

'Someone's there,' Harper said, anticipating Sharpe's thoughts, 'else there'd be no smoke.'

'Sensible thing to do,' Sharpe said, 'is for us to bugger off out of here and go to bed.'

'Sensible thing to do,' Harper said, 'is get out the bloody army and die in bed.'

'But that's not why we joined, is it?'

'Speak for yourself, sir. I just joined to get a square meal,' Harper said. He primed his rifle, then similarly armed the seven-barrel gun. 'Getting killed wasn't really part of the idea at all.'

'I joined so as not to be strung from a gallows,' Sharpe said. He primed his own rifle, then gazed again at the village's moon-washed walls. 'Damn it,' he said, 'I'm going closer.' It was like the game children played when they tried to see how close they could creep to a victim without their movements being observed, and suddenly, in Sharpe's mind, the village assumed a childlike menace, almost as though it were a malevolent but sleeping castle that must be approached with enormous stealth in case it stirred and destroyed him. Yet why bother to risk destruction, he asked himself? And he could give himself no answer to the question, except that he had not come this close to the stronghold of the man who had made himself into Sharpe's bitterest enemy just to turn and walk ignominiously away. 'Watch the windows,' he told his men, then he sneaked along the base of the shadowed wall until at last the stones ran

185

out and there was only a spill of fallen rocks to show where once the wall had stood.

But at least that spill of stones offered a patchy tangle of concealing shadows. Sharpe stared at that tangle, wondering if the shadows were sufficient to hide a man and then he looked up at the village. Nothing stirred except the haze of woodsmoke tugged by the night's small wind.

'Come back, sir!' Harper called softly.

But instead Sharpe took a breath, lay flat and edged out into the moonlight. He was slithering like a snake between the rocks, so slowly that he trusted no watcher would detect his moving shape amidst the patchwork of shadows. His belt and looped uniform kept snagging on stones, but each time he eased himself free and crept a few feet onwards before freezing to listen again. He was anticipating the telltale sound of a musket being cocked, the heavy double click that would presage a crashing shot. He heard nothing except the soft sound of the wind. Not even a dog barked.

He went closer and closer until at last the jumbled stones ended and there was only moonlit open ground between himself and the high wall of the nearest house. He stared up at the window and saw nothing. He could smell nothing but the rank odour of the dungheaps in the town. No smell of tobacco, no saddle-sores, no stink of unwashed uniforms. There was the faint hint of woodsmoke sweetening the stench of dung, but otherwise no suggestion of human presence in the village. Two bats wheeled close to the wall, their ragged wings flickering black against the limewash. Sharpe, now that he was close to the village, could see the signs of neglect. The limewash was wearing thin, slates had slipped from the roofs and the window frames had been torn apart for firewood. The French had displaced San Cristóbal's inhabitants and made it a village of ghosts. Sharpe's heart thumped hard, echoing in his ears as he lay straining for any clue as to what lay behind the blank, silent walls. He cocked his rifle and the clicks sounded unnaturally loud in the night, but no one called a challenge from the village.

'Bugger it.' He had not meant to speak aloud, but had, and as he spoke so he stood up.

He could almost sense Harper taking a nervous breath a hundred paces behind him. Sharpe stood and waited, and no one spoke, no one called, no one challenged and no one shot. He felt suspended between life and death, almost as if the whole spinning earth had become as fragile as a blown-glass ball that could be shattered by a single loud noise.

He walked towards the village that lay just twenty paces away. The loudest noises in the night were the sounds of his boots on the grass and of the breath in his throat. He reached out and touched the cold stone wall, and no one fired and no one challenged, and so Sharpe walked on around the village's edge, past the stone-blocked windows and the wall-barricaded streets until he came at last to the maze-like entrance.

He stopped five paces short of the gate's outer wall. He licked his lips and stared at the dark gap. Was he being watched? Was Loup, like a sorcerer in a tower, drawing him on? Were the French holding their breath and scarcely believing their luck as their victim came to them, step by slow step? Was the night about to explode in stark horror? In gunfire and slaughter, defeat and pain? The thought almost made Sharpe walk away from the village, but his pride stopped him from retreating and the pride was monstrous enough to make him step one pace closer to the labyrinthine gate.

Then another pace, and another, and suddenly he was there, in the gate's opening itself, and nothing moved. Not a breath stirred. In front of him was the blank second wall with its enticing opening off to Sharpe's left. He sidled into the gap, closed off now from the moonlight and from the sight of his riflemen. He was in the maze, in Loup's trap now, and he edged down the narrow gap between the walls with his rifle pointed and his finger on the trigger.

He came to the gap and saw a third blank wall ahead, and so he stepped through into the last narrow passage that led to his right and thus to the final gap in the last wall. His feet scraped on stone, his breath boomed. There was moonlight beyond the third wall, but inside the labyrinth it was dark and cold. He had his back pressed hard against the middle wall and he took an odd comfort from the solid feel of the stone. He edged sideways again, tried to ignore the pumping of his heart, then took a deep breath, dropped to one knee and threw himself sideways in one motion so that he was kneeling in the last entrance to Loup's village with his rifle aimed straight down the stone-paved street towards the whitewashed church.

And in front of him was nothing.

No one called in triumph, no one sneered, no one ordered his capture.

Sharpe let out a long breath. It was a cold night, but sweat was trickling down his face and stinging his eyes. He shivered, then lowered the rifle's muzzle.

And the howling began.

CHAPTER SIX

'He's mad, Hogan,' Wellington said. 'Stark mad. Gibbering. Should be locked up in Bedlam where we could pay sixpence to go and mock him. Ever been to Bedlam?'

'Once, my Lord, just the once.' Hogan's horse was tired and fretful, for the Irishman had ridden long and hard to find the General and he was somewhat confused by the abrupt greeting. Hogan was also in the disobliging mood of a man woken too early, yet he somehow managed to respond to Wellington's jocular greeting in a similar vein. 'My sister wanted to see the lunatics, my Lord, but as I recall we only paid tuppence each.'

'They should lock Erskine up,' Wellington said grimly, 'and charge the populace tuppence apiece to view him. Still, even Erskine should manage this job, eh? All he has to do is stop the place up, not actually capture it.' Wellington was inspecting the grim defences surrounding the French-held town of Almeida. Every now and then a gun would fire from the fortress town and the flat, hard sound of the shot would echo across the rolling country a few seconds after the shot itself had bounced in a flurry of early morning dew and bounded harmlessly off towards fields or woods. Wellington, attended by a dozen aides and gallopers and starkly lit by the long slanting rays of the just risen sun, made a ripe target for the French gunners, but his Lordship ignored their efforts. Instead, almost in mockery of the enemy's marksmanship, he would stop wherever the terrain offered a view and stare at the town which had possessed a peculiar flat-topped appearance ever since the cathedral and castle on Almeida's hill top had exploded in a massive eruption of stored powder. That explosion had forced the British and Portuguese defenders to surrender the fortress town to the French, who in turn were now ringed by British troops under the command of Sir William Erskine. Erskine's men were under orders to contain the garrison, not capture it, and indeed none of Erskine's guns was large enough to make any impression on the massive star-shaped fortifications. 'How many of the scoundrels are in there, Hogan?' Wellington asked, ignoring the fact that Hogan would not have ridden hard across country so early in the day without bringing some important news.

'We think fifteen hundred men, my Lord.'

'Ammunition?'

'Plenty.'

'And how much food do they have?'

'My sources say two weeks on half rations which probably means they can last a month. The French do seem able to subsist on nothing, my Lord. Might I suggest we move before a gunner lays an accurate sight? And might I claim your Lordship's further attention?'

Wellington did not move. 'I am claiming the gunners' whole attention,' the General said with heavy humour, 'as a means of encouraging them to improve their aim. That way, Hogan, they might relieve me of Erskine.' General Erskine was usually drunk, perpetually half blind and reputed to be mad. 'Or so the Horse Guards confessed to me,' Wellington said, expecting Hogan to follow his erratic train of thought. 'I wrote to them, Hogan, and complained at being provided with Erskine and do you know what they wrote back?' Wellington had told Hogan this story at least half a dozen times in the last three months, but the Irishman knew how much the General enjoyed the telling of it and so he indulged his master.

'I fear their reply has momentarily slipped my mind, my Lord.'

'They wrote, Hogan, and I quote, that "no doubt he is sometimes a little mad, but in his lucid intervals he is an uncommonly clever fellow, but he did look a little wild as he embarked"!' Wellington gave his great horse-neigh of a laugh. 'So will Masséna try to relieve the garrison?'

Hogan understood from the General's tone that Wellington knew the answer as well as he did himself, and so he sensibly said nothing. The answer, anyway, was obvious, for both Hogan and Wellington understood that Marshal Masséna would not have left fifteen hundred men in Almeida just so they could be starved into surrender and thus forced to spend the rest of the war in some inhospitable prison camp on Dartmoor. Almeida had been garrisoned for a purpose and Hogan, like his master, suspected the purpose was close to its fulfilment.

A blossom of white smoke marked where a cannon had fired from the ramparts. The ball showed itself to Hogan as a dark vertical line that flickered in the sky, a sure sign that the shot was coming straight towards the observer. Now all depended on whether the gunlayer had judged the elevation right. One half-turn too many on the gun's elevating screw and the ball would fall short, one turn too few and it would scream overhead.

It fell a hundred yards short, then bounced up over Wellington's head to tear through a grove of oaks. Leaves scattered as the shot whipped the branches to and fro. 'Their guns are too cold, Hogan,' the General said. 'They're under-firing.'

'Not by a great deal, my Lord,' Hogan said fervently, 'and the barrels will warm quickly.'

Wellington chuckled. 'Value your life, do you? Well, ride on.' His Lordship clicked his tongue and his horse obediently walked on down the slope past a British gun battery that was screened from the enemy by an earthwork topped by soil-filled baskets. Many of the gunners were stripped to the waist, some were sleeping, and none seemed to notice the army commander passing. Another general might have been annoyed by the battery's casual air, but Wellington's quick eye noted the good condition of the guns and so he merely nodded to the battery commander before waving his aides out of earshot. 'So what's your news, Hogan?'

'Too much news, my Lord, and none of it good,' Hogan said. He took off his hat and fanned his face. 'Marshal Bessières has joined Masséna, my Lord. Brought a deal of cavalry and artillery with him, but no infantry as far as we can gather.'

'Your partisans?' Wellington was inquiring about the source of Hogan's information.

'Indeed, my Lord. They shadowed Bessières's march.' Hogan took out his snuff box and helped himself to a restorative pinch while Wellington digested the news. Bessières commanded the French army in northern Spain, an army devoted wholly to fighting partisans, and the news that Bessières had brought troops to reinforce Marshal Masséna hinted that the French were readying themselves for their attempt to relieve the siege of Almeida.

Wellington rode in silence for a few yards. His route took him up a gentle slope to a grassy crest that offered another view of the enemy fortress. He took out a spyglass and gave the spreading, low walls and the artillery-shattered rooftops a long inspection. Hogan imagined the gunners handspiking their guns around to lay on their new target. Wellington grunted, then snapped the spyglass shut. 'So Masséna's coming to resupply these rascals, is he? And if he succeeds, Hogan, they'll have enough supplies to last out till hell goes cold unless we storm the place first, and storming it will take until midsummer at least, and I can't storm Almeida and Ciudad Rodrigo at the same time, so Masséna will just have to be stopped. It'll go low, I warrant.' This last remark referred to a cannon that had just fired from the walls. The smoke jetted out across the ditch as Hogan tried to catch sight of the missile. The roundshot arrived a second before the sound of the gun. The ball bounced on the slope below the General's party and ricocheted high over his head to crack against an olive tree. Wellington turned his horse away. 'But you know what it will mean, Hogan, if I try to stop Masséna in front of Almeida?'

'The Coa, my Lord.'

'Exactly.' If the British and Portuguese army fought the French close to Almeida then they would have the deep, fast-flowing River Coa at their backs, and if Masséna succeeded in turning Wellington's right flank, which he would assuredly try to do, then the army would be left with one road, just one road, on which it could retreat if it suffered defeat. And that one road led across a high, narrow bridge over the Coa's otherwise uncrossable gorge, and if the defeated army with all its guns and baggage and women and packhorses and wounded were to try and cross that one narrow bridge then there would be chaos. And into that chaos would plunge the Emperor's heavy horses with their sword-wielding troopers and thus a fine British army that had thrown the French out of Portugal would die on the frontier of Spain and there would be a new bridge over the Seine in Paris and it would bear the odd name of Pont Castello Bom in commemoration of the place where André Masséna, Marshal of France, would have destroyed Lord Wellington's army. 'So we shall have to beat Marshal Masséna, won't we?' Wellington said to himself, then turned to Hogan. 'When will he come, Hogan?'

193

'Soon, my Lord, very soon. The stores in Ciudad Rodrigo won't allow them otherwise,' Hogan answered. With the arrival of Bessiéres's men the French now had too many mouths to feed from Ciudad Rodrigo's supply depots, which meant they would have to march soon or starve.

'So how many does Masséna have now?' Wellington asked.

'He can put fifty thousand men into the field, my Lord.'

'And I can't put forty thousand against them,' Wellington said bitterly. 'One day, Hogan, London will come to believe that we can win this war and will actually send us some troops who are not mad, blind or drunk, but till then . . . ?' He left the question unanswered. 'Any more of those damned counterfeit newspapers?'

Hogan was not surprised by the sudden change of subject. The newspapers describing the fictional atrocities in Ireland had been intended to disaffect the Irish soldiers in the British army. The ploy had failed, but only just, and both Hogan and Wellington feared that the next attempt might be more successful. And if that attempt came on the eve of Masséna's crossing of the frontier to relieve Almeida it could be disastrous. 'None, sir,' Hogan said, 'yet.'

'But you've moved the Real Compañía Irlandesa away from the frontier?'

'They should be arriving at Vilar Formoso this morning, my Lord,' Hogan said.

Wellington grimaced. 'At which juncture you will apprise Captain Sharpe of his troubles?' The General did not wait for Hogan's answer. 'Did he shoot the two prisoners, Hogan?'

'I suspect so, my Lord, yes,' Hogan answered heavily. General Valverde had reported the execution of Loup's men to the British headquarters, not in protest at the actual deed, but rather as proof that Loup's raid on the San Isidro Fort had been provoked by Captain Sharpe's irresponsibility. Valverde was riding a high moral horse and loudly proclaiming that Spanish and Portuguese lives could not be trusted to British command. The Portuguese were unlikely to worry overmuch about Valverde's allegations, but the *junta* in Cadiz would be only too eager for any ammunition they could use against their British allies. Valverde was already passing on a litany of other complaints, how British soldiers failed to salute when the Holy Sacraments were being carried through the streets, and how the freemasons among the British officers offended Catholic sensibilities by openly parading in their regalia, but now he had a more bitter and wounding allegation: that the British would fight to the last drop of their allies' blood and the massacre at San Isidro was his proof.

'Damn Sharpe,' Wellington said.

Damn Valverde, Hogan thought, but Britain needed Spanish goodwill more than it needed one rogue rifleman. 'I haven't talked to Sharpe, my Lord,' Hogan said, 'but I suspect he did kill the two men. I hear it was the usual thing: Loup's men had raped village women.' Hogan shrugged as if to imply that such horror was now commonplace.

'It may be the usual thing,' Wellington said acidly, 'but that hardly condones the execution of prisoners. It's my experience, Hogan, that when you promote a man from the ranks he usually takes to drink, but not in Mister Sharpe's case. No, I promote Sergeant Sharpe and he takes to conducting private wars behind my back! Loup didn't attack the San Isidro to destroy Oliveira or Kiely, Hogan, he did it to find Sharpe, which makes the loss of the *caçadores* all Sharpe's fault!'

'We don't know that, my Lord.'

'But the Spanish will deduce it, Hogan, and proclaim it far and wide, which makes it hard, Hogan, damned hard for us to blame Runciman. They'll say we're hiding the real culprit and that we're cavalier with allied lives.'

195

'We can say the allegations against Captain Sharpe are malicious and false, my Lord.'

'I thought he admitted them?' Wellington retorted sharply. 'Didn't he boast to Oliveira about executing the two rogues?'

'So I understand, my Lord,' Hogan said, 'but none of Oliveira's officers survived to testify to that admission.'

'So who can testify?'

Hogan shrugged. 'Kiely and his whore, Runciman and the priest.' Hogan tried to make the list sound trivial, then shook his head. 'Too many witnesses, I'm afraid, my Lord. Not to mention Loup himself. Valverde could well attempt to get a formal complaint from the French and we'd be hard put to ignore such a document.'

'So Sharpe has to be sacrificed?' Wellington asked.

'I fear so, my Lord.'

'God damn it, Hogan!' Wellington snapped. 'Just what the devil was going on between Sharpe and Loup?'

'I wish I knew, my Lord.'

'Aren't you supposed to know?' the General asked angrily.

Hogan soothed his tired horse. 'I've not been idle, my Lord,' he said with a touch of tetchiness. 'I don't know all that happened between Sharpe and Loup, but what does seem to be happening is a concerted effort to sow discord in this army. There's a new man come south from Paris, a man called Ducos, who seems to be cleverer than the usual rogues. He's the fellow behind this scheme of counterfeit newspapers. And I'll guess, my Lord, that there are more of those newspapers on the way, designed to arrive here just before the French themselves.'

'Then stop them!' Wellington demanded.

'I can and shall stop them,' Hogan said confidently. 'We know it's Kiely's whore who brings them over the frontier, but our problem is finding the man who distributes them in our army, and that man is the real danger, my Lord. One of our correspondents in Paris warns us that the French have a new agent in Portugal, a man of whom they expect great things. I would dearly like to find him before he fulfils those expectations. I'm rather hoping the whore will lead us to him.'

'You're sure about the woman?'

'Quite sure,' Hogan said firmly. His sources in Madrid were explicit, but he knew better than to mention their names aloud. 'Sadly we don't know who this new man in Portugal is, but given time, my Lord, and a touch of carelessness on the part of Kiely's whore, we'll find him.'

Wellington grunted. A rumble in the sky announced the passage of a French roundshot, but the General did not even look up to see where the shot might fall. 'Damn all this fuss, Hogan, and damn Kiely and his damned men, and damn Sharpe too. Is Runciman trussed for the sacrifice?'

'He's in Vilar Formoso, my Lord.'

The General nodded. 'Then truss Sharpe too. Put him to administrative duties, Hogan, and warn him that his conduct will be the subject of a court of inquiry. Then inform General Valverde that we're pursuing the matter. You know what to say.' Wellington pulled out a pocket watch and clicked its lid open. An expression of distaste showed on his thin face. 'I suppose, if I'm here, that I'll have to visit Erskine. Or do you think the madman is still in bed?'

'I'm sure his aides will have apprised Sir William of your presence, my Lord, and I can't think he'd be flattered if you were to ignore him.'

'Touchier than a virgin in a barracks room. And mad as well. Just the man, Hogan, to conduct Sharpe and Runciman's court of inquiry. Let us see, Hogan, whether Sir William is experiencing a lucid interval and can thus understand what verdict is required of him. We must sacrifice one good officer and one bad officer to draw Valverde's fangs. God damn it, Hogan, God

damn it, but needs must when the devil drives. Poor Sharpe.'
His Lordship gave one backward glance at the town of Almeida,
then led his entourage towards the besieging force's
headquarters.

While Hogan worried about the narrow bridge at Castello
Bom, about Sharpe and, even more, about a mysterious enemy
come into Portugal to sow discord.

The house with the smoking chimney lay where the street
opened into the small plaza before the church, and it was in
there that the howling had begun. Sharpe, who had been rising
to his feet, had crouched instantly back into the shadows as a
gate beside the house creaked open.

Then the hounds had poured out. They had been pent up
too long and so ran joyously up and down the deserted street.
A figure wearing uniform led a horse and a mule out and then
turned away from Sharpe, evidently planning to leave San
Cristóbal by the gated entrance on the village's far side. One
of the hounds leaped playfully at the mule and received a curse
and a kick for its trouble.

The curse sounded plainly in the street. It was a woman's
voice, the voice of the Doña Juanita de Elia who now put her
foot in the stirrup of the saddled horse, but the hound came
back to plague the mule again just as she tried to haul herself
up into the saddle. The mule, which was loaded with a pair of
heavy panniers, brayed and shied away from the hound and
pulled its leading rein out of Juanita's grip then, frightened by
the excited dogs, it trotted towards Sharpe.

Juanita de Elia cursed again. Her plumed bicorne hat had
fallen off in the commotion so that her long black hair began
to come out of its pins. She pushed it roughly into place as she
hurried after the frightened mule which had come to a stop

just a few paces from Sharpe's hiding place. The hounds ran in the other direction, baptizing the church steps in their joy at being released from confinement in the yard.

'Come on, you bastard,' Juanita told the mule in Spanish. She was wearing the elegant uniform of the Real Compañía Irlandesa.

She leaned to pick up the mule's leading rein and Sharpe stepped out into the moonlight. 'I never know,' he said, 'whether Doña is a title or not. Do I say "good morning, milady"? Or just good morning?' He stopped three paces from her.

It took Juanita a few seconds to recover her poise. She straightened up, glanced at the rifle in Sharpe's hands, then at her horse thirty paces away. She had left a carbine in the saddle holster, but knew she had no chance of reaching the weapon. She had a short sword at her side and her hand went to the hilt, then stopped as Sharpe raised the rifle's muzzle. 'You wouldn't kill a woman, Captain Sharpe,' she said coldly.

'In the dark, milady? With you in uniform? I don't think anyone would blame me.'

Juanita watched Sharpe carefully, trying to judge the veracity of his threat. Then a means of salvation occurred to her and she smiled before giving a brief tuneless whistle. Her hounds stopped and pricked their ears. 'I'll set the dogs on you, Captain,' she said.

'Because that's all you've got left here, isn't it?' Sharpe said. 'Loup has gone. Where?'

Juanita still smiled. 'I've seen my bitches pull down a prime stag, Captain, and turn it into offal in two minutes. The first to reach you will go for your throat and she'll hold you down while the others feed on you.'

Sharpe returned the smile, then raised his voice. 'Pat! Bring 'em in!'

'Damn you,' Juanita said, then she whistled again and the

199

hounds began loping down the street. At the same time she turned and began running towards her horse, but she was slowed by the spurs on her heavy riding boots and Sharpe caught her from behind. He put his left arm round her waist and held her body in front of his like a shield as he backed against the nearest wall.

'Whose throat will they go for now, my lady?' he asked. Her tousled hair was in his face. It smelt of rosewater.

She kicked at him, tried to elbow him, but he was much too strong. The fastest hound came running towards them and Sharpe lowered the rifle with his right hand and pulled the trigger. The sound of the shot was brutally loud in the confined street. Sharpe's aim had been confused by Juanita's struggles, but his bullet caught the attacking animal in the haunch and sent it spinning and yelping to the ground just as Harper led the riflemen through the entrance maze. The Irishman's sudden appearance confused the other hounds. They slowed down, then whined as they clustered about the wounded bitch.

'Put the bugger out of its misery, Pat,' Sharpe said. 'Harris? Go back to Captain Donaju, give him my compliments and tell him to bring his men into the village. Cooper? Get her ladyship's horse. And Perkins? Take her ladyship's sword.'

Harper waded into the hounds, drew his sword bayonet and stooped to the bleeding, snapping bitch. 'Be still, you bugger,' he said gently, then sliced once. 'You poor beast,' he said as he straightened up with his bayonet dripping blood. 'God save Ireland, sir, but look what you found. Lord Kiely's fancy lady.'

'Traitor!' Juanita said to Harper, then spat at him. 'Traitor! You should be fighting the English.'

'Oh, my lady,' Harper said as he wiped the blade on the skirt of his green jacket, 'some time you and me must enjoy a long talk about who should be fighting on whose side, but right now I'm busy with the war I've already got.'

Perkins gingerly extracted the short sword from Juanita's slings, then Sharpe released his grip on her. 'My apologies for manhandling you, ma'am,' he said very formally.

Juanita ignored the apology. She stood straight and stiff, keeping her dignity in front of the foreign riflemen. Dan Hagman was coaxing the mule out of the street corner where it had taken refuge. 'Bring it with you, Dan,' Sharpe said, then led the way up the street towards the house Juanita had vacated. Harper escorted her, making her follow Sharpe into the yard.

The house must have been one of the largest in the village for the gate led into a spacious courtyard that possessed stabling on two sides and an elaborately crowned well in its centre. The kitchen door was open and Sharpe ducked inside to find the fire still smouldering and the remains of a meal on the table. He found some candle stubs, lit them from the fire, and placed them back on the table amidst the litter of plates and cups. At least six people had eaten at the table, suggesting that Loup and his men had left very recently. 'Look round the rest of the village, Pat,' Sharpe told Harper. 'Take half a dozen men and go carefully. I reckon everyone's gone, but you never know.'

'I'll take care, sir, so I will.' Harper took the riflemen out of the kitchen, leaving Sharpe alone with Juanita.

Sharpe gestured at a chair. 'Let's talk, my lady.'

She walked with a slow dignity to the far side of the table, put a hand on the chair back, then suddenly broke away and ran for a door across the room. 'Go to hell,' was her parting injunction. Sharpe was encumbered by the furniture so that by the time he reached the door she was already halfway up a dark flight of stairs. He scrambled after her. She turned right at the stairhead and ran through a door that she slammed behind her. Sharpe kicked it a split second before it would have latched and hurled himself through the opening to see, in the moonlight, that Juanita was sprawled across a bed. She was struggling to free an object from a discarded valise then, as Sharpe crossed the room, she turned with a pistol in her hand. He threw himself at her, slamming his left hand at the pistol just as she pulled the trigger. The bullet cracked into the ceiling as he landed full on her. She gasped from the impact, then tried to claw at his eyes with her free hand.

Sharpe rolled off her, stood and backed to the window. He was panting. His left wrist hurt from the impact of striking the pistol aside. The moonlight came past him to silver the haze of pistol smoke and to shine on the bed that was nothing but a raft of straw-filled mattresses on which a jumble of pelts provided the covers. Juanita half sat up, glared at him, then seemed to realize that her defiance had run its course. She let out a disgruntled sigh and collapsed back onto the furs.

Dan Hagman had heard the pistol shot from the courtyard and now came pounding up the stairs and into the bedroom with his rifle levelled. He looked from the woman prone on the bed to Sharpe. 'Are you all right, sir?'

'Just a disagreement, Dan. No one hurt.'

Hagman looked back at Juanita. 'A right little spitfire, sir,' he said admiringly. 'She probably needs a spanking.'

'I'll look after her, Dan. You get those panniers off the mule. Let's see what the spitfire was taking away, eh?'

Hagman went back downstairs. Sharpe massaged his wrist and looked about the room. It was a large high-ceilinged chamber with dark wood panelling, thick ceiling beams, a fireplace and a heavy linen press in one corner. It was obviously the bedroom of a substantial man and the room that a commanding officer, quartering his men in a small village, would naturally take as his own billet. 'It's a big bed, my lady, too big for just one person,' Sharpe said. 'Are those wolf skins?'

Juanita said nothing.

Sharpe sighed. 'You and Loup, eh? Am I right?'

She stared at him with dark resentful eyes, but still refused to speak.

'And all those days you went hunting alone,' Sharpe said, 'you were coming here to see Loup.'

Again she refused to speak. The moonlight put half her face in shadow.

'And you opened the San Isidro's gate for Loup, didn't you?' Sharpe went on. 'That's why he didn't attack the gatehouse. He wanted to make sure no harm came to you in the fighting. That's nice in a man, isn't it? Looking after his woman. Mind you, he can't have liked the thought of you and Lord Kiely. Or isn't Loup the jealous kind?'

'Kiely was usually too drunk,' she said in a low voice.

'Found your tongue, have you? So now you can tell me what you were doing here.'

'Go to hell, Captain.'

The sound of boots in the street made Sharpe turn to the window to see that the men of the Real Compañía Irlandesa had arrived in the street below. 'Donaju!' he shouted. 'Into the kitchen here!' He turned back to the bed. 'We've got company, my lady, so let's go and be sociable.' He waited for her to stand up, then shook his head when she obstinately refused to move. 'I'm not leaving you on your own, my lady, so you can either go downstairs on your own two feet or have me carry you.'

She stood, straightened her uniform and tried to rearrange her hair. Then, followed by Sharpe, she went down into the candlelit kitchen where El Castrador, Donaju and Sergeant Major Noonan were standing by the table. They gaped at Juanita, then looked at Sharpe who did not feel inclined to offer an immediate explanation of the lady's presence. 'Loup's gone,' Sharpe told Donaju. 'I've got Sergeant Harper making sure the place is empty, so why don't you have your lads man the defences? Just in case Brigadier Loup decides to come back.'

Donaju glanced at Juanita, then turned on Noonan. 'Sergeant Major? You heard the order. Do it.'

Noonan went. El Castrador was watching Hagman unpack the dismounted mule panniers. Juanita had gone to the remnants of the fire where she was warming herself. Donaju looked at her, then gave Sharpe an inquiring look. 'The Doña Juanita,' Sharpe explained, 'is a woman of many parts. She's Lord Kiely's betrothed, General Loup's lover and an agent of the French.'

Juanita's head jerked up at the last phrase, but she made no effort to contradict Sharpe. Donaju stared at her as though he was unwilling to believe what he had just heard. Then he turned back to Sharpe with a frown. 'She and Loup?' he asked.

'Their love nest's upstairs, for Christ's sake,' Sharpe said. 'Go and look if you don't believe me. Her ladyship here let Loup into the fort last night. Her ladyship, Donaju, is a goddamned traitor.'

'Hymn sheets, sir,' Hagman interrupted in a puzzled tone. 'But bloody odd ones. I've seen things like it at church at home, you know, for the musicians, but not like this.' The old poacher had unpacked the panniers to reveal a great pile of manuscripts that were lined with staves and inscribed with words and music.

'They're very old.' Donaju was still dazed by the revelations about Juanita, but now moved across to examine the papers unearthed by Hagman. 'See, Sharpe? Just four staves instead of five. They could be two or three hundred years old. Latin words. Let's see now.' He frowned as he made a mental translation. '"Clap your hands, everyone, call unto God with a voice of victory." The psalms, I think.'

'She wasn't carrying the psalms back to our lines,' Sharpe said, and he seized the top manuscripts off the pile and began sorting through them. It took only seconds to find that there were newspapers hidden beneath the disguising manuscripts.

'These, Donaju' – Sharpe held up the newspapers – 'these are what she was carrying.'

Juanita's only reaction to the discovery was to start biting one of her nails. She glanced at the kitchen door, but Harper had come back to the house and the courtyard was now filled with his riflemen. 'Place is empty, sir. Bugger's gone,' Harper reported, 'and he left in a rare hurry, sir, for the place is still stuffed with plunder. Something drove him out in a hurry.' He nodded respectfully to Captain Donaju. 'Your fellows are manning the defences, sir.'

'They're not American newspapers this time,' Sharpe said, 'but English ones. Learned their lesson last time, didn't they? Make a newspaper too old and no one believes the stories, but these dates are just last week.' He threw the papers on the table one by one. 'The *Morning Chronicle*, the *Weekly Dispatch*, the *Salisbury Journal*, the *Staffordshire Advertiser*, someone's been busy, my lady. Who? Someone in Paris? Is that where these papers are printed?'

Juanita said nothing.

Sharpe plucked another newspaper from the pile. 'Probably printed three weeks ago in Paris and brought here just in time. After all, no one would be astonished to see a two-week-old *Shrewsbury Chronicle* in Portugal, would they? A fast-sailing ship could easily have brought it, and there'll be no drafts of troops to contradict these stories. So what are they saying about us this time?' He leafed through the newspaper, tilting it towards the candles as he turned the pages. 'Apprentice imprisoned for playing football on the Sabbath? Serve the little bugger right for trying to enjoy himself, but I don't suppose his story will drive the troops to mutiny, though something in here will.'

'I've found something,' Donaju said quietly. He had been searching the *Morning Chronicle* and now he folded the paper and held it towards Sharpe. 'A piece about the Irish Division.'

'There isn't an Irish Division,' Sharpe said, taking the newspaper. He found the item that had attracted Donaju's attention and read it aloud. '"Recent disturbances among the Hibernian troops of the army serving in Portugal,"' Sharpe read, embarrassed because he was a slow and not very certain reader, '"have persuaded the government to adopt a new and palliative"' – he had a lot of trouble with that word – '"policy. When the present campaigning season is over the Irish regiments of the army will be brigaded as a division that shall be posted to the garrisons of the Caribbean islands. The exchequer has forbidden the expense of carrying wives, doubting that many so described have benefited from the Almighty's blessing on their union. And in the tropics, doubtless, the hot Irish heads will find a climate more to their liking."'

'The same report is here.' Donaju displayed another paper, then hastily offered El Castrador an explanation of all that was happening inside the smoky kitchen.

The partisan glared at Juanita when her treachery was revealed. 'Traitor!' he spat at her. 'Your mother was a whore,' he said, so far as Sharpe was able to follow the quick, angry Spanish, 'your father a goat. You were given everything, yet you fight for Spain's enemies, while we, who have nothing, fight to save our country.' He spat again and fingered his small bone-handled knife. Juanita stiffened under the onslaught, but said nothing. Her dark eyes went back to Sharpe who had just found another version of the announcement that all the Irish regiments were to be posted to the West Indies.

'It's a clever lie,' Sharpe said, looking at Juanita, 'very clever.'

Donaju frowned. 'Why is it clever?' He had asked the question of Patrick Harper. 'Wouldn't the Irish like to be brigaded together?'

'I'm sure they would, sir, but not in the Caribbean and not without their women, God help us.'

'Half of the men would be dead of the yellow fever within three months of arriving in the islands,' Sharpe explained, 'and the other half dead within six months. Being posted to the Caribbean, Donaju, is a death sentence.' He looked at Juanita. 'So whose idea was it, my lady?'

She said nothing, just chewed on the fingernail. El Castrador shouted at her for her obstinacy and untied the small knife from his belt. Donaju blanched at the stream of obscenities and tried to restrain the big man's anger.

'Well, the story isn't true,' Sharpe interrupted the commotion. 'For a start we wouldn't be so daft as to take the Irish soldiers away from the army. Who'd win the battles else?'

Harper and Donaju smiled. Sharpe felt a quiet exultation, for if this discovery did not justify his breaking orders and marching on San Cristóbal, nothing would. He made a pile of the newspapers, then looked at Donaju. 'Why don't you send someone back to headquarters. Find Major Hogan, tell him what's here and ask him what we should be doing.'

'I'll go myself,' Donaju said, 'but what will you do?'

'I have a few things to do here first,' Sharpe said, looking at Juanita as he spoke. 'Like discovering where Loup is, and why he left in such a hurry.'

Juanita bridled. 'I have nothing to say to you, Captain.'

'Then maybe you'll say it to him.' He jerked his head towards El Castrador.

Juanita gave a fearful glance at the partisan, then looked back at Sharpe. 'When did British officers cease to be gentlemen, Captain?'

'When we began to win battles, ma'am,' Sharpe said. 'So who's it to be? Me or him?'

Donaju looked as though he might make a protest at Sharpe's behaviour, then he saw the rifleman's grim face and thought better of it. 'I'll take a newspaper to Hogan,' he said quietly, then folded the counterfeit *Morning Chronicle* into his pouch and backed from the room. Harper went with him and closed the kitchen door firmly behind him.

'Don't you worry, sir,' Harper said to Donaju once they were in the yard. 'I'll look after the lady now.'

'You will?'

'I'll dig her a nice deep grave, sir, and bury the witch upside down so that the harder she struggles the deeper she'll go. Have a safe ride back to the lines, sir.'

Donaju blanched, then went to find his horse while Harper shouted at Perkins to find some water, make a fire and brew a good strong morning cup of tea.

'You're in trouble, Richard,' Hogan said when he finally reached Sharpe. It was early evening of the day which had begun with Sharpe's stealthy approach to Loup's abandoned stronghold. 'You're in trouble. You've been shooting prisoners. God, man, I don't care if you shoot every damned prisoner between here and Paris, but why the hell did you have to tell anyone?'

Sharpe's only response was to turn from his vantage point among the rocks and wave a hand to indicate that Hogan should keep low.

'Don't you know the first rule of life, Richard?' Hogan grumbled as he tethered his horse to a boulder.

'Never get found out, sir.'

'So why the hell didn't you keep your damned mouth shut?' Hogan clambered up to Sharpe's eyrie and lay down beside the rifleman. 'So what have you found?'

'The enemy, sir.' Sharpe was five miles beyond San Cristóbal, five miles deeper inside Spain, guided there by El Castrador who had ridden back to San Cristóbal with the news that had brought Hogan out to this ridge overlooking the main road that led west out of Ciudad Rodrigo. Sharpe had reached the ridge on Doña Juanita's horse which was now picketed safely out of sight of anyone looking up from the road and there were plenty who might have looked, for Sharpe was staring down at an army. 'The French are out, sir,' he said. 'They're marching, and there are thousands of the buggers.'

Hogan drew out his own telescope. He stared at the road for a long time, then allowed a hiss of breath to escape. 'Dear God,' he said, 'dear sweet merciful God.' For a whole army was on the march. Infantry and dragoons, gunners and hussars, lancers and grenadiers, *voltigeurs* and engineers; a trail of men that looked black in the fading light, though here and there in the long column the dying sun reflected dark scarlet from the flank of a cannon being dragged by a team of oxen or horses. Thick dust clouded up from the wheels of the cannons, wagons and coaches that were keeping to the road itself, while the infantry marched in columns in the fields either side. The cavalry rode on the outermost flanks, long lines of men with steel-tipped lances and shining helmets and tossing plumes, their horses' hooves leaving long bruised marks on the spring grass of the valley. 'Dear God,' Hogan said again.

'Loup's down there,' Sharpe said. 'I saw him. That's why he left San Cristóbal. He was summoned to join the army, you see?'

'Damn it!' Hogan exploded. 'Why couldn't you forget Loup? It's Loup's fault you're in trouble! Why in the name of God couldn't you keep your mouth shut about those two damned fools you shot to death? Now bloody Valverde's saying that the Portuguese lost a prime regiment of men because you stirred up the hornet's nest, and that no sane Spaniard can ever trust a soldier to British officers. What it means, you damned fool, is that we have to parade you in front of the court of inquiry. We have to sacrifice you with Runciman.'

Sharpe stared at the Irish Major. 'Me?'

'Of course! For Christ's sake, Richard! Don't you have the first inkling of politics? The Spanish don't want Wellington as *Generalisimo*! They see that appointment as an insult to their country and they're looking for ammunition to support their cause. Ammunition like some damned fool of a rifleman fighting a private war at the expense of a fine regiment of Portuguese *caçadores* whose fate will serve as an example of what might happen to any Spanish regiments put under the Peer's command.' He paused to stare through his telescope, then pencilled a note on the cuff of his shirt. 'God damn it, Richard, we were going to have a nice quiet court of inquiry, put all the blame on Runciman and then forget what happened at San Isidro. Now you've confused everything. Did you happen to keep notes of what you've seen here?'

'I did, sir,' Sharpe said. He was still trying to come to terms with the idea that his whole career was suddenly in jeopardy. It all seemed so monstrously unfair, but he kept the resentment to himself as he handed Hogan a stiff, folded sheet of the ancient music that had concealed the counterfeit newspapers. On the back of the sheet Sharpe had pencilled a tally of the units he had watched march beneath him. It was an awesome list of battalions and squadrons and batteries, all going towards Almeida and all expecting to meet and trounce the small British army that had to try to stop them from relieving the fortress.

'So tomorrow,' Hogan said, 'they'll reach our positions. Tomorrow, Richard, we fight. And that's why.' Hogan had spotted something new in the column and now pointed far to the west. It took Sharpe a moment to train his telescope, then he saw the vast column of ox-hauled wagons that was following the French troops west. 'The relief supplies for Almeida,' Hogan said, 'all the food and ammunition the garrison wants, enough to keep them there through the summer while we lay siege, and if they can keep us in front of Almeida all summer then we'll never get across the frontier and the Lord alone knows how many Frogs will attack us next spring.' He collapsed his telescope again. 'And talking of spring, Richard, would you like to tell me exactly what you did with the Doña Juanita? Captain Donaju said he left her with you and our knife-happy friend.'

Sharpe coloured. 'I sent her home, sir.'

There was a moment's silence. 'You did what?' Hogan asked.

'I sent her back to the Crapauds, sir.'

Hogan shook his head in disbelief. 'You let an enemy agent go back to the French? Are you entirely mad, Richard?'

'She was upset, sir. She said that if I took her back to the army she'd be arrested by the Spanish authorities and tried by the *junta* in Cadiz, sir, and like as not put in front of a firing squad. I've never been one for fighting against women, sir. And we know who she is, don't we? So she can't do any harm now.'

Hogan closed his eyes and rested his head on his forearm. 'Dear God, in Your infinite mercy please save this poor bugger's soul because Wellington sure as hell will not. Did it not occur to you, Richard, that I would have liked to talk to the lady?'

'It did, sir. But she was frightened. And she didn't want me to leave her alone with El Castrador. I was just being a gentleman, sir.'

'I thought you didn't approve of the gentry fighting wars. So what did you do? Pat her little bum, dry her maidenly tears, then give her a soulful kiss and send her down to Loup so she could tell him how you're stranded in San Cristóbal?'

'I let her go a couple of miles back' – Sharpe jerked his head north and west – 'and made her travel on foot, sir, without any boots. I reckoned that would slow her down. And she did talk to me before she left, sir. It's all written down there if you can make out my handwriting. She says she distributed the newspapers, sir. She took them down to Irish encampments, sir.'

'The only thing that Doña Juanita could distribute, Richard, is the pox. Jesus wept! You let that bitch twist you round her little fingers. For Christ's sake, Richard, I already knew she was the one fetching the newspapers. She was an errand girl. The real villain is someone else and I was hoping to follow her to him. Now you've buggered that up. Jesus!' Hogan paused to contain his anger, then shook his head wearily. 'But at least she left you your bloody jacket.'

Sharpe frowned in puzzlement. 'My jacket, sir?'

'Remember what I told you, Richard? How the Lady Juanita collects the uniforms of every man she sleeps with. Her wardrobes must be vast, but I'm glad to see she won't be hanging a jacket of rifle green along with all the other coats.'

'No, sir,' Sharpe said, and blushed an even deeper red. 'Sorry, sir.'

'It can't be helped,' Hogan said as he wriggled back from the crest. 'You're an idiot for women and always were. If we thrash Masséna then the lady can't do us much harm, and if we don't, then the war's probably lost anyway. Let's get you the hell out of here. You're on administrative duties till your crucifixion.' He backed away from the crest and put his telescope back into a belt pouch. 'I'll do my best for you, God knows why, but your best prayer, Richard, and I hate to tell you this, is that we lose this battle. Because if we do it'll be such a disaster that no one will have the time or energy to remember your idiocy.'

It was dark by the time they reached San Cristóbal. Donaju had returned to the village with Hogan and now he led his fifty men of the Real Compañía Irlandesa back towards the British lines. 'I saw Lord Kiely at headquarters,' he told Sharpe.

'What did you tell him?'

'I told him his lover was an *afrancesada* and that she was sleeping with Loup.' Donaju's tone was stark. 'And I told him he was a fool.'

'What did he say?'

Donaju shrugged. 'What do you think? He's an aristocrat, he has pride. He told me to go to hell.'

'And tomorrow,' Sharpe said, 'we all might do just that.' Because tomorrow the French would attack and he would once again see those vast blue columns drummed forward beneath their eagles and listen to the skull-splitting sound of massed French batteries pounding away. He shuddered at the thought, then turned to watch his greenjackets march past. 'Perkins,' he suddenly shouted, 'come here!'

Perkins had been trying to hide on the far side of the column, but now, sheepishly, he came to stand in front of Sharpe. Harper came with him. 'It isn't his fault, sir,' Harper said hurriedly.

'Shut up,' Sharpe said, and looked down at Perkins. 'Where, Perkins, is your green jacket?'

'Stolen, sir.' Perkins was in shirt, boots and trousers over which his equipment was belted. 'It got wet, sir, when I was carrying water round to the lads so I hung it out to dry and it was stolen, sir.'

'That lady was not so far away, sir, from where he hung it,' Harper said meaningfully.

'Why would she steal a rifleman's jacket?' Sharpe asked, but sensed a blush beginning. He was glad it was dark.

'Why would anyone want Perkins's jacket, sir?' Harper asked. 'It was a threadbare thing at best, so it was, and too small to fit most men. But I reckon it was stolen, sir, and I don't reckon Perkins should pay for it. 'Twasn't his fault.'

'Go away, Perkins,' Sharpe said.

'Yes, sir, thank you, sir.'

Harper watched the boy run back to his file. 'And why would the Lady Juanita steal a jacket? That puzzles me, sir, truly does, for I can't think it was anyone else who took it.'

'She didn't steal it,' Sharpe said, 'the lying bitch earned it. Now keep on going. We've a way to go yet, Pat.' Though whether the road led anywhere good, he no longer knew, for he was a scapegoat and he faced the foregone conclusions of a court of inquiry and in the dark, following his men west, he shivered.

There were only two sentries at the door to the house which served as Wellington's headquarters. Other generals might conclude that their dignity demanded a whole company of soldiers, or even a whole battalion, but Wellington never wanted more than two men and they were only there to keep away the town's children and to control the more importunate petitioners who believed the General could solve their problems with a stroke of his quill pen. Merchants came seeking contracts to supply the army with fouled beef or with bolts of linen stored too long in moth-infested warehouses, officers came seeking redress against imagined slights, and priests arrived to complain that Protestant British soldiers mocked the holy church, and in the midst of these distractions the General tried to solve his own problems: the lack of entrenching tools, the paucity of heavy guns that could grind down a fortress's defences and the ever-pressing duty of convincing a nervous ministry in London that his campaign was not doomed.

So Lord Kiely was not a welcome visitor following the General's customary early dinner of roast saddle of mutton with vinegar sauce. Nor did it help that Kiely had plainly forti-fied himself with brandy for this confrontation with Wellington who, early in his career, had decided that an over-indulgence in alcohol hurt a man's abilities as a soldier. 'One man in this army had better stay sober,' he liked to say of himself, and now, seated behind a table in the room that served as his office, parlour and bedroom, he looked dourly at the flushed, excited

Kiely who had arrived with an urgent request. Urgent to Kiely, if not to anyone else.

Candles flickered on the table that was spread with maps. A galloper had come from Hogan reporting that the French were out and marching on the southern road that led through Fuentes de Oñoro. That news was not unexpected, but it meant that the General's plans were now to be subjected to the test of cannon fire and musket volleys. 'I am busy, Kiely,' Wellington said icily.

'I ask only that my unit be allowed to take the forefront of the battle line,' Kiely said with the careful dignity of a man who knows that liquor might otherwise slur his words.

'No,' Wellington said. The General's aide, standing in the window, gestured towards the door, but Kiely ignored the invitation to leave.

'We have been ill used, my Lord,' he said unwisely. 'We came here at the request of my sovereign in good faith, expecting to be properly employed, and instead you have ignored us, denied us our supplies –'

'No!' The loudness of the word was such that the sentries at the house's front step were visibly startled. Then they looked at each other and grinned. The General had a temper, though it was rarely seen, but when Wellington did choose to unleash the full fury of his personality it was an awesome thing.

The General stared up at his visitor. His voice dropped to a conversational level, but it still reeked of scorn. 'You came here, sir, ill prepared, unwanted, unfunded, and expected me, sir, to provide both your men's livelihoods and their accoutrements, and in return, sir, you have offered me insolence and, worse, betrayal. You did not come at His Majesty's bidding, but because the enemy desired you to come, and it is now my desire that you should go. And you shall go, sir, with honour because it is unthinkable that we should send away King Ferdinand's household troops in any other condition, but that honour, sir, has been earned at the expense of other men. Your troops, sir, shall serve in the battle, for there will be no opportunity to remove them before the French arrive, but they shall serve as guards on my ammunition park. You may choose to command them or to sulk in your tent. Good day to you, my Lord.'

'My Lord?' The aide addressed Kiely tactfully, stepping towards the door.

But Lord Kiely was blind to tact. 'Insolence?' He pounced on the word. 'My God, but I command King Ferdinand's guard and –'

'And King Ferdinand, sir, is a prisoner!' Wellington snapped. 'Which does not speak, sir, for the efficacy of his guard. You came here, sir, with your adulterous whore, flaunting her like a prinked bitch, and the whore, sir, is a traitor! The whore, sir, has been doing her best to destroy this army and the only providence that has saved this army from her ministrations is that her best, thank God, is no better than your own! Your request is denied, good day.'

Wellington looked down to his papers. Kiely had other complaints to make, chief of them the way in which he had been manhandled and insulted by Captain Sharpe, but now he stood insulted by Wellington too. Lord Kiely was just summoning his last reserves of courage to protest this treatment when the aide took firm hold of his elbow and pulled him towards the door and Kiely found himself powerless to resist. 'Perhaps your Lordship requires some refreshment?' the aide inquired emolliently as he steered the furious Kiely out into the hallway where a group of curious officers looked with pity at the disgraced man. Kiely shook the aide's hand away, seized his hat and sword from the hall table, and stalked out of the front door without another word. He ignored the two sentries as they presented arms.

'Nosey saw him off fast enough,' one of the sentries said, then snapped to attention again as Edward Pakenham, the Adjutant General, climbed the steps.

Kiely seemed oblivious of Pakenham's cheerful greeting. Instead he walked down the street in a blind rage, passing long lines of guns that were slowly negotiating the town's narrow lanes, but he saw nothing and understood nothing except that he had failed. Just as he had failed at everything, he told himself, but none of the failure was his fault. The cards had run against him, and that was how he had lost what small fortune his mother had left to him after she had squandered her wealth on the damned church and on the damned Irish rebels who always managed to end up on British gallows, and the same bad luck explained why he had failed to win the hand of at least two Madrid heiresses who had preferred to marry Spaniards of the blood rather than a peer without a country. Kiely's self-pity welled up at the memories of their rejections. In Madrid he was a second-class citizen because he could not trace his lineage back to some medieval brute who had fought against the Moors, while in this army, he decided, he was an outcast because he was Irish.

Yet the worst insult of all was Juanita's betrayal. Juanita the wild, unconventional, clever and seductive woman whom Kiely had imagined himself marrying. She had money, she had noble blood and other men had looked enviously at Kiely when Juanita was at his side. Yet all along, he supposed, she had been deceiving him. She had given herself to Loup. She had lain in Loup's arms and Kiely presumed she had told all his secrets to Loup, and he imagined their laughter as they lay entangled in their bed and once again the anger and the pity swelled inside him. There were tears in his eyes as he realized he would be the laughing stock of all Madrid and all this army.

He entered a church. Not because he wanted to pray, but

because he could think of nowhere else to go. He could not face going back to his quarters in General Valverde's lodgings where everyone would look at him and whisper that he was a cuckold.

The church was crowded with dark-shawled women waiting to make their confessions. Phalanxes of candles glimmered in front of statues, altars and paintings. The small lights glittered off the gilded pillars and from the massive silver cross on the high altar that still had its white Easter frontal.

Kiely went to the altar steps. His sword clattered on the marble as he knelt and stared at the rood. He was being crucified too, he told himself, and by smaller men who did not understand his noble aims. He took a flask from his pocket and tipped it to his lips, sucking at the fierce Spanish brandy as though it would save his life.

'Are you well, my son?' A priest had come soft-footed to Kiely's side.

'Go away,' Kiely said.

'The hat, my son,' the priest said nervously. 'This is God's house.'

Kiely snatched the plumed hat from his head. 'Go away,' he said again.

'God preserve you,' the priest said and walked back into the shadows. The women waiting to make their confessions glanced nervously at the finely uniformed officer and wondered if he was praying for victory over the approaching French. Everyone knew the blue-coated enemy was coming again and householders were burying their valuables in their gardens in case Masséna's dreaded veterans beat the British aside and came back to sack the town.

Kiely finished the flask. His head spun with liquor, shame and anger. Behind the silver rood in a niche above the high altar was a statue of Our Lady. She wore a diadem of stars, a blue robe,

218

and carried lilies in her hands. It had been a long time since Kiely had stared at such an image. His mother had loved such things. She had forced him to confession and to the sacrament, and had chided him for failing her. She had used to pray to the Virgin, claiming a special kinship with Our Lady as another disappointed woman who had known a mother's sadness. 'Bitch,' Kiely said aloud, staring at the blue-robed statue, 'bitch!' He had hated his mother, just as he hated the church. Juanita had shared Kiely's contempt for the church, but Juanita was another man's lover. Maybe she had always been another man's lover. She had lain with Loup and God knows how many other men and all the while Kiely had been planning to make her a countess and to show off her beauty in all the great capitals of Europe. Tears trickled down his cheeks as he thought of her betrayal and as he remembered his humiliation at the hands of Captain Sharpe. That last memory filled him with a sudden fury. 'Bitch!' he shouted at the Virgin Mary. He stood up and hurled the empty flask at her statue behind the altar. 'Whore bitch!' he cried as the flask bounced harmlessly off the Virgin's blue robe.

The women screamed. The priest ran towards his Lordship, then stopped in terror because Kiely had drawn the pistol from his holster. The click of the gun's lock echoed loud in the cavernous church as Kiely thumbed back the heavy hammer.

'Bitch!' Kiely spat the word at the statue. 'Lying, whoring, thieving, two-faced, leprous bitch!' Tears poured down his cheeks as he aimed the pistol.

'No!' the priest implored as the women's shrieks filled the church. 'Please! No! Think of the blessed Virgin, please!'

Kiely turned on the man. 'Call her a virgin, do you? You think she'd be a virgin after the Legions had hammered through Galilee?' He laughed wildly, then turned back to the statue. 'You whore bitch!' he shouted as he trained the pistol again. 'You filthy whore bitch!'

219

'No!' the priest cried despairingly.

Kiely pulled the trigger.

The heavy bullet smashed through his palate and punched out a palm-sized patch of his skull as it exited. Blood and brain splashed as high as the Virgin's diadem of stars, but none landed on Our Lady. Instead the gore spattered across the sanctuary steps, doused a handful of candles, then trickled down to the nave. Kiely's dead body fell back, his head a mangled horror of blood, brain and bone.

The screams in the church slowly died to be replaced by the rumble of wheels in the street as more guns were dragged towards the east.

And towards the French. Who were coming to reclaim Portugal and break the insolent British at a narrow bridge across the Coa.

PART TWO

CHAPTER SEVEN

The Real Compañía Irlandesa bivouacked on the plateau north and west of Fuentes de Oñoro. The village lay astride the southernmost road leading from Ciudad Rodrigo to Almeida and in the night Wellington's army had closed about the village that now threatened to become a battlefield. The dawn mist hid the eastern countryside where the French army readied itself, while up on the plateau Wellington's forces were a smoke-obscured chaos of troops, horses and wagons. Guns were parked on the plateau's eastern crest, their barrels pointing across the Dos Casas stream that marked the army's forward line.

Donaju discovered Sharpe squinting sideways into a scrap of mirror in an attempt to cut his own hair. The sides and the front were easy enough to trim, the difficulty always lay in the rear. 'Just like soldiering,' Sharpe said.

'You've heard about Kiely?' Donaju, suddenly in command of the Real Compañía Irlandesa, ignored Sharpe's gnomic comment.

Sharpe snipped, frowned, then tried to repair the damage by snipping again, but it only made things worse. 'Blew his head off, I heard.'

Donaju flinched at Sharpe's callousness, but made no protest. 'I can't believe he would do such a thing,' he said instead.

'Too much pride, not enough sense. Sounds like most bloody aristocrats to me. These damn scissors are blunt.'

Donaju frowned. 'Why don't you have a servant?'

'Can't afford one. Besides, I've always looked after myself.'

'And cut your own hair?'

'There's a pretty girl among the battalion wives who usually cuts it,' Sharpe said. But Sally Clayton, like the rest of the South Essex, was far away. The South Essex was too shrunken by war to serve in the battle line and now was doing guard duty on the army's Portuguese depots and thus would be spared Marshal Masséna's battle to relieve Almeida and cut the British retreat across the Coa.

'Father Sarsfield is burying Kiely tomorrow,' Donaju said.

'Father Sarsfield might be burying a lot of us tomorrow,' Sharpe said. 'If they bury us at all. Have you ever seen a battle-field a year after the fighting? It's like a boneyard. Skulls lying about like boulders, and fox-chewed bones everywhere. Bugger this,' he said savagely as he gave his hair a last forlorn chop.

'Kiely can't even be buried in a churchyard' – Donaju did not want to think about battlefields on this ominous morning – 'because it was suicide.'

'There aren't many soldiers who get a proper grave,' Sharpe said, 'so I wouldn't grieve for Kiely. We'll be lucky if any of us get a proper hole, let alone a stone on top. Dan!' he shouted to Hagman.

'Sir?'

'Your bloody scissors are blunt.'

'Sharpened them last night, sir,' Hagman said stoically. 'It's like my father always said, sir, only a bad workman blames his tools, sir.'

Sharpe tossed the scissors across to Hagman, then brushed the cut strands of hair from his shirt. 'You're better off without Kiely,' he told Donaju.

'To guard the ammunition park?' Donaju said bitterly. 'We would have done better to stay in Madrid.'

'To be thought of as traitors?' Sharpe asked as he pulled on his jacket. 'Listen, Donaju, you're alive and Kiely isn't. You've got yourself a good company to command. So what if you're guarding the ammunition? You think that isn't important? What happens if the Crapauds break through?'

Donaju did not seem cheered by Sharpe's opinions. 'We're orphans,' he said self-pityingly. 'No one cares what happens to us.'

'Why do you want someone to care?' Sharpe asked bluntly. 'You're a soldier, Donaju, not a child. They issued you with a sword and a gun so you could take care of yourself, not have others take care of you. But as it happens, they do care. They care enough to send the whole lot of you to Cadiz, and I care enough to tell you that you've got two choices. You can go to Cadiz whipped and with your men knowing they've been whipped, or you can go back with your pride intact. It's up to you, but I know which one I'd choose.'

This was the first Donaju had heard of the Real Compañía Irlandesa's proposed move to Cadiz and he frowned as he tried to work out whether Sharpe was being serious. 'You're sure about Cadiz?'

'Of course I'm sure,' Sharpe said. 'General Valverde's been pulling strings. He doesn't think you should be here at all, so now you're off to join the rest of the Spanish army.'

Donaju digested the news for a few seconds, then nodded approval. 'Good,' he said enthusiastically. 'They should have sent us there in the first place.' He sipped his mug of tea and made a wry face at the taste. 'What happens to you now?'

'I'm ordered to stay with you till someone tells me to go somewhere else,' Sharpe said. He did not want to admit that he was facing a court of inquiry, not because he was ashamed of his conduct, but because he did not want other men's sympathies. The court was a battle that he would have to face when the time came.

'You're guarding the ammunition?' Donaju seemed surprised.

'Someone has to,' Sharpe said. 'But don't worry, Donaju, they'll take me away from you before you go to Cadiz. Valverde doesn't want me there.'

'So what do we do today?' Donaju asked nervously.

'Today,' Sharpe said, 'we do our duty. And there are fifty thousand Frogs doing theirs, and somewhere over that hill, Donaju, their duty and our duty will get bloody contradictory.'

'It will be bad,' Donaju said, not quite as a statement and not quite as a question either.

Sharpe heard the nervousness. Donaju had never been in a major battle and any man, however brave, was right to be nervous at the prospect. 'It'll be bad,' Sharpe said. 'The noise is the worst, that and the powder fog, but always remember one thing: it's just as bad for the French. And I'll tell you another thing. I don't know why, and maybe it's just my imagination, but the Frogs always seem to break before we do. Just when you think you can't hold on for a minute longer, count to ten and by the time you reach six the bloody Frogs will have turned tall and buggered off. Now watch out, here's trouble.'

The trouble was manifested by the approach of a thin, tall and bespectacled major in the blue coat of the Royal Artillery. He was carrying a sheaf of papers that kept coming loose as he tried to find one particular sheet among the rest. The errant sheets were being fielded by two nervous red-coated privates, one of whom had his arm in a dirty sling while the other was struggling along on a crutch. The Major waved at Sharpe and Donaju, thus releasing another flutter of paper. 'The thing is,' the Major said without any attempt to introduce himself, 'that the divisions have their own ammunition parks. One or

226

the other, I said, make up your mind! But no! Divisions will be independent! Which leaves us, you understand, with the central reserve. They call it that, though God knows it's rarely in the centre and, of course, in the very nature of things, we are never told what stocks the divisions themselves hold. They demand more, we yield, and suddenly there is none. It is a problem. Let us hope and pray the French do things worse. Is that tea?' The Major, who had a broad Scottish accent, peered hopefully at the mug in Donaju's hand.

'It is, sir,' Donaju said, 'but foul.'

'Let me taste it, I beg you. Thank you. Pick up that paper, Magog, the day's battle may depend upon it. Gog and Magog,' he introduced the two hapless privates. 'Gog is bereft one arm, Magog one leg, and both the rogues are Welsh. Together they are a Welshman and a half, and the three of us, or two and a half if I am to be exact, comprise the entire staff complement of the central reserve.' The Major smiled suddenly. 'Alexander Tarrant,' he introduced himself. 'Major in the artillery but seconded to the Quartermaster General's staff. I think of myself as the Assistant-Assistant-Assistant Quartermaster General, and you, I suspect, are the new Assistant-Assistant-Assistant-Assistant Quartermaster Generals? Which means that Gog and Magog are now Assistant-Assistant-Assistant-Assistant-Assistant Quartermaster Generals. Demoted, by God! Will their careers ever recover? This tea is delicious, though tepid. You must be Captain Sharpe?'

'Yes, sir.'

'An honour, Sharpe, 'pon my soul, an honour.' Tarrant thrust out a hand, thus releasing a cascade of paper. 'Heard about the dickie-bird, Sharpe, and confess I was moved mightily.' It took Sharpe half a second to realize that Tarrant was talking about the eagle that Sharpe had captured at Talavera, but before he could respond the Major was already talking again. 'And you must be Donaju of the royal guard? 'Pon my soul, Gog, but we're in elevated company! You'll have to mind your manners today!'

'Private Hughes, sir,' Gog introduced himself to Sharpe, 'and that's my brother.' He gestured with his one arm at Magog.

'The Hughes brothers,' Tarrant explained, 'were wounded in their country's service and reduced to my servitude. Till now, Sharpe, they have been the sole guard for the ammunition. Gog would kick intruders and Magog shake his crutch at them. Once recovered, of course, they will return to duty and I shall be provided with yet more cripples to protect the powder and shot. Except today, Donaju, I have your fine fellows. Let us examine your duties!'

The duties were hardly onerous. The central reserve was just that, a place where hard-pressed divisions, brigades or even battalions could send for more ammunition. A motley collection of Royal Wagon Train drivers augmented by muleteers and carters recruited from the local population were available to deliver the infantry cartridges while the artillery usually provided their own transport. The difficulty of his own job, Tarrant said, was in working out which requests were frivolous and which desperate. 'I like to keep the supplies intact,' the Scotsman said, 'until we near the end of an engagement. Anyone requesting ammunition in the first few hours is either already defeated or merely nervous. These papers purport to describe the divisional reserves, though the Lord alone knows how accurate they are.' He thrust the papers at Sharpe, then pulled them back in case Sharpe muddled them. 'Lastly, of course,' Tarrant went on, 'there is always the problem of making certain the ammunition gets through. Drivers can be' – he paused, looking for a word – 'cowards!' he finally said, then frowned at the severity of the judgement. 'Not all, of course, and some are wonderfully stout-hearted, but the quality isn't consistent.

Perhaps, gentlemen, when the fighting gets bloody, I might rely on your men to fortify the drivers' bravery?' He made this inquiry nervously, as though half expecting that Sharpe or Donaju might refuse. When neither offered a demurral, he smiled. 'Good! Well, Sharpe, maybe you'd like to survey the landscape? Can't despatch ammunition without knowing whither it's bound.'

The offer gave Sharpe a temporary freedom. He knew that both he and Donaju had been shuffled aside as inconveniences and that Tarrant needed neither of them, yet still a battle was to be fought and the more Sharpe understood of the battlefield the better. 'Because if things go bad, Pat,' he told Harper as the two of them walked towards the gun line on the misted plateau's crest, 'we'll be in the thick of it.' The two carried their weapons, but had left their packs and greatcoats with the ammunition wagons.

'Still seems odd,' Harper said, 'having nothing proper to do.'

'Bloody Frogs might find us work,' Sharpe said dourly. The two men were standing at the British gun line that faced east into the rising sun that was making the mist glow above the Dos Casas stream. That stream flowed south along the foot of the high, flat-topped ridge where Sharpe and Harper were standing and which barred the French routes to Almeida. The French could have committed suicide by attacking directly over the stream and fighting up the ridge's steep escarpment into the face of the British guns, but barring that unlikely self-destruction there were only two other routes to the besieged garrison at Almeida. One led north around the ridge, but that road was barred by the still formidable ruins of Fort Concepción, and Wellington had decided that Masséna would try this southern road that led through Fuentes de Oñoro.

The village lay where the ridge fell to a wide, marshy plain above which the morning mist now shredded and faded. The road from Ciudad Rodrigo ran white and straight across that flat land to where it forded the Dos Casas stream. Once over the stream the road climbed the hill between the village houses to reach the plateau where it forked into two roads. One road led to Almeida a dozen miles to the north-west and the other to Castello Bom and its murderously narrow bridge across the deep gorge of the Coa. If the French were to reach either road and so relieve the besieged town and force the redcoats back to the bottleneck of the narrow bridge, then they must first fight up the steep village streets of Fuentes de Oñoro which was garrisoned with a mix of redcoats and greenjackets.

The ridge and the village both demanded that the enemy fight uphill, but there was a second and much more inviting option open to the French. A second road ran west across the plain south of the village. That second road ran through flat country and led to the passable fords that crossed the Coa further south. Those fords were the only place Wellington could hope to withdraw his guns, wagons and wounded if he was forced to retreat into Portugal, and if the French threatened to outflank Fuentes de Oñoro by looping deep around the southern plain then Wellington would have to come down from the plateau to defend his escape route. If he chose not to come down from the heights then he would abandon the only routes that offered a safe crossing of the River Coa. Such a decision to let the French cut the southern roads would commit Wellington's army to victory or to utter annihilation. It was a choice Sharpe would not have wanted to make himself.

'God save Ireland,' Harper suddenly said, 'but would you look at that?'

Sharpe had been looking south towards the inviting flat meadows that offered such an easy route around Fuentes de Oñoro's flank, but now he looked east to where Harper was staring.

And to where the mist had thinned to reveal a long, dark grove of cork oaks and holm oaks, and out of that grove, just where the white road left the dark trees, an army was appearing. Masséna's men must have bivouacked on the trees' far side and the smoke of their morning fires had melded with the mist to look like cloud, but now, in a grimly threatening silence, the French army debouched onto the plain that lapped wide about the village.

Some of the British gunners leaped to their guns' trails and began handspiking the cannons around so that the barrels were aimed at the place where the road came from the trees, but a gunner colonel trotted along the line and shouted at the crews to hold their fire. 'Let them come closer! Hold your fire! Let's see where they place their batteries! Don't waste your powder. Morning, John! Nice one again!' the Colonel called to an acquaintance, then touched his hat in a polite greeting to the two strange riflemen. 'You boys will have some trade today, I don't doubt.'

'You too, Colonel,' Sharpe said.

The Colonel spurred on and Sharpe turned back to the east. He drew out his telescope and leaned on a gunwheel to steady the spyglass's long barrel.

French infantry was forming at the tree line just behind the deploying batteries of French artillery. The guns' teams of oxen and horses were being led back into the shelter of the oaks while squads of gunners hoisted the hugely heavy cannon barrels out of their rear travelling trunnion holes and moved them into the forward fighting holes where other men used hammers to fasten the capsquares over the newly placed trunnions. Other gunners were piling ammunition close to the guns: squat cylinders of roundshot ready-strapped to their canvas bags of gunpowder. 'Looks like solid shot,' Sharpe told Harper. 'They'll be aiming for the village.'

The British gunners near Sharpe were making their own

preparations. The guns' ready magazines held a mixture of roundshot and case shot. The roundshot were solid iron balls that would plunge wickedly through advancing infantry, while the case shot was Britain's secret weapon: the one artillery projectile that no other nation had learned to make. It was a hollow iron ball filled with musket bullets that were packed about a small powder charge that was ignited by a fuse. When the powder exploded it shattered the outer casing and spread the musket balls in a killing fan. If the case shot was properly employed it would explode just above and ahead of the advancing infantry and the secret to that horror lay in the missile's fusing. The fuses were wooden or reed tubes filled with powder and marked into lengths, each small division of the marked length representing half a second of burning time. The fuses were cut for the desired time, then pushed into the case shot and ignited by the firing of the gun itself, but a fuse that had been left too long would let the shot scream safely over the enemy's heads while one cut too short would explode prematurely. Gunner sergeants were cutting the fuses in different lengths, then laying the ammunition in piles that represented the different ranges. The first shells had fuses over half an inch long that would delay the explosion until the shot had carried eleven hundred yards while the shortest fuses were tiny stubs measuring hardly more than a fifth of an inch that would ignite the charge at six hundred and fifty yards. Once the enemy infantry was inside that distance the gunners would switch to roundshot alone and after that, when the French had closed to within three hundred and fifty yards, the guns would employ canister: tin cylinders crammed with musket balls that spread apart at the very muzzle of the cannon as the thin tin was shredded by the gun's powder charge.

These guns would be firing down the slope and over the stream so that the French infantry would be exposed to shell or shot for their whole approach. That infantry was now forming its columns. Sharpe tried to count the eagles, but there were so many standards and so much movement among the enemy that it was hard to make an accurate assessment. 'At least a dozen battalions,' he said.

'So where are the others?' Harper asked.

'God knows,' Sharpe said. During his reconnaissance with Hogan the night before he had estimated that the French were marching to Almeida with at least eighty infantry battalions, but he could only see a fraction of that host forming their attack columns at the edge of the far woods. 'Twelve thousand men?' he guessed.

The last mist evaporated from the village just as the French opened fire. The opening salvo was ragged as the gun captains fired in turn so that they could observe the fall of their shot and so make adjustments to their guns' aim. The first shot fell short, then bounced up over the few houses and walled gardens on the far bank to plough into a tiled roof halfway up the village slope. The sound of the gun arrived after the crash of falling tiles and splintering beams. The second shot cracked into an apple tree on the stream's eastern bank and scattered a small shower of white blossom before it ricocheted into the water, but the next few rounds were all aimed straight and hammered into the village houses. The British gunners muttered grudging approval of the enemy gunners' expertise.

'I wonder what poor sods are holding the village,' Harper said.

'Let's go and find out.'

'I'm honestly not that curious, sir,' Harper protested, but followed Sharpe along the plateau's crest. The high ground ended just above the village where the plateau bent at a right angle to run due west back into the hills. In the angle of the bend, directly above the village, were two rocky knolls on one of which was built the village church with its stork's ragged nest perched precariously on the bell tower. The church's grave-yard occupied the east-facing slope between the church and the village, and riflemen were crouched behind the mounded graves and canted stones, just as they were crouched among the outcrops of the second rocky knoll. Between the two stone peaks, on a saddle of short springy turf where yellow ragweed grew and where the Almeida road reached the high ground after zigzagging up beside the graveyard, a knot of staff officers sat on their horses and watched the French cannonade which had begun to cloud the distant view with a dirty bank of smoke that twitched each time a roundshot blasted through. The cannon balls were crashing remorselessly into the village, smashing tile and thatch, splintering beams and toppling walls. The sound of the gunfire was a pounding that was palpable in the warm spring air, yet here, on the high ground above Fuentes de Oñoro, it was almost as though the battle for the village was something happening far away.

Sharpe led Harper on a wide detour behind the group of staff officers. 'Nosey's there,' he explained to Harper, 'and I don't need him glaring at me.'

'In his bad books, are we?'

'More than that, Pat. I'm facing a bloody court of inquiry.' Sharpe had not been willing to confess the truth to Donaju, but Harper was a friend and so he told him the story, and the bitterness of his plight could not help but spill over. 'What was I supposed to do, Pat? Let those raping bastards live?'

'What will the court do to you?'

'Christ knows. At worst? Order a court martial and have me thrown out of the army. At best? Break me down to lieutenant. But that'll be the end of me. They'll make me a storekeeper again, then put me in charge of bloody lists at some bloody depot where I can drink myself to death.'

'But they have to prove you shot those buggers! God save Ireland, but none of us will say a word. Jesus, I'd kill anyone who said different!'

'But there are others, Pat. Runciman and Sarsfield.'

'They won't say a word, sir.'

'May be too late anyway. General bloody Valverde knows, and that's all that matters. He's got his knife stuck into me and there's bugger all I can do about it.'

'Could shoot the bastard,' Harper said.

'You won't catch him alone,' Sharpe said. He had dreamed of shooting Valverde, but doubted he would have the opportunity. 'And Hogan says that bloody Loup might even send an official complaint!'

'It isn't fair, sir,' Harper complained.

'No, Pat, it isn't, but it hasn't happened yet, and Loup might walk into a cannon ball today. But not a word to anyone, Pat. I don't want half the bloody army discussing it.'

'I'll keep quiet, sir,' Harper promised, though he could not imagine the news not getting round the army, nor could he imagine how anyone would think justice might be served by sacrificing an officer for shooting two French bastards. He followed Sharpe between two parked wagons and a brigade of seated infantry. Sharpe recognized the pale-green facings of the 24th, a Warwickshire regiment, while beyond them were the kilted and bonneted Highlanders of the 79th. The Highlanders' pipers were playing a wild tune to the tattoo of drums, trying to rival the deeper percussive blasts of the French cannonade. Sharpe guessed the two battalions formed the reserve poised to go down into Fuentes de Oñoro's streets if the French looked like capturing the village. A third battalion was just joining the reserve brigade as Sharpe turned towards the sound of breaking tiles and cracking stone.

'Right, down here,' Sharpe said. He had spotted a track that

235

led beside the graveyard's southern wall. It was a precipitous track, probably made by goats, and the two men had to use their hands to steady themselves on the steep top portion of the slope, then they ran down the last few yards to the scanty cover of an alleyway where they were greeted by the sudden appearance of a nervous redcoat who came round the corner with levelled musket. 'Hold your fire, lad!' Sharpe called. 'Anyone who comes down here is probably on your side, and if they're not you're in trouble.'

'Sorry, sir,' the boy said, then ducked as a scrap of tile whistled overhead. 'They're a bit lively, sir,' he added.

'Time to worry, lad, is when they stop firing,' Sharpe said, 'because that means the infantry are on their way. Who's in charge here?'

'Don't know, sir. Unless it's Sergeant Patterson.'

'I doubt it, lad, but thanks anyway.' Sharpe ran from the alley's end, turned down a side street, dodged right into another street, jumped down a steep flight of stone stairs littered with broken tiles and so found himself in the main street which ran down the hill in a series of sharp twists. A roundshot hit the street's centre just as he ducked down beside a dungheap. The ball ploughed up a patch of stone and earth, then bounced to smash into a reed-thatched cattle byre as another roundshot splayed apart some roof beams across the street. Still more shots crashed home as the French gunners put in a sudden energetic spell. Sharpe and Harper took temporary cover in a doorway that bore the fading chalk marks from both armies' billeting officers; one mark read 5/4/60 meaning that five men of number four company of the 60th Rifles had been billeted in the tiny cottage, while just above it was a legend saying that seven Frenchmen, the mark carried the enemy's strange cross-bar on the shank of the 7, of the 82nd of the Line had once been posted to the house that now lacked its roof. Dust drifted like mist in what had been the front room where a torn sacking curtain fluttered forlornly at a window. The village's inhabitants and their belongings had been carried in army wagons to the nearby town of Frenada, but inevitably some of the villagers' possessions had been left behind. One doorway was barricaded with a child's cot while another had a pair of benches as a firestep. A mixture of riflemen and redcoats garrisoned the town and they were sheltering from the cannonade by crouching behind the thickest walls of the deserted houses. The stone walls could not stop every French roundshot and Sharpe had already passed three dead men put out in the street and seen a half-dozen wounded men making their slow way back up towards the ridge. 'What unit are you?' he called to a sergeant sheltering behind the cot across the street.

'Third Division Light Companies, sir!' the sergeant called back.

'And the First Division!' another voice chimed in. 'Don't forget the First Division!'

It seemed the army had collected the cream of two divisions, their skirmishers, and put them into Fuentes de Oñoro. Skirmishers were the brightest men, the ones trained to fight independently, and this village was no place for men who could only stand in the battle line and fire volleys. This was going to be a place of sharpshooting and street brawls, a place where men would be separated from their officers and forced to fight without orders. 'Who's in charge of you all?' Sharpe asked the sergeant.

'Colonel Williams of the 60th, sir. Down there, in the inn.'

'Thanks!' Sharpe and Harper edged down the side of the street. A roundshot rumbled overhead to drive into a roof. A scream sounded, then was cut off. The inn was the very same tavern where Sharpe had first met El Castrador and where now, in the same garden with the half-severed vine, he found Colonel Williams and his small staff.

'It's Sharpe, isn't it? Come to help us?' Williams was a genial Welshman from the 60th Rifles. 'Don't know you,' he said to Harper.

'Sergeant Harper, sir.'

'You look handy to have in a scrap, Sergeant,' Williams said. 'Damned noisy today, eh?' he added in mild complaint of the cannonade. He was standing on a bench that gave him a view over the garden wall and the roofs of the lower houses. 'So what brings you here, Sharpe?'

'I'm just making sure we know where to deliver ammunition, sir.'

Williams offered Sharpe an owlish gaze of surprise. 'Got you fetching and carrying, have they? Seems a waste of time for a man of your talents, Sharpe. And I don't think you'll find much custom here. My boys are all well supplied. Eighty rounds a man, two thousand men, and as many cartridges again stacked up in the church. Sweet Jesus!' This last imprecation was caused by a roundshot that must have gone within two feet of the Colonel's head, forcing him to duck hard down. It crashed into a house, there was a tumble of falling stone and then, quite suddenly, silence.

Sharpe tensed. The silence, after the crash of the guns and the splintering thunder of the roundshots' destructive impacts, was unnerving. Maybe, he thought, it was just a strange pause, like the sudden coincidental silence that could descend on a room of lively talkers during that moment when an angel was said to be passing over the room, and maybe an angel had flickered across the gunsmoke and all the French cannon had found themselves momentarily unloaded. Sharpe almost found himself praying for the guns to start again, but the silence stretched and stretched, threatening to be replaced by something much worse than a cannonade. Somewhere in the village a man coughed and a musket lock clicked. A horse whinnied up on the ridge where the pipes played. Rubble fell in a house where a wounded man whimpered. Out in the street a spent French cannon ball rolled gently downhill, then lodged against a fallen beam.

'I suspect we'll have company soon, gentlemen,' Williams said. He climbed down from the bench and brushed white dust from his faded green jacket. 'Very soon. Can't see a thing from here. Gunsmoke, you see. Worse than fog.' He was talking to fill the ominous silence. 'Down to the stream, I think. Not that we can hold them there, not enough loopholes, but once they're in the village they'll find life a bit difficult. At least I hope so.' He nodded agreeably to Sharpe, then ducked out of the door. His staff ran after him.

'We're not staying here, are we, sir?' Harper asked.

'Might as well see what's happening,' Sharpe said. 'Got nothing better to do. Are you loaded?'

'Just the rifle.'

'I'd have the volley gun ready,' Sharpe said. 'Just in case.' He began loading his own rifle just as the British guns on the ridge opened fire. Their smoke jetted sixty feet out from the crest and their noise punched at the wounded village as the shots screamed overhead towards the advancing French battalions.

Sharpe stood on the bench to see the dark columns of infantry emerging from the French gunsmoke. The first British case shot exploded above and ahead of the columns, each explosion staining the air with a smear of grey-white smoke riven with fire. Solid shots seared into the massed ranks, but none of the missiles seemed to make an ounce of difference. The columns kept coming: twelve thousand men under their eagles being drummed across the flat land towards the hammering artillery and the waiting muskets and the primed rifles beyond the stream. Sharpe looked left and right, but saw no other enemies apart from a handful of green-coated

239

dragoons patrolling the southern fields. 'They're coming straight in,' he said, 'no messing. One attack, Pat, hard at the village. No buggering round the edge yet. Looks like they think they can come straight through here. There'll be more brigades behind, and they'll throw them in one after the other till they get the church. After that it's downhill all the way to the Atlantic, so if we don't stop them here we'll not stop them anywhere.'

'Well, as you say, sir, we've got nothing better to do.' Harper finished loading his seven-barrelled gun, then picked up a small rag doll that had been discarded under the garden bench. The doll had a red torso on which a mother had stitched a white crossbelt to imitate a British infantryman's uniform. Harper propped the doll in a niche in the wall. 'You keep guard now,' he said to the rag bundle.

Sharpe half drew his sword and tested the edge. 'Didn't get it sharpened,' he said. Before a battle he liked to have the big blade professionally honed by a cavalry armourer, but there had been no time. He hoped it was not an omen.

'You'll just have to bludgeon the bastards to death then,' Harper said, then crossed himself before reaching into his pocket to make sure his rabbit's foot was in its proper place. He looked back to the rag doll and was suddenly overwhelmed by a certainty that his own fate hung on the doll surviving in the wall's niche. 'You take care now,' he told the doll, then gave fate a nudge by jamming a scrap of stone across the niche's face to try and imprison the small rag toy.

A crackling sound like the tearing of calico announced that the British skirmishers had opened fire. The French *voltigeurs* had been advancing a hundred paces in front of their columns, but now were stopped by the fire of the riflemen concealed among the gardens and hovels on the stream's far bank. For a few minutes the skirmish fire stuttered loud, then the outnumbering *voltigeurs* threatened to surround the British skirmishers

240

and the whistles of the officers and sergeants sounded shrilly to call the greenjackets back through the gardens. Two riflemen were limping, a third was being carried by two of his comrades, but most splashed unscathed through the stream and up into the labyrinthine maze of cottages and alleys.

The French *voltigeurs* crouched behind the garden walls on the stream's far bank and began trading fire with the village's defenders. The stream became fogged with a lacy veil of powder smoke that drifted south in the day's small wind. Sharpe and Harper, still waiting in the inn, could hear the French drummers sounding the *pas de charge*, the rhythm that had driven Napoleon's veterans over half Europe to fell their enemies like ninepins. The drums suddenly paused and both Sharpe and Harper instinctively mouthed the words along with twelve thousand Frenchmen, '*Vive l'Empereur.*' Both men laughed as the drums started again.

The guns on the ridge had abandoned the case shot and were smashing roundshot down into the columns and now that the enemy's main formations were almost at the village's eastern gardens Sharpe could see the damage being done by the iron balls as they slashed through file and rank to fling men aside like bloody rags before bouncing in sprays of misted blood to smash into yet more ranks of men. Again and again the missiles lanced through the massed files, yet again and again, doggedly, unstoppably, the French closed up their ranks and kept on coming. The drummers beat on, the eagles flashed in the sun as brightly as the bayonets on the muskets of the leading ranks.

The drums paused again. '*Vive l'Empereur!*' the mass of Frenchmen called, but this time they drew out the last syllable into a long cheer that sustained them as they were released to the attack. The columns could not march in close order through the maze of walled gardens on the village's eastern bank and so the attacking infantry was let off the leash and ordered to charge pell-mell through the vegetable plots and small orchards, across the stream and up into the fire of Colonel Williams's defenders.

'God save us,' Harper said in awe as the French attack engulfed the far bank like a dark wave. The enemy were cheering as they ran and as they overwhelmed the small walls and trampled down the spring crops and splashed into the shallow stream.

'Fire!' a voice shouted and the muskets and rifles cracked from the loopholed houses. A Frenchman went down, his blood thick in the water. Another fell on the clapper bridge and was unceremoniously pushed into the ford by the men crowding behind. Sharpe and Harper both fired from the inn garden, their bullets spinning over the lower roofs to plough into the mass of attackers who were now shielded from the artillery on the ridge by the village itself.

The first French attackers burst against the village's eastern walls. Bayonets clashed against bayonets. Sharpe saw a Frenchman appear on a top of a wall, then jump down into a hidden yard. More Frenchmen followed him across the wall. 'Sword on, Pat,' Sharpe said and drew his own sword as Harper clicked the sword bayonet onto his rifle. They ducked through the garden door and ran down the main street to find their progress blocked by a double rank of redcoats who were waiting with charged muskets and fixed bayonets. Twenty yards further down the street there were more redcoats who were firing over a makeshift barricade of window shutters, doors, tree branches and a pair of commandeered handcarts. The barricade was shaking from the assault of the French on the far side and every few seconds a musket would be thrust through the entanglement and blast fire, smoke and bullet at the defenders.

'Ready to open files!' the redcoat Lieutenant called. He looked to be about eighteen years old, but his West Country voice was firm. He nodded a greeting to Sharpe, then looked back to the barricade. 'Steady now, boys, steady!'

Sharpe knew he would not need the sword yet, so sheathed it and reloaded his rifle instead. He bit the bullet off the cartridge, then held the round in his mouth as he pulled the rifle's hammer back one click to the half cock. He could taste the acrid, salty powder in his mouth as he poured a pinch of powder from the cartridge into the lock's open pan. He held tight to the rest of the cartridge as he pulled the frizzen full up to close the pan cover, then, with the rifle so primed, he let its brass stock fall to the ground. He poured the rest of the cartridge's powder into the muzzle, crammed the empty waxed cartridge paper on top of the powder to serve as wadding, then bent his head to spit the bullet into the gun. He yanked out the steel ramming rod with his left hand, spun the ramrod so that the splayed head faced downwards and thrust the rod hard down the barrel. He pulled it out, spun it again and let it fall into its holding rings, then tossed the rifle up with his left hand, caught it under the lock with his right and pulled the hammer back through a second click so that the weapon was at full cock and ready to fire. It had taken him twelve seconds and he had not thought once about what he was doing, nor even looked at the gun while he loaded it. The manoeuvre was the basic skill of his trade, the necessary skill that had to be taught to new recruits and then practised and practised until it was second nature. As a new recruit, just sixteen years old, Sharpe had dreamed about loading muskets. He had been forced to do it again and again until he had been bored rigid by the drill and was ready to spit at the sergeants for making him do it one more time and then, on a damp day in Flanders, he had found himself doing it for real and suddenly he had fumbled the cartridge and lost his ramrod and forgotten to prime the musket. He had somehow survived that fight, and afterwards he had practised again until at last he could do it without thinking. It was the same skill that he had laboured to drive into the Real Compañía Irlandesa during their unhappy stay in the San Isidro Fort.

Now, as he watched the defenders back away from the collapsing barricade, he found himself wondering how many times he had loaded a gun. Except there was no time to make a guess for the barricade's defenders were running back up the street and the victory roar of the French was swelling as they dismantled the last pieces of the obstacle.

'Open files!' the Lieutenant shouted and the two ranks of men obediently opened their files out from the centre to let the barricade's defenders stream through. At least three red-jackcted bodies were left on the street. A wounded man collapsed and pulled himself into a doorway, then a red-faced captain with grey side whiskers ran through the gap and shouted at the men to close ranks.

The files closed again. 'Front rank, kneel!' the Lieutenant shouted when his two ranks were again arrayed across the street. 'Wait for it!' he called, and this time his voice cracked with nervousness. 'Wait for it!' he called again more firmly, then drew his sword and gave the slim blade a couple of tentative strokes. He swallowed as he watched the French finally burst through the wreckage and charge up the hill with their bayonets fixed.

'Fire!' the Lieutenant shouted, and the twenty-four muskets crashed in unison to choke the road with smoke. Somewhere a man was screaming. Sharpe fired his rifle and heard the distinctive sound of a bullet hitting a musket stock. 'Front rank, stand!' the Lieutenant called. 'At the double! Advance!'

The smoke cleared to show a half-dozen blue-coated bodies down on the stones and earth of the road. Burning scraps of wadding flickered like candle flames. The enemy retreated fast from the threat of the bayonets, but then another mass of blue uniforms appeared at the bottom edge of the village.

'I'm ready, Pollard!' a voice called behind Sharpe, and the Lieutenant, hearing it, halted his men.

'Back, boys!' he shouted and the two ranks, unable to advance against the new mass of the enemy, broke files and retreated uphill. The new attackers had loaded muskets and some stopped to aim. Harper gave them the seven barrels of his volley gun, then followed Sharpe up the hill as the smoke of the big gun spread between the houses.

The grey-whiskered Captain had formed a new defence line that opened to let the Lieutenant's men through. The Lieutenant formed his men into their two ranks a few paces behind the Captain's men and shouted at the redcoats to reload. Sharpe reloaded with them. Harper, knowing he would not have time to reload the volley gun, strapped it across his back and spat a bullet into his rifle.

The drums were still beating the *pas de charge*, while on the ridge behind Sharpe the pipes were rivalling the sound with their feral music. The cannon on the ridge were still firing, presumably aiming case shot at the distant French artillery. The small village reeked of powder smoke, reverberated with musket shots and echoed with the screams and shouts of frightened men.

'Fire!' the Captain ordered and his men poured a volley down the street. It was answered by a French volley. The enemy had decided to use their firepower rather than try to rush the defenders, and it was a battle the Captain knew he must lose. 'Close on me, Pollard!' he shouted and the young Lieutenant took his men down to join the Captain's troops.

'Fire!' Pollard shouted, then made a mewing sound that was momentarily drowned by the crash of his men's muskets. The Lieutenant staggered back, blood showing on the white facings of his elegant coat. He staggered again and let go of his sword which clattered on a doorstep.

'Take him back, Pat,' Sharpe said. 'Meet me at the top of the cemetery.'

Harper lifted the Lieutenant as though he was a child and ran back up the street. The redcoats were reloading, their ramrods rising and falling over their dark shakoes. Sharpe waited for the smoke to clear and looked for an enemy officer. He saw a moustached man carrying a sword, aimed, fired and thought he saw the man twist backwards, but the smoke obscured his view and then a great rush of Frenchmen pounded up the street.

'Bayonets!' the Captain called.

One redcoat backed away. Sharpe put his hand in the small of the man's back and shoved him hard back into his rank. He slung his rifle and drew his sword again. The French charge stalled in the face of the unbroken ranks with their grim steel blades, but the Captain knew he was outgunned and outnumbered. 'Pace backwards!' he ordered. 'Slow and steady! Slow and steady! If you're loaded, boys, give them a shot.'

A dozen muskets fired, but at least twice as many Frenchmen returned the volley and the Captain's ranks seemed to shudder as the balls struck home. Sharpe was serving as a sergeant now, keeping the files in place from behind, but he was also looking back up the street to where a mixture of redcoats and green-jackets were retreating haphazardly from an alley. Their ragged retreat suggested the French were not far behind them and in a moment or two, Sharpe reckoned, the Captain's small company might be cut off. 'Captain!' he shouted, then pointed with his sword when he had the man's attention.

'Back, lads, back!' The Captain grasped the danger immediately. His men turned and ran up the street. Some were helping their comrades, a few ran hard to find safety, but most stayed together to join the larger number of British troops who were forming in the small cobbled space at the village's centre. Williams had held three reserve companies in the safer houses at the upper end of the village and those men had now come down to stem the rising French tide.

The French burst out of the alley just as the company went past its mouth. A redcoat went down to a bayonet, then the Captain slashed his sword in a wild cut that sliced open the face of the Frenchman. A big French sergeant swung his musket stock at the Captain, but Sharpe lunged into the man's face with his sword and though the blow was off balance and feeble, it served to check the man while the Captain got away. The Frenchman rammed his bayonet at Sharpe, had it parried away, then Sharpe skewered the sword low and hard, twisting the blade to stop it being gripped by the man's flesh. He ripped it clear of the Frenchman's belly and went back up the hill, one pace, two, watching for more attacks, then a hand pulled him into the reformed British ranks in the open space. 'Fire!' someone shouted, and Sharpe's ears rang with the deafening bellow of serried muskets exploding all around his head.

'I want that alley cleared!' Colonel Williams's voice called. 'Go on, Wentworth! Take your men down. Don't let them stand!'

A group of redcoats charged. There were French muskets firing from the windows of the houses and some of the men burst through the doors to drive the French out. More enemy came up the main street. They came in small groups, stopping to fire, then running up into the square where the battle was ragged and desperate. One small group of redcoats was overrun by a rush of Frenchmen who came out of a side alley and there were screams as the enemy's bayonets rose and fell. A boy somehow escaped the massacre and scrambled over the cobbles. 'Where's your musket, Sanders?' a sergeant shouted.

The boy swore, turned to look for his fallen weapon and

was shot in the open mouth. The French, exhilarated by their victory over the small group, charged over the boy's body to attack the larger mass of men who were trying to hold the mouth of the recaptured alley. They were met by bayonets. The clash of steel on steel and of steel on wood was louder than the muskets, for few men now had time to load a musket and so they used their blades or the stocks of their guns instead of bullets. The two sides stood poised just feet from each other and every now and then a brave group of men would summon the courage to make a charge into the enemy ranks. Then the voices would rise to hoarse shouts and the clash of steel would begin again. One such assault was led by a tall, bareheaded French officer who drove two redcoats aside with whip-quick slashes of his sword, then lunged at a British officer who was fumbling with his pistol. The red-coated officer stepped back and so exposed Sharpe. The tall Frenchman feinted left and managed to draw Sharpe's sword away in the parry, then reversed his stroke and was already gritting his teeth for the killing lunge, but Sharpe was not fighting by the rules of some Parisian fencing master and so he kicked the man in the crotch, then hammered the heavy iron hilt of the sword down onto his head. He kicked the man out of the ranks, and back-cut his heavy sword at a French soldier who was trying to drag a musket and bayonet out of a redcoat's hand. The blade's edge, unsharpened, served as a cudgel rather than a sword, but the Frenchman reeled away with his head in his hands.

'Forward!' a voice shouted and the makeshift British line advanced down the street. The enemy retreated from Williams's reserve who now threatened to take back the whole lower part of the village, but then a vagary of wind swirled away a patch of dust and gunsmoke and Sharpe saw a whole new wave of French attackers swarming over the gardens and walls on the stream's eastern bank.

'Sharpe!' Colonel Williams called. 'Are you spoken for?'

Sharpe elbowed back through the tight ranks of redcoats. 'Sir?'

'I'd be damned grateful if you were to find Spencer on the ridge and tell him we could use a few reinforcements.'

'At once, sir.'

'Lost a couple of my aides, you see,' Williams began to explain, but Sharpe had already left on the errand. 'Good man!' Williams called after him, then turned back to the fight that had degenerated into a series of bloody and desperate brawls in the murderous confines of the alleys and back gardens. It was a fight Williams feared losing for the French had committed their own reserves and a new mass of blue-coated infantry was now pouring into the village.

Sharpe ran past wounded men dragging themselves uphill. The village was clouded with dust and smoke and he took one wrong turning and found himself in a blind alley of stone walls. He backtracked, found the right street again, and emerged on the slope above the village where a crowd of wounded men waited for help. They were too weak to climb the slope and some called out as Sharpe ran past.

He ignored them. Instead he climbed up the goat path beside the graveyard. A group of worried officers were standing beside the church and Sharpe shouted at them to see if any knew where General Spencer was. 'I've got a message!' he called.

'What is it?' a man called back. 'I'm his aide!'

'Williams wants reinforcements. Too many Frogs!'

The staff officer turned and ran towards the brigade that was waiting beyond the crest while Sharpe paused to catch his breath. His sword was in his hand and its blade was sticky with blood. He cleaned the steel on the edge of his jacket, then jumped in alarm as a bullet smacked hard into the stone wall beside him. He turned and saw a puff of musket smoke showing between some broken beams at the upper edge of the village and he realized the French had taken those houses and were now trying to cut off the defenders still inside Fuentes de Oñoro. The greenjackets in the graveyard opened fire, their rifles cutting down any enemy foolish enough to show himself at a window or door for too long.

Sharpe sheathed his cleaned sword then went over the wall and crouched behind a slab of granite on which a rough cross had been chiselled. He loaded the rifle, then aimed it at the broken roof where he had seen the musket smoke. The flint had skewed in the doghead and he released the screw, adjusted the leather patch that gripped the flint, then tightened it down. He thumbed the cock back. He was bitterly thirsty, the usual fate of any man who had been biting into salty gunpowder cartridges. The air was foul with the stench of smoke.

A musket appeared between the beams and, a second later, a man's head showed. Sharpe fired first, but the rifle's smoke hid the bullet's mark. Harper slid down the graveyard's slope to land beside Sharpe. 'Jesus,' the Irishman said, 'Jesus.'

'Bad in there.' Sharpe nodded down to the village. He primed the rifle, then upended the weapon to charge the muzzle. He had left his ramrod conveniently propped against the grave.

'More of the buggers coming over the stream,' Harper said. He bit a bullet and was forced to silence until he could spit it into the rifle. 'That poor lieutenant. Died.'

'It was a chest wound,' Sharpe said, ramming the ball and charge hard down the barrel. 'Not many survive chest wounds.'

'I stayed with the poor bugger,' Harper said. 'His mother's a widow, he told me. She sold the family plate to buy his uniform and sword, then said he'd be as great a soldier as any there was.'

'He was good,' Sharpe said. 'He kept his nerve.' He cocked the rifle.

'I told him that. Gave him a prayer. Poor wee bugger. First

250

battle, too.' Harper pulled the trigger. 'Got you, you bastard,' he said and immediately fished a new cartridge from his pouch while he pulled the hammer to half cock. More British defenders were emerging from between the houses, forced out of the village by the sheer weight of French numbers. 'They should send some more men down there,' Harper said.

'They're coming,' Sharpe said. He laid the rifle's barrel on the gravestone and looked for a target.

'Taking their time, though,' Harper said. On this occasion he did not spit the bullet into the rifle, but first wrapped it in the small patch of greased leather that would grip the barrel's rifling and so make the ball spin as it was fired. It took longer to load such a round, but it made the Baker rifle far more accurate. The Irishman grunted as he forced the patched bullet down the barrel that was caked with the deposits of gun-powder. 'There's some boiling water behind the church,' he said, telling Sharpe where to go if he needed to clean the fouled powder from his rifle's barrel.

'I'll piss down it if I have to.'

'If you've got any piss. I'm dry as a dead rat. Jesus, you bastard.' This was addressed at a bearded Frenchman who had appeared between two of the houses where he was beating down a greenjacket with a pioneer's axe. Sharpe, already loaded, took aim through the sudden spray of the dying rifleman's blood and pulled the trigger, but at least a dozen other green-jackets in the churchyard had seen the incident and the bearded Frenchman seemed to quiver as the bullets whipped home. 'That'll teach him,' Harper said, and laid his rifle on the stone. 'Where the hell are those reinforcements?'

'Takes time to get them ready,' Sharpe said.

'Lose a bloody battle just because they want straight ranks?' Harper asked scornfully. He looked for a target. 'Come on, someone, show yourself.'

More of Williams's men retreated out of the village. They tried to form ranks on the rough ground at the foot of the graveyard, but by abandoning the houses they had yielded the stone walls to the French who could hide as they loaded, fire, then duck back into hiding again. Some British were still fighting inside the village, but the musket smoke betrayed that their fight had shrunk to a small group of houses at the very top of the main street. One more push by the French, Sharpe thought, and the village would be lost, and then there would a bitter fight up through the graveyard for mastery of the church and the rock outcrop. Lose those two summits, he thought, and the battle was done.

The French drumming rose to a new fervour. There were Frenchmen coming out of the houses to form small squads that tried to outflank the retreating British. The riflemen in the graveyard fired at the daring sallies, but there were too many French and not enough rifles. One of the wounded men tried to crawl away from the advancing enemy and was bayoneted in the back for his trouble. Two Frenchmen ransacked his uniform, searching for the small hoard of coins most soldiers hid away. Sharpe fired at the plunderers, then turned his rifle on the French who were threatening to find cover behind the graveyard's lower wall. He loaded and fired, loaded and fired until his right shoulder felt like one massive bruise hammered into the bone by the rifle's brutal recoil, then suddenly, blessedly, there was a skirl of pipes and a rush of kilted men spilt over the crest of the ridge between the church and the rocks to charge down the main road into the village.

'Look at the bastards!' Harper said with pride. 'They'll give the Frogs a right beating.'

The Warwicks appeared to Sharpe's right and, like the Scots, just poured over the edge and scrambled down the steeper slope towards Fuentes de Oñoro. The leading French attackers paused for a second to judge the weight of the counterattack, then hurried back into the cover of the houses. The Highlanders were already in the village where their war cries echoed between the walls, then the Warwicks went into the western alleyways and drove hard and deep into the tangle of houses.

Sharpe felt the tension drain out of him. He was thirsty, he ached, he was tired and his shoulder was agony. 'Jesus,' he said, 'and it wasn't even our fight.' The thirst was galling and he had left his canteen with the ammunition wagons, but he felt too tired and dispirited to go and find water. He watched the broken village, noting how the gunsmoke marked the British advance right back down to the stream's edge, but he felt little elation. It seemed to Sharpe that all his hopes had stalled. He faced disgrace. Worse, he felt a sense of failure. He had dared to hope that he could turn the Real Compañía Irlandesa into soldiers, but he knew, staring down at the gunsmoke and the shattered houses, that the Irishmen needed another month of training and far more goodwill than Wellington had ever been prepared to give them. Sharpe had failed with them just as he had failed Hogan, and the twin failures raked at his spirits, then he realized he was feeling sorry for himself just as Donaju had felt self-pity in the morning mist. 'Jesus,' he said, disgusted at himself.

'Sir?' Harper asked, not having heard Sharpe.

'Never mind,' Sharpe said. He felt the loom of disgrace and the bite of regret. He was a captain on sufferance and he supposed he would never now make major. 'Bugger them all, Pat,' he said and wearily stood. 'Let's find something to drink.'

Down in the village a dying redcoat had found Harper's rag doll jammed into the niche of the wall and had shoved it into his mouth to stop himself crying out in his pain. Now he died and his blood welled and spilt from his gullet so that the small, damaged doll fell in a welter of red. The French had pulled back beyond the stream where they took cover behind the garden walls to open fire on the Highlanders and the Warwicks who hunted down the last groups of trapped French survivors in the village. A disconsolate line of French prisoners straggled up the slope under a mixed guard of riflemen and Highlanders. Colonel Williams had been wounded in the counterattack and was now carried by his riflemen to the church which had been turned into a hospital. The stork's nest on the bell tower was still an untidy tangle of twigs, but the adult birds had been driven out by the noise and smoke of the battle to leave their nestlings to starve. The sound of musketry crackled across the stream for a while, then died away as both sides took stock of the first attack.

But not, both sides knew, the last.

CHAPTER EIGHT

The French did not attack again. They stayed on the stream's eastern bank, while behind them, at the distant line of oaks that straddled the straight white road, the rest of their army slowly deployed so that by nightfall the whole of Masséna's force was encamped and the smoke of their fires mingled to make a grey wash that darkened to a hellish black as the sun sank behind the British ridge. The fighting in the village had stopped, but the artillery kept up a desultory battle till nightfall. The British had the best of it. Their guns were emplaced just back from the plateau's crest so that all the French could aim for was the skyline itself and most of their shots were fired too high and rumbled impotently over the British infantry concealed by the crest. Shots fired too low merely thumped into the ridge's slope which was too steep for the roundshot to bounce up to their targets. The British gunners, on the other hand, had a clear view of the enemy batteries and one by one their long-fused case shot either silenced the French artillery or persuaded the gunners to drag their cannon back into the cover of the trees.

The last gun fired as the sun set. The flat echo of the sound crashed and faded across the shadowed plain while the smoke from the gun's barrel curled and drifted in the wind. Small fires flickered in the village ruins, the flames glimmering luridly on broken walls and snapped beams. The streets were crammed with dead men and pitiful with the wounded who cried through the night for help. Behind the church, where the luckier casualties had been safely evacuated, wives searched for husbands, brothers for brothers and friends for friends. Burial parties looked for patches of soil on the rocky slopes while officers auctioned the possessions of their dead mess-fellows and wondered how long it would be before their own belongings were similarly knocked down for puny prices. Up on the plateau the soldiers stewed newly slaughtered beef in their Flanders cauldrons and sang sentimental songs of greenwoods and girls.

The armies slept with their weapons loaded and ready. Picquets watched the dark as the big guns cooled. Rats scampered through the fallen stones of Fuentes de Oñoro and gnawed at dead men. Few of the living slept well. The British footguards had been infected with Methodism and some of the guardsmen gathered for a midnight prayer meeting until a Coldstreamer officer growled at them to give God and himself a bloody rest. Other men prowled in the dark to seek the dead and wounded for plunder. Now and then an injured man would call out in protest and a bayonet would glint quickly in the starlight and a wash of blood ebb into the soil as the newly dead man's uniform was searched for coins.

Major Tarrant had at last heard about Sharpe's impending ordeal by court of inquiry. He could hardly have avoided learning of it for a succession of officers came to the ammunition park to give Sharpe their condolences and to complain that an army which persecuted a man for killing the enemy must be an army led by idiots and administered by fools. Tarrant did not understand Wellington's decision either. 'Surely the two men deserved to die? I agree they hardly endured the proper processes of the law, but even so, can anyone doubt their guilt?'

Captain Donaju, who was sharing Tarrant's late supper with Sharpe, nodded agreement.

'It's not about two men dying, sir,' Sharpe said, 'but about bloody politics. I've given the Spanish reason to distrust us, sir.'

'No Spaniards died!' Tarrant protested.

'Aye, sir, but too many good Portuguese did, so General Valverde's claiming that we can't be trusted with other nations' soldiers.'

'This is too bad!' Tarrant said angrily. 'So what happens to you now?'

Sharpe shrugged. 'There's a court of inquiry, I'm blamed, which means a court martial. The worst they can do to me, sir, is take away my commission.'

Captain Donaju frowned. 'Suppose I speak to General Valverde?'

Sharpe shook his head. 'And ruin your career, too? Thank you, but no. What this is really about,' he explained, 'is who should become *Generalisimo* of Spain. We reckon it should be Nosey, but Valverde doesn't agree.'

'Doubtless because he wants the job himself!' Tarrant said scornfully. 'It is too bad, Sharpe, too bad.' The Scotsman frowned down at the dish of liver and kidney that Gog and Magog had cooked for his supper. Traditionally the officers received the offal of newly slaughtered cattle, a privilege Tarrant would happily have foregone. He tossed a peculiarly nauseating piece of kidney to one of the many dogs that had attached themselves to the army, then shook his head. 'Is there any chance at all that you might avoid this ridiculous court of inquiry?' he asked Sharpe.

Sharpe thought of Hogan's sarcastic remark that Sharpe's only hope lay in a French victory that would obliterate all memories of what had happened at San Isidro. That seemed a dubious solution, yet there was another hope, a very slender hope, but one Sharpe had been thinking about all day.

'Go on,' Tarrant said, sensing that the rifleman was hesitant about offering an answer.

Sharpe grimaced. 'Nosey's been known to pardon men for good behaviour. There was a fellow in the 83rd who was caught red-handed stealing money from a poor-box in Guarda and he was condemned to be hanged for it, but his company fought so well at Talavera that Nosey let him go.'

Donaju gestured with his knife towards the village that was beyond the eastern skyline. 'Is that why you fought down there all day?' he asked.

Sharpe shook his head. 'We just happened to find ourselves down there,' he said dismissively.

'But you took an eagle, Sharpe!' Tarrant protested. 'What more gallantry do you need to display?'

'A lot, sir.' Sharpe winced as his sore shoulder gave a stab of pain. 'I'm not rich, sir, so I can't buy a captaincy, let alone a majority, so I have to survive by merit. And a soldier's only as good as his last battle, sir, and my last battle was San Isidro. I have to wipe that out.'

Donaju frowned. 'It was my only battle,' he said softly and to no one but himself.

Tarrant scorned Sharpe's pessimism. 'Are you saying, Sharpe, that you have to perform some ridiculous act of heroism to survive?'

'Yes, sir. Exactly that, sir. So if you've got some horrid errand tomorrow then I want it.'

'Good God, man.' Tarrant was appalled. 'Good God! Send you to your death? I can't do that!'

Sharpe smiled. 'What were you doing seventeen years ago, sir?'

Tarrant thought for a second or two. ''Ninety-four? Let's see now . . .' He counted off on his fingers for another few seconds. 'I was still at school. Construing Horace in a gloomy

258

schoolroom beneath the walls of Stirling Castle and being beaten every time I made an error.'

'I was fighting the French, sir,' Sharpe said. 'And I've been fighting one bugger or another ever since, so don't you worry about me.'

'Even so, Sharpe, even so.' Tarrant frowned and shook his head. 'Do you like kidney?'

'Love it, sir.'

'It's all yours.' Tarrant handed his plate to Sharpe. 'Get your strength up, Sharpe, it seems you might need it.' He twisted around to look at the red flame glow that lit the night above the fires of the French encampments. 'Unless they don't attack,' he said wistfully.

'The buggers aren't going away, sir, until we drive them away,' Sharpe said. 'Today was just a skirmish. The real battle hasn't started yet, so the Crapauds will be back, sir, they'll be back.'

They slept close to the ammunition wagons. Sharpe woke once as a small shower hissed in the embers of the fire, then slept again until an hour before dawn. He awoke to see a small mist clinging to the plateau and blurring the grey shapes of soldiers tending their fires. Sharpe shared a pot of hot shaving water with Major Tarrant, then pulled on his jacket and weapons and walked westwards in search of a cavalry regiment. He found an encampment of hussars from the King's German Legion and exchanged a half-pint of issue rum for an edge on his sword. The German armourer bent over his wheel as the sparks flew and when he was done the edge of Sharpe's heavy cavalry sword was glinting in the dawn's small light. Sharpe slid the blade carefully into its scabbard and walked slowly back towards the gaunt silhouetted shapes of the wagon park.

The sun rose through a cloud of French cooking smoke. The enemy on the stream's eastern bank greeted the new day with a fusillade of musketry that rattled among Fuentes de Oñoro's houses, but died away as no shots were returned. On the British ridge the gunners cut new fuses and piled their ready magazines with case shot, but no French infantry advanced from the distant trees to be the beneficiaries of their work. A large force of French cavalry rode southwards across the marshy plain where they were shadowed by horsemen from the King's German Legion, but as the sun rose higher and the last pockets of mist evaporated from the lowland fields it dawned on the waiting British that Masséna was not planning any immediate attack.

Two hours after dawn a French *voltigeur* picquet on the stream's eastern bank called out a tentative greeting to the British sentry he knew was hidden behind a broken wall on the west bank. He could not see the British soldier, but he could see the blue haze of his pipe smoke. 'Goddam!' he called, using the French nickname for all British troops. 'Goddam!'

'Crapaud?'

A pair of empty hands appeared above the French-held wall. No one fired and, a moment later, an anxious moustached face appeared. The Frenchman produced an unlit cigar and mimed that he would like a light.

The greenjacket picquet emerged from hiding just as warily, but when no enemy fired at him he walked out onto the clapper bridge that had lost one of its stone slabs in the previous day's fighting. He held his clay pipe out over the gap. 'Come on, Frenchie.'

The *voltigeur* walked onto the bridge and leaned over for the pipe that he used to light his cigar. Then he returned the pipe with a short length of garlic sausage. The two men smoked companionably, enjoying the spring sunshine. Other *voltigeurs* stretched and stood, just as the greenjackets relaxed in their positions. Some men took off their boots and dangled their feet in the stream.

In Fuentes de Oñoro itself the British were struggling to remove the dead and the wounded from the crammed alleys. Men wrapped cloth strips about their mouths to drag the blood-black and heat-swollen bodies from the piles that marked where the fighting had been fiercest. Other men fetched water from the stream to relieve the thirst of the wounded. By mid-morning the truce across the stream was official and a company of unarmed French infantry arrived to carry their own casualties back across the bridge that had been patched with a plank taken from the watermill on the British bank. French ambulances waited at the ford to carry their men to the surgeons. The vehicles had been specially constructed for carrying wounded men and had springs as lavish as any city grandee's coach. The British army preferred to use farm carts that jolted the wounded foully.

A French major sat drinking wine and playing chess with a greenjacket captain in the inn's garden. Outside the inn a work party loaded an ox-drawn wagon with the dead who would be carried up to the ridge and buried in a common grave. The chess-players frowned when a burst of raucous laughter sounded loud and the British Captain, annoyed that the laughter was not fading away, went to the gate and snapped at a sergeant for an explanation. 'It was Mallory, sir,' the Sergeant said, pointing to a shamefaced British rifleman who was the butt of French and British amusement. 'Bugger fell asleep, sir, and the Frogs was loading him up with the dead 'uns.'

The French Major took one of the Englishman's castles and remarked that he had once almost buried a living man. 'We were already throwing earth in his grave when he sneezed. That was in Italy. He's a sergeant now.'

The rifle Captain might have been losing the game of chess, but he was determined not to be outdone in stories. 'I've met two men who survived hangings in England,' he remarked.

261

'They were pulled off the scaffold too soon and their bodies sold to the surgeons. The doctors pay five guineas a corpse, I'm told, so they can demonstrate their damned techniques to their apprentices. I'm told the corpses revive far more often than you'd think. There's always an unseemly scramble round the gallows as the man's family tries to cut the body down before the doctors get their wretched hands on it, and there doesn't seem anyone in authority to make sure the villain's properly dead before he's unstrung.' He moved a bishop. 'I suppose the authorities are being bribed.'

'The guillotine makes no such mistakes,' the Major said as he advanced a pawn. 'Death by science. Very quick and certain. I do believe that is checkmate.'

'Damn me,' the Englishman said, 'so it is.'

The French Major stowed away his chess set. His pawns were musket balls, half limewashed and half left plain, the court pieces were carved from wood and the board was a square of painted canvas that he wrapped carefully about the chessmen. 'It seems our lives have been spared this day,' he said, glancing up at the sun that was already past the meridian. 'Maybe we shall fight tomorrow instead?'

Up on the ridge the British watched as French troops marched south. It was clear that Masséna would now be trying to turn the British right flank and so Wellington ordered the Seventh Division to deploy southwards and thus reinforce a strong force of Spanish partisans who were blocking the roads the French needed to advance artillery as part of their flanking manoeuvre. Wellington's army was now in two parts; the largest on the plateau behind Fuentes de Oñoro was blocking the approach to Almeida while the smaller part was two and a half miles south astride the road along which the British would need to retreat if they were defeated. Masséna put a telescope to his one eye to watch as the small British division moved south. He kept expecting the division to stop before it left the protective artillery range of the plateau, but the troops kept marching and marching. 'He's made a bollocks of it,' he told an aide as the Seventh Division finally marched way beyond the range of the strong British artillery. Masséna collapsed the telescope. 'Monsieur Wellington has made a bollocks of it,' he said.

André Masséna had begun his military career as a private in the ranks of Louis XVI's army and now he was a marshal of France, the Duke of Rivoli and the Prince of Essling. Men called him 'Your Majesty', yet once he had been a half-starved wharf rat in the small town of Nice. He had also once possessed two eyes, but the Emperor had shot one of the eyeballs away in a hunting accident. Napoleon would never acknowledge the responsibility, but nor would Marshal Masséna ever dream of blaming his beloved Emperor for the eye's loss, for he owed both his royal status and his high military rank to Napoleon who had recognized the wharf rat's skills as a soldier. Those skills had made André Masséna famous inside the Empire and feared outside. He had trampled through Italy winning victory after victory, he had smashed the Russians on the borders of Switzerland and rammed bloody defeat down Austrian throats before Marengo. Marshal André Masséna, Duke of Rivoli and Prince of Essling, was not a pretty soldier, but by God he knew how to fight, which was why, at fifty-two years old, he had been sent to retrieve the disasters besetting the Emperor's armies in Spain and Portugal.

Now the wharf rat turned prince watched in disbelief as the gap between the two parts of the British army opened still wider. For a few seconds he even toyed with the idea that perhaps the four or five thousand red-coated infantrymen marching southwards were the Irish regiments that Major Ducos had promised would mutiny before the battle, but

Masséna had never put much hope in Ducos's stratagem and the fact that these nine battalions were flying their flags as they marched suggested that they were hardly in revolt. Instead, miraculously, it seemed that the British were offering them up as a sacrifice by isolating them out in the southern plain where they would be far from any help. Masséna watched as the enemy regiments finally stopped just short of a village far to the south. According to his map the village was called Nave de Haver and it lay nearly five miles from Fuentes de Oñoro. 'Is Wellington tricking us?' Masséna asked an aide.

The aide was just as incredulous as his master. 'Perhaps he believes he can beat us without keeping to the rules?' he suggested.

'Then in the morning we will teach him about the rules of war. I expected better of this Englishman! Tomorrow night, Jean, we shall have his whores as our own. Does Wellington have whores?'

'I don't know, Your Majesty.'

'Then find out. And make sure I get the pick of the bunch before some filthy grenadier gives her the clap, you hear me?'

'Yes, Your Majesty,' the aide said. His master's passion for women was as tiresome as his appetite for victory was inspiring, and tomorrow, it seemed, both hungers would be satisfied.

By mid-afternoon it was plain that the French were not coming that day. The picquets were doubled, and every battalion kept at least three companies under arms, but the other companies were released to more usual duties. Cattle were herded onto the plateau and slaughtered for the evening meal, bread was fetched from Vilar Formoso and the rum ration distributed.

Captain Donaju sought and received Tarrant's permission to take a score of men to attend Lord Kiely's burial which was taking place four miles behind Fuentes de Oñoro. Hogan also insisted that Sharpe attend and Harper wanted to come as well. Sharpe felt awkward in Hogan's company, especially as the Irishman seemed blithely unaware of Sharpe's bitterness over the court of inquiry. 'I invited Runciman,' Hogan told Sharpe as they walked along the dusty road west from Vilar Formoso, 'but he didn't really want to come. Poor fellow.'

'In a bad way, is he?' Sharpe asked.

'Heartbroken,' Hogan said callously. 'Keeps claiming that nothing was his fault. He doesn't seem to grasp that isn't the point.'

'It isn't, is it? The point is that you'd prefer to keep bloody Valverde happy.'

Hogan shook his head. 'I'd prefer to bury Valverde, and preferably alive, but what I really want is for Wellington to be *Generalisimo*.'

'And you'll sacrifice me for that?'

'Of course! Every soldier knows you must lose some valuable men if you want to win a great prize. Besides, what does it matter if you do lose your commission? You'll just go off and join Teresa and become a famous partisan: El Fusilero!' Hogan smiled cheerfully, then turned to Harper. 'Sergeant? Would you do me a great service and give me a moment's privacy with Captain Sharpe?'

Harper obligingly walked on ahead where he tried to overhear the conversation between the two officers, but Hogan kept his voice low and Sharpe's exclamations of surprise offered Harper no clue. Nor did he have any chance to question Sharpe before the three British officers turned a corner to see Lord Kiely's servants and Captain Donaju's twenty men standing awkwardly beside a grave that had been recently dug in an orchard next to a graveyard. Father Sarsfield had paid the village gravediggers to dig the hole just feet away from consecrated

265

ground for, though the laws of the church insisted that Lord Kiely's sins must keep him from burial in holy ground, Sarsfield would nevertheless place the body as near as he could to consecrated soil so that on Judgment Day the exiled Irishman's soul would not be utterly bereft of Christian company.

The body had been stitched into a dirty white canvas shroud. Four men of the Real Compañía Irlandesa lowered the corpse into the deep grave, then Hogan, Sharpe and Harper took off their hats as Father Sarsfield said the prayers in Latin and afterwards spoke in English to the twenty guardsmen. Lord Kiely, the priest said, had suffered from the sin of pride and that pride had not let him endure disappointment. Yet all Irishmen, Sarsfield said, must learn to live with disappointment for it was given to their heritage as surely as the sparks flew upwards. Yet, he went on, the proper response to disappointment was not to abandon hope and reject God's gift of life, but to keep the hope glowing bright. 'We have no homes, you and I,' he said to the sombre guardsmen, 'but one day we shall all inherit our earthly home, and if it is not given to us then it will come to our children or to our children's children.' The priest fell silent and stared down into the grave. 'Nor must you worry that his Lordship committed suicide,' he finally continued. 'Suicide is a sin, but sometimes life is so unbearable that we must risk the sin rather than face the horror. Wolfe Tone made that choice thirteen years ago.' The mention of the Irish patriot rebel made one or two of the guardsmen glance at Sharpe, then they looked back to the priest who went on in his gentle, persuasive voice to tell how Wolfe Tone had been held captive in a British dungeon and how, rather than face the enemy's gallows, he had slit his own throat with a penknife. 'Lord Kiely's motives might not have been so pure as Tone's,' Sarsfield said, 'but we don't know what sadness drove him to his sin and in our ignorance we must therefore pray for his soul and forgive him.' There were tears in the priest's eyes as he took a small phial of holy water from the haversack at his side and sprinkled its drops on the lonely grave. He offered the benediction in Latin, then stepped back as the guardsmen raised their muskets to fire a ragged volley over the open grave. Birds panicked up from the orchard's trees, then circled and flew back as the smoke dissipated among the branches.

Hogan took charge as soon as the volley had been fired. He insisted that there was still some danger of a French attack at dusk and that the soldiers should all return to the ridge. 'I'll follow soon,' he told Sharpe, then he ordered Kiely's servants back to his Lordship's quarters.

The soldiers and servants left, the sound of their boots fading in the late afternoon air. It was sultry in the orchard where the two gravediggers waited patiently for the signal to fill up the grave beside which Hogan now stood, hat in hand, staring down at the shrouded corpse. 'For a long time,' he said to Father Sarsfield, 'I've carried a pillbox with some Irish earth inside so that if I should die I would rest with a little bit of Ireland all through eternity. I seem to have mislaid it, Father, which is a pity for I'd have liked to sprinkle a wee bit of Ireland's soil onto Lord Kiely's grave.'

'A generous thought, Major,' Sarsfield said.

Hogan stared down at Kiely's shroud. 'The poor man. I hear he was hoping to marry the Lady Juanita?'

'They spoke of it,' Sarsfield said drily, his tone implying his disapproval of the match.

'The lady's doubtless in mourning,' Hogan said, then put his hat back on. 'Or maybe she's not mourning at all? You've heard that she's gone back to the French? Captain Sharpe let her go. He's a fool for women, that man, but the Lady Juanita can easily make a fool of men. She did of poor Kiely here, did she not?' Hogan paused as a sneeze gathered and exploded. 'Bless me,' he said, wiping his nose and eyes with a vast red hand-kerchief. 'And what a terrible woman she was,' he went on. 'Saying she was going to marry Kiely, and all the while she was committing adultery and fornication with Brigadier Guy Loup. Is fornication a mere venial sin these days?'

'Fornication, Major, is a mortal sin.' Sarsfield smiled. 'As I suspect you know only too well.'

'Crying out to heaven for revenge, is it?' Hogan returned the smile, then looked back to the grave. Bees hummed in the orchard blossoms above Hogan's head. 'But what about forni-cating with the enemy, Father?' he asked. 'Isn't that a worse sin?'

Sarsfield took the scapular from around his neck, kissed it, then carefully folded the strip of cloth. 'Why are you so worried for the Doña Juanita's soul, Major?' he asked.

Hogan still looked down at the dead man's coarse shroud. 'I'd rather worry about his poor soul. Do you think it was discovering that his lady was humping a Frog that killed him?'

Sarsfield flinched at Hogan's crudity. 'If he did discover that, Major, then it could hardly have added to his happiness. But he was not a man who knew much happiness, and he rejected the hand of the church.'

'And what could the church have done? Changed the whore's nature?' Hogan asked. 'And don't tell me that Doña Juanita de Elia is not a spy, Father, for I know she is and you know the selfsame thing.'

'I do?' Sarsfield frowned in puzzlement.

'You do, Father, you do, and God forgive you for it. Juanita is a whore and a spy, and a better whore, I think, than she is a spy. But she was the only person available for you, isn't that so? Doubtless you'd have preferred someone less flamboyant, but what choice did you have? Or was it Major Ducos who made the choice? But it was a bad choice, a very bad choice.

Juanita failed you, Father. We found her when she was trying to bring you a whole lot of these.' Hogan reached into his tail pocket and produced one of the counterfeit newspapers that Sharpe had discovered in San Cristóbal. 'They were wrapped in sheets of sacred music, Father, and I thought to myself, why would they do that? Why church music? Why not other newspapers? But, of course, if she was stopped and given a cursory search then who would think it odd that she was carrying a pile of psalms to a man of God?'

Sarsfield glanced at the newspaper, but did not take it. 'I think, maybe,' he said carefully, 'that grief has deranged your mind.'

Hogan laughed. 'Grief for Kiely? Hardly, Father. What might have deranged me is all the work I've been having to do in these last few days. I've been reading my correspondence, Father, and it comes from all sorts of strange places. Some from Madrid, some from Paris, some even from London. Would you like to hear what I've learned?'

Father Sarsfield was fidgeting with the scapular, folding and refolding the embroidered strip of cloth. 'If you insist,' he said guardedly.

Hogan smiled. 'Oh, I do, Father. For I've been thinking about this fellow, Ducos, and how clever everyone says he is, but what really worries me is that he's put another clever fellow behind our lines, and I've been hurting my mind wondering just who that new clever fellow might be. And I was also wondering, you see, just why it was that the first newspapers to arrive in the Irish regiments were supposed to be from Philadelphia. Very odd choice that. Am I losing you?'

'Go on,' Sarsfield said. The scapular had come loose and he was meticulously folding it again.

'I've never been to Philadelphia,' Hogan said, 'though I hear it's a fine city. Would you like a pinch of snuff, Father?'

Sarsfield did not answer. He just watched Hogan and went on folding the cloth.

'Why Philadelphia?' Hogan asked. 'Then I remembered! Actually I didn't remember at all; a man in London sent me a reminder. They remember these things in London. They have them all written down in a great big book, and one of the things written in that great big book is that it was in Philadelphia that Wolfe Tone got his letter of introduction to the French government. And it was there, too, that he met a passionate priest called Father Mallon. Mallon was more of a soldier than a priest and he was doing his best to raise a regiment of volunteers to fight the British, but he wasn't having a whole lot of success so he threw his lot in with Tone instead. Tone was a Protestant, wasn't he? And he never did have much fondness for priests, but he liked Mallon well enough because Mallon was an Irish patriot before he was a priest. And I think Mallon became Tone's friend as well, for he stayed with Tone every step of the way after that first meeting in Philadelphia. He went to Paris with Tone, raised the volunteers with Tone, then sailed to Ireland with Tone. Sailed all the way into Lough Swilly. That was in 1798, Father, in case you'd forgotten, and no one has seen Mallon from that day to this. Poor Tone was captured and the redcoats were all over Ireland looking for Father Mallon, but there's not been a sight nor smell of the man. Are you sure you won't have a pinch of snuff? It's Irish Blackguard and hard to come by.'

'I would rather have a cigar, if you have one,' Sarsfield said calmly.

'I don't, Father, but you should try the snuff one day. It's a grand specific against the fever, or so my mother always said. Now where was I? Oh yes, with poor Father Mallon on the run from the British. It's my belief he got back to France, and I think from there he was sent to Spain. The French couldn't use

270

him against the English, at least not until the English had forgotten the events of '98, but Mallon must have been useful in Spain. I suspect he met the old Lady Kiely in Madrid. I hear she was a fierce old witch! Lived for the church and for Ireland, even though she saw too much of the one and had never seen the other. D'you think Mallon used her patronage as he spied on the Spanish for Bonaparte? I suspect so, but then the French took over the Spanish throne and someone must have been wondering where Father Mallon could be more usefully employed, and I suspect Father Mallon pleaded with his French masters to be employed against the real enemy. After all, who among the British would remember Father Mallon from '98? His hair will be white by now, he'll be a changed man. Maybe he's put on weight like me.' Hogan patted his belly and smiled.

Father Sarsfield frowned at the scapular. He seemed surprised that he was still holding the vestment and so he carefully stowed it in the haversack slung from his shoulder, then just as carefully brought out a small pistol. 'Father Mallon might be a changed man,' he said as he opened the frizzen to check that the gun was primed, 'but I would like to think that if he was still alive he would be a patriot.'

'I imagine he is,' Hogan said, apparently unworried by the pistol. 'A man like Mallon? His loyalty won't change as much as his hair and belly.'

Sarsfield frowned at Hogan. 'And you're not a patriot, Major?'

'I like to think so.'

'Yet you fight for Britain.'

Hogan shrugged. The priest's pistol was loaded and primed, but for the moment it hung loose in Sarsfield's hand. Hogan had played a game with the priest, a game he had expected to win, but this proof of his victory was not giving the Major any pleasure. Indeed, as the realization of his triumph sank in, Hogan's mood became ever bleaker. 'I worry about allegiance,'

Hogan said, 'I surely do. I lie awake sometimes and wonder whether I'm right in thinking that what's best for Ireland is to be a part of Britain, but I do know one thing, Father, which is that I don't want to be ruled by Bonaparte. I think maybe I'm not so brave a man as Wolfe Tone, but nor did I ever agree with his ideas. You do, Father, and I salute you for it, but that isn't why you're going to have to die. The reason you're going to have to die, Father, is not because you fight for Ireland, but because you fight for Napoleon. The distinction is fatal.'

Sarsfield smiled. '*I* shall have to die?' he asked in wry amusement. He cocked the pistol, then raised it towards Hogan's head.

The sound of the shot pounded across the orchard. The two gravediggers jumped in terror as smoke drifted out from the hedge where the killer had been concealed just twenty paces from where Hogan and Sarsfield had been standing. The priest was now lying on the mound of excavated soil where his body jerked twice and then, with a sigh, lay still.

Sharpe stood up from behind the hedge and crossed to the grave to see that his bullet had gone plumb where he had aimed it, straight through the dead man's heart. He stared down at the priest, noting how dark the blood looked on the soutane's cloth. A fly had already settled there. 'I liked him,' he told Hogan.

'It's allowed, Richard,' Hogan said. The Major was upset and pale, so pale that for a moment he looked as if he might be sick. 'One of mankind's higher authorities enjoins us to love our enemies and He said nothing about them ceasing to be enemies just because we love them. Nor can I recall any specific injunction in Holy Scripture against shooting our enemies through the heart.' Hogan paused and suddenly all his usual flippancy seemed to drain out of him. 'I liked him too,' he said simply.

'But he was going to shoot you,' Sharpe said. Hogan, talking privately with Sharpe on their way to the burial, had warned the rifleman what might happen and Sharpe, disbelieving the prediction, had nevertheless watched it happen and then done his part.

'He deserved a better death,' Hogan said, then he pushed the corpse with his foot and thus toppled it into the grave. The priest's body landed awkwardly so that it seemed as if he was sitting on the shrouded head of Kiely's corpse. Hogan tossed the counterfeit newspaper after the body, then took a small round box from his pocket. 'Shooting Sarsfield doesn't fetch you any favours, Richard,' Hogan said sternly as he prised the lid off the box. 'Let's just say I now forgive you for letting Juanita go. That damage has been contained. But you still might need to be sacrificed for the happiness of Spain.'

'Yes, sir,' Sharpe said resentfully.

Hogan caught the resentment in the rifleman's voice. 'Of course life isn't fair, Richard. Ask him.' He nodded down at the dead, white-haired priest then sprinkled the contents of his small box onto the corpse's faded and bloodied soutane.

'What's that?' Sharpe asked.

'Just soil, Richard, just soil. Nothing important.' Hogan tossed the empty pillbox onto the two bodies, then summoned the gravediggers. 'He was a Frenchman,' he told them in Portuguese, certain that such an explanation would make them sympathize with the murder they had just witnessed. He gave each man a coin, then watched as the double grave was filled with earth.

Hogan walked back with Sharpe towards Fuentes de Oñoro. 'Where's Patrick?' the Major asked.

'I told him to wait in Vilar Formoso.'

'At an inn?'

'Aye. The one where I first met Runciman.'

'Good. I need to get drunk, Richard.' Hogan looked bleak, almost as if he might weep. 'One less witness of your confession in San Isidro, Richard,' he said.

'That's not why I did it, Major,' Sharpe protested.

'You did nothing, Richard, absolutely nothing.' Hogan spoke fiercely. 'What happened in that orchard never happened. You saw nothing, heard nothing, did nothing. Father Sarsfield is alive, God knows where, and his disappearance will become a mystery that will never be explained. Or perhaps the truth is that Father Sarsfield never even existed, Richard, in which case you can't possibly have killed him, can you? So say no more about it, not a word.' He sniffed, then looked ahead at the blue evening sky which was unbruised by any gunsmoke. 'The French have given us a day of peace, Richard, so we shall celebrate by getting bloody drunk. And tomorrow, God help us sinners both, we'll bloody fight.'

The sun sank behind layers of western cloud so that the sky seemed shot with glory. For a time the shadows of the British guns reached monstrously across the plain as they stretched towards the oaks and the French army and it was then, in the dying minutes of the full light, that Sharpe rested his telescope on the chill barrel of a nine-pounder gun and trained the glass across the low-lying land until he could see the enemy soldiers around their cooking fires. It was not the first time that day he had searched the enemy lines through the glass. All morning he had wandered restlessly between the ammunition park and the gun line where he had stared fixedly at the enemy and now, back from Vilar Formoso with a sour belly and a head thick with too much wine, he looked once again into Masséna's lines.

'They won't come now,' a gunner lieutenant said, thinking that the rifle Captain feared a dusk assault. 'Froggies don't like fighting at night.'

'No,' Sharpe agreed, 'they won't come now,' but he kept his eye to the telescope as he inched it along the shadowed line of trees and fires and men. And then, suddenly, he checked the glass.

For he had seen the grey uniforms. Loup was here after all and his brigade was a part of Masséna's army which had spent the whole day preparing for the attack that would surely come with the returning sun.

Sharpe watched his enemy, then straightened from the gun barrel and closed the glass. His head spun with the effects of the wine, but he was not so drunk that he did not feel a shudder of fear as he thought of what would come across those cannon-scarred fields when the sun next shone on Spain.

Tomorrow.

CHAPTER NINE

The horsemen came out of the mist like creatures from nightmare. The Frenchmen rode big horses that galloped through the marshland to explode water with every stride, then the leading squadrons reached the higher ground about the village of Nave de Haver where the Spanish partisans had bivouacked and the sound of the French cavalry's hooves turned into a thunder that shook the earth itself. A trumpet urged the horsemen on. It was dawn and the sun was a silver disc low in the fogbank that veiled the eastern fields from which death was erupting.

The Spanish sentinels fired one hasty volley, then retreated before the overwhelming enemy numbers. Some of the partisans were asleep after standing guard through the night, and they woke only to stumble out from their requisitioned houses and be cut down with slashing blades and dipping lance heads. The partisan brigade had been placed in Nave de Haver to watch the allies' southern flank and no one had expected them to face a full French attack, but now the heavy cavalry was streaming in through the alleys and crashing their big horses through the gardens and orchards beside the huddle of houses that lay so far to the south of Fuentes de Oñoro. The partisan commander shouted at his men to withdraw, but the French were slashing at defenders as they frantically tried to reach their frightened horses. Some men refused to retreat, but ran at the enemy with all the passionate hatred of the *guerrillero*. Blood spilt on the streets and splashed on the house walls. One street was blocked when a Spaniard shot a dragoon's horse and the beast fell thrashing to the cobbles. The Spaniard bayoneted the rider, then was hurled backwards as a second horse, unable to stop its charge, tripped and stumbled over the bleeding corpses. A knot of Spaniards fell on the second horse and its rider. Knives and swords hacked down, then more partisans scrambled over the dying, bloody beasts to fire a volley at the milling riders trapped by the carnage. More Frenchmen fell from their saddles, then a troop of lancers entered the street behind the Spanish defenders and the lance heads dropped to the level of a man's waist as the horses were spurred forward. The Spaniards, trapped between dragoons and lancers, tried to fight back, but now it was the turn of the French to be the killers. A few partisans escaped through the houses, but only to find the streets beyond the back doors were also filled with blood-crazed horsemen in glittering uniforms being urged to the slaughter by the frantic, joyous notes of the trumpeters.

Most of Nave de Haver's Spanish defenders fled into the mists west of the village where they were pursued by *cuirassiers* in high black-plumed helmets and shining steel breastplates. The big swords hacked down like meat axes; one such blow could cripple a horse or crush a man's skull. To the north and south of the *cuirassiers*, troops of lightly mounted *chasseurs à cheval* raced like steeplechasers to cut off the Spaniards. They whooped hunting calls. The *chasseurs* carried light, curved sabres that slashed wicked wounds across their enemies' heads and shoulders. Unhorsed Spaniards reeled in agony across the meadows and were ridden down by horsemen practising their sword cuts or lance thrusts. Dismounted dragoons hunted through the houses and cattle sheds of Nave de Haver, finding the survivors one by one and shooting them with carbines or pistols. One group of Spaniards took refuge in the church, but the copper-helmeted dragoons forced their way in through the priest's door at the back of the sacristy and fell on the defenders with swords. It was Sunday morning and the priest had hoped to say a Mass for the Spanish troops, but now he died with his congregation as the French ransacked the small, blood-soaked church for its plate and candlesticks.

A French work party dragged the corpses out of the village's main street so that the advancing artillery could pass through. It took half an hour's work before the guns could crash and rattle between the blood-splashed houses. The first guns were the light and mobile cannon of the horse artillery; six-pounder guns dragged by horses ridden by gunners resplendent in gold and blue uniforms. Larger cannons were coming behind, but the horse artillery would lead the attack on the next village upstream where the British Seventh Division had taken its position. Infantry columns followed the horse artillery, battalion after battalion marching beneath their gilded eagles. The mist was burning off to show a village smoking with abandoned cooking fires and reeking of blood where the victorious dragoons were remounting their horses to join the pursuit. Some of the infantry tried to march through the village, but staff officers forced them to go around Nave de Haver's southern flank so that none of the battalions would be slowed by plundering. The first aides galloped back to Masséna's headquarters to say that Nave de Haver had fallen and that the village of Poco Velha, less than two miles upstream, was already under artillery fire. A second division of infantry marched to support the men who were already turning the allies' southern flank and were now marching due north towards the road that led from Fuentes de Oñoro to the fords across the River Coa.

Opposite Fuentes de Oñoro itself the French main gun

batteries opened fire. The cannon had been dragged to the tree line and roughly embrasured with felled trunks to give their crews some protection from the British guns on the ridge. The French fired common shell, iron balls filled with a fused powder charge that cracked apart in a burst of smoke to shatter the casing on the plateau's skyline, while short-barrelled howitzers lobbed shells into the broken streets of Fuentes de Oñoro to fill the village with the stench of burned powder and the rattle of exploded iron. During the night a battery of mixed four-and six-pounder guns had been moved into the gardens and houses on the stream's eastern bank and those guns opened up with roundshot that cracked fiercely on the defenders' walls. The *voltigeurs* in the gardens fired at British loopholes and cheered whenever a roundshot brought down a length of wall or collapsed a broken roof onto a room of crouching redcoats. A shell set light to some collapsed thatch and the flames crackled up to spread thick smoke across the upper village where riflemen sheltered behind the cemetery's gravestones. French shells drove into the burial ground, overturning headstones and grubbing up the earth around the graves so that it looked as though a herd of monstrous pigs had been truffling the soil to reach the buried dead.

The British guns returned a sporadic fire. They were holding the bulk of their ammunition for the moment when the French columns were launched across the plain towards the village, though every now and then a case shot exploded at the tree line to make the French gunners duck and curse. One by one the aim of the French guns was shifted from the ridge onto the burning village where the spreading smoke gave evidence of the damage being done. Behind the ridge the redcoat battalions listened to the cannonade and prayed they would not be asked to go down into the maelstrom of fire and smoke. Some chaplains raised their voice over the sound of the cannon as they read Morning Prayer to the waiting battalions. There was a comfort in the old words, though some sergeants barked at the men to mind their damned manners when they tittered at the line in the day's epistle which enjoined the congregation to abstain from fleshly lusts. Then they prayed for the King's Majesty, for the royal family, for the clergy, and only then did some chaplains add a prayer that God would preserve the lives of His soldiers on this Sabbath day on the border of Spain.

Where, three miles south of Fuentes de Oñoro, the *cuirassiers* and *chasseurs* and lancers and dragoons were met by a force of British dragoons and German hussars. The horsemen clashed in a sudden and bloody mêlée. The allied horse were outnumbered, but they were properly formed and fighting against an enemy force strung out by the excitement of the pursuit. The French faltered, then retreated, but on either flank of the allied squadrons other French horsemen raced ahead to where two battalions of infantry, one British and one Portuguese, waited behind the walls and hedges of Poco Velha. The British and German cavalry, fearing that they would be surrounded, hurried out of danger's way as the excited French horse ignored them and charged at the village's defenders instead.

'Fire!' a *caçador* colonel shouted and ragged smoke whiplashed from the garden walls. Horses screamed and fell, while men were plucked backwards from saddles as the musket and rifle balls cracked straight through the *cuirassiers'* steel breastplates. There was a frantic trumpet call and the charging French horse checked, turned and rode back to re-form, leaving behind a tideline of struggling horses and bleeding men. More French horsemen were arriving to join the attack; imperial guardsmen mounted on big horses and carrying carbines and swords, while beyond the cavalry the leading foot artillery unlimbered in the meadows and opened fire to add their heavier missiles to the six-pounder guns of the horse artillery. The first twelve-pounder cannon balls fell short, but the next rounds crashed into Poco Velha's defenders and tore great gaps in their protective walls. The French cavalry had drawn to one side to re-form its ranks and to open a path for the infantry who now appeared behind the guns. The infantry battalions formed themselves into two attack columns that would move like human avalanches at the thin line of Poco Velha's defenders. The French drummer boys tightened their drumskins, while beyond Poco Velha the remaining seven battalions of the British Seventh Division waited for the attack that the drums would inspire. Horse artillery guarded the infantry's flanks, but the French were bringing still more horses and still more guns against the isolated defenders. The British and German cavalry, which had been driven away westwards, now trotted in a wide circle to rejoin the beleaguered Seventh Division.

French skirmishers ran ahead of the attacking column. They splashed through a streamlet, passed the artillery gun line and ran out to where the dead horses and dying men marked the limit of the cavalry's first attack. There the skirmishers split into their pairs to open fire. British and Portuguese skirmishers met them and the crackle of muskets and rifles carried across the marshy fields to where Wellington stared anxiously southwards. Beneath him the village of Fuentes de Oñoro was a smoking shambles being pounded by a continuous cannonade, but his gaze was always to the south where he had sent his Seventh Division beyond the protective range of the British cannon on the plateau.

Wellington had made a mistake, and he knew it. His army was split in two and the enemy was threatening to overwhelm the smaller of the two parts. Gallopers brought him news of a broken Spanish force, then of ever mounting numbers of French infantry crossing the stream at Nave de Haver to join the attack on the Seventh Division's nine battalions. At least two French divisions had gone south for that attack, and each of those divisions was stronger than the newly formed and still under-strength Seventh Division which was not only under attack by infantry, but also seemed assailed by every French horseman in Spain.

French infantry officers urged the columns forward and the drummers responded by beating the *pas de charge* with a frantic energy. The French attack had rolled over Nave de Haver, had brushed aside the allied cavalry and now it had to keep up the momentum if it was to annihilate Wellington's right wing. Then the victorious attack could lance at the rear of Wellington's main force while the rest of the French army hammered through his battered defences at Fuentes de Oñoro.

The *voltigeurs* pushed back the outnumbered allied skir-mishers who ran back to join a main defence line being shredded and torn by French canister. Wounded men crawled back into Poco Velha's small streets where they tried to find a patch of shelter from the terrible storm of canister. French cavalrymen were waiting on the village's flanks, waiting with blade and lance to pounce on the broken fugitives who must soon stream back from the columns' attack.

'*Vive l'Empereur!*' the attackers shouted. The mist had gone now, replaced by a clear sunlight that flickered off thousands of French bayonets. The sun was shining into the defenders' eyes, a great blinding blaze out of which loomed the huge dark shapes of the French columns trampling the fields to the sounds of drums and cheering and the thunder of marching feet. The *voltigeurs* began firing at the main British and Portuguese line. The sergeants shouted at the files to close up, then looked nervously at the enemy cavalry waiting to charge from the flanks.

The British and Portuguese battalions shrank towards their centres as the dead and wounded left the files. 'Fire!' the British

Colonel ordered and his men began the rolling volleys that rippled smoke up and down the line as the companies fired in turn. The Portuguese battalion took up the volleys so that the whole eastern face of the village flashed flame. Men in the leading ranks of the French columns went down and the columns divided so that the files could walk round the wounded and dead, then the ranks closed up again as the cheering Frenchmen came stolidly on. The Portuguese and British volleys became ragged as the officers let men fire as soon as they were loaded. Smoke rolled thick to hide the villages. A French galloper gun unlimbered on the village's northern flank and slashed a roundshot into the *caçadores'* ranks. The drummers paused in the *pas de charge* and the columns let out their great war cry, '*Vive l'Empereur!*' and then the drums began again, beating even faster as the columns crashed through the fragile vegetable gardens on the outskirts of the village. Another round-shot seared in from the north, slathering a gable end with blood.

'Withdraw! Withdraw!' The two battalions had no hope of holding the village and so, almost overrun by the enemy, the redcoats and Portuguese ran back through the village. It was a poor place with a tiny church no bigger than a dissenting chapel. The grenadier companies of both battalions formed ranks beside the church. Ramrods scraped in barrels. The French were in the village now, their columns breaking apart as the infantry found their own paths through the alleyways and gardens. The cavalry was closing on the village's flanks, looking for broken ranks to charge and decimate. The leading French attackers came into sight of the church and a Portuguese officer gave the order to fire and the two companies hurled a volley that choked the narrow street with dead and wounded Frenchmen. 'Back! Back!' the Portuguese officer shouted. 'Watch your flanks!'

A roundshot splintered part of the church roof, showering

the retreating grenadiers with shards of broken tile. French infantry appeared in an alleyway and spilt out to make a crude firing line that brought down two *caçadores* and a redcoat. Most of the two battalions were clear of the village now and retreating towards the other seven battalions that were formed in square to deter the circling French cavalry. That cavalry feared it would be cheated of its prey and some of the horsemen charged Poco Velha's withdrawing garrison. 'Rally, rally!' a redcoat officer called as he saw a squadron of *cuirassiers* wheel around to charge at his men. His company shrank into the rally square, a huddle of men forming an obstacle large enough to deter a horse from charging home. 'Hold your fire! Let the buggers get close!'

'Leave him be!' a sergeant shouted when a man ran out of the rally square to help a wounded comrade.

'Hive! Hive!' another captain shouted and his men rallied into a hasty square. 'Fire!' Maybe a third of his men were loaded and they loosed a ragged volley that made one horse scream and rear. The rider fell, crashing heavily to earth with all the weight of his breastplate and back armour dragging him down. Another horseman rode clear through the musket balls and galloped wildly along the face of the crude square. A redcoat darted out to lunge at the Frenchman with his bayonet, but the rider leaned far from his saddle and screamed in triumph as he whipped his sword across the infantryman's face.

'You bloody fool, Smithers! You bloody fool!' his captain shouted at the blinded redcoat who was screaming and clutching a face that was a mask of blood.

'Back! Back!' the Portuguese Colonel urged his men. The French infantry had advanced through the village and was forming an attack column at its northern edge. A British galloper gun fired at them and the roundshot skipped on the ground and bounced up to crack into the village houses.

'*Vive l'Empereur!*' a French colonel bellowed and the drummer boys began to sound the dreaded *pas de charge* that would drive the Emperor's infantry onwards. The two allied battalions were streaming in clumps across the fields pursued by the advancing infantry and harried by horsemen. One small group was ridden down by lancers, another panicked and ran towards the waiting squares only to be hunted down by dragoons who held their swords like lances to spear into the redcoats' backs. The two largest masses of horsemen were those that stalked the colour parties, waiting for the first sign of panic that would open the clustered infantrymen to a thunderous charge. The flags of the two battalions were lures to glory, trophies that would make their captors famous throughout France. Both sets of flags were surrounded by bayonets and defended by sergeants carrying spontoons, the long, heavy, lance-headed pikes designed to kill any horse or man daring to thrust in to capture the fringed silk trophies.

'Rally! Rally!' the English Colonel shouted at his men. 'Steady, boys, steady!' And his men doggedly worked their way westwards while the cavalry feinted charges that might provoke a volley. Once the volley was fired the real charge would be led by lancers who could reach across the infantry's bayonets and unloaded muskets to kill the outer ranks of defenders. 'Hold your fire, boys, hold your fire,' the Colonel called. His men passed close to one of the outcrops of rock that studded the plain and for a few seconds the redcoats seemed to cling to the tiny scrap of high ground as though the lichen-covered stone would offer them a safe refuge, then the officers and sergeants moved them on to the next stretch of open grassland. Such open land was heaven-sent for horsemen, a cavalryman's perfect killing ground.

Dragoons had unholstered their carbines to snipe at the colour parties. Other horsemen fired pistols. Bloody trails followed the redcoats and *caçadores* as they marched. The hurrying French infantry were shouting at their own horsemen to clear a line of fire so that a musket volley could tear the defiant colour parties apart, but the horsemen would not yield the glory of capturing an enemy standard to any foot soldier and so they circled the flags and blocked the infantry fire that might have overwhelmed the retreating allied infantrymen. Marksmen among the British and Portuguese picked their targets, fired, then reloaded as they walked. The two battalions had lost all order; there were no more ranks or files, just clusters of desperate men who knew that salvation lay in staying close together as they edged their way back towards the dubious safety of the Seventh Division's remaining battalions who still waited in square and watched aghast as the boiling maelstrom of cavalry and cannon smoke inched ever nearer.

'Fire!' a voice shouted from one of these battalions and the face of a square erupted with smoke to shatter an excited troop of sabre-wielding *chasseurs*. The retreating infantry had come close to the other battalions now and the horsemen saw their first chance of fame slipping away. Some *cuirassiers* wound their swords' wrist straps tight, called encouragement to one another and then spurred their big horses into the gallop as a trumpeter sounded the charge. They rode booted knee to booted knee, a phalanx of steel and horse flesh designed to batter the nearest colours' defenders into broken shreds that could be slaughtered like cattle. This was a lottery: fifty horsemen against two hundred frightened men and if the horsemen broke the rally square then one of the surviving *cuirassiers* would ride back to Marshal Masséna with a king's flag and another would carry the bullet-scarred remnants of the 85th's yellow colour and both would be famous.

'Front rank, kneel!' the 85th's Colonel shouted.

'Take aim! Wait for it!' a captain called. 'Damn your eager-ness! Wait!'

The redcoats were from Buckinghamshire. Some had been recruited from the farms of the Chilterns and from the villages of Aylesbury's vale, while most had come from the noisome slums and pestilent prisons of London which sprawled on the county's southern edge. Now their mouths were dry from the salt gunpowder of the cartridges they had bitten all morning and their battle had shrunk to a terrifying patch of foreign land that was surrounded by a victorious, rampaging, screaming enemy. For all the men of the 85th knew they might have been the last British troops alive and now they faced the Emperor's horse as it charged at them with plumed men holding heavy swords and behind the *cuirassiers* a tangled mass of lancers, dragoons and *chasseurs* followed to snap up the broken remnants of the colour party's rally square. A Frenchman screamed a war cry as he rammed his spurs hard back along his horse's flanks and, just as it seemed that the redcoats had left their one volley too late, their Colonel called the word.

'Fire!'

Horses tumbled in bloody agony. A horse and cavalryman struck by a volley kept moving forward, turned in an instant from war's gaudiest killers into so much overdressed meat, but the meat could still smash a square's face apart by its sheer dead weight. The leading rank of the cavalry charge fell to smear its dying blood along the grass. Horsemen screamed as they were crushed by their own rolling horses. The riders coming behind could not avoid the carnage in front and the second rank rode hard into the flailing remnants of the first and the horses shrieked as their legs broke and as they tumbled down to slide to a halt just yards from the redcoats' lingering gunsmoke.

The rest of the charge was blocked by the horror before them and so it split into two streams of horsemen that galloped ineffectually down the sides of the rally square. Redcoats fired as the cavalry passed and then the charge was gone and the Colonel was telling his men to move on westwards. 'Steady, boys, steady!' he called. A man ran out and cut a horsehair-plumed helmet from the corpse of a Frenchman, then ran back into the rally square. Another volley came from the battalions waiting in square and suddenly the battered, harried fugitives of Poco Velha's defenders were back amidst the rest of the Seventh Division. They formed in the division's centre, just where a wide road led south and west between deep ditches. It was the road that went to the safe fords across the Coa, the road which went home, the road to security, but all that was left to guard it were the nine squares of infantry, a battery of light guns and the cavalry who had survived the fight south of Poco Velha.

The two battalions from Poco Velha formed small squares. They had suffered in the village's streets and on the spring grass of the meadows outside the village, yet their colours still flew: four bright flags amidst a division flying eighteen such flags, while around them circled the Empire's cavalry and to their north there marched two whole divisions of the Empire's foot soldiers. The two beleaguered battalions had reached safety, but it looked as though it would be short-lived for they had survived only to join a division that was surely doomed. Sixteen thousand Frenchmen now threatened four and a half thousand Portuguese and Britons.

The French horsemen wheeled away from the musket fire to re-form ranks made ragged by the morning's charge. The French infantry stopped to form for their new attack, while from the east, from across the stream, there came new French artillery fire that aimed to batter the nine waiting squares into carnage.

It was two hours after dawn. And in the meadows south of Fuentes de Oñoro and far from any help an army seemed to be dying. While the French marched on.

* * *

'He has a choice,' Marshal Massén...
The Marshal did not really want to be...
on this morning of his triumph, but Ducos...
who had an inexplicable sway with the Empero...
Masséna, Marshal of France, Duke of Rivoli and...
Essling, found time after breakfast to make certain...
understood the day's opportunities and, more important,...
whom this day's laurels would belong.

Ducos had ridden out of Ciudad Rodrigo to witness the
battle. Officially Masséna's attack was merely an effort to move
supplies into Almeida, but every Frenchman knew the stakes
were much higher than the relief of one small garrison stranded
behind the British lines. The real prize was the opportunity to
cut Wellington off from his base and then destroy his army in
one glorious day of bloodletting. Such a victory would end
British defiance in Spain and Portugal for ever and would bring
in its wake a roll call of new titles for the wharf rat who had
joined the French royal army as a private. Maybe Masséna
would earn a throne? The Emperor had redistributed half the
chairs in Europe by making his brothers into kings, so why
should not Marshal Masséna, Prince of Essling, become the
king of somewhere or other? The throne in Lisbon needed a
pair of buttocks to keep it warm, and Masséna reckoned his
bum was as good for the task as any of Napoleon's brothers.
And all that was needed for that glorious vision to come true
was victory here at Fuentes de Oñoro and that victory was now
very close. The battle had opened as Masséna had intended
and now it would close as he intended.

'You were saying, Your Majesty, that Wellington has a choice?'
Ducos prompted the Marshal who had drifted into a momentary daydream.

'He has a choice,' Masséna confirmed. 'He can abandon his
right wing which means he also abandons any chance of retreat,

case we shall break his centre in Fuentes de Oñoro and hunt his army down in the hills for the next week. Or he can abandon Fuentes de Oñoro and try to rescue his right wing, in which case we shall fight him to the death on the plain. I'd rather he offered me a fight on the plain, but he won't. This Englishman only feels safe when he has a hill to defend, so he'll stay in Fuentes de Oñoro and let his right wing go to a hell of our making.'

Ducos was impressed. It had been a long time since he had heard a French officer sound so optimistic in Spain, and a long time too since the eagles had marched into battle with such confidence and alacrity. Masséna deserved applause and Ducos happily offered the Marshal the compliments he desired, but he also added a caution. 'This Englishman, Your Majesty,' he pointed out, 'is also skilled at defending hills. He defended Fuentes de Oñoro on Friday, did he not?'

Masséna sneered at the caution. Ducos had elaborated such devious schemes to undermine British morale, but they only sprang from his lack of faith in soldiers, just as Ducos's presence in Spain sprang from the Emperor's lack of faith in his marshals. Ducos had to learn that when a marshal of France put his mind to victory then victory was certain. 'On Friday, Ducos,' Masséna explained, 'I tickled Fuentes de Oñoro with a pair of brigades, but today we shall send three whole divisions into that little village. Three big divisions, Ducos, full of hungry men. What chance do you think that little village has?'

Ducos considered the question in his usual pedantic way. He could see Fuentes de Oñoro clearly enough; the village was a meagre sprawl of peasants' hovels being pounded to dust by the French artillery. Beyond the dust and smoke Ducos could see the graveyard and battered church where the road angled uphill to the plateau. The hill was steep, to be sure, but not very high, and on Friday the attackers had cleared the village of its defenders and gained a lodgement among the lower stones of the graveyard and one more attack would surely have driven the eagles clear across the ridge's crest and into the soft belly of the enemy beyond. And now, out of sight of that enemy, three whole divisions of French infantry were waiting to attack, and in the van of that attack Masséna planned to put the elite of his attacking regiments, the massed companies of grenadiers with their plumed bearskins and fearful reputation. The cream of France would march against a raddled army of half-broken men.

'Well, Ducos?' Masséna challenged the Major for his verdict.

'I must congratulate Your Majesty,' Ducos said.

'Which means, I suppose, that you approve of my humble plan?' Masséna asked sarcastically.

'All France will approve, Your Majesty, when it brings victory.'

'Bugger the victory,' Masséna said, 'so long as it brings me Wellington's whores. I'm tired of my present bunch. Half of them are poxed, the other half are pregnant and the fat one bawls her eyes out every time you strip the bitch for duty.'

'Wellington has no whores,' Ducos said icily. 'He controls his passions.'

The one-eyed Masséna burst into laughter. 'Controls his passions! God on his cross, Ducos, but you'd make smiling a crime. Controls his passions, does he? Then he's a fool, and a defeated fool at that.' The Marshal wheeled his horse away from the Major and snapped his fingers at a nearby aide. 'Let the eagles go, Jean, let them go!'

The drums called for the muster and three divisions stirred themselves for action. Men drained coffee dregs, stowed knives and tin plates in haversacks, checked their cartridge pouches and plucked their muskets from the pyramid stacks. It was two hours after a Sunday dawn and time to close the battle's jaws as all along the Marshal's line, from south in the plain to north where the village smoked under its numbing cannonade, the French smelt victory.

"Pon my soul, Sharpe, but it's unfair. Unfair! You and me both to stand trial?' Colonel Runciman had been unable to resist the lure of witnessing the day's high drama and so he had come to the plateau, though he had taken care not to step too close to the ridge's crest which was occasionally churned by a high French roundshot. A pyre of smoke marked where the village endured its bombardment while further south, way down on the plain, a second smudge of musket smoke betrayed where the French flank attack was driving across the low ground.

'Waste of time complaining about unfairness, General,' Sharpe said. 'Only the wealthy can afford to preach about fairness. The rest of us take what we can and try hard not to miss what we can't take.'

'Even so, Sharpe, it's unfair!' Runciman said reprovingly. The Colonel looked pale and unhappy. 'It's the disgrace, you see. A man goes home to England and expects to be decently treated, but instead I'll be vilified.' He ducked as a French roundshot rumbled far overhead. 'I had hopes, Sharpe! I had hopes!'

'The Golden Fleece, General? Order of the Bath?'

'Not just those, Sharpe, but of marriage. There are, you understand, ladies of fortune in Hampshire. I've no ambition to be a bachelor all my life, Sharpe. My dear mother, God rest her, always claimed I'd make a good husband so long as the lady was possessed of a middling fortune. Not a great fortune, one must not be unrealistic, but a sufficiency to keep our good selves in modest comfort. A pair of coaches, decent stables, cooks that know their business, smallish game park, a dairy, you know the sort of place.'

'Makes me homesick, General,' Sharpe said.

The sarcasm sailed airily over Runciman's head. 'But now, Sharpe, can you imagine any woman of decent family allying herself with a vilified name?' He thought about it for a moment, then gave a slow despairing shake of the head. 'Good God! I might have to marry a Methodist!'

'It hasn't happened yet, General,' Sharpe said, 'and a lot could change today.'

Runciman looked alarmed. 'You mean I could be killed?'

'Or you could make a name for bravery, sir,' Sharpe said. 'Nosey always forgives a man for good conduct.'

'Oh, good Lord, no! Dear me, no. 'Pon my soul, Sharpe, no. I ain't the type. Never was. I went into soldiering because my dear father couldn't find a place for me anywhere else! He purchased me into the army, you understand, because he said it was as good a billet as I could ever expect from society, but I'm not the fighting sort. Never was, Sharpe.' Runciman listened to the terrible noise of the cannonade pounding Fuentes de Oñoro, a noise made worse by the splintering sound of *voltigeur* muskets firing over the stream. 'I'm not proud of it, Sharpe, but I don't think I could endure that kind of thing. Don't think I could at all.'

'Can't blame you, sir,' Sharpe said, then turned as Sergeant Harper shouted for his attention. 'You'll forgive me, General?'

'Off you go, Sharpe, off you go.'

'Trade, sir,' Harper said, jerking his head towards Major Tarrant who was gesticulating at a wagon driver.

Tarrant turned as Sharpe came near. 'The Light Division is ordered south, Sharpe, but its ammunition reserve is stuck to the north. We're to replace it. Would you mind if your rifles accompanied it?'

Sharpe did mind. He instinctively wanted to stay where the battle would be fiercest and that was in Fuentes de Oñoro, but he could not say as much to Tarrant. 'No, sir.'

293

'In case they get bogged down, d'you see, and have to spend the rest of the day fighting off Frenchmen, so the General wants them to have a plenitude of ammunition. Rifle and musket cartridges, mixed. Artillery are looking after themselves. One wagon should do it, but it needs an escort, Sharpe. French cavalry are lively down there.'

'Can we help?' Captain Donaju had overheard Tarrant's hurried explanation of Sharpe's errand.

'Might need you later, Captain,' Tarrant said. 'I have a feeling today's likely to be lively all round. Never seen the Frogs so uppity. Have you, Sharpe?'

'They've got their tails up today, Major,' Sharpe agreed. He looked up at the wagon driver. 'Are you ready?'

The driver nodded. His wagon was an English four-wheeled farm vehicle with high splayed sides to which were harnessed three Cleveland Bays in single file. 'Had four beasts once,' the driver remarked as Sharpe climbed up beside him, 'but a Frenchie shell got Bess, so now I'm down to three.' The driver had woven red and blue woollen braiding into the horses' manes and had decorated his wagon's flanks with discarded cap-plates and thrown horseshoes that he had nailed to the planking. 'You know where we're going?' he asked Sharpe as Harper ordered the riflemen to climb onto the boxes of ammunition stacked on the wagon's bed.

'After them.' Sharpe pointed to his right where the plateau offered a gentler slope down to the southern lowlands and where the Light Division was marching south beneath its banners. It was Sharpe's old division, made up of riflemen and light infantry, and it regarded itself as the army's elite division. Now it was marching to save the Seventh Division from annihilation.

A mile away, across the Dos Casas stream and close to the ruined barn that served as his headquarters, Marshal André

Masséna saw the fresh British troops leaving the plateau's protection to march south towards the beleaguered redcoats and Portuguese. 'The fool,' he said to himself, then louder in a gleeful voice, 'the fool!'

'Your Majesty?' an aide inquired.

'The first rule of war, Jean,' the Marshal said, 'is never to reinforce failure. And what is our whore-free Englishman doing? He's sending more troops to be massacred by our cavalry!' The Marshal put the telescope back to his eye. He could see guns and cavalry going south with the new troops. 'Or maybe he's withdrawing?' he mused aloud. 'Maybe he's making sure he can get back to Portugal. Where's Loup's brigade?'

'Just north of here, Your Majesty,' the aide answered.

'With his whore, no doubt?' Masséna asked sourly. Juanita de Elia's flamboyant presence with the Loup Brigade had drawn the attention and jealousy of every Frenchman in the army.

'Indeed, Your Majesty.'

Masséna snapped the telescope shut. He disliked Loup. He recognized his ambitions and knew that Loup would trample over any man to gain those ambitions. Loup wanted to be a marshal like Masséna, he had even lost an eye like Masséna, and now he wanted those grand titles with which the Emperor rewarded the brave and the lucky. But Masséna would not help Loup secure those ambitions. A man remained a marshal by suppressing his rivals, not encouraging them, so this day Brigadier Loup would be given a menial task. 'Warn Brigadier Loup,' Masséna told the aide, 'that he's to untangle himself from his Spanish whore and be ready to escort the wagons through Fuentes de Oñoro when our soldiers have opened the road. Tell him Wellington's shifting his position to the south and the road to Almeida should be open by midday, and that his brigade's job will be to escort the supplies into Almeida while the rest of us finish off the enemy.' Masséna smiled. Today was a day for Frenchmen to win glory, a day to capture a haul of enemy colours and to soak a river bank with the blood of Englishmen, but Loup, Masséna had decided, would share no part of it. Loup would be a common baggage guard while Masséna and the eagles made all Europe shudder with fear.

The Seventh Division retreated towards a slight ridge of ground above the Dos Casas stream. They were retreating north, but facing south as they tried to block the advance of the massive French force that had been sent around the army's flank. In the distance they could see the two enemy infantry divisions re-forming their ranks in front of Poco Velha, but the immediate danger came from the enormous number of French cavalry that waited just outside the effective range of the Seventh Division's muskets. The equation facing the nine allied battalions was simple enough. They could form squares and know that even the bravest cavalry would be slaughtered if they tried to charge the mass of compacted muskets and bayonets, but infantry in square was cruelly vulnerable to artillery and musket fire; the moment the Seventh Division contracted into squares the French would batter the allied ranks with gunfire until the Portuguese and redcoats were shredded bloody and the cavalry could ride unchallenged over the crazed survivors.

British and German cavalry came to the rescue first. The allied horse was outnumbered and could never hope to defeat the swirling mass of plumed and breast-plated Frenchmen, but the hussars and dragoons made charge after charge that kept the enemy cavalry from harrying the infantry. 'Keep them in hand!' a British cavalry major kept shouting at his squadron. 'Keep them in hand!' He feared that his men would lose their sense and make a mad charge to glory instead of retiring after each short attack to re-form and charge again, and so he kept encouraging them to show caution and keep their discipline. The squadrons took turns to hold off the French cavalry, one fighting as the others retreated after the infantry. The horses were bleeding, sweating and trembling, but time after time they trotted into their ranks and waited for the spurs to throw them back into the fight. The men tightened their grips on sword and sabre and watched the enemy who shouted insults in an attempt to entice the British and Germans to a mad galloping assault that would open their tightly ordered ranks and turn the controlled charges into a frantic mêlée of swords, lances and sabres. In such a mêlée the French numbers were bound to win, but the allied officers kept their men in hand. 'Damn your eagerness! Hold her in, hold her in!' a captain called to a trooper whose horse broke into a trot too early.

The dragoons were the allied heavy cavalry. They were big men mounted on big horses and carried long heavy straight-bladed swords. They did not charge at the gallop, but rather waited until an enemy regiment threatened to charge and then they made their countercharge at walking pace. Sergeants shouted at the men to hold the line, to keep close and curb their horses, and only at the very last moment, when the enemy was within pistol shot, did a trumpeter sound the charge and the horses would be spurred to a gallop and the men would scream their war cries as they hacked at the enemy horsemen. The big swords could do horrid work. They battered the lighter sabres of the French *chasseurs* aside and forced the riders to duck low over their horses' necks as they tried to avoid the butchers' blades. Steel clashed on steel, wounded horses screamed and reared, then the trumpet would call for the withdrawal and the allied horse would disengage and wheel away. A few French were bound to pursue, but the British and Germans were working close to their own infantry and any Frenchman tempted to pursue too close to the Portuguese and

British battalions became easy meat for a company of muskets. It was hard, disciplined, inglorious work, and each counter-charge paid a price in men and horses, but the threat of the enemy cavalry was checked by it and the nine infantry battalions marched steadily north because of it.

The retreating Seventh Division's flanks were covered by the fire of the horse artillery. The gunners fired canister that could turn a horse and man into a mangled horror of flesh, cloth, leather, steel and blood. The guns would fire four or five rounds while the infantry retreated, then the horse teams were hurried forward, the gun's trail lifted into the limber's pintle, and the gunners would scramble onto the horses' backs and whip the animals into a frantic dash before the vengeful French caval-rymen could catch them. As soon as the team reached the protection of the infantry's muskets it would slew around to make the gun's skidding wheels throw up a fountain of mud or dust, and the gunners would slide off the horses' backs even before they had stopped running. The gun was unhitched, the horses and limber led away and in seconds the next round of canister would shriek down the field to drive another French squadron bloodily away.

The French artillery concentrated their fire on the infantry. Their roundshot and shells whipped through the ranks, spraying blood ten feet high as the missiles plunged home. 'Close up! Close up!' the sergeants shouted and prayed that the excitable enemy cavalry would mask their own guns and thus stop the bombardment, but the cavalry was learning to let the gunners and the French infantry do some of the work before the horsemen garnered all the glory. The French cavalry pulled aside to let the muskets and cannons fight the battle and to rest their horses while the Portuguese and British infantry died.

And die they did. The roundshot whipped through the columns and musket fire raked the files to slow the already agonizingly slow retreat. The nine shrinking battalions left trails of crushed and bloodied grass as they crawled northwards and the crawl was threatening to come to a full halt when all that would be left of the division would be nine bands of survivors clustered round their precious colours. The French cavalry saw their enemy dying and were content to wait for the perfect moment to pounce and deliver the *coup de grâce*. One group of *chasseurs* and *cuirassiers* rode towards a slight rise in the ground where a long wood was planted. The cavalry's commander reckoned the wood would hide his men as they worked their way to the rear of the dying battalions and so give him a chance to launch a surprise attack that might capture a half-dozen flags in one glorious charge. He led the two troops up the slope, his men trailing behind, when suddenly the tree line exploded with gunsmoke. There were not supposed to be enemy troops among the trees, but the volley ripped the advancing cavalry into chaos. The *cuirassier* commander went backwards off his horse's rump with his breastplate holed three times. One of his boots was trapped in a stirrup and he screamed as his terrified and wounded horse dragged him bouncing across the grass to leave great splashes of blood. Then his foot came free and he twitched on the grass as he died. Eight other horsemen fell, some had merely been unhorsed and those men ran to find an unwounded mount while their comrades turned and spurred to safety.

Green-jacketed riflemen ran out of the woods to pillage the dead and wounded cavalrymen. The deeply bellied breastplates worn by the *cuirassiers* were valued as shaving bowls or skillets and even a bullet-holed breastplate could be patched up by a friendly blacksmith. More greenjackets showed at the woods' southern end, then a battalion of redcoats appeared behind them and with the redcoats came a squadron of fresh cavalry and another battery of horse artillery. A regimental band was playing 'Over the Hills and Far Away' as yet more redcoats and greenjackets marched into view.

The Light Division had arrived.

The ammunition wagon lumbered across the fields in the wake of the fast-marching Light Division. One of the wagon's axles squealed like a soul in torment, an annoyance for which the driver apologized, 'but I've greased her,' he told Sharpe, 'and greased her again. I've greased her with the best pig's fat rendered down, but that squeak still don't want to go away. It started the day our Bess got killed and I reckons that squeak is our Bess letting us know she's still kicking somewhere.' For a time the driver followed a cart track, then Sharpe and his riflemen had to dismount and put their shoulders to the wagon's rear to help the vehicle over a bank and into a meadow. Once back on top of the ammunition boxes the greenjackets decided the wagon was a stage coach and began imitating the calls of the post horns and singing out the stops. 'Red Lion! Fine ales, good food, we change the horses and leave in a quarter-hour! Ladies will find their convenience catered for in the passage behind the lounge.' The wagon driver had heard it all before and showed no reaction, but Sharpe, after Harris had hollered for ten minutes about pissing in the passage, turned and told them all to shut the hell up whereupon they pretended to be cowed by him and Sharpe had a sudden pang of regret at the things he would miss if he were to lose his commission. Ahead of the wagon the rifles and muskets cracked. An occasional French roundshot that had been fired too high came bounding across the nearby fields, but the three horses plodded on as patiently as though they were harnessed to a plough instead of lumbering into battle. Only once did an enemy threaten and so force Sharpe's score of riflemen off the wagon to form a rank beside the road. A troop of fifty green-coated dragoons appeared way off to the west where their commander spotted the wagon and turned his men in for the attack. The wagon driver stopped the vehicle and was waiting with a knife poised in case he needed to cut the traces. 'We takes the horses,' he advised Sharpe, 'and leaves the Frenchies to ransack the wagon. That'll keep the buggers busy while we makes off.' His horses munched the grass contentedly while Sharpe measured the range to the French dragoons whose copper helmets glinted gold in the sunlight.

Then, just when he had decided that he might be forced to take the wagon driver's advice and retreat, a squadron of blue-coated cavalrymen intervened. The newcomers were British light dragoons who tempted the French into a running fight of sword against sabre. The driver put away his knife and clicked his tongue, provoking the horses forward. The riflemen scrambled back aboard as the wagon swayed on towards a tree line that obscured the source of the growing powder smoke whitening the southern sky.

Then a crash of heavy guns sounded to the north and Sharpe twisted on the wagon's box to see that the rim of the British-held plateau was thick with smoke as the main batteries fired thunderous volleys towards the east. 'Frogs are attacking the village again,' Sharpe said.

'Nasty place to fight,' Harper said. 'Be glad we're out here instead, boys.'

'And pray the buggers don't cut us off out here,' Sergeant Latimer added gloomily.

'You've got to die somewhere, ain't that right, Mister Sharpe?' Perkins called out.

'Make it your own bed, Perkins, with Miranda beside you,' Sharpe answered. 'Are you looking after that girl?'

'She's not complaining, Mister Sharpe,' Perkins said, thereby provoking a chorus of teasing jeers. Perkins still lacked his green jacket and was touchy about the loss of the coat with its distinguishing black armband denoting that he was a Chosen Man, a compliment that was paid only to the best and most reliable riflemen.

The wagon lurched onto a deep-rutted farm track that led south through the trees towards the distant villages overrun by the French. The Seventh Division was marching north from the woods, going back to the plateau, while the newly arrived Light Division deployed across the broader road that led back into Portugal. The retiring battalions marched slowly, forced to the snail's pace by the number of wounded in their ranks, but at least they marched undefeated beneath flying colours.

The wagon driver hauled on the reins to stop the horses among the trees where the Light Division had established a temporary depot. Two surgeons had spread their knives and saws on tarpaulins laid under holm oaks, while a regimental band played a few yards away. Sharpe told his riflemen to stay with the wagon while he sought orders.

The Light Division was arrayed in squares on the plain between the trees and the smoking villages. The French cavalry trotted across the faces of the squares trying to provoke wasteful volleys at too long a range. The British cavalry was being held in reserve, waiting until the French horse came too close. Six guns of the horse artillery were firing at the French cannon while groups of riflemen were occupying the rocky outcrops that studded the fields. General Crauford, the Light Division's irascible commander, had brought three and a half thousand men to the rescue of the Seventh Division and now those three and half thousand were faced by four thousand French cavalry and twelve thousand French infantrymen. That infantry was advancing in its attack columns from Poco Velha.

'Sharpe? What the hell are you doing here? Thought you'd

deserted us, gone to join the bumboys in Picton's division.' Brigadier General Robert Crauford, fierce-faced and scowling, had spotted Sharpe.

Sharpe explained he had brought a wagonload of ammunition that was now waiting among the trees.

'Waste of time bringing us ammunition,' Crauford snapped. 'We've got plenty. And what the hell are you doing delivering ammunition? Been demoted, have you? I heard you were in disgrace.'

'I'm on administrative duties, sir,' Sharpe said. He had known Crauford ever since India and, like every other skirmisher in Britain's army, Sharpe had a mixed regard for 'Black Bob', sometimes resenting the man's hard, unforgiving discipline, but also recognizing that in Crauford the army had a soldier almost as talented as Wellington himself.

'They're going to sacrifice you, Sharpe,' Crauford said with unholy relish. He was not looking at Sharpe, but instead watched the great horde of French cavalry that was preparing for a concerted charge against his newly arrived battalions. 'You shot a pair of Frogs, ain't that right?'

'Yes, sir.'

'No wonder you're in disgrace,' Crauford said, then gave a bark of laughter. His aides sat their horses in a tight group behind the General. 'Come alone, Sharpe, did you?' Crauford asked.

'I've got my greenjackets here, sir.'

'And the buggers can remember how to fight?'

'I think they can, sir.'

'Then skirmish for me. Those are your new administrative duties, Mister Sharpe. I have to keep the division a safe distance in front of the Frog infantry which means we'll all have to endure the attentions of their gunners and horse, but I'm expecting my rifles to plague the horses and kill the damn guns,

303

and you can help them.' Crauford twisted in his saddle. 'Barratt? Distribute the ammunition and send the wagon back with the wounded. Go to it, Sharpe! And keep a good lookout, we don't want to abandon you out here on your own.'

Sharpe hesitated. It was a risky business asking questions of Black Bob, a man who expected instant obedience, but the General's words had intrigued him. 'So we're not staying here, sir?' he asked. 'We're going back to the ridge?'

'Of course we're bloody going back! Why the hell do you think we marched out here? Just to commit suicide? You think I came back from leave just to give the bloody Frogs some target practice? Get the hell on with it, Sharpe!'

'Yes, sir.' Sharpe ran back to fetch his men and felt a sudden mingled surge of fear and hope.

For Wellington had abandoned the roads back to Portugal. There could be no safe withdrawal now, no steady retreat across the Coa's fords, for Wellington had yielded those roads to the enemy. The British and Portuguese must stand and fight now, and if they lost they would die and with them would die all hopes of victory in Spain. Defeat now did not just mean that Almeida would be relieved, but that the British and Portuguese army would be annihilated. Fuentes de Oñoro had become a battle to the death.

CHAPTER TEN

Sunday's first attack on Fuentes de Oñoro was made by the same French infantrymen who had attacked two days before and who had since been occupying the gardens and houses on the stream's eastern bank. They assembled silently, using the stone walls of the orchards and gardens to disguise their intentions and then, without an opening volley or even bothering to throw out a skirmish line, the blue-coated infantry swarmed across the tumbled walls and plunged down to the stream. The Scottish defenders had time for one volley, then the French were in the village, clawing at the barricades or clambering over the walls thrown down by the howitzer shells that had fallen among the houses in the two hours since dawn. The French drove the Scots deep into the village where one surge trapped two companies of Highlanders in a cul de sac. The attackers turned on the cornered men in a frenzy, filling the alley's narrow confines with a storm of musketry. Some of the Scots tried to escape by pushing down a house wall, but the French were waiting on the far side and met the wall's collapse with more volleys of musket fire. The surviving Highlanders barricaded themselves in houses bordering the stream, but the French poured fire at windows, loopholes and doors, then brought up galloper guns to fire across the stream until at last, with all their officers killed or wounded, the dazed Highlanders surrendered.

The attack on the cornered Highlanders had drained men from the main uphill assault which stalled in the village's centre. The Warwicks, again in reserve, came down from the plateau to help the remaining Scots and together they first stopped the French, then drove them back towards the stream. The fight was fought at murderously close range. Muskets flamed just feet from their targets, and when these were empty men used their guns as clubs or else stabbed forward with bayonets. They were hoarse from shouting and from breathing the smoky dust that filled the air in the narrow, twisting streets where gutters ran with blood and bodies piled to block each door and entryway. The Scots and Warwicks fought their way downhill, but each time they tried to push the French out of the last few houses the newly emplaced guns in the orchards would open fire with canister to fill the village's lower streets and alleys with a rattling sleet of death. Blood trickled to the stream. The village's defenders were deafened by the echo of muskets and the crash of artillery in the streets, but they were not so deaf that they did not hear the ominous tattoo of approaching drummers. New French columns were crossing the plain. The British guns on the ridge were slashing roundshot into the advancing ranks and blasting case shot that exploded above their heads, but the columns were vast and the defenders' cannons few, and so the great mass of men marched on into the eastern gardens from where, with a vast shout, a horde of men in shaggy black bearskin hats swept over the stream and up into the village.

These new attackers were the massed grenadiers: the biggest men and bravest fighters that the attacking divisions could muster. They wore moustaches, epaulettes and plumed bearskins as marks of their special status and they stormed into the village with a roar of triumph that lasted as they swept up the streets with bayonets and musket fire. The tired

Warwicks went back and the Scots went with them. More Frenchmen crossed the stream, a seemingly never-ending flood of blue coats that followed the elite grenadiers into the alleys and up through the houses. The fight in the lower half of the village was the hardest for the attackers, for although sheer impetus carried the assault far into the village heart they were constantly obstructed by dead or wounded. Grenadiers slipped on stones made treacherous by blood, yet sheer numbers forced the attackers on and the defenders were now too few to stop them. Some redcoats tried to clear streets with volley fire, but the grenadiers swarmed through back alleys or over garden walls to outflank the redcoat companies which could only go back uphill through the dust and tiles and burning thatch of the upper village. Wounded men called out pathetically, beseeching their comrades to carry them to safety, but the attack was coming too fast now and the Scots and Englishmen were retreating too quickly. They abandoned the village altogether, fleeing from the upper houses to find a refuge in the graveyard.

The leading French grenadiers charged from the village towards the church above and were met by a volley of muskets fired by men waiting behind the graveyard wall.

The front men fell, but those behind leaped over their dying comrades to assault the graveyard wall. Bayonets and musket stocks slashed over the stone, then the big French soldiers surged over the wall, even pushing it down in some places to begin hunting the survivors up through the heaped graves and fallen stones and shattered wooden crosses. More Frenchmen came from the village to bolster the attack, then a splintering deluge of rifle and musket fire flashed from the stony outcrops just above the blood-greased slope. Grenadiers fell and rolled downhill. A second British volley whipped over the gun-churned graves as still more redcoats arrived to line the ridge's crest and fire their rolling volleys from beside the church and from the saddle of grassland where Wellington had watched aghast as this spring French tide had risen almost to his horse's hooves.

And there, for a while, the attack stalled. The French had first filled the village with dead and wounded, then they had captured it, and now they held the graveyard too. Their soldiers crouched behind graves or behind their enemy's piled dead. They were just feet from the ridge's summit, just feet from victory, while behind them, on a plain gouged by roundshot and scorched by shell and littered with the bodies of dead and dying men, still more French infantry came to help the attackers on.

The day needed just one more push, then the eagles of France would fly free.

The Light Division had formed its battalions into close columns of companies. Each company formed a rectangle four ranks deep and anything from twelve to twenty files wide, then the ten companies of each battalion paraded in column so that from the sky each battalion now resembled a stack of thin red bricks. Then, one by one, the battalion columns turned their backs on the enemy and began marching north towards the plateau. The French cavalry gave immediate pursuit and the air rang with a brassy cacophony as trumpet after trumpet sounded the advance.

'Form square on the front division!' the Colonel of the redcoat battalion nearest Sharpe shouted.

The Major commanding the battalion's leading division of companies called for the first brick to halt and for the second to form alongside it so that two of the bricks now made one long wall of men four ranks deep and forty men wide. 'Dress ranks!' the sergeants shouted as the men shuffled close together and looked right to make sure their rank was ruler straight. While the leading two companies straightened their ranks the Major was calling orders to the succeeding companies. 'Sections outward wheel! Rear sections close to the front!' The French trumpets were pealing and the earth was vibrating from the mass of hooves, but the sergeants' and officers' voices sounded coolly over the threat. 'Outward wheel! Steady now! Rear sections close to the front!' The six centre companies of the battalion now split into four sections each. Two sections swung like hinged doors to the right and two to the left, the innermost men of each section reducing their marching pace from thirty to twenty inches, while the men swinging widest lengthened their stride to thirty-three inches and so the sections pivoted outward to begin forming the twin faces of the square whose anchoring wall was the first two companies. Mounted officers hurried to get their horses inside the rapidly forming square that was, in reality, an oblong. The northward face had been made by the two leading companies, now the two longer sides were formed by the next six companies wheeling outward and closing hard up, while the last companies merely filled in the vacant fourth side. 'Halt! Right about face!' the Major in command of the rear division shouted to the last two companies.

'Prepare to receive cavalry!' the Colonel shouted dutifully, as if the sight of the massed French horse was not warning enough. The Colonel drew his sword, then swatted with his free hand at a horsefly. The colour party stood beside him, two teenage ensigns holding the precious flags that were guarded by a squad of chosen men commanded by hard-bitten sergeants armed with spontoons. 'Rear rank! Port arms!' the Major called. The innermost rank of the square would hold its fire and so act as the battalion's reserve. The cavalry was a hundred paces away and closing fast, a churning mass of excited horses, raised blades, trumpets, flags and thunder.

'Front rank, kneel!' a captain called. The front rank dropped and jammed their bayonet-tipped muskets into the earth to make a continuous hedge of steel about the formation.

'Make ready!' The two inside ranks cocked their loaded guns, and took aim. The whole manoeuvre had been done at a steady pace, without fuss, and the sudden sight of the levelled muskets and braced bayonets persuaded the leading cavalrymen to sheer away from the steady, stolid and silent square. Infantry in square were just about as safe from cavalry as if they were tucked up at home in bed, and the redcoat battalion, by forming square so quickly and quietly, had made the French charge impotent.

'Very nice,' Sergeant Latimer said in tribute to the battalion's professionalism. 'Very nicely done. Just like the parade ground at Shorncliffe.'

'Gun to the right, sir,' Harper called. Sharpe's men were occupying one of the rocky outcrops that studded the plain and which gave the riflemen protection from the marauding cavalry. Their job was to snipe at the cavalry and especially at the French horse artillery which was trying to take advantage of the British squares. Men in square were safe from cavalry yet horribly vulnerable to shell and roundshot, but gunners were equally vulnerable to the accuracy of the British Baker rifles. A galloper gun had taken position two hundred paces away from Sharpe and the gun's crew was lining the barrel on the newly formed square. Two men lifted the ammunition chest off the gun's trail while a third double-shotted the gun's blackened barrel by ramming a round of canister on top of a roundshot.

Dan Hagman fired first and the man ramming the shot slewed round, then held onto the protruding rammer's handle as though it was his grip on life itself. A second bullet cracked off the cannon's barrel to leave a bright scratch in the jaded brass. Another gunner fell, then one of the gun's horses was hit and it reared up and kicked at the horse harnessed next to it. 'Steady does it,' Sharpe said, 'take aim, boys, take aim. Don't waste the shots.' Three more greenjackets fired and their bullets persuaded the beleaguered gunners to crouch behind the cannon and its limber. The gunners shouted at some green-coated dragoons to go and dig the damned riflemen out from their rocky eyrie. 'Someone take care of that dragoon captain,' Sharpe said.

'Square's going, sir!' Cooper warned Sharpe as Horrell and Cresacre fired at the distant horseman.

Sharpe turned and saw the redcoat square was shaking itself into a column again to resume its retreat. He dared not get too far away from the protection of the redcoats' muskets. His danger, like that facing every small group of riflemen who covered the retreat, was that his men might be cut off by the cavalry and Sharpe doubted that the long-suffering French horsemen would be willing to take prisoners this day. Any greenjacket caught in the open would most likely be used for sword or lance practice. 'Go!' he shouted, and his men scrambled away from the rocks and ran for the cover of the redcoat battalion. The dragoons turned to pursue, then the leading ranks of horsemen were thrown sideways and turned bloody as a blast of canister fired from a British galloper gun smashed into them. Sharpe saw a clump of trees just to the left of the redcoat battalion's line of march and shouted at Harper to lead the men to the small wood's cover.

Once safe among the oaks the greenjackets reloaded and looked for new targets. To Sharpe, who had served on a dozen battlefields, the plain offered an extraordinary sight: a mass of cavalry was churning and spilling between the steadily with-drawing battalions, yet for all their noise and excitement the horsemen were achieving nothing. The infantry were steady and silent, performing the intricate drill that they had practised for hours and hours and which now was saving their lives, and doing it in the knowledge that just one mistake by a battalion commander would be fatal. If a column was just a few seconds too slow to form square then the rampaging *cuirassiers* would be through the gap on their heavy horses and gutting the imperfect square from the inside. A disciplined battalion would be turned in an instant into a rabble of panicking fugitives to be ridden down by dragoons or slaughtered by lancers, yet no battalion made any mistake and so the French were being frustrated by a superb display of steady soldiering.

The French kept searching for an opportunity. Whenever a battalion was marching in a column of companies and so looked ripe for attack a sudden surge of horses would flow across the field and the trumpets would rally yet more horse to join the thunderous charge, but then the redcoats' column would break, wheel and march into square with the same precision as if they were drilling on the parade ground of their home barracks. The troops would mark time for an instant as the square was achieved, then the outer rank would kneel, the whole formation would bristle with bayonets and the horsemen would sheer away in impotent rage. A few impetuous Frenchmen would always try to draw blood and gallop too close to the square only to be blasted from their saddles, or maybe a British galloper gun would bloody a whole troop of dragoons or *cuirassiers* with a blast of canister, but then the cavalry would gallop out of range and the horses would be rested while the square trudged back into column and marched stoically on. The horsemen would watch them go until another flurry of trumpets summoned the whole flux of mounted men to chase yet another opportunity far across the field and once again a battalion would contract into square and once again the horsemen would wheel away with unblooded blades.

And always, everywhere, ahead and behind and in between the slowly withdrawing battalions, groups of greenjackets sniped and harried and killed. French gunners became reluctant to advance while the more sober horsemen took care to avoid the small nests of riflemen that stung so viciously. The French had no rifles because the Emperor despised the weapon as being too slow for battle use, but today the rifles were making the Emperor's soldiers curse.

The Emperor's soldiers were also dying. The calm redcoat battalions were leaving scarcely any bodies behind, but the cavalry was being flayed by rifle and cannon fire. Unhorsed cavalrymen limped southwards carrying saddles, bridles and weapons. Some riderless horses stayed with their regiments, forming in the ranks whenever a squadron regrouped and charging along with the other horses when the trumpets threw the squadron into the attack. Far behind the milling cavalry the French infantry divisions hurried to join the battle, but the Light Division was outmarching the advancing French infantry. When a battalion did form column to continue the retreat it would go at the rifle speed of a hundred and eight paces to the minute – faster than any other infantry in the world. The French marching pace was shorter than the British and the speed of their march much slower than that of the specially trained troops of Crauford's Light Division and so, despite the need to stop and form square and see off the cavalry, Crauford's men were still outpacing the pursuing infantry while far to the north of the Light Division the main British line was being remade so that Wellington's defence now followed the edge of the plateau to make a right angle with Fuentes de Oñoro at its corner. All that was needed now was for the Light Division to come safely home and the army would be complete again, ensconced behind slopes and daring the French to attack.

Sharpe took his men back another quarter-mile to a patch

of rocks where his riflemen could find cover. A pair of British guns was working close to the rocks, blasting roundshot and shell at a newly placed French battery beside the wood Sharpe had just abandoned. The flow of horse began to thicken in this part of the field as the cavalry sought out a vulnerable battalion. Two regiments, one of redcoats and the other Portuguese, were retreating past the battery and the sweating horsemen stalked the two columns. Eventually the press of horse became so thick that the columns marched into squares. 'Buggers are everywhere,' Harper said, firing his rifle at a *chasseur* officer. The two British guns had switched their aim to fire canister at the cavalry in an attempt to drive them away from the two infantry squares. The guns crashed back on their trails to jar the wheels up in the air. The gunners swabbed out the barrel, rammed down a new charge and canister, pricked the powder bag through the touch-hole, then ducked aside after putting the smoking linstock to the powder fuse. The guns cracked deafeningly, smoke punched sixty feet out from the muzzles and the grass lay momentarily flat as the blast whipped overhead. A horse screamed as the musket balls spread out and thumped home.

A surge and eddy in the mass of horse presaged another move, but instead of riding back across the fields to harry a marching column the cavalry suddenly turned on the two guns. Blood dripped from horses' flanks as riders spurred frantically towards the desperate gunners who now picked up their guns' trails, turned the weapons and dropped the trail-hooks over the limbers' pintles. The team horses were run into place, the harnesses attached and the gunners scrambled up onto the guns or horses, but the French cavalry had timed their charge well and the gunners were still whipping their tired animals into motion as the leading *cuirassiers* swept down on the battery.

A charge of British light dragoons saved the guns. The blue-coated horsemen slashed in from the north, sabres cutting down at plumed helmets and parrying swords. More British cavalry arrived to flank the guns that were now galloping frantically northwards. The heavy cannons bounced over the rough ground, the gunners clung to the limbers' handles, the whips cracked, and all about the galloping horses and blurring wheels the cavalry hacked at each other in a running fight. A British dragoon reeled out of the fight with a face turned into a mask of blood while a *cuirassier* fell from his saddle to be mangled by the hooves of the gun teams then crushed by the iron-rimmed wheels of limber and cannon. Then a rippling crash of musketry announced that the rolling chaos of guns, horses, swordsmen and lancers had come into range of the Portuguese square's face and the cheated French cavalry swerved away as the two guns galloped on to safety. A cheer for the gunners' escape went up from the two allied squares, then the guns slewed about in an eruption of grass and dust to open fire again on their erstwhile pursuers.

Sharpe's men had slipped away from the rocks to join another battalion of redcoats. They marched among the companies for a few minutes, then broke off to take position in a tangle of thorns and boulders. A small group of *chasseurs* in green coats, black silver-looped shakoes and with carbines slung on hooks on their white crossbelts trotted close by. The French had not noticed the small group of riflemen crouched among the thorns. They were continually taking off their shakoes and wiping sweat from their faces with their frayed red cuffs. Their horses were white with sweat. One had a leg matted with blood, but it was somehow keeping up with its companions. The officer stopped his troop and one of the men unclipped his carbine, cocked the weapon and aimed at a British gun that was unlimbering to the east. Hagman put a rifle bullet into the man's head before he could pull the trigger and suddenly the *chasseurs* were cursing and trying to spur their horses out of rifle range. Sharpe fired, his rifle's report lost in the crackle of sound as his men sent a volley after the enemy troop. A half-dozen of the *chasseurs* galloped out of range, but they left as many bodies behind. 'Permission to rake the bastards over, sir?' Cooper asked.

'Go on, but equal shares,' Sharpe said, meaning that whatever plunder was found had to be shared among the whole squad.

Cooper and Harris ran out to filch the bodies while Harper and Finn carried bundles of empty water bottles to a nearby stream. They filled the bottles while Cooper and Harris slit the seams of the dead men's green coats, cut open the pockets of their white waistcoats, searched inside the shako linings and tugged off the short, white-tasselled boots. The two riflemen came back with a French shako half filled with a motley collection of French, Portuguese and Spanish coins. 'Poor as church mice,' Harris complained while he split the coins into piles. 'You having a share, sir?'

''Course he is,' Harper said, distributing the precious water. Every man was parched. Their mouths had been dried and soured by the acrid, salty gunpowder in the cartridges and now they swilled the water round their mouths and spat it out black before drinking the rest.

A distant crackling sound made Sharpe turn. The village of Fuentes de Oñoro was a mile away now and the sound seemed to be coming from its narrow, death-choked streets where a plume of smoke climbed into the sky. More gunsmoke showed at the plateau's edge, evidence that the French were still attacking the village. Sharpe turned back to look at the tired, hot cavalrymen who spread across the plain. He was looking for grey uniforms and seeing none.

'Time to go, sir?' Hagman called, hinting that the riflemen would be cut off if Sharpe did not withdraw soon.

'Back we go,' Sharpe said. 'Run to that column.' He pointed to some Portuguese infantry.

They ran, easily reaching the Portuguese before a half-hearted pursuit of vengeful *chasseurs* could get close to the riflemen, but the *chasseurs'* small charge attracted a flow of other cavalrymen, enough to make the Portuguese column shake itself into square. Sharpe and his men stayed in the square and watched as the cavalry streamed around the battalion. Brigadier General Crauford had also taken shelter in the square and now observed the surrounding French from under the battalion's colours. He looked a proud man, and no wonder. His division, which he had disciplined into becoming the best in all the army, was performing magnificently. They were outnumbered, they were surrounded, yet no one had panicked, not one battalion had been caught deployed in column, and not one square had been rattled by the horsemen's proximity. The Light had saved the Seventh Division and now it was saving itself with a dazzling display of professional soldiering. Pure drill was defeating French verve, and Masséna's attack, which had swept around the British right flank with over-whelming force, had been rendered utterly impotent. 'You like it, Sharpe?' Crauford called from his horse.

'Wonderful, sir, just wonderful.' Sharpe's compliment was heartfelt.

'They're scoundrels,' Crauford said of his men, 'but the devils can fight, can't they?' His pride was understandable, and it had even persuaded the irascible Crauford to unbend and indulge in conversation. It was even a friendly conversation. 'I'll put a word in for you, Sharpe,' Crauford said, 'because a man shouldn't be disciplined for killing the enemy, but I don't suppose my help will do you any good.'

'It won't, sir?'

'Valverde's an awkward bugger,' Crauford said. 'He don't like the British, and he won't want Wellington given a Spanish *Generalisimo*'s hat. Valverde reckons he'd make a better *Generalisimo* himself, but the only time the bugger fought the

French he pissed his yellow pants yellower and lost three good battalions doing it. But it ain't about soldiering, Sharpe, it's about politics, all about damned politics, and the one thing every soldier should know is not to get tangled up in politics. Slimy bastards, politicians, should all be killed. Every last damned one of them. I'd tie the whole bloody pack of lying bastards to cannon muzzles and blow them away, blow them away! Fertilize a field with the bastards, dung the world with the breed. Them and lawyers.' The thought of the twin professions had put Crauford into a bad mood. He scowled at Sharpe, then twitched his reins to take his horse back towards the battalion's colours. 'I'll speak for you, Sharpe.'

'Thank you, sir,' Sharpe said.

'Won't help you,' Crauford said curtly, 'but I'll try.' He watched the nearest French cavalry move away. 'I think the buggers are looking for other meat,' he called to the Portuguese battalion's Colonel. 'Let's march on. Should be back in the lines for luncheon. Day to you, Sharpe.'

The Seventh Division had long reached the safety of the plateau and now the leading battalions of the Light Division climbed the slope under the protection of British artillery. The British and German cavalry, that had charged again and again to hold off the hordes of French horsemen, now walked their weary and wounded horses up the hill where riflemen with dried mouths and bruised shoulders and fouled rifle barrels trudged towards safety. The French horsemen could only watch their enemy march away and wonder why in over three miles of pursuit across country made by God for cavalrymen they had not managed to break one single battalion. They had succeeded in catching and killing a handful of redcoat skirmishers in the open land at the bottom of the ridge, but the overall price of the morning's fight had been dozens of dead troopers and scores of butchered horses.

The last of the Light Division columns climbed the hill beneath its colours where bands played to greet the battalion's return. The British army that had been so dangerously divided was now whole again, but it was still cut off from home and it still faced the larger of the two French attacks.

For in Fuentes de Oñoro, whose streets were already choked with blood, a whole new French attack was following the drums.

Marshal Masséna felt annoyance as he watched the two parts of the enemy's army recombine. Good God, he had sent two divisions of infantry and all his cavalry and still they had let the enemy slip away! But at least all the British and Portuguese forces were now cut off from their retreat across the Coa so that now, when they were defeated, the whole of Wellington's army must try to find safety in the wild hills and deep gorges of the high borderland. It would be a massacre. The cavalry which had frittered away the morning so uselessly would hunt the survivors through the hills, and all that was needed to begin that wild and slaughterous chase was for Masséna's infantry to break through the last defences above Fuentes de Oñoro.

The French now held the village and the graveyard. Their leading soldiers were just feet beneath the ridge's summit that was crowned with redcoats and Portuguese blasting volleys that fountained soil among the graves and rattled sharply against the village walls. The surviving Highlanders had retreated to the ridge with the Warwickshire men who had lived through the mauling fight in the streets and now they had been joined by Portuguese *caçadores*, redcoats from the English shires, skirmishers from the valleys of Wales and Hanoverians loyal to King George III; all mingled as they stood shoulder to shoulder to hold the heights and drown Fuentes de Oñoro in smoke and lead. And in the village the streets were crowded with French infantry who were waiting for the order to make the last victorious assault up and out of the smoking houses, across the broken graveyard wall, over the humped graves and broken stones of the cemetery and then across the ridge's crest and into the enemy's vulnerable rear. To the left of their charge would be the white-walled, bullet-scarred church on its ledge of rock, while to the right would be the tumbled grey boulders of the stony summit where the British riflemen lurked, and in between those two landmarks the road climbed the grassy, blood-slicked chute up which the blue-coated infantry needed to attack to bring France a victory.

Masséna now tried to make the victory certain by sending forward ten fresh battalions of infantry. Wellington, he knew, could defend the slope above the village only by bringing in men who were guarding other parts of the ridge. If Masséna could weaken another section of the ridge it would open an alternative path to the plateau, but to do that he must first turn the saddle of grassland above the village into a place of death. The French reinforcements crossed the plain in two great columns and their appearance provoked the fire of every British cannon on the ridge. Case shot slashed across the stream to burst in livid smoke, roundshot crashed through the ranks while shells lobbed from the short-barrelled howitzers fizzed to leave smoky trails arcing in the sky before cracking open in the columns' hearts.

Yet still the columns came. Drummer boys beat them on and the eagles showed bright above as they marched past the dead of the previous attacks. It seemed to some of the French that they walked towards the very gate of hell, towards a smoke-wreathed maw spitting flame and stinking from three days of death. To north and south the meadows lay in spring freshness, but on the banks of Fuentes de Oñoro's stream there was nothing but blasted trees, burned houses, fallen walls, dead,

320

dying and screaming men, and on the plateau's crest above the village there was just smoke and more smoke as the cannons and rifles and muskets hammered at the men waiting to make their huge assault.

The battle had been shrunken to this one place, to these last few feet of the slope above Fuentes de Oñoro. It was midday and the sun was fierce and the shadows short as the ten new battalions broke their ranks to run through the gardens and down the eastern bank of the stream. They splashed through the water and ran up into streets choked with bloody bodies and groaning, slow-moving wounded men. The fresh attackers cheered as they ran, encouraging themselves and the waiting French infantry to one last, supreme effort. They filled the streets, then they burst in huge streams from the alley and laneway entrances at the top of the village, and there were so many attackers that the last of the newly arrived columns were still crossing the stream as the leading companies swarmed over the graveyard wall and up into the volley fire. Men fell to the allied volleys, but more men came behind to clamber over the dead and the dying and to struggle across the graves. Other men ran up the road alongside the cemetery. One whole battalion swerved to the right to fire up at the riflemen on the rocky knoll and their musket fire overwhelmed and drove the greenjackets back from the boulders. A Frenchman climbed to the knoll's summit where he waved his hat before pitching down with a rifle bullet in his lungs. More Frenchmen clambered up the slabs from where they could look down on the great victorious surge of their comrades who were fighting up the last few bloody inches of the slope. The attackers passed the Frenchmen left dead from the previous attacks, they climbed at last onto grass untouched by blood, and then they reached the ragged place where the wadding of the allied muskets had scorched and burned the turf, and still they climbed, and still their officers and sergeants shouted them on, and still the drummer boys beat their attack rhythm to drive this vast wave up and across the plateau's lip. Masséna's infantrymen were doing all that the Marshal had wanted them to do. They were climbing into the horror of the rolling volleys and climbing over their own dead, so many dead that the survivors seemed dipped in blood, and the British and Portuguese and Germans were being forced back step by step as still more men came from the village to press up behind and replace the men who fell to the awful volley fire.

A cheer arose as the leading Frenchmen gained the ridge's summit. A whole company of *voltigeurs* had run to the church to use its wall and rock foundations as a shelter from the musketry and now those men clambered up the last few feet and bayoneted some redcoats defending the church door, then burst inside to find the flagged floor filled with wounded men. Doctors sawed at shattered arms and bleeding legs as the French *voltigeurs* ran to the windows and opened fire. One of the *voltigeurs* was hit by a rifle bullet and left a sliding trail of blood on the whitewashed wall as he sagged to the floor. The other *voltigeurs* ducked as they reloaded, but when they took aim across the window ledges they could see deep across the plateau into the heart of Wellington's position. Close by they could see the wagons of the ammunition park and one of the *voltigeurs* laughed as he made an English officer scamper for safety with a shot that drove a long splinter out of a wagon's side. The doctors shouted a protest as the noise and smoke of the musketry filled the church, but the *voltigeur* commander told them to shut the hell up and keep on working. On the road outside the church a surge of French attackers reinforced the heroes who had captured the ridge's crest and who now threatened to break the enemy army in two before they scattered it to the merciless blades of the frustrated cavalry.

Masséna saw his blue coats gain the far skyline and he felt a great burden drop from his soul. Sometimes, he thought, the hardest part of being a general lay in the necessity of disguising worry. All day he had pretended a confidence he had not altogether felt, for the wretched Major Ducos had been right when he said that Wellington loved nothing better than defending a hill, and Masséna had watched Fuentes de Oñoro's hill and worried that his brave men would never spill over its lip to the rich harvest of victory beyond. Now they were over, the battle was won, and Masséna had no further need to hide his anxiety. He laughed aloud, smiled on his entourage and accepted a flask of brandy with which to toast his victory. And victory was sweet, so sweet. 'Send Loup forward,' Masséna now commanded. 'Tell him to clear the road through the village. We can't deliver supplies through streets choked with dead. Tell him the battle's won so he can take his whore with him if he can't bear to untie her apron strings from round his neck.' He laughed again for life was suddenly so very very good.

There were two battalions standing ready near the church; one famous and the other infamous. The famous battalion was the 74th, Highlanders all, and known for their hard steadiness in battle. The Scotsmen were eager to take revenge for the losses suffered by their sister regiment in Fuentes de Oñoro's bloody streets, and to help them was the 88th, the infamous battalion, reckoned to be as near ungovernable as any regiment in the army, though no one had ever complained about their ability in battle. The 88th was a hard brawling regiment, its men as proud of their fighting record as of their homeland, and that homeland was the wild, bleak and beautiful west of Ireland. The 88th were the Connaught Rangers and now, with the 74th from the Scottish mountains, they would be sent to save Wellington's army.

323

The French hold on the ridge's crest was tightening as more men reached the road's summit. There was no time to deploy the Scots or Irish into line, only to throw them forward in columns of sections at the very centre of the enemy's line. 'Bayonets, boys!' an officer shouted, then the two battalions were running forward. Pipes played the Scotsmen on and wild cheers marked the Connaught advance. Both regiments went fast, eager to get the moment over. The thin mingled line of allied infantry split to let the columns through, then fell in behind as the front ranks of the Irish and Scots slammed into the advancing French. There was no time for musketry and no chance for men to hold back from hand-to-hand fighting. The French knew that victory was theirs if they could just defeat this last enemy effort, while the Scots and Irish knew that their only chance of victory depended on them throwing the French off the ridge's crest.

And so they struck home. Most infantry would have checked their charge a few paces short of an enemy line to pour in a volley of musketry in the hope that the enemy would retreat rather than accept the challenge and horror of hand-to-hand fighting, but the Highlanders and the men of Connaught offered the French no such chance. The front ranks charged bodily into the French attackers and used their bayonets. They screamed war cries in Gaelic and Erse, they clawed and spat and clubbed and kicked and stabbed and all the time more men piled in behind as the rear ranks of the columns collapsed onto the fight. Highland officers slashed with their heavy claymores, while the Irish officers stabbed with the lighter infantry sword. Sergeants drove spontoons hard into the mass of Frenchmen, skewering them with the pikehead, twisting it free and driving it forward again. Inch by inch the counter-attack advanced. This was fighting as the Highlanders had always known it, hand to hand and smelling your enemy's blood as you killed him, and it was the kind of fighting for which the Irish were as feared in their own army as among the enemy. They thrust forward, at times so close packed with the enemy that it was the sheer weight of men rather than the edge of their weapons that forced progress. Men slipped and sprawled on the bodies that lay on the saddle's lip, but the press of men behind thrust the men in front onwards and suddenly the French were going back down the steep hill and their grudging retreat became a spilling flight for the safety of the houses.

Riflemen retook the knoll of rocks as Portuguese soldiers hunted down and killed the *voltigeurs* inside the church. Irishmen and Scotsmen led the wild, screaming, bloody countercharge down through the graveyard and for a moment it seemed as though the ridge, the battle and the army were saved.

Then the French struck again.

Brigadier Loup understood that Masséna would not offer him a chance to make a name in the battle, but that did not mean he would accept the Marshal's animosity. Loup understood Masséna's distrust and did not particularly object, for he believed that a soldier made his own chances. The art of advancement was to wait patiently until an opportunity offered itself and then to move as fast as a striking snake, and now that his brigade had been ordered to its menial task of clearing the main road through and beyond the village of Fuentes de Oñoro the Brigadier would watch for any opportunity that would allow him to release his superbly trained and hard-fighting men to a task more suited to their skills.

His journey across the plain was placid. The fighting boiled at the top of the pass above the village, but the British guns seemed not to notice the advance of a single small brigade. A couple of roundshot struck his infantrymen, and one case shot exploded wide of his grey dragoons, but otherwise the Loup Brigade's advance was untroubled by the enemy. The brigade's two infantry battalions marched in column either side of the road, the dragoons flanked them in two large squadrons while Loup himself, beneath his savage wolf-tailed banner, rode in the centre of the formation. Juanita de Elia rode with him. She had insisted on witnessing the battle's closing stages and Marshal Masséna's confident assurance that the battle was won had persuaded Loup it was safe enough for Juanita to ride at least as far as the Dos Casas's eastern bank. The paucity of British artillery fire seemed to vindicate Masséna's confidence.

Loup dismounted his dragoons outside the village gardens. The horses were picketed in a battered orchard where they would remain while the dragoons cleared the road east of the stream. There were not many obstructions here to slow the progress of the heavy baggage wagons carrying Almeida's relief supplies, merely one collapsed wall and a few blackening corpses left from the British gunfire, so once the dragoons had cleared the passage they were ordered to cross the ford and start on the larger job inside the village proper. Loup ordered Juanita to stay with the horses while he marched his two battalions of infantry around the village's northern flank so that they could begin clearing the main street from the top of the hill, working their way down to meet the dragoons coming up from the stream. 'You don't have to be careful with the wounded,' he told his men, 'we're not a damned rescue mission. Our job is to clear the street, not nurse injured men, so just throw the casualties aside until the doctors arrive. Just clear the way, that's all, because the sooner the road's clear the sooner we can put some guns on the ridge to finish off the Goddams. To work!'

He led his men up around the village. A few scattered skirmishers' bullets came from the heights above to remind the grey-clad infantry that this was still not a battle won and Loup, striding eagerly ahead of his men, noted that the fighting was still very close to the plateau's lip, and then a great cheer from the ridge announced that the battle could yet be lost.

For the cheer marked the moment when a phalanx of red-coated infantry drove in the French attack and thrust it back across the crest. Now, beneath their bright flags, the British counterattack was storming down the slope towards the village. French *voltigeurs* were abandoning the high rocks and fleeing down the slope to find safety behind the village's stone walls. A sudden panic had gripped the leading French grenadiers who were giving ground to the vengeful redcoats, but Loup felt nothing but elation. God, it seemed, was working to a different plan than Marshal André Masséna. The street clearance could wait, for suddenly Loup's opportunity had come.

Providence had placed his brigade on the left flank of the Irish counterattack. The redcoats were screaming down the hill, bayoneting and clubbing their enemies, oblivious of the two waiting battalions of fresh infantry. Behind the Irish came a disorganized mass of allied infantry, all sucked pell-mell into this new battle for mastery of Fuentes de Oñoro's blood-glutted streets.

'Fix bayonets!' Loup called and drew his own straight-bladed dragoon sword. So Masséna had thought to keep his brigade from glory? Loup turned to see that his pagan banner of wolf tails hanging from an eagle's cross-bar was held high, and then, as the counterattacking British troops poured into the village streets, he ordered the advance.

Like a whirlpool that sucked every scrap of flotsam into its destructive vortex, the village had again become a place of close-quarter killing. '*Vive l'Empereur!*' Loup shouted, and plunged into the fight.

* * *

Sharpe eased the green jacket off the dead rifleman. The man had been one of the sharpshooters on the rocky knoll, but he had been shot by a *voltigeur* at the high point of the French attack and now Sharpe pulled the bloody jacket off the stiff, awkward arms. 'Perkins! Here!' He threw the green jacket to the rifleman. 'Get your girl to shorten the sleeves.'

'Yes, sir.'

'Or do it yourself, Perkins,' Harper added.

'I'm no good with a needle, Sarge.'

'That's what Miranda says too,' Harper said, and the riflemen laughed.

Sharpe walked to the rocks above the village. He had brought his riflemen back unscathed from their errand to the Light Division, only to find that Major Tarrant had no new orders for him. The battle had become a vicious fight over mastery of the village, its graveyard and the church above, and men were not using ammunition so much as sword, bayonet and musket stock. Captain Donaju had wanted permission to join the men firing at the French from the crest's ridge, but Tarrant had been so worried by the proximity of the attackers that he had ordered the Real Compañía Irlandesa to stay close to the ammunition wagons that he was busily having harnessed to their horses or oxen. 'If we must retreat,' he had told Sharpe, 'it'll be chaos! But a man must be ready.' The Real Compañía Irlandesa made a thin line between the wagons and the fighting, but then the attack of the 74th Highlanders and the Connaught Rangers had eased Tarrant's urgency.

''Pon my soul, Sharpe, but it's hot work.' Colonel Runciman had been hovering around the ammunition wagons, fidgeting and worrying, but now he came forward to catch a glimpse of the turmoil in the village beneath. He gave his horse's reins to one of the riflemen and peered nervously over the crest at the fighting beneath. It was hot work indeed. The village, left

328

reeking and smoking from the earlier battles fought through its streets, was once again a maelstrom of musket smoke, screams and blood. The 74th and 88th had driven deep into the labyrinth of houses, but now their progress was slowing as the French defences thickened. The French howitzers on the other stream bank had begun lobbing shells into the grave-yard and upper houses, adding to the smoke and noise. Runciman shuddered at the horrid sight, then stepped back two paces only to stumble on a dead *voltigeur* whose body marked the deepest point of penetration reached by the French. Runciman frowned at the body. 'Why do they call them vaulters?' he asked.

'Vaulters?' Sharpe asked, not understanding the question.

'*Voltigeur*, Sharpe,' Runciman explained. 'French for vaulter.'

Sharpe shook his head. 'God knows, sir.'

'Because they jump like fleas, sir, when you shoot at them,' Harper offered. 'But don't worry yourself about that one, sir.' Harper had seen the look of worry on Runciman's face. 'He's a good *voltigeur*, that one. He's dead.'

Wellington was not far away from Sharpe and Runciman. The General was sitting on his horse on the bloody dip of land where the road crossed the ridge between the church and the rocks, and behind him was nothing except the army's baggage and ammunition park. To the north and west his divisions guarded the plateau against the French threat, but here, in the centre, where the enemy had so nearly broken through, there was nothing left. There were no more reserves and he would not thin the ridge's other defenders and so open a back door to French victory. The battle would have to be won by his Highlanders and Irishmen, and so far they were rewarding his faith by retaking the village house by bloody house and cattle shed by burning cattle shed.

Then the grey infantry struck from the flank.

Sharpe saw the wolf-tail banner in the smoke. For a second he froze. He wanted to pretend he had not seen it. He wanted an excuse, any excuse, not to go down that awful slope to a village so reeking with death that the air alone was enough to make a man vomit. He had fought once already inside Fuentes de Oñoro, and once was surely enough, but his hesitation was only for a heartbeat. He knew there was no excuse. His enemy had come to Fuentes de Oñoro to claim victory and Sharpe must stop him. He turned. 'Sergeant Harper! My compliments to Captain Donaju and ask him to form column. Go on! Hurry!' Sharpe looked at his men, his handful of good men from the bloody, fighting 95th. 'Load up, lads. Time to go to work.'

'What are you doing, Sharpe?' Runciman asked.

'You want to beat our court of inquiry, General?' Sharpe asked.

Runciman gaped at Sharpe, not understanding why the question had been asked. 'Why, yes, of course,' he managed to say.

'Then go over to Wellington, General,' Sharpe said, 'and ask his Lordship's permission to lead the Real Compañía Irlandesa into battle.'

Runciman blanched. 'You mean . . . ?' he began, but could not articulate the horror. He glanced down at the village that had been turned into a slaughterhouse. 'You mean . . . ?' he began again and then his mouth fell slackly open at the very thought of going down into that smoking hell.

'I'll ask if you don't,' Sharpe said. 'For Christ's sake, sir! Gallantry forgives everything! Gallantry means you're a hero. Gallantry gets you a wife. Now for Christ's sake! Do it!' he shouted at Runciman as though the Colonel was a raw recruit.

Runciman looked startled. 'You'll come with me, Sharpe?' He was as frightened of approaching Wellington as he was of going towards the enemy.

'Come on!' Sharpe snapped, and led a flustered Runciman towards the sombre knot of staff officers who surrounded Wellington. Hogan was there, watching anxiously as the tide of struggle in the village turned against the allies once again. The French were inching uphill, forcing the redcoats and the Portuguese and the German infantry back out of the village, only this time there were no ranks of muskets waiting at the crest of the ridge to blast the enemy as they climbed the road and overran the churned-up graveyard.

Runciman hung back as the two men reached the staff officers, but Sharpe pushed his way through the horses and dragged the reluctant Colonel with him. 'Ask him,' Sharpe said.

Wellington heard the words and frowned at the two men. Colonel Runciman hesitated, snatched off his hat, tried to speak and only managed an incoherent stutter.

'General Runciman wants permission, my Lord –' Sharpe began coldly.

'– To take the Irish into battle.' Runciman managed to complete the sentence in a barely coherent rush. 'Please, my Lord!'

Some of the staff officers smiled at the thought of the Wagon Master General leading troops, but Wellington twisted in his saddle to see that the red-jacketed Real Compañía Irlandesa had formed column. It looked a pathetically small unit, but it was there, formed, armed and evidently eager. There was no one else. The General looked at Sharpe and raised an eyebrow. Sharpe nodded.

'Carry on, Runciman,' Wellington said.

'Come on, sir.' Sharpe plucked the fat man's sleeve to pull him away from the General.

'One moment!' The General's voice was frigid. 'Captain Sharpe?'

Sharpe turned back. 'My Lord?'

'The reason, Captain Sharpe, why we do not execute enemy prisoners, no matter how vile their behaviour, is that the enemy will reciprocate the favour on our men, no matter how small their provocation.' The General looked at Sharpe with an eye as cold as a winter stream. 'Do I make myself clear, Captain Sharpe?'

'Yes, sir. My Lord.'

Wellington gave a very small nod. 'Go.'

Sharpe dragged Runciman away. 'Come on, sir!'

'What do I do, Sharpe?' Runciman asked. 'For God's sake, what do I do? I'm not a fighter!'

'Stay at the back, sir,' Sharpe said, 'and leave everything else to me.' Sharpe scraped his long sword free. 'Captain Donaju!'

'Captain Sharpe?' Donaju was pale.

'General Wellington requests,' Sharpe shouted loudly enough for every man in the Real Compañía Irlandesa to hear him, 'that the King of Spain's bodyguard goes down to the village and kills every goddamn Frenchman it finds. And the Connaught Rangers are down there, Captain, and they need a morsel of Irish help. Are you ready?'

Donaju drew his own sword. 'Perhaps you would do the honour of taking us down, Captain?'

Sharpe beckoned his riflemen into the ranks. There would be no skirmishers here, no delicate long-range killing, only a blood-soaked brawl in a godforsaken village on the edge of Spain where Sharpe's sworn enemy had come to turn defeat into victory. 'Fix bayonets!' Sharpe called. For a second or two he was assailed with the strange thought that this was just how Lord Kiely had wanted his men to fight. His Lordship had simply wanted to throw his men into a suicidal battle, and this place was as good as any for that kind of gesture. No training could prepare a man for this battle. This was gutter fighting and it was either born into a man's bones or it was absent for ever. 'And forward!' Sharpe shouted. 'At the double!' And he led the small unit up the road to the ridge's crest where the soil was torn by enemy roundshot, then over the skyline and down. Down into the smoke, the blood and the slaughter.

CHAPTER ELEVEN

Bodies lay sprawled on the upper slope. Some were motionless, others still stirred slowly with the remnants of life. A Highlander vomited blood, then collapsed across a grave that had been so churned by shell and roundshot that the pelvic and wrist bones of a corpse lay among the soil. A French drummer boy sat beside the road with his hands clasped over his spilt guts. His drumsticks were still stuck in his crossbelt. He looked up mutely as Sharpe ran past, then began to cry. A greenjacket lay dead from one of the very first attacks. A bent French bayonet was stuck in his ribs just above a distended, blackened belly that was thick with flies. A shell cracked apart beside the body and scraps of its casing whistled past Sharpe's head. One of the guardsmen was hit and fell, tripping two men behind him. Harper shouted at them to leave the man alone. 'Keep running!' he called harshly. 'Keep running! Let the bugger look after himself! Come on!'

Halfway to the village the road curved sharply to the right. Sharpe left the road there, jumping down a small embankment into a patch of scrubland. He could see the Loup Brigade not far ahead. The grey infantry had plunged into the village from the north and were now threatening to cut the 88th into two parts. Loup's attack had first arrested the momentum of the British counterattack then reversed it, and to Sharpe's right he

334

could see redcoats retreating out of the village to find shelter behind the remnants of the graveyard wall. A swarm of Frenchmen was pushing up from the village's lower houses, roused to one last brave effort by the example of Loup's brigade.

But Loup's brigade now had an enemy of its own, a small enemy, but one with something to prove. Sharpe led the Real Compañía Irlandesa through the scrubland, over a tiny plot of parched beans, then he was leaping down another low embankment and running hard towards the flank of the nearest grey infantry battalion. 'Kill them!' Sharpe shouted, 'kill them!' It was a horrid, savage and appropriate battle cry for the Real Compañía Irlandesa was outnumbered and unless they fell on the enemy with a hungry ferocity they would be repelled and broken. This fight would depend on savagery. 'Kill the bastards!' Sharpe screamed. Fear was huge inside him, making his voice harsh and desperate. His belly was sour with terror, but he had long learned that the enemy suffered just the same fear and that to yield to it was to invite disaster. The key to this fight's survival lay in closing on the enemy fast, in crossing the open space where their muskets could kill and so getting his men hard into the enemy's ranks where the fight would degenerate into a street brawl.

And so he screamed his awful encouragement even as he wondered if his courage would fail and drive him to seek shelter behind one of the broken walls, but at the same time he was judging the enemy ahead. There was an alley crammed with enemy immediately in front of Sharpe, and to its left a low wall enclosing a garden. Some of Loup's men had crossed a fallen wall into the garden, but most were pushing through the alley towards the bigger fight raging in the village's centre. Sharpe headed for the alley. Frenchmen turned and called in warning. One man fired his musket to shroud the alley's entrance with white smoke, then Sharpe crashed into the rearmost grey ranks and slammed his sword forward. The relief of contact was enormous, releasing a terrible energy that he poured into the wickedly sharp sword blade. Men arrived either side of him with bayonets. They were screaming and stabbing, men in whom terror was similarly being turned into a barbaric frenzy. Other guardsmen had gone to clear the garden, while Donaju was fighting his way into another alley lower down the slope.

It was a gutter fight, and if for the first few moments Sharpe's men found it easier than they had expected that was because they had assaulted the rearmost of Loup's ranks, the place where the men least enthusiastic about fighting like animals in narrow streets had taken refuge. Yet the longer Sharpe's men fought, the closer they came to Loup's best fighters and the harder the fight proved. Sharpe saw a big moustached sergeant working his way back through the ranks and rallying the men as he came. The Sergeant was shouting, hitting men, forcing the cowardly to turn and use their bayonets on the new attackers, but then his head snapped back and was surrounded with a momentary red mist of blood droplets as a rifle bullet killed him. Hagman and Cooper had found a rooftop from which to serve as sharpshooters.

Sharpe stepped over bodies, hammered muskets aside, then stabbed with his sword. There was no room for slashing strokes, only a tight space in which to jab and ram and twist the blade. The only leadership required of him now was to be seen fighting and the Real Compañía Irlandesa followed him willingly. It was as if they had been let off a leash and they fought like fiends as they cleared first one alley and then the next. The French retreated from the bitter attack, looking for an easier place to defend. Donaju, his face and uniform spattered with blood, rejoined Sharpe in a small triangular plaza where the two alleys met. A dead Frenchman lay on a dungheap, another blocked a door. There were bodies shoved into the gutters, bodies piled inside houses and bodies heaped against walls. The piles of dead showed the battle's progression, with skirmishers from the first day covered with Frenchmen, then Highlanders, then French grenadiers in their massive bearskin hats beneath more redcoats and now Loup's grey uniforms made a new top layer. The stench of death was thick as fog. The ruts in the earthen road, where they showed between the corpses, were flooded with blood. The streets were glutted by death and choked with men seeking to glut them more.

Hagman and Cooper jumped from one broken roof to another. 'Bastards to your left, sir!' Cooper called from his eyrie, indicating an alley that ran crookedly downhill from the small triangular plaza. The French had withdrawn far enough to give Sharpe's men a pause in which they could reload or else wrap dirty strips of cloth round slashed hands and arms. Some men drank from their hoarded rum issue. A few were wholly drunk, but they would fight all the better for it and Sharpe did not mind. 'Bastards are coming, sir!' Cooper called in warning.

'Bayonets!' Sharpe called. 'Now come on!' He drew out the last word as he led his men into the alley. It was scarcely six feet wide, no room to swing a sword. The first bend was just ten feet away and Sharpe reached it at the same time as a rush of Frenchmen. Sharpe felt a bayonet catch in his jacket, heard the cloth rip, then he was punching the iron hilt of his sword into a moustached face. He was fighting a grenadier who snarled through bleeding lips with yellow rotted teeth as he tried to kick Sharpe in the crotch. Sharpe hammered the sword down, but the blow was cushioned by the black greasy fur of the thick bearskin. The man's breath was fetid. The grenadier had let go of his musket and was trying to throttle Sharpe, but Sharpe seized the upper blade of his sword with his left hand, kept tight hold of the hilt with his right and rammed the blade hard into the Frenchman's throat. He pushed the grenadier's head

337

back so far that he could see the whites of his eyes and still the man would not let go of his throat so Sharpe just slid the blade to his right, slid once and his world turned red as the sword sliced into the Frenchman's jugular.

He clambered over the twitching body of the dying grenadier. Rum-crazed guardsmen were slashing with bayonets, hitting with musket stocks, kicking and screaming at an enemy who could not match this ferocity. Guardsman Rourke had broken his musket and had picked up a blackened roof beam instead and was now ramming the heavy timber forward at the Frenchmen's faces. The enemy began to edge backwards. An officer from Loup's brigade tried to rally them, but Hagman picked him off from a rooftop and the enemy's grudging retreat turned into a sudden rout. One Frenchman took refuge in a house where he lost his head by firing from a window on the advancing guardsmen. A rush of Irishmen stormed the house and killed every French fugitive inside.

'God save Ireland.' Harper dropped down beside Sharpe. 'Jesus, but it's hard work.' He was breathing hoarsely. 'Christ, sir, have you seen yourself? Drenched in blood, so you are.'

'Not mine, Pat.' Sharpe cuffed blood out of his eyes. He had reached the corner of a street which led into the village's heart. A dead French officer lay in the centre of the street, his mouth open and crawling with flies. Someone had already cut open his pockets, seams and pouches and discarded a crude chess set with a board made of painted canvas, court pieces of carved wood and pawns from musket balls. Sharpe could smell the corpse as he crouched at the street corner and tried to divine the battle's course from the tangle of noise and smoke. He sensed he was behind the enemy now and that if he could just attack to his right then he would be threatening to cut off Loup's grey infantry and the bearskinned grenadiers who were now inextricably mixed together. If the enemy thought they were about to be surrounded they would probably retreat, and that retreat could lead to a wholesale French withdrawal. It could lead to victory.

Harper peered round the corner. 'Thousands of the buggers,' he said. He was carrying a spontoon that he had picked up from a dead Connaught sergeant. He had snapped off four feet of the pike to make it a handier weapon for the grim business of killing in a confined space. He looked at the plundered French officer in the street. 'No money in that chess set,' he said grimly. 'Do you remember that sergeant at Busaco who found the silver chess men?' He hefted the spontoon. 'Just send me a rich dead officer, please God.'

'No one will get rich off me,' Sharpe said grimly, then peered round the corner to see a barricade of dead grenadiers blocking the street with a mass of French infantry waiting behind them. 'Who's loaded?' Sharpe asked the men crouching near him. 'To the front,' he ordered the half-dozen men who raised their hands. 'Hurry now! We go round the corner,' he told them, 'you wait for my word, you kneel, you fire, then you charge like hell. Pat? You bring the rest five paces behind.' Sharpe was leading a mongrel mix of riflemen, Connaught Rangers, Highlanders, guardsmen and *caçadores*. 'Ready, boys?' He grinned at them from a face smeared with enemy blood. 'Then come on!'

He screamed the last word as he led his men around the corner. The French behind the barricade obliged Sharpe by firing straightaway, panicked by the awful screams of the attackers into firing too soon and firing too high. 'Halt! Kneel!' Sharpe stood among the kneeling men. 'Aim!' Harper was already leading the second charge out of the alley. 'Fire!' Sharpe shouted and the volley whipped over the dead grenadiers as Sharpe's men charged out of the smoke and scrambled over the warm heap of bloody dead. The French ahead of Sharpe were desperately reloading, but their fixed bayonets impeded their ramrods and they were still trying to load their muskets when Sharpe's charge smashed home and the killing began again. Sharpe's sword arm was weary, his throat was hoarse from shouting and his eyes were stinging from powder smoke, sweat and blood, but there could be no rest. He rammed the sword home, twisted it, pulled it out, then rammed it forward again. A Frenchman aimed his musket at Sharpe, pulled the trigger and was rewarded with a hangfire as the powder in the pan caught fire, but did not set off the charge inside the barrel. The man screamed as the sword stabbed home. Sharpe was so weary from the killing that he was holding the big sword two-handed, his right hand on the hilt and his left gripping the lowest part of the blade so that he could shove it hard into the press of men. The crush of bodies was so great that there were times when he could hardly move and so he would claw at the faces nearest him, kick and bite and butt with his head until the damned French moved or fell or died and he could climb over another body and snarl forward with the bloody sword dripping.

Harper caught up with him. The spontoon's foot-long sharpened steel spearhead had a small cross-bar at its base to prevent the weapon being driven too deep into an enemy horse or man and Harper was repeatedly burying the blade clear to the cross-piece, then kicking and twisting to loosen the weapon before thrusting forward again. Once, when a French sergeant tried to rally a group of men, Harper lifted a dying man on the end of the truncated spear and used his thrashing body as a bleeding and screaming battering ram that he slammed into the enemy ranks. A pair of bloody-faced Connaught Rangers had attached themselves to Harper and the three were chanting their war cries in Irish.

A rush of Highlanders came out of a lane on Sharpe's right. He sensed that the battle was turning. They were attacking downhill now, not defending uphill, and the grey infantry of Loup's brigade was going back with the rest. He unclenched his left hand from the lower blade of the sword and saw he had cut his palm open. A musket flamed from a window to his left and a guardsman went spinning down, gasping. Captain Donaju led a charge into the roofless house that echoed with shouts as French fugitives were hunted through the tiny rooms and back into the pig shed. A terrible roar of triumph sounded to Sharpe's right as a company of Connaught Rangers trapped two companies of Frenchmen in a blind alley. The Irish began working their bloody way to the alley's end and no officer dared try to stop their slaughter. Down on the grassland north of Poco Velha this battle had seen the most delicate of drill manoeuvres save the Light Division, now it was witnessing a primitive wild fighting out of the most gruesome nightmare that might yet save the whole army.

'Left!' Harper called and Sharpe turned to see a rush of grey-uniformed Frenchmen coming through an alley. The guardsmen no longer needed orders to counterattack, they just swarmed into the alley and screamed a wild, keening noise as they laid into the enemy. The Real Compañía Irlandesa had been caught up by the sublime joy of a victorious and killing fight. One man took a bullet in the chest and noticed nothing, but just went on stabbing and swinging his musket. Donaju had long ceased trying to exercise control. Instead he was fighting like his men, grinning horribly from a face made awful by blood, smoke, sweat and strain. 'Seen Runciman?' Sharpe asked him.

'No.'

'He'll live,' Sharpe said. 'He ain't the kind to die in battle.'

'And we are?' Donaju asked.

'God knows.' Sharpe was resting for a moment in an angle of wall. His breath came in great gasps. 'Have you seen Loup?' he asked Harper.

'Not a sign of the bugger, sir,' Harper answered. 'But I'm saving this for him.' He touched the clustered barrels of his volley gun that was slung on his back.

'Bastard's mine,' Sharpe said.

A cheer announced another rush forward somewhere in the village. The French were going back everywhere and Sharpe knew this was the time to keep the enemy from holding or regrouping. He led a squad of men through a house, stepping over two French corpses and one dead Highlander to emerge into the small backyard. He kicked open the yard's gate and saw Frenchmen just yards away. 'Come on!' He screamed the last word as he ran into the street and led his men against the remnants of a barricade. Muskets flared and flamed, something slapped against the stock of Sharpe's slung rifle, then he was hacking the sword over the barricade and guardsmen were hauling the carts and benches and burning straw bales aside. A house was on fire nearby and the smoke made Sharpe cough as he kicked his way through the last obstacles and parried a bayonet lunged by a small wiry French sergeant. Harper skewered the man with his spontoon. The stream was just feet away. A French gun fired, blasting canister up the main road and twitching a dozen Highlanders aside, then the French gunners were masked as a rush of Frenchmen tried to escape the vengeful allied counter-attack by fleeing back over the Dos Casas stream.

A bellowing voice sounded to Sharpe's right and he saw it was Loup himself trying to rally the French. The Brigadier was standing on the remnants of the old stone clapper bridge where he swore at the running Frenchmen and tried to turn them back with his sword. Harper unslung his seven-barrelled gun, but Sharpe pushed it down. 'Bugger's mine, Pat.'

Some redcoats were pursuing the French over the stream as Sharpe ran towards the bridge. 'Loup! You bastard! Loup!' he shouted. 'Loup!'

The Brigadier turned and saw the blood-soaked rifleman running towards him. Loup jumped off the bridge as Sharpe splashed into the stream and the two men met halfway, thigh-deep in a pool made by a dam of bodies and discoloured by their blood. The swords clashed, Loup lunged, but Sharpe parried and swung, only to have his own blow parried. He kicked at Loup's knee, but the deep water impeded him and he almost fell and opened himself to a scything swing of Loup's straight sword, but Sharpe recovered at the last moment and deflected the blow with the hilt of his sword which he rammed forward at Loup's wall-eye. The Brigadier stepped hurriedly back, tripped, but gained his balance with another vicious swing of the sword. The wider battle was still being fought, but both the British and the French left the two swordsmen alone. The French were going to earth in the walls and gardens of the stream's eastern bank where their first attacks of the day had started, while the British and Portuguese were hunting the last enemy out of the village proper. While in the stream the two battle-crazed men swung their clumsy swords like clubs.

They were evenly matched. Loup was the better swordsman, but he lacked Sharpe's height and reach and he was more accustomed to fighting on horseback than on foot. The two swung, stabbed and parried in a grotesque mockery of the fine art of fencing. Their movements were slowed by the stream and by their tiredness, while the finesse of swordfighting was wasted on blades as long and cumbersome as heavy cavalry swords. The sound of the two swords was reminiscent of a blacksmith's shop.

'Bastard,' Sharpe said, and cut. 'Bastard,' he said again and rammed the point forward.

Loup parried the lunge. 'This is for my two murdered men,' he said and cut the sword upward, forcing Sharpe to an awkward parry. Loup spat an insult then lunged his sword at Sharpe's face, making the rifleman stagger sideways. Sharpe returned the lunge and shouted in triumph as his sword sliced into Loup's midriff, but he had only succeeded in piercing the Frenchman's sabretache that now trapped the point of his sword as Loup waded forward to give the killing blow. Sharpe stepped forward as well, closing the gap to stop the lunge and butting with his head as he got close. The Frenchman avoided the butt and brought up his knee. Sharpe hit him with his left hand, then wrenched his sword free and hit Loup with the hilt just as the Brigadier's sword guard clouted him stingingly on the left side of his head.

The two men reeled apart. They stared at each other, but they no longer traded insults for they needed all their strength for the fight. Muskets snapped across the stream, but still no one interfered with the duellists, recognizing that they were fighting the battle of honour that belonged to them alone. A group of grey-uniformed men watched from the eastern bank while a mix of riflemen, guardsmen, Rangers and Highlanders cheered Sharpe from the west.

Sharpe scooped water up with his left hand and splashed it on his mouth. He licked his lips. 'Time to finish you,' he said thickly and waded forward. Loup raised his sword as Sharpe swung, parried the blow, then parried again. Sharpe had found a new, desperate energy and he gave the Frenchman stroke after stroke, huge strokes, great slashing cuts of the heavy sword that beat down Loup's guard and followed each other so fast that the Frenchman had no time to disengage and turn his own blade into the attack. He went back, beaten by Sharpe's strength, and blow by blow his defence weakened as Sharpe, teeth gritted, went on swinging. One last blow rang on Loup's upheld sword to drive the grey Frenchman down onto his knees in the water and Sharpe screamed his victory as he raised the sword for one last terrible strike.

'Watch out, sir!' Harper called desperately.

Sharpe glanced to his left to see a grey-uniformed dragoon mounted on a grey horse and with a plume of black, shining hair hanging from his helmet to his waist. He was holding a short-barrelled carbine aimed dead at Sharpe. Sharpe stepped back, checking the killing stroke, and saw that the black hair was not a helmet's plume at all. 'Juanita!' he shouted. She would save Loup just as she had once kept Lord Kiely alive, only she had saved Kiely to preserve her excuse for staying behind British lines while she would keep Loup alive for love. 'Juanita!' Sharpe called, appealing to that one memory of a grey dawn in a grey wolf's bed in the high hills.

She smiled. She fired. She turned to flee, but Harper was in the shallows with the seven-barrelled gun at his shoulder and his volley snatched Juanita off her horse in an eruption of blood. Her death screech ended before her falling body struck the ground.

Sharpe was also falling. He had taken a terrible blow under his right shoulder and the pain was already flickering like fire down his suddenly nerveless hand. He staggered and went to one knee and Loup was suddenly over him, sword aloft. Smoke from a burning house wafted over the stream as Loup shouted his victory and brought the sword slamming down.

Sharpe hooked the Frenchman's right ankle with his left hand and tugged. Loup shouted as he fell. Sharpe snarled and dived forward, going beneath the falling sword, and he grabbed his own sword blade with his blood-encrusted left hand so that he was holding the three-foot blade like a quarterstaff that he rammed hard across his enemy's neck. Blood from his shoulder was running down to the stream as he drove the Brigadier beneath the water, drove him down to the stream's gravel bed and held him there with the sword. He locked his right arm straight and held the sword tip with his left and clenched his teeth against the pain in his arm as he used all his weight to hold the smaller man down under the hurrying stream. Bubbles showed in the bloody water and were whirled away. Loup kicked and thrashed, but Sharpe held him there, kneeling in the stream so that only his head and bloody shoulder were above water and he kept the sword hard over the dying man's throat to drown the Frenchman like a man would drown a rabid dog.

Rifles and muskets splintered from the western bank as Sharpe's men drove away Loup's infantry from the eastern bank. Those grey infantry had come forward to rescue their Brigadier, but Loup was dying, choking on water and steel, blacking out under the stream. A bullet slapped the water close to Sharpe, but he stayed there, ignoring the pain, just holding the sword hard across his enemy's throat. And slowly, slowly, the last bubbles faded, and slowly, slowly, the struggles beneath Sharpe ceased, and slowly, slowly, Sharpe understood that he had scotched the beast and that Loup, his enemy, was dead and slowly, slowly, Sharpe eased away from the body that floated up to the surface as he staggered, bloody and hurting, back to the western bank where Harper caught up with him and hurried him back into the shelter of a bullet-chipped wall. 'God save Ireland,' Harper said as he eased the wet sword out of Sharpe's hand, 'but what have you done?'

'Won, Pat, bloody well won.' And, despite the pain, he grinned. For he was a soldier, and he bloody well had won.

'Stay still, man, for God's sake.' The surgeon's voice was slurred and his breath reeked of brandy. He grimaced as he manipulated the probe that was sunk deep in Sharpe's shoulder. The surgeon also held a small pair of tweezers that he constantly darted in and out of the open wound to give jabs of pure agony. 'The goddamn bullet drove in scraps of your uniform,' he said. 'Why the hell don't you wear silk? That doesn't fall to pieces.'

'Can't afford silk,' Sharpe said. The church stank of blood, pus, faeces and urine. It was night time and Fuentes de Oñoro's church was crammed with the wounded of two armies who lay in the smoking rushlight as they waited their turn with the surgeons who would be busy with their hooks and saws and blades all night long.

'God knows if you'll live.' The doctor plucked another scrap of bloody wool out of the wound and scraped it off the tweezer's jaws onto his stained apron. He belched a fetid brandy-flavoured breath over Sharpe, then shook his head wearily. 'The wound will probably turn septic. They usually do. You'll stink like a leper's latrine, your arm will drop off and in ten days' time you'll be dead. Lots of fever before then, you'll gibber like a lunatic and sweat like a horse, but you'll be a hero back home. Of course it hurts, man. Stop whining like a damned child, for Christ's sake! I never could stand whining bloody children. And sit still, man!'

Sharpe sat still. The pain of the probe was excruciating, like having a white-hot flesh-hook jammed and twisted into his shoulder joint. He closed his eyes and tried not to listen to the grating sound caused by the surgeon's probe scraping against the bone as he searched for the carbine ball. 'Got the little bastard. Hold still.' The surgeon found a narrow-nosed set of forceps and eased them into the wound after the probe. 'You say a woman did it?'

'A woman did it,' Sharpe said, keeping his eyes closed. A prisoner from Loup's brigade had confirmed that Juanita had indeed advanced with the dragoons. No one in Loup's brigade had thought the French would be dislodged from the village and thrown back over the stream and so no one had told Juanita the danger. Not that she would have listened. She had been an adventuress who loved the smell of fighting, and now she was dead.

So was Loup, and with their death had died General Valverde's last chance of finding a witness to Sharpe's confession to having killed the French prisoners and so precipitating the fiasco at San Isidro. There was only one witness left alive and he had come at dusk to the church where Sharpe had been waiting for the surgeon. 'They asked me,' Runciman had told Sharpe excitedly. The Colonel had been in the village throughout the fight, and though no one was claiming that the erstwhile Wagon Master General had taken a leading role in the battle, nor was anyone denying that Colonel Runciman had been in the place of greatest danger where he had neither flinched nor shrunk from the fight.

'Who asked you what, General?' Sharpe had responded.

'Wellington and that wretched Spanish General.' Runciman gabbled in his excitement. 'Asked me directly, straight to my face. Had you admitted to shooting two Frenchies? That's what they asked me.'

Sharpe flinched as a man screamed under the surgeon's knife. The amputated arms and feet made a grisly pile beside the altar that served as an operating table. 'They asked you,' Sharpe said, 'and you don't tell lies.'

'So I didn't!' Runciman said. 'I said it was a preposterous question. That no gentleman would do such a thing and that you were an officer and therefore a gentleman and that with the greatest of respect to his Lordship I found the question offensive.' Runciman bubbled with joy. 'And Wellington backed me up! Told Valverde he wanted to hear no more allegations against British officers. And there's to be no court of inquiry either, Sharpe! Our conduct today, I am told, obviates any need to question the sad events of San Isidro. Quite right too!'

Sharpe had smiled. He had known he was exonerated from the moment that Wellington, just before the Real Compañía Irlandesa's counterattack on the village, had reprimanded him for shooting the French prisoners, but Runciman's excited news was a welcome confirmation of that release. 'Congratulations, General,' Sharpe said. 'So what now?'

'Home, I think. Home. Home.' Runciman smiled at the thought. 'Maybe I can be of some use in the Hampshire militia? I suggested as much to Wellington and he was kind enough to agree. The militia, he said, needed men with martial experience, men of vision and men with an experience of command, and he was kind enough to suggest I possessed all three qualities. He's a very kind man, Wellington. Haven't you discovered that, Sharpe?'

'Very kind, sir,' Sharpe said drily, watching the orderlies hold down a man whose leg was quivering as the surgeons cut at the thigh.

'So I'm off to England!' Runciman said with delight. 'Dear England, all that good food and sensible religion! And you, Sharpe? What of your future?'

'I'll go on killing Frogs, General. It's all I'm good for.' He glanced at the doctor and saw the man was nearly finished with his previous patient and he braced himself for the pain to come. 'And the Real Compañía Irlandesa, General,' he asked, 'what happens to them?'

'Cadiz. But they go as heroes, Sharpe. A battle won! Almeida still invested and Masséna scuttling back to Ciudad Rodrigo. 'Pon my word, Sharpe, but we're all heroes now!'

'I'm sure your father and mother always said you'd be a hero one day, General.'

Runciman had shaken his head. 'No, Sharpe, they never did. They were hopeful for me, I don't deny it, and no wonder for they were blessed with only the one child and I was that fortunate blessing, and they gave me great gifts, Sharpe, great gifts, but not, I think, heroism.'

'Well, you are a hero, sir,' Sharpe said, 'and you can tell anyone who asks that I said as much.' Sharpe held out his right arm and, despite the pain, shook Runciman's hand. Harper had just appeared at the church doorway and was holding up a bottle to show that there was some consolation waiting when Sharpe's bullet was extracted. 'I'll see you outside, sir,' Sharpe told Runciman, 'unless you want to watch the surgeon pull out the bullet?'

'Oh, good Lord, no, Sharpe! My dear parents never thought I'd have the stomach to study medicine and I fear they were right.' Runciman had gone pale. 'I shall let you suffer alone,' he said and backed hastily away with a handkerchief held over his mouth in case the noxious effusions of the hospital gave him a sickness.

Now the doctor pulled the bullet free of the wound before ramming a dirty rag against Sharpe's shoulder to staunch the flow of blood. 'No bones broken,' he said, sounding disappointed, 'but there are some bone chips off the rib that'll hurt you for a few days. Maybe for ever, if you live. You want to keep the bullet?' he asked Sharpe.

'No, sir.'

'Not as a keepsake for the ladies?' the doctor asked, then took a flask of brandy from a pocket of his blood-stiffened apron. He took a deep swallow, then used a corner of his bloody apron to wipe the tips of the forceps clean. 'I know a man in the artillery who has dozens of spent bullets mounted in gold and hung on chains,' the surgeon said. 'He claims each one lodged near his heart. He's got the scar, you see, to prove it, and he presents a bullet to every woman he wants to roger and tells each silly bitch that he dreamed of a woman who looked just like her when he thought he was dying. It works, he says.

He's a pig-ugly scoundrel but he reckons the women can't wait to claw his breeches down.' He offered Sharpe the bullet again. 'Sure you don't want the damn thing?'

'Quite sure.'

The doctor tossed the bullet aside. 'I'll get you wrapped up,' he said. 'Keep the bandage damp if you want to live and don't blame me if you die.' He walked unsteadily away, calling for an orderly to bandage Sharpe's shoulder.

'I do hate bloody doctors,' Sharpe said as he joined Harper outside the church.

'My grand-da said the same thing,' the Irishman said as he offered Sharpe the bottle of captured brandy. 'He only saw a doctor once in all his life and a week later he was dead. Mind you, he was eighty-six at the time.'

Sharpe smiled. 'Is he the same one whose bullock dropped off the cliff?'

'Aye, and bellowed all the way down. Just like when Grogan's pig fell down a well. I think we laughed for a week, but the damned pig wasn't even scratched! Just wet.'

Sharpe smiled. 'You must tell me about it some time, Pat.'

'So you're staying with us then?'

'No court of inquiry,' Sharpe said. 'Runciman told me.'

'They should never have wanted one in the first place,' Harper said scornfully, then took the bottle from Sharpe and tipped it to his mouth.

They wandered through an encampment smeared with the smoke of cooking fires and haunted with the cries of wounded men left on the battlefield. Those cries faded as Sharpe and Harper walked further from the village. Around the fires men sang of their homes far away. The singing was sentimental enough to give Sharpe a pang of homesickness even though he knew his home was not in England, but here, in the army, and he could not imagine leaving this home. He was a soldier and he marched where he was ordered to march and he killed the King's enemies when he arrived. That was his job and the army was his home and he loved both even though he knew he would have to fight like a gutter-born bastard for every step of advancement that other men took for granted. And he knew too that he would never be prized for his birth or his wit or his wealth, but would only be reckoned as good as his last fight, but that thought made him smile. For Sharpe's last battle had been against the best soldier France had and Sharpe had drowned the bastard like a rat. Sharpe had won, Loup was dead, and it was over at last: Sharpe's battle.

HISTORICAL NOTE

The royal guard of Spain in Napoleonic times consisted of four companies: the Spanish, American, Italian and Flemish companies, but alas, no Real Compañía Irlandesa. There were, however, three Irish regiments in Spanish service (de Irlanda, de Hibernia and de Ultonia), each composed of Irish exiles and their descendants. The British army, too, had more than its share of Irishmen; some English county regiments in the Peninsula were more than one third Irish and if the French could ever have disaffected those men then the army would have been in a desperate condition.

It was in a fairly desperate condition in the spring of 1811 anyway, not because of disaffection, but simply because of numbers. The British government had yet to realize that in Wellington they had at last discovered a general who knew how to fight and they were still niggardly in sending him troops. The shortfall was partly remedied by the fine Portuguese battalions that were under Wellington's command. Some divisions, like the Seventh, had more Portuguese than British soldiers and every account of the war pays tribute to the fighting qualities of those allies. The relationship with the Spanish was never so easy nor so fruitful, even after General Alava became liaison officer to Wellington. Alava became a close friend to Wellington and was with him, indeed, on the field of Waterloo. The Spanish did eventually appoint Wellington the *Generalisimo* of their armies, but they waited until after the battle of Salamanca in 1812 had driven the French out of Madrid and central Spain.

But in 1811 the French were still very close to Portugal which they had occupied twice in the previous three years. Ciudad Rodrigo and Badajoz barred Wellington's progress into Spain and until those twin fortresses fell (in early 1812) no one could be certain that the French would not attempt another invasion of Portugal. Such an invasion became much less likely after the battle of Fuentes de Oñoro, but it would not have been impossible.

Fuentes de Oñoro was never one of Wellington's 'favourite' battles, which were those that he could recall with some pleasure at his own generalship. Assaye, in India, is the battle of which he was most proud and Fuentes de Oñoro is probably the one of which he was least proud. He made one of his rare mistakes when he allowed the Seventh Division to march so far from the rest of the army, but he was rescued by the brilliant performance of the Light Division under Crauford on that Sunday morning. It was a display of soldiering that impressed everyone who witnessed it; the Division was far from help, it was surrounded, yet it withdrew safely and took only a handful of casualties. The fighting in the village itself was far worse, little more than a slaughterous brawl that left the streets glutted with the dead and dying, yet in the end, despite the French bravery and their one glorious moment when they did capture the church and the crest, the British and their allies held the ridge and denied Masséna the road to Almeida. Masséna, disappointed, distributed the rations he had been carrying for Almeida's garrison among his own hungry army, then marched back to Ciudad Rodrigo.

So Wellington, despite his mistake, was left with a victory, but it was a victory soured by the escape of Almeida's garrison.

That garrison was being blockaded by Sir William Erskine who, sadly, did not have too many 'lucid intervals'. The letter from the Horse Guards describing Erskine's madness is genuine and shows one of the problems Wellington had in trying to prosecute a war. Erskine did nothing when the French blew up Almeida's defences and slept while the garrison slipped away in the night. The whole lot of them should have been made prisoner, but instead they escaped a feeble blockade and went to reinforce the vast French armies in Spain.

Most of those armies were fighting *guerrilleros*, not British soldiers, and in another year some of them would be fighting an even more terrible enemy: the Russian winter. But the British too have their hardships to come, hardships that Sharpe and Harper will share, endure and, happily, survive.

SHARPE'S STORY

I'm often asked where Sharpe came from; whether I modelled him on some real person whose memoirs I had found, or whether he is based on a friend of mine, but the truth is that he is entirely fictional. I do recall writing an early story about him, though he was not called Sharpe then. I was producing television then which I liked, but I had always wanted to be a novelist, and ever since reading Hornblower as a child I had tried to find a series of books which did for Wellington's army what C.S. Forester had done for Nelson's navy. No one wrote the series, so one wet day in Belfast I made a start. It went nowhere.

Then, in 1979, I met Judy, an American. Cupid's arrow struck me with the accuracy of a rifle bullet fired by Daniel Hagman. Judy, for all sorts of good reasons, could not move from the States, so I decided I would abandon television, give up Belfast and go to America. The trouble was that the US government, in its wisdom, refused me a work permit, so I airily promised Judy that I would earn a living as a writer, and the only thing I wanted to write was that Hornblower-as-a-soldier series. So I put a typewriter on a kitchen table in New Jersey and started again. This time, unlike my first effort in Belfast, things were more desperate. If Sharpe failed me or, more likely, if I failed Sharpe, then the course of true love would hit a massive roadblock. What little money I possessed would not last long, so speed was of the essence and *Sharpe's Eagle* was written in a hurry. What did I know of my hero? I knew he would be a rifleman, because the rifle was unique to Wellington's troops and that would give him an edge over the enemy. I knew he could not stay with his beloved 95th Rifles because then I would be limited to describing only those actions in which the 95th fought and I wanted the freedom for him to be at every possible action. I knew he was an officer who had come up from the ranks, because that would give him some problems in his own army, but beyond that, not much. I described him at the beginning of the book as tall and black-haired, which was fine till Sean Bean came along, after which I tried not to mention his hair colour ever again. I gave him a scarred cheek, though for the life of me I can never remember which cheek has the scar and I suspect it changes from book to book. What I did not give him was a name because I was looking for something as memorable and quirky as Horatio Hornblower. Day after day passed, more pages piled up in the kitchen, and still he was called Lieutenant XXX. I made lists of names, none of which worked, and it began to annoy me, even hold up the writing, so I decided to give this rifleman a temporary name. I called him Richard Sharpe after the great Cornwall and England rugby player, Richard Sharp, and thought I would change it when the right name came along. But of course the new name stuck. Within a day or two I was already thinking of him as Sharpe, and so he has remained.

Patrick Harper was easier to name. I had been living in Belfast in the years immediately prior to writing Sharpe and had acquired a fondness for Ireland which has never abated. I had a friend in Belfast called Charlie Harper who had a son named Patrick. The problem was that the Harper family were not fond of the British, nor did they have cause to be, and I worried they would be offended if I named a soldier in Britain's army after their son. I asked their permission which was gladly given and so Harper has marched with Sharpe ever since.

The book was finished in about six months, and I had no idea whether it was any good, but I found a London literary agent and he found a publisher, and so *Sharpe's Eagle* was issued in 1981. I have never re-read it but not so long ago a reader told me his reaction to that first Sharpe book. 'I thought it would be like every other book,' he said, 'but when Sharpe killed Berry I knew it was different. Other heroes would never have done that. They're all officers and gentlemen, but not Sharpe.' So right from the beginning Sharpe was a rogue. Berry was a fellow-British officer who managed to upset Sharpe, which is never a wise thing to do, perhaps because Sharpe is so fuelled by anger. It is the anger of an unhappy childhood, of a man who has been forced to fight for every advantage that others were given, and that rage has always driven Sharpe. It makes him very different from Hornblower who is so fair-minded and honourable. Sharpe is a rogue, and a dangerous one, but he is a rogue on our side.

'He could never carry that sword,' an expert told me after *Sharpe's Eagle* was published. 'That sword' was the 1796 pattern Heavy Cavalry sword, a beast of a blade, ill-balanced and ineffective, but I liked the idea of Sharpe, a tall man, carrying such a butcher's weapon. I spent some money I could not afford on buying a trooper's sword (I was assured by the vendor that it was carried at Waterloo, and I like to think that is true) and I discovered that it could be carried. I slung it from a belt and it hung just fine, so that was all right, and Sharpe carried the sword from that day on.

The story of the siege of Badajoz in 1812 is one of the great tales of the war. It was the story I really wanted to tell in the first

Sharpe book, but I reckoned I might not have the skills to do it as a first-time author, and so I began Sharpe in 1809. The story of Badajoz with all its horror and heroism comes in the third Sharpe book, *Sharpe's Company*. That book also introduces the malevolent Sergeant Obadiah Hakeswill. I have no idea where he came from. I was driving one day and the name simply popped into my head. Hakeswill. It's a marvellously villainous name, and he proved to be a terrific villain. But why was Hakeswill's neck 'obscenely mutilated'? Because he had survived a judicial hanging. I remember writing that and pausing. Would anyone believe me? Was I stretching, not just Obadiah's neck, but credulity? I almost cut it out, thinking I would receive scornful letters, but somehow it seemed absolutely right for Obadiah to have been hanged and to have survived it, and so I left it in. Then, months later, I discovered that so many folk survived judicial hangings that the Royal College of Surgeons had a by-law dealing with how such survivors were to be treated by their members. The bodies of hanged felons were sold to the surgeons for dissection, and enough proved to be alive when they reached the hospitals to make the by-law necessary (they were resuscitated, and then, mostly, sent off to Australia). Far from being unlikely it seemed that Obadiah's history was almost commonplace. Obadiah, who was so marvellously portrayed by Pete Postlethwaite in the TV series, was one of those characters who come out of nowhere to enliven a book, and another was Lucille, the Frenchwoman with whom Sharpe will spend the rest of his life, and of all the things Sharpe has ever done, settling in France surprised me the most! I knew his marriage to Jane Gibbons was well on the rocks, but I assumed he would find himself some other woman and settle down to a life in the English countryside. I always intended Lucille to be a consolation prize for Sharpe's close friend, William Frederickson, who had endured a lot for Sharpe, but had never been fortunate in love. I thought Lucille Castineau would be perfect for 'Sweet William', but, perversely, Sharpe fell in love with her. I tried to prevent it, but when a character takes off on their own like that, there's very little a writer can do, and so Sharpe and Lucille fall hopelessly in love, and poor Frederickson is both offended and jilted.

It astonished me that Sharpe went to live in France, yet now it seems inescapable. Sharpe was always an outsider and he could never have been content in Britain after the war. But as a British soldier living among the erstwhile enemy he is as happy as when he was a man from the ranks surviving in the officers' mess. He likes being the square peg. And he loves Lucille. Lucky Sharpe, though I doubt he believed he was lucky when, out of the blue, the Emperor escaped from Elba and Sharpe finds himself thrust unexpectedly into the campaign of Waterloo. The drama of that campaign is such that no fictional plot can live beside it. Not just the drama of the day itself when, till the very last moment, it seemed the French must win, but the human drama of the two greatest soldiers of the age at last meeting on a battlefield.

No one would dispute Napoleon's place in the pantheon of great military leaders, but Wellington, to my mind, is a much greater battlefield general. Wellington, of course, was never a 'war leader' like Napoleon. He did not play dice with nations. He operated at a more modest level, as the leader of an army, and it is remarkable that, unlike the Emperor, he never suffered a battlefield defeat. He had a great talent for soldiering, a clear eye, a decisive mind, and a comprehensive grasp of what his men were capable of doing. His men liked him. They did not love him as the French soldiers loved Napoleon, but the Emperor was a politician who knew how to tweak men's affections. In return they worshipped him. But Wellington? He did not want to be worshipped. He had, he said, no small talk. He did not know how to talk to common soldiers, indeed he was an unashamed snob, yet his men liked him because they knew he did not risk their lives unnecessarily. In battle he protected them, usually by placing them on a reverse slope where they were out of sight of the enemy, and the soldiers in his army knew that he did not throw away their lives lightly. After Austerlitz a French general lamented the vast number of French dead on the battlefield and received a scornful look from Napoleon. 'The women of Paris,' the Emperor said, 'can replace those men in one night.' Wellington would never have said that.

It was only in sieges that Wellington lost his ability to keep casualties to a minimum, but he was never at his best besieging fortresses. In battle, because he knew how difficult it was to replace the dead and wounded, he did his best to keep his men safe until the moment came to expose them. He was once asked what was the greatest compliment he had ever received, and he told how he had visited the wounded after the battle of Albuera. That was a dreadful battle in which the British were commanded by General Beresford and it nearly ended in disaster. British casualties were horribly high. 'The enemy,' the French commander said, 'was beaten, but did not know it.' The battle was won, but at an awful price and two days later Wellington visited the wounded. As usual he was tongue-tied when he had to speak to the common soldiery. He came to a large room in the convent where scores of redcoats were lying in pain. He claimed he did not know what to say, so cleared his throat and, rather lamely, said that he was sorry to see so many of them there. 'My lord,' a corporal spoke up from among the injured, 'if you had been at the battle then not so many of us would be here.' It was, indeed, a great compliment.

Behind almost all the Sharpe books is the relationship between Wellington and Sharpe. They are not men who would instinctively like each other. The Duke, as he became, is cold and taciturn. He did not approve of men like Sharpe. He did not like seeing officers promoted from the ranks; 'they always take to drink,' he said dismissively. Sharpe, on the other hand, is scornful of men like Wellington who were born with the privileges of rank, money and connections. Sharpe cannot buy his way up the army's ladder, yet that is how Wellington gained his first promotions. Yet the two men are inextricably tied because Sharpe once saved Wellington's life. The general is aware that he ought to be grateful, and is, in a grudging way. Sharpe, who ought to dislike the general, admires him instead. He knows a good soldier when he sees one. Birth and privilege have nothing to do with it, efficiency is all. They will never be friends, they will always be distant, but they need each other. They even, I think, like each other, but neither knows how to bridge the gap to express that liking. And Sharpe is always doing over-dramatic things, of which the Duke disapproves. He liked steady officers, unflashy, who quietly did their duty, and he was quite right to approve of such good men. Sharpe is anything but quietly dutiful. He is the odd man out, but still a very useful man on the battlefield.

I always thought Waterloo would mark the end of the Sharpe series. I had written eleven novels, the same number as in Forester's Hornblower series, and I had taken Sharpe from Talavera to Waterloo, and now his world was at peace. Sharpe could go back to Normandy and to Lucille, while I would try my hand at other books. Sharpe was finished.

Then things grew complicated. Actually they had grown complicated a couple of years earlier when a television production company had announced that they wanted to make a series about Sharpe. I was, of course, delighted even though I did not believe that any such films would ever be made. But there was a chance that a Spanish production company would invest in the project. What the producers needed, therefore, was a new story set at the beginning of Sharpe's career which would include a Spanish hero. I still did not think the project would get anywhere, but it was foolish to ignore the chance that it might, so I wrote *Sharpe's Rifles* with Blas Vivar as the Spaniard who could provoke the desired cheque. The book was published and I heard no more about any television series and I deduced that the proposed films had been a flash in the pan. A flash in the pan is when a musket flint fires the priming powder in the lock, but doesn't set off the main charge in the barrel. But I was wrong, the films were to be made, a crew was in the Ukraine, actors were there, and then, just as suddenly, it was all over again. The actor playing Sharpe had a dreadful accident while playing football against the Ukrainian extras, and he was not going to be able to walk for six months, and the whole project seemed doomed. Somehow they rescued it, but they now needed a new actor to play Sharpe, and they needed him on very short notice. There was no time for auditions, and the only actor available was Sean Bean who unexpectedly found himself on a plane to Simferopol (known to all the film crew as Simply-Awful). That was a lucky accident because I cannot imagine Sharpe as anyone else; I hear Sean's voice when I write Sharpe. It is a wonderful coincidence of actor and character.

Before this, having abandoned any hope of seeing the television series, I had started the Starbuck books, the tale of a young northerner who finds himself fighting for the Confederacy in the American Civil War. I was enjoying those books but once the Sharpe filming was underway it became clear that I should go back to writing Sharpe, and that meant taking Sharpe all the way back to India.

* * *

India had always been a part of Sharpe's 'back-story'. Even in the very first book, *Sharpe's Eagle*, India is mentioned. It helped explain much about Sharpe; how he had learned to read and, crucially, how he had saved Wellington's life and was thus rewarded with a commission. So India had been useful to me, but I never had any intention of telling the Indian stories. I knew very little about India, and sources for the Indian campaigns of Sir Arthur Wellesley (as Wellington was then called) were very skimpy compared with the vast amount written about his Peninsular and Waterloo campaigns. I also had a conviction that I could not write convincingly about any battle unless I had visited the place, and I had never been to India and was wary of going because I expected the battlefields to have changed beyond recognition. Yet those Indian battlefields turned out to be the least altered sites I have ever visited. Seringapatam, where *Sharpe's Tiger* is set, was a considerable town when the British laid siege to it in 1799. I suspected that I would have to scratch around in back alleys to find even a remnant of the town Sharpe knew, but discovered that Seringapatam had shrunk to a village so that the impressive ramparts surround a great area of vacant land. It is a marvellous place.

One of the joys of writing historical novels is to 'explain' the small dark inexplicable corners of real history. One of those mysteries is what caused the terrible explosion at Almeida, described in *Sharpe's Gold*, and another is how the Tippoo Sultan died at Seringapatam. We know he was shot in the Watergate, a tunnel leading through the ramparts, but the British soldier who killed him was never discovered. He would have been rewarded, but he never volunteered his action, probably because the Tippoo, when he died, was festooned with jewels. That unknown soldier became very rich that day and he undoubtedly feared that his ill-gotten plunder would be confiscated. So Sharpe takes his place.

Sharpe begins *Sharpe's Tiger* as a private and ends it as a sergeant. He has also learned to read in the Tippoo's dungeons, so now has two of the necessary qualifications to be promoted from the ranks. That promotion occurs in the second Indian adventure, *Sharpe's Triumph*, which tells the extraordinary story of the battle of Assaye and at the heart of that battle is another of those small mysteries. We know that Sir Arthur Wellesley, while galloping across the field from one wing of his army to the other, was stranded in the enemy gun line. His horse, Diomed, had been piked in the chest, the general slid from the saddle and was surrounded by his Mahratta enemies. He survived, yet he was ever reluctant to describe exactly what happened. In a career that was remarkable for his frequent proximity to mortal danger and his avoidance of anything other than the most trifling wounds, that survival was the Duke of Wellington's closest brush with death. Yet what happened? He would not say, but I needed an event that would catapult Sharpe into the officers' mess. That event had to be a display of extraordinary bravery and Wellesley's miraculous survival gave me the perfect opportunity. In all Sharpe's career that is the crucial moment. It brings him to Wellesley's notice, it makes him an officer and it begins his reputation.

Sharpe, of course, had to return from India, and it occurred to me, somewhat mischievously, that his homeward voyage must inevitably take him not far from Cape Trafalgar and, as his last fight in India was in 1804 and because the battle of Trafalgar was fought in 1805, it seemed an irresistible mischief. Hornblower, after all, never got to Trafalgar, but why should not Sharpe fight there? So he did, one of the few men (I have discovered two others) present at both Trafalgar and Waterloo.

I am frequently asked how many more Sharpe novels will be written and I always answer five. I said that when there were only five novels in print, again when there were six, and keep saying it. I say five because it is an easier answer than trying to work out the real answer, which is that I do not know. I only know there will be more stories, and some, like the twenty-first in the series, will surprise me. Judy and I were invited to a wedding in Jerez de la Frontera, a town not far from Cadiz in southern Spain, and a long way from any place where Wellington fought. But close to Cadiz is Barrosa, a small seaside resort, and it was at Barrosa that the British, under the leadership of Sir Thomas Graham, captured the first of the many French eagles they were to take in the wars. I thought it would be interesting to see the battlefield, even though it had nothing whatever to do with Sharpe or Wellington, and so, under the influence of a massive hangover (Spanish weddings are spectacular), we drove to Barrosa. There is almost nothing left of the battlefield now, but I stood on the hill where Major Browne's makeshift battalion marched to certain death and I looked past the construction cranes on the lower ground where Major Gough's Irish took the eagle of the French 8th and I thought Sharpe has to be here. I had no idea how to get him to Cadiz, but the thought of writing Barrosa was irresistible, and so *Sharpe's Fury* was born.

There will be more Sharpe books (five more, perhaps?). I do not know now what stories they will tell, but I do know they will be a tribute to the heroism of the British soldier. There is an odd idea (I heard it being trotted out by a professor on Radio Four not long ago) that Wellington's army was a mass of gutterborn scum commanded by aristocrats and disciplined by brutality. That is glib rubbish. You cannot win wars with such an instrument. There were very few aristocrats, most of the officers were what we would call middle-class, and by the war's end many, like Sharpe, had been promoted from the ranks. The army's morale was high and memoir after memoir reveals the mutual respect between officers and men. They joked, they survived, they did endure terrible punishments, but they fought like devils and they won battle after battle. Sharpe is one of them. I have always thought of him as a rogue, but that may not be a bad thing. I once talked with a retired Warrant Officer who was running a programme for teenaged drug addicts and he told me that 'a soldier fights battles for those who cannot fight for themselves.' I think that is the most brilliant summation of a soldier's purpose that I have ever heard, and I have used it in the Sharpe books more than once. Sharpe fights for those who cannot fight for themselves, and he fights dirty, which is why he is so effective. It's also why I like him, and one day Sharpe and Harper will march again.

Bernard Cornwell

The SHARPE Series
(in chronological order)

The SHARPE Series
(in order of publication)

Also by Bernard Cornwell

The MAKING OF ENGLAND Series
The Last Kingdom
The Pale Horseman
The Lords of the North
Sword Song
The Burning Land
Death of Kings

The GRAIL QUEST Series
Harlequin
Vagabond
Heretic

Azincourt

Stonehenge: a novel of 2000 BC